Silkwin's Edge

A Novel

Harvey Bateman
and
Judy Schwinkendorf

Strategic Book Group

Strategic Book Group
P.O. Box 333
Durham CT 06422
www.StrategicBookClub.com

ISBN: 978-1-60911-449-7

Printed in the United States of America

Book Design: Suzanne Kelly

IN MEMORY OF MY WIFE, VIRGINIA

Virginia Bateman passed away August 9, 2007, after a yearlong struggle with cancer. She was a very devoted and caring person. Her support and encouragement made this novel possible. She is truly missed, and life will never be the same without her.

DISCLAIMER

THIS IS A WORK OF FICTION. Names, characters, places, dates, and events are the product of the authors' imagination. Any resemblance to actual persons living or dead, events, or locales is coincidental. Some products or services may not actually have existed during that period of time.

ACKNOWLEDGEMENTS

I WOULD LIKE TO THANK MY SON Gary and my grand-son Josh for their creative help on the book cover, and for their support and encouragement, which helped in making this novel possible.

Thanks to Juli for her positive support, attention to detail and her dedication to this book and family.

In addition, I would also like to thank Jan, Mabel, Jake, Jean, Clara, and any other family members or friends who were instrumental in helping my daughter and me resurrect this novel and make it a reality. With their insight and help, I was able to complete this journey.

Harvey Bateman

You're probably wondering why a guy like me in his early eighties wrote a novel. My resounding answer is—Why Not!

Harvey Bateman

PROLOGUE

OKLAHOMA, 1936

"THE BOY'S STRANGE!" HIRAM WALDEN YELLED. He rubbed his bristling salt-and-pepper beard and faced Martha Silkwin, his only daughter. "But what'n the hell would 'ya expect—marryin' a half-breed."

"Howard's a good man and I love him," Martha said, trying to control the anger in her voice. "Why can't you accept things as they are instead of raising so much hell—especially with Eric being a rare and gifted child?"

Martha Silkwin looked out the kitchen window at her daughter Ellen and son Eric playing in the backyard.

Hiram Walden hesitated a moment, then continued ranting. "Gifted! For what? He's a boy!" He took another swig of whiskey, wiped his mouth with his sleeve, and pointed his bony finger at his wife. "It's your fault, woman, pushin' the Book at him and sayin' he's special."

"I'm tired hearin' it!" Bessie Walden yelled back at her husband. "You old fool! The way you carry on, and the book you're talkin' bout is the Bible." Her voice suddenly softened. "They're our own flesh and blood. We haven't seen 'em in over a year. They're leavin' tomorrow for some place in Illinois. That's quite a stretch away, and you don't know when—or if—you'll see 'em again."

"I'm fed up! I've had bout all I can take. Workin' myself to death on this backbreakin' farm." He slammed his fist down on the table. "On top of everthin' else, I got the wrath of them self-righteous bankers' breathin' down my neck." Hiram Walden stared at his wife. "You tell me . . .What's the use of anythin' anymore?"

"That's whiskey talkin'!" Bessie Walden said, her voice rising, "I swear, it's the devil hisself, comin' right outta that jug you're holdin' . . . Everybody's got hard times. There's nothin' we can do bout it. Maybe if you started prayin' serious-like instead of feelin' sorry for yourself."

A rare grin appeared on his weather-beaten face. "What about your prayin', woman?"

"If you'd pray with me—oh, what's the use?" Martha's mother said with an edge in her voice.

Ellen came in the house when she heard the yelling. "Are you talking about Eric?" she said. "Kids at school say Eric is kinda—touched."

"You see, the girl knows!" Hiram Walden said. "He's always fightin' or quotin' the Book—err, the Bible. Folks think he's—"

"The boy's *chosen,* Hiram," Bessie Walden said, her voice barely above a whisper. "I saw the sign on him the day he was born. I tried tellin' ya, but you just mocked me."

A short time later, Eric also hearing the yelling, came in the house. "You leave my mom and grandma alone!" Eric cried.

"You got spunk, boy. I'll say that much for ya."

The following morning, the July sun showed signs of another scorching day. Hiram Walden spit out a stream of tobacco juice, mumbled something, and stuck his head back under the hood of his battered old Ford pickup. His daughter ignored his moaning and patiently waited. Finally, he slammed down the hood and loaded Martha's battered suitcases.

Hiram wiped his face, looked out over his sun-scorched fields, and cursed while his daughter and grandchildren said their goodbyes. Martha's mother hugged the kids and faced her daughter. "Don't mind your paw. It's mostly the times and whiskey. He's afraid of losin' the farm, with the bank closings and all. Your father's fightin' somethin' he can't do anythin' about or can't understand."

Martha stared at her mother's faded print dress sagging around her bony shoulders and embraced her. "I know. Don't worry—when we get settled I'll write and . . ."

"I'll be prayin'. Remember, I got the faith," Martha's mother said.

Martha took one last look at the white, paint-peeled, two-story farmhouse. She couldn't help remembering the way the place used to be. The farm showed signs of slowly decaying from age, neglect, and broken dreams—something her father would never have let happen a few years ago. She wondered if she would ever see that home again.

"Hey girl—we gotta get movin'!" her father yelled.

Martha and the children waved to her mother as they pulled out of the driveway.

Moments later, Martha stared at fields of corn badly in need of rain and better days. The feeling of defeat and depression hung over the land like a fog.

The scattered farmhouses, many deserted, in the barren flatlands of Oklahoma reflected the widespread sign of the times. Mile after mile, Martha would see people standing near the road. Usually there were small children, digging their toes in the dirt, with the same haunted look as their parents. "You can even see the hopelessness in the children's faces. It's so heartbreaking," Martha said.

"Damn right!" Her father spit out the words. "I want ya to always remember the look of defeat in these people's faces. It's our own brand of hell on earth."

"Hectic" was the word that came to Martha's mind the last two weeks. She, Ellen, and Eric had stayed with her parents while her husband Howard went to see his brother in Illinois about a job. She understood her father's bitterness over the bank and the weather, but not with her husband. The tension between her and her father was still there, even in silence. She couldn't help feeling sadness, relief, and excitement all rolled into one.

The kids in back pecked on the truck window with a new-found enthusiasm Martha hadn't seen for a long time. After miles of awkward silence, she said, "Howard's worked with the shoe repair trade in the Army. His brother knows a man who owns a shoe repair shop, and he's going to work with Howard for a while. When Howard can take over the shop, then the man's going to retire. We have a little money saved and maybe we can have our own business."

"You think your half-breed got a chance of ownin' his own business? You been out in the sun too long, girl!" her father said with familiar bitterness.

"We'll see." Martha clutched her husband's letter, praying for the beginning of a new life while trying to ignore her father's contempt.

"Why'd he get outta the Army? The country's in the worst mess it's been in years. At least you were sure of three meals a day and a roof over your head."

"Howard, like any man, wants his independence," Martha said. "I don't think he would've left the Army if he didn't have a job. We want a home and roots for our children."

"I'll bet he couldn't take orders. Indians don't like bein' ordered around."

"And you do?"

A rare smile crossed her father's face. "Howard's taken his share of orders for years," Martha said. "We felt it was time to find a place to belong. I know you don't like to hear it, but he's more like you than you think."

Her father's smile vanished as quickly as it appeared. "I hope you know what you're doin.'" He grunted and stared at the road ahead.

Martha welcomed the silence and took out her handkerchief to try to wipe off some of the perspiration. A few minutes later, she was relieved when she saw the train station up ahead. Her father unloaded their suitcases, wiped his forehead, and faced Eric. "I don't know what's gonna become of you, boy."

Eric looked him straight in the eye. "Grandpa, I'll be led." Eric extended his hand and his grandfather shook it.

"Yeah. I know—you're *chosen!*" He turned to face Ellen and put his hand on her shoulder. "Sometimes girl, I think you're the only one in the family that's got the common sense. You take care of yourself and help your maw."

"I will Grandpa, I promise."

He faced his daughter. "Write your mother, and keep your wits 'bout ya." He unloaded the suitcases and tugged awkwardly at his suspenders while glaring at the only other couple boarding the train.

"It's time," Martha said with a sudden softness in her voice that surprised her. She searched for the father she knew a few short years ago. She looked into her father's mad gray eyes. *How could this be the same man who a few years ago had braved a winter storm to get her a fountain pen for Christmas?*

"You know President Roosevelt signed that Social Security thing." She looked into his eyes. "It could be a blessing for all of us. I—I have the faith."

"You sound like your maw. Miracles are not for folks like us." Her father watched the train like it was a foreign object. He stared at the road leading back to the only life he knew. "You and that half-breed'll be back. You'll see!" For an instant, Martha thought she saw a flicker of emotion, maybe a tear in her father's eye, but he quickly turned and walked away.

CHAPTER ONE

ILLINOIS, 1947

IN THE EARLY MORNING SILENCE of a modest ranch home, twenty-year-old Eric Silkwin struggled with a strange dream. *"Reach out to me!"* the little girl with twisted legs cried. *"Your thoughts could touch me and make me whole if you trust your faith. I'm reaching as far as I can."* A moment later, her tears turned into a big smile.

Suddenly, the face of an Indian appeared above the little girl. His eyes glistened like clear black glass. An aura of a radiant, pale blue light surrounded his head. The Indian gently placed his huge hands on her shoulder, and raised them to the top of her head. The light changed to a brilliant white. "I am the spirit of a medicine man who offers the gift of healing," he said, with a voice that sounded like distant thunder. "I pass to you the healing touch of the Great Spirit, if your heart so desires. The choice must be yours!"

"Wait!" Eric shouted in his sleep. He jumped when his father shook him, and suddenly became aware of cool perspiration on his face as he struggled between sleep and consciousness. He stared at the early morning light shining through the tree branches outside his window.

———

"Eric, you better come in the kitchen," his father said

"Give me a couple of minutes." Eric groped his way down the hallway and switched on the bathroom light. He ran cold water over his face and looked at the familiar reflection of his Cheyenne heritage starring back at him.

He entered the kitchen where his mother, father and sister were waiting. The kitchen clock and the percolating coffee pot were the only sounds in the early morning silence. Eric's twenty-three-year-old sister, Ellen, stared at him with a look of disgust through bold brown eyes. At this hour, he couldn't blame her.

Eric got a cup of coffee and took his place at the table. He looked from one to another, "I had a dream about that little Indian girl—I know how this is going to sound, but she asked me to touch her."

"Really," Ellen said, impatiently drumming her fingers on the table. "Do you have any idea of what you are saying—I know we've gone along with some of this—but how can you?" She trailed off and shook her head.

Their mother went to the living room, returned and opened her Bible. "It's the Holy Spirit working through you!" Martha said. "It's in I Corinthians: 'To another the gift of healing by the spirit.' It's Eric's calling. Can't you see that?" She pressed her Bible against her breast.

"Wait a minute. We don't know," Howard replied.

Ellen held up her hand and said, with obvious impatience, "I'm sure we're all tired. Besides, we've been through all this before."

"It's almost six and I have a busy day at the shop," Howard said.

After Ellen and her father left, his mother said to Eric, "Dreams are signs. Your father and sister don't understand. It's your destiny!"

Later, alone in his room, Eric wondered about last night's dream. He thought of the embarrassment almost a year ago that still haunted him. It was so sudden when an uncontrollable blast of words poured from him during church service. When it ended, he stood staring self-consciously into the stunned faces of the congregation.

Suddenly, that self-conscious silence was broken. *"Halle-lujah!"* shouted a woman. *"Praise the Lord,"* rang out a chorus of voices, finally interrupting the silence, followed by a blur of confusion and congratulations.

After the incident, he overheard one woman whisper to another, "That Silkwin boy could be possessed." Eric wondered if it was because he was only nineteen or if he possessed a power they could not control or understand. The Bible came alive for him in ways he couldn't explain. When the congregation sang, even the music, at times, lifted him beyond any reasonable explanation.

At breakfast the next morning, Ellen whispered to Eric, "I've heard rumors about you and a certain waitress at Mabel's cafe. Any comment?"

He grinned. "None, what an imagination—and this early in the morning."

"What're you two whispering about?" their mother asked.

"Nothing important," Eric said, but his thoughts shifted to Rita, the tall, thin, outspoken blond waitress. She was a little rough around the edges, but she had a great sense of humor and probably the biggest heart in Benford.

"Eric, what's the big deal about you joining the service?" his father asked.

"I don't want to worry about the draft later."

"Maybe you're right—it could be worse later. I guess there's nothing else to say," his mother said. Eric saw the beginning of tears she was trying to control. She quickly left the table and went to the stove.

"What's Frank think about this?" his father asked, trying to ease the tension.

"Not much, you know how he is."

"Frank should've stayed in high school," his father said. "He's a good-hearted kid, but, he's confused and torn between his feelings and loyalty he has for his father."

3

"With his accident and the trouble he had with his courses, he lost interest in about everything," Eric said. "I'm going over there now. I'll see you later."

Eric recalled when Frank his best friend, fell after the start of his junior year. He injured his ankle while picking apples. Although the injury was not serious, it left him with a slight limp and shattered his dream of playing semi-pro baseball.

In Frank's own words, "It was my only chance of really being somebody—even the coach said I was a good prospect— all because of a few lousy apples."

"It's about time Eric," Frank said as he put his pocket book aside. "That Mike Hammer is some private eye. Did you listen to the game last night? I told ya the Cardinals would pull it out. My old man and I argued over the ball game last night. First time we've really talked in quite a while."

"Maybe you can work things out," Eric said.

"I've tried, but I have a hard time forgetting what happened when my mom had an appendicitis attack. What really got to me, and something I can't get outta my mind, was my dad being so drunk I couldn't wake him!"

Eric wasn't sure what to say. Finally he asked, "Is he still a night watchman?"

"Yeah," Frank said. "Mullaird's gave him that job because of the years he had in as a lab technician. From what I heard, he was a good one until the booze took over."

"I'm gonna talk to the Air Force recruiter," Eric said.

"You think that's the answer, huh—to get away?" Frank grunted. "I know it's not the draft, it's the people who give you that strange look, even at church. It's also the pressure from your mom. To quote one of your idols, 'You can run, but you can't hide.'"

Eric's only reply was a smile.

The recruiting sergeant flashed his smile with the eagerness of a hunter closing in on its prey. He had the classic military look Eric expected. "When would you like to join us?"

"As soon as possible," Eric said.

The sergeant's smile never faded. "Fill out these forms and I'll make arrangements for your physical." They shook hands and Eric joined Frank, who muttered something about Eric losing his mind.

"Well?" Eric's father asked. He put the newspaper crossword puzzle under the counter and puffed on his cigar. He groaned as he slowly lifted his six-foot, two hundred-pound frame off the stool.

"I'm in if I pass the physical."

"I hope you know what you're doing."

With the end of the war and Mullaird's and Wyatt's expansion, Benford's two leading industries, his father's business, along with others in Benford, grew rapidly. Eric walked to the back of the shop and flipped the canvas off a roughly chiseled log. The dust hung in the air like a fog. His father joined him and said, "I guess we got a ways to go." They stood silently staring at the crude form of a totem pole.

"That's for sure," Eric said. They both looked at their project they had started six or seven years ago. Eric placed his hand on it, as if somehow expecting some kind of reaction. His father took a big puff on his cigar, glanced at Eric, and they both laughed.

"I still think the totem pole was a good idea," Eric said. "I just don't have the enthusiasm I had."

"I can tell you got something else on your mind."

"I can't bring myself to ask Mom what's behind her obsession with me being special, and following my so-called destiny, especially after this dream I had."

His father looked off in the distance for a moment, and then said. "Your Grandmother Walden saw a sign on you at birth.

5

She was—to put it mildly—a religious fanatic. The more she quoted the Bible, the more your grandfather drank. He swore, if their daughter married an Indian—a 'heathen' was the way he put it—he wanted no part of her." Eric's father took another puff off his cigar and returned to the past. "The night before we left, your grandmother made your mother swear to dedicate her life and her children to the Bible—especially you." They walked back to the front of the store and sat down. Eric saw his father wince from the arthritis in his hip.

"She saw the tension between your mother and your grandfather because of me," his father continued. "She knew he was so bullheaded he'd never change. Your grandmother knew your mother and I loved each other. She encouraged us to get married. She died of a heart attack just before they foreclosed on the farm."

"Whatever happened to him?"

"Nobody knows. We went to her funeral, but he never showed up. At least we didn't see him. I talked to his neighbor, Mr. Snipes, who said the last time he had seen him was a couple of weeks before her death. He was drunk and muttered something about losin' a worthless farm."

"What was Mothers' reaction to her father?"

"To quote your mother: 'Thou will honor thy father and mother.' Years ago, before one bad time followed the others, she loved her father. Evidently, he was charming enough when he was sober, although I never saw any evidence of it."

"She never talks about her family. I'm beginning to understand why," Eric said. "What I didn't mention about the dream: There was an Indian with the little girl."

"What can I say? Naturally, your mother thinks your dreams are some high, spiritual power. With my Cheyenne background, it's more than likely communication from our ancestors. I can't tell your mother that! You'd better walk softly, but keep your guard up. For some reason, the two-edged sword comes to mind." The weather was cool for September. The relief of the weekend showed in the faces of the Saturday evening crowd. Eric took his time walking along the streets, which were lined with large oak trees. He climbed the familiar steps, where pots of his mother's faded geraniums crowded the front porch. The aroma of meatloaf filled the living room. "Dad's gotta rush job; he'll be a little late."

"Supper's almost ready," his mother said.

Eric ate quickly, lit a Camel and sipped his coffee. It was one of those rare awkward moments of silence. Finally, Eric said. "I gotta take off. I'm meeting Frank."

Two hours later, the light was still on next to his mother's over-stuffed easy chair. Weariness showed in her face. She removed her glasses, brushed back her long, reddish blond hair and carefully closed the timeworn Bible in her lap. "The more I read the Bible," she said in that familiar tone, "the more I realize what a blessing your gift is."

"Sometimes I wonder," Eric said, "especially that speaking in tongues—well the whole church incident bothers me."

"Put that behind you. God works in mysterious ways. There's a reason for everything when you're working for the Lord. I'm going to bed; leave the porch light on for Ellen."

After settling in bed, Eric reached for his cigar box. He took out an acorn and thought of his Grandfather Silkwin. He quickly dismissed his tortured memories of his paternal grandparents' death when their farmhouse perished in flames almost twelve years ago.

Eric forced his thoughts to the special Sundays and holidays at his grandparents' farm. He could almost smell the cured ham and fresh baked bread. His most vivid memory was the old kerosene lamp on the red and white checkered tablecloth that cast flickering, eerie shadows throughout the kitchen.

He also remembered his parents explaining that questioning the church's views and the elders were disrespectful for an eight-year-old boy. He could still hear his Grandfather Silkwin say, "I told your father, we'd have a talk," He winked and added, "This is just between us."

"I know, Grandpa—man to man."

7

"I'm gonna explain some things."

"I know, go in the closet, like Jesus says."

"Right. You see, some folks don't understand like we do—this is what God's existence means to me." He bent down, picked up an acorn, and handed it to Eric. "You keep this, to remind you of something entirely of God's making—something you can hold in the palm of your hand."

Eric gazed out over the big backyard and screamed, "Look at the acorns. God is everywhere!" The last thing he remembered before falling asleep was the smile on his grandfather's face.

The next morning he heard his father shout from the hallway. "It's almost nine. I don't want to be late for church." Eric woke with the feeling of the small acorn still in his hand. The smell of bacon and eggs filled the hallway, along with voices from the kitchen. "I got home about twelve," Eric heard his sister say, "I'm not a little girl anymore. Well, good morning Reverend Silkwin; are you going to preach today?"

"Ellen, you shouldn't say those things," their mother said. Eric glanced at his sister. He could not blame her. She had worked hard to become one of Mullaird's leading secretaries. His reputation hadn't exactly helped her career.

"I mean, you are our guiding light! Sorry, this evidently is not one of my best mornings."

"Maybe if you'd come home earlier," their father said.

"*Howard*!" Eric's mother shouted at her husband.

Frank came in, helped himself to coffee, and joined Eric at the table. "You know, Karen is helping me. Your cousin finally got through to me—that I'd be stuck in a dead-end job if I didn't get my high school diploma."

"I'm aware I've got an honor student for a cousin. Are you two getting a little serious?"

"More than a little, I . . ."

Ellen sipped some coffee, patted Frank's cheek, and laughed. "You look very handsome today." His face turned a pale red, the same color as his tie

"Thanks," he muttered, watching her hurry away. Eric thought of the contrast between him and Frank. He was a little less than six feet, with the olive complexion of his Cheyenne heritage, while Frank was six-three and light skinned.

———————

When Eric and Frank arrived in front of the courthouse, Frank stopped and looked up at the curved arches topped with a large clock, centered over four massive stone pillars. "Hey Eric, I got this problem. Karen asked me to describe Benford to someone who's never seen it."

Eric grinned. "That sounds like Karen, all right. Let's see, Benford is a small town near the Missouri and Illinois state lines. I think the population is a little over ten thousand. I can't think of anything outstanding. You could mention our industries—Mullaird's Appliance Corporation and the Wyatt lock factory."

"That's important, but Karen is gonna ask me what is so special about Benford. You know—-maybe history or something like that."

Eric hesitated a moment, then said, "The only thing I remember about the founders is they were the Hedwicks and the Wyatts. Rumor had it that George Rogers Clark and his rangers stopped at this courthouse on their way to Vincennes. I forget the details."

"Hey, a guy can't remember everything. That's really something—George Rogers Clark and his rangers, huh?"

"Yeah, if I remember right, we were told about that in the seventh or eighth grade."

Frank broke out in a broad grin. "I must have missed that class."

Eric laughed, and then added, "Mention our statue of the Second World War."

"Yeah," Frank said, "Some time ago Karen and her brother Bryan told me about being awakened in the middle of the night because their father had nightmares about the war."

"A few months ago, my Uncle David and I watched the construction of the statue," Eric said. "I remember my uncle saying, 'I wonder if most of the guys wouldn't rather have had the money to take care of their families instead of having a statue.'"

His uncle had served in an Infantry division until the end of the war, but that was the only time Eric had heard him talk about it.

"I was wondering, why do you and Bryan argue about religion and the Bible?" Frank asked.

"Bryan and I have always challenged each other since we were kids. It was always something."

"Come on, Eric! I know part of it is Bryan's resentment of his Cheyenne heritage."

"I admit that really bugs me," Eric said. "He refuses to respect or even consider his heritage. He hides his family ties, like he's ashamed."

"Forget Bryan. What about Linda?"

"Strictly friends; besides, I've seen her with Bill Hausler."

"How about you and Alice Dawsher?" Frank asked.

"She's very shy," Eric said as they arrived at the small, white, wood frame church.

"Hi' ya Cousin," Karen greeted Eric. "You going to reveal your thoughts this morning or should they be censored?" Karen cocked her strawberry-blond head to one side and then turned to Frank. "How about you, handsome?" she said, with that deep laugh of hers. "Would your thoughts be censored, too?" She grabbed an arm from each of them, and with her head held high, gracefully escorted them up the front steps.

Suddenly Bryan appeared before them. "I'm ready for you, Cousin," he said. He looked more intense than ever, with his dark, moody eyes that emphasized his seriousness.

At twenty-three, Bryan Silkwin, an expediter for Mullaird's Corporation, considered himself a Bible authority and accepted his role of religious fanatic gracefully.

Reverend Langtree wiped perspiration from his brow and glanced at his restless, uncomfortable congregation. Ushers passed out fans and raised the windows, but the bright sunlight streaming through the windows made conditions worse. The men tugged at their ties and women pulled at their dresses, trying to find a comfortable position.

Eric motioned for Alice to join them. She blushed as Eric stood and whispered, "You're late." She stared straight ahead, and then suddenly glanced at him. Eric smiled and she quickly turned her head.

"We are blessed with a beautiful Sunday morning, although a bit warm," the Reverend said. "If the Sunday school teachers will gather their classes, it will be cooler."

Eric waited for Alice, and then said, "Are you all right?"

Her face reddened, but she managed a smile, "Yes. I bumped my knee on the car door a couple days ago. It was so clumsy of me."

"Those things happen. I'll help you down the basement steps." Eric guided her, as everyone hurried to their classes.

Eric's Uncle David sat in the front of the class and opened his Bible. "Last week, we left off discussing the spiritual gifts mentioned in Chapter Twelve, when Paul explains these gifts are available to everyone. Who wants to tell us what their views are?"

"Eric, do you believe we possess spiritual gifts?" Bryan asked, wasting no time. "If so, come forward and tell us about it."

"I think we should explore the possibility," Eric said.

"I firmly believe those gifts existed only for His disciples," Bryan said. "You're taking your brief attempt at speaking in tongues too seriously."

"It's what you believe in," Eric said.

Eric's uncle quickly interrupted. "Anybody else? Alice?"

She glanced at Eric, and then quickly looked away. "Well I . . . I think it's a matter of faith. If you mean laying on of hands, yes I do." The discussion went on for several minutes, mainly between Bryan and Eric. It wasn't long before the class ended.

"Why don't we try healing your knee?" Eric said to Alice.

Alice glanced at Frank. "Hey, don't mind me, I'll help," Frank said.

"I feel a little. . ." Alice whispered, and then blushed. "Do you have to put your hands on my knee?"

"Yeah. . . I don't know how else we can do it. Frank'll put his hands on your head and I'll place mine on your knee."

"I guess you're right," Alice said.

Eric placed a pillow on the floor in front of Alice. She closed her eyes as Eric carefully placed his hands on her knee. She

11

quickly covered his hands with hers. He suddenly felt energy passing through his body and out his hands. The shock and sudden reaction started his hands to vibrate. Alice flinched and began to tremble, her breathing becoming much faster. Her eyes stared into his, carefully following his hands with hers. Beads of perspiration covered her forehead. "Frank, would you please get me a glass of water?" Alice whispered.

"Yeah, I'll be right back." He hurried to the back of the church.

Alice shifted in her chair, with an expression of unbelief. "I feel heat coming from your hands. I can't believe this! Eric— *Eric,* what's wrong with you?"

Eric's throat was so dry he could hardly speak. "My—my hands! I can't control 'em."

"*You have to!*" Alice whispered.

"I left my purse down here somewhere. I ..." They heard the woman's voice just before she appeared. For a moment, she looked shocked, and then suddenly her voice rang throughout the church basement. "What are you doing with your hands up that girl's dress?"

CHAPTER TWO

ERIC TRIED TO STAND, BUT HIS LEGS cramped. He fell off balance and sprawled on the floor.

Alice, her face turning a crimson red, quickly jumped off the chair. Eric glanced up just in time to see Frank drop the glasses of water. "Damn!" he said, as the sound of breaking glass echoed through the basement. Frank froze, his face pale and his mouth wide open.

"What's going on down here?" The startled woman yelled, then screamed again, bringing people rushing from the church service upstairs.

"Mrs. Dunley, what happened?" Eric heard someone ask.

"Eric Silkwin had his hands up her dress. I couldn't believe it!"

Alice's mother rushed toward her daughter. "What in the world are you doing, girl? Wait until your father hears about this!"

"We weren't doing anything wrong. We were trying to heal my knee," Alice said.

"You were what?"

Alice looked her mother straight in the eye, and repeated, "Healing my knee."

"It's my fault," Eric said. Alice's mother glared at him, then faced her daughter again.

Reverend Langtree, who had finally worked his way through the crowd, said, "Please, let's have some order, and try to get some control of ourselves."

A few minutes later, the church committee dismissed the congregation. Alice, Eric and Frank sat facing the church's two senior members. Mrs. Edna Dunley, a tall, thin attractive lady with wavy, iron gray hair, and Nathan Lewis Winslow, a short, balding, overweight bank manager in his early sixties, took charge. Mrs. Dunley was, until last year, a charming woman, especially around the traditional winter holidays. Her disposition changed after the death of her husband, a retired railroad worker who died after a short illness. It shattered their dreams of traveling across the country.

Eric's mother focused her attention on Nathan Winslow—clearly in charge. Her husband, Eric's father, showed no emotion. He sat quietly with his hands folded in his lap.

Alice's mother watched the proceedings carefully; her face showed anxiety as she nervously twisted her handkerchief. She had the same blue eyes and dark hair as her daughter. Alice's father watched carefully his daughter's response. He was a loan officer at the First National Bank; Nathan Winslow was his supervisor, which increased the pressure.

"Alice, we'll open the discussion with you," the reverend said. "You tell us, in your own words, exactly what happened."

She self-consciously tugged at her dress, and stared at the committee members. "We were studying healing as a spiritual gift in Sunday school. We wondered if healing was possible today."

"You believed they could heal?" Mrs. Dunley asked.

"I was skeptical, but I figured why not try it." Alice stared back at her. "You got the wrong impression."

"Nevertheless, he did have his hand on your leg," Mrs. Dunley pressed.

"My knee!" Alice countered, with surprising control. Reverend Langtree called Eric for questioning.

"It's like Alice said. Please try and understand it was a very emotional time," Eric said.

"I'll bet it was," Mrs. Dunley taunted.

"Can you explain what you felt during the healing?" the reverend hesitated, ignoring the subdued laughter, and then quickly continued. "Was there any mental or physical reaction?"

14

"Yes," Eric said. "I felt heat and the sensation of a mild electrical current flowing through my body and out my hands. I can't explain it any other way." He looked directly at Mrs. Dunley and added, "If I'd had something other than healing in mind, I would've asked Frank to go upstairs."

"The committee can consider all the facts later. It's getting late. Any objections?" Reverend Langtree asked.

"It'll do for now—but should be reviewed," Winslow said. He wiped his brow. "It's damn—err, too hot and stuffy in here. Eric, could you wait a minute? We need to talk."

Eric joined Winslow after the others had left. "It seems some of the church members," Winslow began carefully, "object to the notoriety and attention your practice of certain, err, healing rituals can bring, along with some unfavorable publicity. You think you could handle it in a different way and maybe confine it to some other…"

"I think I know what you mean," Eric said. "I'll take care of it." He immediately thought of his parents and what the church meant to them—especially his mother.

"I appreciate it. You know I admire and respect your parents," Winslow said, carefully wiping his forehead with his handkerchief. "That makes it even more awkward for me. Personally, I have to think of the church members. This type of notoriety can upset some rather influential people. The fact that you will be in the regular service should ease some of the pressure for all concerned." Eric left to meet Frank, he had a lot to think about.

"Hey, what happened?" Frank said.

"He wants me to keep my healing under control."

Frank smiled. "Hey, forget it; I know it was about Alice."

"Not entirely—I was really serious about the healing." When they arrived at Eric's house, his mother glanced at him and shook her head. He headed for the living room before she could start asking questions.

"I heard you created a little trouble in church." Ellen said. "You're really something. Won't you ever learn?"

Eric looked out the window. "Forget it. Uncle David and the family are here."

After getting settled, Karen said with a mischievous grin. "Eric, Frank, you can sit with me." She scooted to the center of the couch. Frank looked uneasy. He pulled at his tie and seemed unable to follow the conversation while trying to ignore Karen's legs. Her eyes gleamed as she slowly crossed her legs. "What'd you think, Eric?"

Her mother glared at her. "Karen, have you no shame!"

"Karen! Enough is enough." her father yelled.

"All right, Pop." Her father winced. She saw his expression and took off for the kitchen.

Eric watched his father and his uncle huddled together. His uncle was about thirty pounds lighter and four years younger, but they looked almost the same.

"How about that Jackie Robinson!" Frank added. "Talk about guts. He's the first black to sign with a major baseball club. Can you imagine the trouble he's gonna have?"

"That's nothing," Karen added, rejoining the men. "Is that all you guys think about—sports? How about those reports of flying saucers?"

Frank laughed. "You would notice that bunk. I think I'll stick with Mickey Spillane."

"All right, everybody, dinner is ready," Martha said.

"The important thing is," Howard said, "President Roosevelt and Henry Ford gave many people a way to help themselves when they needed it the most. I don't know about this Truman fella, but he seems to take charge and know what he's doing."

"I hope you're right," his brother added.

Eric's father continued his favorite subject. "History will record how great President Roosevelt was." Later, after Eric's uncle and the family left, his father stared at him. Finally he said, "Tell me about it." Although he never talked much, Eric somehow knew what he meant.

"When I read the Bible the other night, Apostle Paul talked about spiritual gifts and healing," Eric said. "I know it sounds strange, but it was as if I were a part of it."

"That's what caused this thing with Alice?"

"Yes. My intentions were good, but I guess—"

The phone rang, startling them. "Alice and her parents are coming over," Eric's mother said after hanging up the phone. "She said it was important." Eric's father remained silent while his mother sat calmly, running her finger over the pattern in the tablecloth.

When they heard a car, his mother hurried to the door. "Won't you come in? This is an unexpected pleasure."

"I know we're imposing," Edith, Alice's mother, said, pausing to catch her breath. "Alice's swelling on her knee has almost completely vanished. It's very strange. Look, no bruise! I can hardly believe it myself."

Eric looked at Alice's knee, but said nothing.

"Thank God, I've always known Eric has contact with spiritual forces," Eric's mother said. "I told you, Howard. Now maybe you'll believe me!"

"How will we explain this?" Alice's father asked. "I do think we should keep it to ourselves until we can find out what this is all about."

"I agree," Eric's father added.

"We must go." Alice's mother said. "We apologize—but you can imagine our shock"

After the Dawshers left, Eric said, "I'm goin' for a walk. I need time to think. I'll be back later." He did not feel like answering questions he knew his mother would be asking.

The evening was still warm, with a spring-like freshness in the air. He wasn't sure why, but he knew exactly where he was going. He knocked. Almost immediately, the door opened. "Hello Eric," Linda said. "I haven't seen you for quite a while."

"I know. That's my loss," he said, then followed with the obvious, the expected, "You look fabulous, as always."

"Thank you," she said. Linda tossed her dark auburn hair to one side in that familiar way of hers, and turned on that smile that drew immediate attention. Her flair for the dramatics, along with Eric's offbeat reputation, seemed to attract her in some odd way. They had become friends after a class debate.

"I thought we might go to a movie or something," Eric said.

"How about setting on the porch swing and talk?"

17

He felt the awkward silence between them. Finally, he asked, "How's the fashion world at Garlan's department store?"

"All right. It's a job, I guess—definitely not a career. I have heard about you and the Air Force." Linda looked across the street at the neighbor's barking dog, then turned to face him. "I find it hard to picture you in a military environment."

Eric shrugged. "Maybe it will make a man of me."

"It could do just the opposite," Linda replied.

On an impulse, he told her about the church incident. "You and Alice Dawsher—in church?" She started to laugh. "I'm sorry. I can't help it—the picture I have in mind. You're so unpredictable. You never cease to amaze me. Why is it when you mention her name you ..."

"I admit she's been on my mind."

She turned to face him with those big gray eyes and said, "Tell her how you feel, Eric."

She hesitated a moment then added, "I guess you and about everyone in town know about Bill Hausler and me. We're becoming engaged."

He had seen them together several times. It was obvious they would make a very attractive couple. William Hausler was the only son of Steven Hausler, one of the most prominent lawyers in Benford, as was his father before him. Although there was a younger daughter, from what Eric had heard, Steven Hausler focused most of his attention on his only son. The Hauslers lived in a large, Southern-styled mansion. Like most similar houses, they were in the western part of town.

"You can't be that surprised," Linda continued. "I never gave you the impression that we were anything but casual friends. Eric, I value our friendship, and I hope you feel the same."

"I do. Knowing you has been quite an experience. There was one thing that never got settled—we never got together."

It was one of the few times he ever saw her blush. "Now, Eric—"

"Sorry, that was outta line. But I meant it as a compliment."

She looked out over the porch railing at her neighbors carrying groceries in the house with their dog barking at their heels.

"In your own strange way," she said, choosing her words carefully, "and knowing you as I do, I believe you."

"I guess it's just the feeling of maybe losing you," Eric said.

She smiled as only she could. "We'll always be friends."

"I hope so," Eric said. "We've had some good times and we could always talk. I wish you both the best. I mean it. I think it's time for me to take off." Linda started to say something, but she quickly went in the house. He left and, unlike before, didn't look back.

———————

Eric sat at the soda fountain in Grover's drugstore, sipping coffee. A couple stood over the jukebox, with their faces reflecting the glow of the machine. Soon, someone was singing about lonely nights and lost loves.

Eric stared at the big clock surrounded by paper signs advertising the latest specials. He could not get Alice off his mind. After a few minutes, he went to the phone and dialed Alice's number. He waited until he heard her voice. "Alice," Eric said, "I wanna see you."

"You mean tonight? I just finished washing my hair. At this moment, my head's wrapped in a big towel," Alice said, with laughter in her voice. "Why?"

"You have been on my mind," Eric said.

"My parents are asleep. Maybe for just a few minutes."

Alice opened the door before he could knock. "Hello, Eric. Won't you come in?" She smiled, self-consciously tugging the white fluffy towel around her head. She quickly lowered her head, almost losing the towel, and blushed.

"You look cute in a towel," he said softly.

"I don't know what to say to something like that. What'd you want to see me about?"

"I wondered if we could date or something."

"Aren't you going with Linda Maynard? I've seen you with her a couple times."

"We're just friends. Besides, she's becoming engaged to Bill Hausler, and I'm joining the Air Force." He looked into her big blue eyes and smiled. "How about enlisting with me on the buddy plan?"

She laughed and said, "I don't think so."

Eric shrugged. "They'd probably split us up anyway."

Her blush deepened. "You may call me. Right now—it's getting late." When Eric looked back, she was still standing in the doorway.

The next day, Eric received word he had passed his physical. Eric stood in front of the Air Force recruiter's desk. The calendar on the desk read, "11-SEPTEMBER-1947."

The sergeant stood up from his desk and shook hands. "You're almost one of us." He smiled, pausing long enough to make a dramatic effect. "You will leave here September twenty-fifth, two weeks from today. You will take a bus to Cutler City and be sworn in, after which you'll board the train, along with several others, for Landish Air Force base in Dennard, Texas."

Eric left the recruiting office and stopped at his father's shop. "I passed my physical," he told his father. "I'm suppose to leave September twenty-fifth."

"It's your decision," he said. "Don't tell your mother, but maybe it's best if you do get away from here for a while. For some reason, you can't resist getting involved in some controversy."

"It does seem to follow me," Eric said. "As far as Bryan is concerned, we always got into it—I think it's because of me speaking in tongues at church."

"I agree, but you have to get beyond this petty stuff. The healing of Alice's knee is important, but beyond that, the healing gift is the most important of all—and it's going to bring more controversy; there is no way to avoid it," his father said. "It seems to me you're leaving about the right time."

"I agree," Eric said. "What'll you say we knock off for supper?"

Eric finished supper and watched his mother clear away the dishes. His father shut off the radio and handed Eric a stone. "It was passed down from my grandfather."

The small stone was bluish in color, and seemed to cast a glowing light.

"According to my father," Howard said, "this is a healing stone used by your great grandfather. As far as I know, there was never a calling for us to use it. I think after what you told me, it should be yours."

Eric held the stone and wondered if the sensation of heat was real or his imagination. "I don't know what to say."

His mother stood in the doorway. "It's Indian superstition," she said. Her expression matched her words. "You don't need something like that. Yours is a spiritual path!"

Eric put it in his pocket and said quietly, "I'll see you later. I'm goin' for a walk." He didn't want to hear the conversation that would follow. He'd heard it before.

There were very few people in Grover's drugstore when Eric walked in the door. He was surprised to see Alice sitting at the counter. He walked up behind her and said quietly, "Mind if I join you?"

Startled, she almost knocked over her sundae. After regaining her composure, she whispered, "I guess so." He noticed how the royal blue dress brought out the color of her eyes.

"The usual, Jeff," Eric said to the boy behind the counter. "I'm surprised to see you."

She smiled. "I had a dress alteration, so I thought I might treat myself." She laughed self-consciously. A few minutes later, she watched him for a moment and said, "I never saw anyone have a chocolate sundae with chocolate ice cream and syrup. Unbelievable—and you add peanuts on top." She laughed and shook her head.

"It's great. You should try it." Eric replied.

She made a face. "It's getting late, I better be going," Alice said.

"I feel I should walk my patient home. On an evening like this, maybe a stroll through the park. It's on our way."

"We'll see," she said. A few minutes later, they walked through the park entrance. As they approached the pool area, the exterior lights were turned off. "The pool's closing. It's later than I thought. Maybe we should go back."

"How about the scenic route—over by the bandstand?" Eric tried to take her hand, but she pulled it away.

"It's too dark," she said with a nervous little laugh.

Eric tried to lead her, but she held back. "I don't like this very much." She finally let him take her hand and lead her to a nearby picnic table. He put his arm around her and kissed her. When he kissed her again, she pulled away. "I think you have the wrong idea about me."

She grabbed his hand when he touched her leg and said suddenly. "You'd better not try to force me or I'll smack you silly. *Damn!* I can't believe I said that."

Eric couldn't resist laughing. He tried taking her in his arms. When her body stiffened, she took a deep breath, and said, "You definitely have the wrong idea about me."

"Relax." He reached for her, and she pushed him away.

"No. No!" Alice jumped up, and screamed, "You really don't care for me or you wouldn't . . ."

Eric felt his control slipping away. "I do care for you more than you realize."

"I'm going!" she yelled. When they left the park, she refused to speak until they arrived under the streetlight near her home. "This is far enough," Alice said. "Was I to be your conquest before you left? You tell me! Would Linda be out here like this?" Eric tried to put his arms around her, but she pushed him away and ran down the street.

"You're wrong Alice. I ..." He yelled, but she kept running away from him.

When Eric walked through the front door, his mother was still reading her Bible. A familiar hymn from the phonograph filled the room. The vanilla-colored shawl draped around her shoulders made her look older. She looked up and said, "You look upset, what's the matter?"

"Nothing. I'm just a little tired."

A couple of days later Eric helped his father at his shop. After work, he walked by the Griffin Insurance agency where Alice worked. He started to enter but quickly turned and walked home. After supper he felt depressed and knew the only cure was fresh air and a long walk.

A few minutes later he heard a woman's voice, which he recognized as Rita's. "Hi, Eric, mind if I walk with you?"

At first he was surprised. "My pleasure," he said, remembering Ellen's comments about rumors of him and a waitress at Mabel's Café.

"You're sure I won't embarrass you?"

"I'll take my chances," Eric said. In the evening shadows, he noticed she had less makeup on and a stylish blue print dress, with a light colored tan sweater. Her general appearance was just the opposite when she was on duty. "You look pretty sharp this evening."

"What a line," Rita said. "I've heard some pretty amazing things about you lately." She lowered her voice as they passed another couple walking along the sidewalk.

"What can I say? Don't believe everything you hear," Eric said.

"That's for sure. I'm going to the movies. I've heard so much about this new movie, I just have to see it."

"The late show, huh? Mind if I join you?"

"I don't think they should see us together, at least not till we get inside," Rita said, then she laughed. "Although I don't know whose reputation would suffer the most."

A few minutes later, he bought his ticket and headed for the balcony. It was so dark he couldn't see her. Eric walked down one aisle, then half way down the other before he heard her voice. "Over here." He slipped into the seat next to her. Almost immediately, he became aware of her perfume. Eric put his arm around her and kissed her. The effect of her contact spread through him like a wildfire.

He moved his hand toward her breast. "This is not the place," she whispered, "I'll meet you at Elm and Main in a little while. If you'll excuse the pun, things are getting out of hand."

He suddenly lost interest in the movie. "Don't be too long," Eric said, his voice much too loud. He left the theater and walked to the designated location. He stopped under the street light and lit a cigarette. A few minutes later, he glanced at his watch. *"It's been almost half an hour. Where in the world is she?"*

"Do you always talk to yourself?" Rita asked. She stepped out of the shadows. "A little patience goes a long way. Why do I feel this is going to be an experience?"

He took her by the hand and started across the nearby schoolyard. "Where're we going? There's cars out here," Rita said.

"How about that school fire escape?"

"You're kidding. I can't believe this!"

"Where's your spirit of adventure?" Eric lifted her up where she could reach the lower rung of the fire escape, and boosted her up.

"I'll be damned. This is a first for me." Rita grabbed the cool steel bars of the fire escape landing, and pulled herself into the shadows.

Eric spread his jacket on the landing. He shivered, but only for a moment. He slipped his arm around her, and kissed her. She responded, and he kissed her harder. He moved his hand up her leg. "Easy Eric, let me help you," she whispered. Several moments later, her desire met his. They lay in silence, as the sounds of the night returned.

A few moments later Rita whispered, "I'll say one thing: What you lack in experience, you make up for in enthusiasm," she laughed. She quickly covered her mouth with her hand. "We have to get off this thing. We're pressing our luck."

"I—I really enjoyed it. Did you, I mean?"

Rita laughed. "That's enough! Let's get outta here." Eric helped her down the iron steps of the fire escape. Suddenly, they heard voices coming from around the corner.

He grabbed her hand and they ran across the schoolyard.

"Wait, I'm out of breath," Rita said, slowing to a walk after they were back among the shadows. They watched the crowd of people coming out the school's side door.

"Close, huh?"

"Yeah," Eric said. "You're something else."

"I'm not sure what that would be—but let's not make any more out of it," Rita said. Her deep voice suddenly became serious. "Let's face it—I'm almost, *notice I said almost*, old enough to be your mother."

"I don't believe it," Eric said. "Even if you were, I. . ."

"Let it go Eric—for both our sakes. Hey, I heard about you and the Air Force. Tell you what, I have Friday night off, why don't I fix you a farewell dinner?"

"You're on," Eric said. "What wine would you like?"

She patted his cheek, "The choice is yours. I'll see ya later." She strolled off into the night with that special laugh of hers ringing in his ears. The scent of her perfume lingered in the still evening air like a solid object.

CHAPTER THREE

ERIC ARRIVED AT GROVER'S DRUGSTORE for his pre-arranged meeting with Karen. He saw her waiting at the soda fountain. She smiled, "What do I call you—Private Silkwin?"

"Not yet," Eric said. "Let's get a booth and talk." A few moments later, they huddled over coffee. "I don't know exactly how to put this, but here goes: How do you see me? Like, maybe Alice would . . ."

"Eric, if you'll excuse the expression, you're definitely not handsome. Your attraction is a kind of mystical curiosity. Your personality is complex—it seems to consist of moods and contradictions. How about this Silkwin edge you are always talking about? That's where your charisma is, if that's what you want to call it."

Eric laughed.

"You know how I am." Her laughter matched his. "I'm going to tell you how I really see it—otherwise, what would be the point?"

"That's why I needed to talk to you. You say what you really mean. As for Linda, I knew it wasn't goin' anywhere. Alice is something else."

"I suspected that." She glanced at her watch and added, "Thanks for the coffee and the break from my routine, but I must be going, I know you well enough to quote your own words, 'If it's meant to be, it'll work out.' I'll see you later."

Eric arrived at Rita Luckner's little white cottage, which was almost buried under shaggy cedar which appeared to be fighting for its own existence. He knocked, feeling a little foolish, wondering whether he brought the right kind of wine.

"Hello Eric," she said. "I hope you like roast beef."

"Very much." He handed her the sack, feeling awkward.

Rita seemed reserved and soft-spoken, which surprised him. She was not at all like the loud, fun loving waitress he knew. He glanced around the room, and then wandered over to the bookcase, which contained mostly classics and poetry.

She stood in the doorway watching him. "Surprised?"

"You read these?"

"Yes, at least once. It's my secret passion."

"I'm impressed," he said.

"The dinner was great. I'll never forget it." He helped her carry the dishes to the sink. They engaged in small talk and sipped coffee. Eric could not get over the personality change.

"I'm going to come right out and tell you: My ex-husband is coming over later. If you were expecting something. . ."

"It's all right. There's a girl I got on my mind—It's Alice Dawsher, the girl I gave a healing to in church."

She smiled, and then added. "What can I say? It happens that way sometimes."

It was time to go.

"Goodbye Eric." Rita kissed his cheek, and added, "I wish you the best of luck, and somehow I think you're going to need it."

———————

"Alice, this is Eric. I need to see you. I'll be at your house at eight o'clock. If the porch light is on I'll come to the door."

He watched the clock until it was seven-thirty, and then walked past Alice's house to the end of the block and waited for the porch light that failed to appear. He glanced at his watch and looked back again before heading home.

———————

"Eric—you left the porch light on—never mind—I'll get it," his mother said. A moment later she shouted, "There's someone walking along the street."

Eric looked out the window at the lone figure walking across the street.

"It's Alice. She probably changed her mind, and can't decide what to do." He heard laughter as he ran out the door.

"Alice!" Eric yelled. He ran across the street.

"Oh, Eric, my mother turned the light off by mistake. When I found out, it was after eight and I didn't know what to do."

He put his arms around her. "I'm just happy you're here."

"I feel so foolish. Your family will think I am crazy and now it is starting to rain." Eric put his jacket around her and said, "I'll walk you home. I've missed you."

After they arrived at her house, she glanced at him. "I've missed you too." He kissed her while trying to ignore her mother looking out the window.

"I want to see you as much as possible before I leave," Eric said.

Her smile in the dim porch light agreed with him. The following week, they were inseparable.

"Hey, Eric I got my car back," said Frank. "All it needed was a tune-up. It's ready to roll." Frank's pride and joy was his '46 maroon Ford. "I couldn't do without my Ford, although when it comes to the payments and repair bills, I'm not so sure. Hey, how about you and Alice meeting Karen and me at Grover's about six? How'd you like to do something different tonight?"

Eric matched his grin and said, "Let's hear about it."

"There's a special church in Mayville that has a message service Saturday evenings. It's about an hour's drive from here. Hey, like I said, the Ford is ready to roll." Frank sensed Eric's hesitation, but pressed forward, "If anybody should be interested, it's you."

"I'm not so sure. You think the girls will go for it?"

"We'll worry about it later. I'll see you at Grover's at six."

Alice's mother greeted him at the door. "Hello Eric, won't you please come in?" Her pleasant greeting failed to match the sound in her voice. "You and my daughter have been seeing a lot of each other lately—and something about a dinner tomorrow."

"Yes. It's my going-away dinner," Eric said. It was strange she never mentioned the healing. It was as if nothing happened.

When Alice and Eric arrived at Grover's, the sound of the jukebox and the conversations were drowning each other out. Karen motioned from a table in the back.

"Now hear this," Karen said, glancing at her watch. "We're engaged as of fifteen minutes ago. There's more. We'll get into that later."

Frank explained their plans for the evening.

"I don't believe you guys," Karen said, "At least it's different. I'm game if Alice is."

Less than an hour later, they arrived at the small grey church on the outskirts of Mayville. "This has gotta be it," Frank said.

At first, it appeared like the usual church service, but a feeling that was different—something he could not explain. Later, a tall, thin man gave a brief sermon, followed by a message service. "The young lady in back with the red dress!" the voice from the platform called. Alice glanced at Eric, then at the platform.

"Would you please acknowledge?"

Alice, who was stunned, finally answered. "Yes thank you."

"You and the young lady next to you will have more in common than you realize," he said. He gave several messages, including one for Frank.

Later, a middle-aged lady took over the message service. Her face shone with an almost unbelievable radiance. "You— the young man beside the girl in the red dress. I know you are new to this chapel, but you were led here—you are familiar with healing, which surrounds you." The lady seemed unable to control the flow of words. "You have powerful doctors and guides working through you from the spirit side."

Eric was not surprised. He looked at Alice and Karen, who looked stunned. After the service, the lady who gave the messages approached Eric and said, "My name is Elaine Caulfield. I wanted you to know how strong the vibration was. I seldom get a message with such clarity, and I see you in some type of military uniform."

Eric felt the warmth and compassion of these people he had never met before. He explained his enlistment in the Air Force.

The woman smiled, and introduced the man they had seen earlier. "I'd like you to meet Steven Loulder." The group shook hands.

"Your aura impressed me," Loulder said. He saw the look on their faces and smiled.

"Maybe I should explain in more detail. You have a deep sense of compassion for others. Red in your aura suggests streaks of temper and frustration."

"You will have difficulties," Mrs. Caulfield added. "I'm afraid you have a difficult road ahead, with several challenging decisions."

"What can I say?" Eric replied.

After the service they drove toward Benford. Frank laughed about his involvement with books and schools.

Karen was silent, which was unusual, and then suddenly she remarked, "Well Eric, did you find out what you needed to know?"

"I'm not sure."

"It was bizarre. Unusual. I don't know why, but I was fascinated and uncomfortable simultaneously. What about you, Alice?"

"Strange and unorthodox. I don't know what else to say."

"There's more to it," Karen said. "And I'm not sure I want to know."

"Strictly entertainment." Frank added, "What do you think Eric? You're the closest thing we have to a prophet, but don't tell Bryan I said that."

"I'm not sure, but I think there is much more to it."

"Hey, don't worry about it. Can you imagine me working in a business suit? Let's get something at Cookie's and go to the park. It's your last Saturday night at home."

Lights surrounded the picnic area. A warm breeze crossed their picnic table. Music drifted from the jukebox, on the patio near the swimming pool. They all broke out in laughter when someone sang about a gypsy.

"Talk about timing!" Karen added.

Most of the people taking advantage of the warm, late-summer evening were on the patio.

"Now for something more serious and pressing," Karen began slowly. "There's only one way to say this, I missed my period. I mean . . . Oh, hell, you know what I mean." For a few moments, the distant sounds of the area seemed to fade.

"I'm afraid we were a little careless," Frank said, as he put his arm around Karen. "It seems we are about to become parents."

"We screwed up all right," Karen blurted out.

Frank sighed, "Talk about a play on words."

"I don't know what to say," Eric said. He looked at Frank, who had a sheepish look on his face. "I wouldn't wait to long before telling your parents. It'll only make it worse."

"I'll see the doctor this week to be sure," Karen said. "In any event, I'm not about to ruin this evening. Let's have some wine and get on with it."

"We'll just tell your parents we love each other," Frank said slowly.

"For some reason, I have a hard time picturing that," Karen added.

Frank took Karen's hand. "We're going for a walk. You two need some time alone."

Karen laughed, "I'll bet—see you later."

"You want to go for a walk?" Eric said, watching her reaction.

"Yeah . . . Maybe we should take some wine with us, I kinda like it," Alice said.

They walked to the swings. "Push me," she said. She finished her wine and said, "Do you notice how Karen is kinda outspoken?"

Eric laughed. "I've noticed that, but once you get to know her, very few things will surprise you."

"I think you're trying to get me to make love with you?" Alice said. She started to hiccup.

"Hold your breath and count to ten," Eric told her. He tried to keep from laughing, but he could not avoid it. After getting control of himself, he said, "Coffee for you." They walked back to the table, where Karen and Frank were waiting for them. "Alice is . . ."

"Just a little bit tipsy," Alice interrupted.

"I'll go along with that," Karen said. Then she glanced at Alice, laughed, and said, "I'm sorry, Alice, but the expression on your face defies description." After black coffee at Cookie's drive-in, they dropped Alice and Eric off at her house.

Eric walked her to the door. "Should I come in?"

"For a little while, mom and dad are in bed so we have to be quiet." She opened the door and saw the note by the phone. "My uncle is sick so they're checking on him." Alice looked at Eric and said, "Why am I whispering?"

"I don't know." Eric grinned.

He picked up the picture on the end table. "I've been meaning to ask you: Who's this girl with you in the picture?"

"My sister Paula. She's five years older than I am," Alice said. "She married a reporter whom my father didn't approve of, that can't seem to hold a job. My mother wonders why they never had any children. Actually, we are not as close as we used to be—too much conflict, I guess. I don't know what else to say but they live in Chicago."

"I just never heard you mention her before."

"She drops in every once in a while, usually around the holidays. She is pretty, isn't she?" Alice said. "You will meet her one of these days, although I would not even guess when, or what time of day. Paula is the opposite of me—very outgoing—and, to quote my father, 'self-centered and crude.'"

Eric studied the picture then faced Alice. "Yes she is pretty, but she looks so—sad. I am sorry. I can see it makes you uncomfortable. We could change the subject."

"My sentiments exactly, Mr. Silkwin." She turned on the radio. A reddish glow from the radio lit the room as they danced. "This will be our last night alone together for a long time," she whispered.

"I know." Suddenly, they stopped dancing. He put his arms around her and kissed her.

"I don't know how to handle this. It's very awkward." Alice whispered, "Maybe if we took it one step at a time."

The awkward moment of silence seemed to go on forever. Finally, she said slowly, "You want to unzip me?"

"Yes," Eric whispered softly.

"Wait. Give me a minute," she said softly.

Eric lit a cigarette, surprised to see his hand shake.

"I'm ready." Alice stood in the hallway in a red nightgown. He stared at her, wanting to take in the vision that he never dreamed possible. He put out his cigarette and followed her to her bedroom. Eric took his time, afraid of making the wrong move. Slowly he caressed her until he felt she responded. Uneasy at first at the sudden intimacy, Alice slowly melted into his arms. Eric kissed her softly, again.

"I love you," Eric said. She shuddered as the woman in her came alive. Suddenly, it was over. He held her, listening to music that would take on new meaning in their lives.

"I'll never forget this song," Alice said. "I must get you outta here. I'm suddenly getting a little nervous."

Early Sunday morning, Eric felt the people staring at him and Alice as they walked down the aisle of the church.

"My sermon this morning will be 'While we are apart, one from another.'" Reverend Langtree smiled at Alice and Eric.

The going-away dinner was crowded. Finally, the younger group moved to the back yard. It was a warm, sunny, almost-perfect fall day, with a gentle breeze, and a few brightly colored leaves drifting to the ground.

"Eric," Bryan said slowly, "That healing business at church; I've given it a lot of thought. I figure that was nature's way of exerting herself. It's ridiculous to think it miraculous."

"Oh, Bryan, let it go," Karen said coldly. "This is Eric's last day before leaving and he doesn't need this discussion."

The late evening air grew chilly, so they went back inside. The remaining crowd wished Eric luck and left.

Bryan extended his hand.

"See you at the bus station," Karen called as they left.

Alice and Eric walked silently up the steps. Her mother opened the door and said, "We were just having a cup of tea. Won't you join us in the kitchen?"

While still standing, Eric took Alice's hand in his, and with a deep breath announced, "I'm in love with your daughter." Alice's face reddened.

"Was it a pleasant dinner?" her mother asked calmly.

"Very pleasant, but a little sad," Alice said.

"How do you feel, Alice, about what Eric just told us?" Her father asked. He pushed his rimless glasses farther down on his nose and peered over them at Alice.

She focused on her mother. "I've had a crush on Eric for a long time. When we fought and separated, I knew it was much more than infatuation. Our time together this last week has only confirmed those feelings."

"Maybe I'm rushing it," Eric said, "but I want Alice and me to be engaged."

"Isn't this just a last-minute thing because you're leaving tomorrow?" her mother asked. "That was my first impression."

Eric reached in his pocket and pulled out a little box. He took out a ring and placed it on Alice's finger. "I had no idea," Alice whispered in shock.

"I'm going to be blunt, because my daughter's future is at stake," her mother said with an edge in her voice. "We have a responsible reputation in the community. As for the healing—if that's what it was—I'm afraid it is unorthodox and misleading of our Christian beliefs. Maybe I—we don't know—or what this type of, err, healing it is. It could be ..."

"Mother! How can you say that?" Alice said. "This is a gift—Eric's gift. He could help people. And I assure you—I'm not Paula!"

"There are too many people that are against this sort of thing."

"I'm sorry you feel that way," Eric said.

Her mother watched Eric very closely. "Do you know who Claude Stratman is?"

"Not personally. I think he's a reporter for the Benford *Daily News.*"

"Yes. He most certainly is," Alice's mother said. "He tried questioning us this morning about what went on at the church with Alice's . . . healing!"

"I didn't know," Eric said. "Why wouldn't he contact me?"

"He couldn't get a hold of you. Evidently he'd just heard about it," Alice's father said. "We hadn't planned on anything like this."

"Me either," Eric said. "I'll try to contact him before I leave."

"This has nothing to do with your Indian heritage. I have respect for your parents."

"It's strange you would mention my Indian heritage," Eric said calmly, "if it hadn't been on your mind."

"I'm accepting this engagement, with or without your blessing!" Alice said, close to tears. The tense moments before her mother answered seemed to go on forever.

"Under those conditions, I don't seem to have much of a choice—seems like I've been through this before," she said very slowly, and then quickly regained her composure. "I'll accept this, err, engagement with the obvious test of time." Close to tears herself now, she continued, "The whole town will know. As for the publicity . . ."

Alice's father interrupted. "I don't like it either. I promised I'd hold my temper. I was afraid something like this would happen, but we will try to handle the situation as best we can. The best line of defense is to refuse to comment." After a few awkward moments, Alice's mother embraced her daughter, with tears in her eyes and kissed her cheek. "You may not realize it, but your happiness is all that really matters."

Alice wiped her tears away and broke into a big smile. "We will be happy, you'll see."

"We'll leave you two alone," her father said. "I don't want trouble. It's just hard for us—especially when we have been through something like this before with Paula."

"I'm sorry it has to be this way," Alice said.

"I understand. You're not Paula, whatever that may mean," Eric said. "I'd better go."

"I'll see you at the bus station," she said. "I'll probably cry, but not in front of you."

"If you do I won't be able to get on the bus," Eric said, and tried to smile. He kissed her and hurried out the door.

When he arrived home, his mother asked, "Don't you think Karen and Frank are too close?"

"It's my understanding they love each other," Eric replied.

"A couple of kids like that—both at times a little scatter-brained to begin with. They don't know what love is."

"Does anybody?" His father laughed.

His mother shook her head. "Eric, you hear me? You're drifting off again. Sometimes I wonder about you, too!"

"Has anybody tried to contact you from the paper?" Eric asked. "A reporter from the Benford *Daily News* has contacted the Dawshers about Alice's healing!"

"What in the world are you talking about?" his mother asked.

"It was just a matter of time," his father replied. "I'll handle it. I was hoping somehow . . . ."

"Don't you worry about it," his father said. "You're going to have your hands full."

"The Dawshers must be so upset," his mother said.

"Yes. Very much," Eric said. He tried the phone. "I can't get a hold of the reporter. I'll try again in the morning. I'm gonna turn in."

Before drifting off to sleep, he held the healing stone in his hand, and wondered why the Indian or the crippled little girl in his dreams had not contacted him.

The next morning Eric's parents and, surprisingly enough, Ellen, were waiting in the kitchen.

Eric grabbed the phone. He waited several minutes and hung up. "I still can't get the guy. Some secretary said he's out on assignment."

Ellen surprised Eric by saying, "I've had a little experience in public relations. I will do what I can. This thing was bound to come out one way or another."

"You eat this breakfast. No telling what those people will feed you," his mother said.

Eric ate quickly. "I'm running a little late."

Ellen hugged him. "You take care of yourself, I don't know why we—you know—never mind." She rushed out the door.

'I'll say goodbye here, Dad." They shook hands. "I know you'll take care of things."

"Bye, son. You stand tall. Don't let 'em get to you."

His mother kissed his cheek and started crying. "I promised myself I wouldn't do this, but what do I know?"

"I'll be home for Christmas," he told her. "Don't worry about a thing." He picked up his bag and started out the door.

"You gonna see Alice?" his mother asked.

"Yes, at the bus station. I gave her a ring last night. We're engaged."

"What are you talking about? I...."

The last thing Eric saw when he waved was his mother's mouth wide open and his father's smile, with his arm around her shoulder.

"You're playing it close buddy," Frank said, shaking Eric's hand, "You know if I could ...."

"I know," Eric said. Karen quickly kissed him, and then stepped aside when the bus pulled in the station.

Alice was in his arms. "I love you, Eric Silkwin," she said.

"I love you. Remember; tell Stratman or anybody else you have no comment. If he presses you, tell him I'll talk to him when I get home."

"I will," Alice said.

"Keep your chin up. I'll write when I can!" Eric shouted as he boarded the bus. He grabbed a seat next to the window and waved at the curly-headed girl with the big blue eyes until she was out of sight.

CHAPTER FOUR

"WYLER IN TWENTY MINUTES," the driver announced. A few minutes later, the bus came to a stop and a handful of passengers got on board.

A tall, thin guy with uncontrollable, wavy red hair sat next to Eric. "Weren't you at the recruiter's the other day? Name's Jason Corkland. I get the feeling we're in the same boat. I signed up in Benford, but I live in Wyler."

"Eric Silkwin from Benford." They shook hands.

"You think we know what we're doing?"

"I hope so," Eric said, although right then he was not sure.

"Cutler City in thirty minutes," the driver announced.

When they arrived, Eric and Jason stood in line with several recruits. After their briefing and paperwork, the recruits raised their right hands to be sworn in. A little later, they boarded the train.

"I overdid it a little bit last night," Jason said, forcing a smile. "I've got a hangover. Hey, you wouldn't happen to have a cigarette, would you?"

Eric handed him a Camel.

Jason took a deep drag, coughed, and said, with a lopsided grin, "I kinda like Luckys myself." They introduced themselves to the other recruit, who sat across from them. Ted Faulkland had one of those button-nosed impish faces. He looked no more than seventeen—boyish, blond, and blue-eyed, with a shy smile—but Ted was twenty-one and the oldest of the three. His intense look gave the impression he was a very serious young man.

Whatever the situation, Jason seemed just the opposite. He seemed carefree and took everything in stride.

Several of the guys played poker and shot dice. The afternoon slowly turned into darkness, as the train roared through the night.

The following morning Eric awoke to the call for breakfast. He poked Jason, who slowly shook his head. "Damn, it's for real. I was hoping this was just a bad dream."

After breakfast, Jason asked the porter, "Are we in Texas yet?"

He smiled. "Not for a few hours yet."

Eric wondered how often this porter answered the same question. After becoming bored with the poker game, the conversation led to anything that came to mind.

"This has gotta be Texas," Jason said later. "You guys better get a load of this."

The recruits looked out the train windows. Suddenly all the humor faded as the train gradually slowed and pulled into the station. The reality of their immediate future for the next several weeks was suddenly before them.

"I've got a feeling this party's over," Jason said, with an unusual tone. His familiar, good-natured expression faded as he, along with the others, stared at the military bus and men in uniform waiting for them.

"All right you guys, over here—on the double!" Corporal Avery shouted. Eric, Jason, and Ted fell in line with the other recruits. "When I call your name, sound off, pick up your personal belongings and board this bus." He waited, and then yelled, "*I can't hear you!*"

"Yes, sir!" The corporal smiled, but only for a moment. After miles of dry, dusty, barren country, they reached the entrance to Landish Air Force Base. When they stopped, a military policeman boarded the bus, checked them out, and waved the driver through. Eric stared at the endless rows of two-story barracks. The bus stopped. When the recruits filed off, a formation of guys in fatigues marched by. Their sergeant yelled, "*I gotta gal in San Antoine,*" and the squad echoed, "*I gotta a gal in*

San Antoine," then the sergeant again, *"She don't like to sleep alone."* And the echo: *"She don't like to sleep alone."*

"Ten-hut!" the corporal shouted. The recruits attempted a formation, which brought on a mixture of laughter and obvious frustration. "Knock it off," the corporal yelled. "When I call your name, line up over here with your personal belongings." Suddenly a sergeant appeared out of nowhere and joined the corporal. Eric stared at the tanned, slim, six-foot sergeant, and the image of a recruiting poster came to mind.

"My name is Baulkner. Sergeant Baulkner. You *will* know my face—and my commands. If you do not, believe me—you *will* before I'm through with you! It's my job to pressure you misfits—regardless of what I have to work with—to become airmen in twelve weeks, or you'll be held over by my demand. *Do you read me?"*

"Yes, sir!" They shouted. "This is Corporal Avery," Baulkner said. He was a tall, thin man with curly brown hair and a face that looked as if he was only now recovering from the early stages of adolescence. "From the looks of you, we're gonna attempt the impossible." He walked from one end of the formation to the other, staring into faces.

"You'll be sor-ry!" shouted another group marching by, followed by a swearing, frustrated sergeant.

"That was a formation of airmen," Baulkner yelled. "If first impressions count, you guys got a long way to go. Leave your belongings here. As difficult as it sounds, we're gonna try and march to supply." The recruits spent the hot, humid day standing in endless lines—for shots, lectures and a combination of uniforms. Finally, after being very frustrated they received the closest haircuts Eric had ever seen. They took showers, dressed in fatigues, and headed back to the barracks and were assigned bunks. The only time Eric saw anyone smile was after the haircuts, but that did not last long.

"Fall out in front of the barracks in five minutes," the sergeant, barked. A weary, frustrated, pitiful-looking group finally managed a lopsided formation. "Tallest man in front. Get with it, we're going to chow." Eric watched as they rushed hundreds of men in and out of the mess hall. After chow, they marched back to the barracks.

"You men gather around over here," Baulkner said. "Corporal Avery and I will show you how to make a bunk." The men watched closely. "Any questions? Get the rest of your gear straightened out. I want each man to get his bunk squared away. You got an hour before lights out. We'll really get under way tomorrow."

Sergeant Baulkner walked away, shaking his head. Later, he came out of his room at the end of the barracks and shouted "Lights out in fifteen minutes."

Eric thought of home. He was certain he was not alone.

Next morning the nightmare returned. "Fall out. Up and at 'em!" Baulkner walked up and down the aisle, yelling, *"Move it! Move it!"* The men groaned, grabbed their shaving kits, bumping into each other, and headed for the latrine. "Roll call in ten minutes. Full fatigue dress in front of the barracks, and all bunks must be made," Baulkner shouted, "It's a half hour past daylight. The day's half-over."

Somehow, a formation assembled in front of the barracks. Baulkner looked from one end of the group to the other. "Don't you think you're taller than the guy in front of you?" He shouted in someone's ear. "Get the hell in front of this guy."

"Yes, sir," the recruit snapped back. "No, sir . . . I mean . . ."

"We'll get better acquainted after chow." Baulkner grinned.

"You mean this crap is supposed to be scrambled eggs?" one of the guys said. Eric joined the others in laughter.

––––––––––––––––

When the recruits returned to the barracks, Baulkner shouted, "Every man will be at attention in front of his bunk. You've got five minutes. Fall out."

"What in the hell do you call this?" Baulkner yelled. He ripped the blanket and sheet off the bunk and threw it on the floor. "All recruits who are not sure how to make a bunk, fall in over here. Pay attention, your very existence may depend on it."

Everyone in the lower bay crowded in around the bunk. Sergeant Baulkner looked at the frustrated group. "I get stuck with a bunch of misfits who're lucky if they know their ass from a hole in the ground." The men watched him make up the bunk slowly.

"Each man will check his bunk," Baulkner instructed. "You got ten minutes. Corporal Avery will take the upper bay and I'll take the lower. *Hit it!*" A blur of green fatigues swept the barracks. Somehow, a few minutes later, they had the bunks squared away. "Each man will, I repeat, will, know his exact place in formation. You will know it so well you can find it in your sleep. Ten-hut! Eyes front—don't look right, left, up or down. Keep your eyes straight ahead. Do you hear me?"

"Yes, sir."

"I can't hear you."

"Yes, sir!"

"What's your name, Son?" Baulkner stared into the eyes of a recruit who made the mistake of looking down. "What in the hell did I just tell you? What's your name?"

"Morris, Sir. You—you make me nervous—sir."

"That's the most brilliant observation I've heard all day Misfit Morris. Where are you from, boy?"

"Nebraska, sir."

"Evidently they didn't raise clowns like you to respect my authority," Baulkner yelled in his ear. "For a minute, I thought you were losing respect for me . . . but that would never happen—would it, Private Morris?"

"Yes sir . . . I mean no sir." Baulkner shook his head and moved down the line. "Why in the hell didn't you shave, boy?"

Jason smiled. "Well, you see it's this way, Sarge . . ."

"Sarge! Wipe that smile off your face!" Jason snapped to attention. "Have you ever heard the expression, familiarity breeds contempt? Give me ten push-ups—*now!*" Baulkner quickly turned to the recruit beside him. "Since you think, it's so damn funny, you join him." Both finished and stood at attention. "Corkland, go to the latrine and shave, and since you get

off on it," Baulkner said, turning to the recruit who laughed, "you bring back his whiskers and show me. You've got five minutes." Baulkner checked his watch. "Move out! What a bunch of clowns. What'd you think, Avery?"

"I dunno, Sarge, looks hopeless. What'll we do with 'em?"

"Hard work: close-order drills, marches, inspections. This will be our ultimate challenge to prove we can make something out of next to nothing." Corkland and the other guy ran out of the barracks and fell back in formation. Sergeant Baulkner stood in front of Corkland. "What in the hell is that on your chin, Private Corkland?"

"Toilet paper, I nicked myself, sir."

"Where are those whiskers?"

"Here, sir," the guy said.

Sergeant Baulkner raised his hand, "Put them here." Avery walked up and looked at them. "What do you think, Avery?"

The sergeant quickly turned to face the squad. "What's so damn funny?"

Eric, along with a few others could not keep from smiling. "You men find this funny? Step forward," Baulkner shouted to Eric. He stared into Eric's eyes. "What's your name?"

"Silkwin, sir."

"Silkwin! What the hell kind of name is that. You look part Indian."

"Yes, sir. I'm part Cheyenne, sir."

"Where you from, Silkwin?"

"Illinois, sir."

"You man enough to represent the Land of Lincoln?" Before Eric could answer he shouted, "I've heard you Indians are hard asses, with guts. We'll see." Baulkner never cracked a smile, but his eyes gave him away. "I want these men in the athletic field for close-order drill. Move 'em out!" Baulkner stalked off.

"I'm going to show you the basic commands," Avery told them. "Watch closely. This may not be one of his best days."

It seemed like the day went on forever. Hours later, they headed back to the barracks and, a few minutes after that, they marched to chow. "Each man will take a shower every evening," Baulkner ordered. "If I hear of any man not taking one, Avery and I will personally give him one. Believe me. He will never forget it. Another thing," Baulkner continued, "Each man will write home. Lights out in half an hour. We have a very busy and hectic day tomorrow."

Across the aisle, Jason lay moaning. "I hurt in places I didn't know I had," he said to no one in particular. He wandered over and sat on Eric's bunk. "Did I tell you about my girl back home? She's blond, blue-eyed, and just a little top-heavy, but carries it well," Jason said. "She's a typist for a construction company. When she smiles, its sunshine."

"Sunshine—how original," one of the guys yelled. "When do we meet her?" Several guys joined in, along with whistles throughout the barracks.

"Forget it," Jason yelled. "Hey when do we get mail?"

Baulkner grunted on the way to his room.

"He's something else, isn't he?" Ted Faulkland said.

Jason laughed. "Yeah, but what?"

"Up and at 'em. Fall out in ten minutes," Avery shouted as the lights came on. The groans began. On the way back from chow, Baulkner halted the formation after Ted kept bumping into Youder, the guy in front of him.

"Faulkland, you and Youder, from all appearances, have about as much coordination as a fence post."

He picked up a stone and ordered Ted to the front. "In order for you to know your left foot from your right, you carry this in your left hand until you can execute."

Ted's face reddened, he whispered, "Yes sir."

Baulkner turned to the guy Ted kept bumping into. "Youder, since you seem to get such a charge out of Faulkand's dilemma, you'll keep the stone in your possession at all times when Faulkland is not in formation—is that clear?"

"Yes sir," Youder said.

45

The day was another long one, but routine slowly began to take over. The next few weeks, the men, including Ted and Youder, marched together in a reasonable formation.

Eric quickly showered and shaved.

"Mail," Corporal Avery announced. The recruits' faces lit up. Eric got a feeling they were really going to make it through Basic. "Silkwin, Eric," Avery shouted. He sat on his bunk, and opened the letter from Karen.

"Hey, you guys, I'm going to be a father," some guy yelled.

"That's great, why don't you do the right thing and marry the girl?" someone else yelled. Everybody laughed, releasing the tension of another long, hot, frustrating day.

Eric opened his letter from Karen and grinned.

Dear Cousin,

The rabbit flipped over and died. From the above I guess you know I am pregnant. Frank and I talked to my parents last night and they took it a lot better than we thought. Frank tried to take all the blame, but we know better than that don't we? We are going to be married this Saturday in church. Mother has been running around with rushed invitations. I am afraid she is fighting a losing battle. I feel a little sorry for her, but dad is taking it in stride. I keep picturing you looking like a bald eagle.

Write when you can. I hope this letter finds you happy despite basic training.

As ever, Karen and Frank

"Lights out in ten minutes." The familiar call echoed throughout the barracks.

———————

"Up and at 'em. Move it! We've got a busy day ahead," Avery called. The sound of his voice was becoming familiar.

That evening everybody wandered into the barracks dog-tired. At mail call, Eric received letters from Alice and his parents.

Dear Son,

We hope you are doing well in basic training. Things are the same here, except Karen and Frank are getting married. I bet you knew, didn't you? Dad said to hang in there.

Ellen misses you. Those talks were as much for her benefit as yours. It's hard for her to write. You know how she is. Remember your dreams and study your Bible. It's still the best book in the world.

Love Mom and Dad

Dear Eric

I hope everything is going well. Karen and Frank are getting married Saturday and I am invited. We are so close, yet I find it hard knowing what to write. I guess so much of what we share comes from silent communication.

I worry about you Eric; I know it's been only a month you have been away. It seems longer. I know they keep you busy. I must close. Remember. I love you. Write when can.

Love and kisses, your Alice

Eric closed his eyes and tried to picture the freckles on that little turned-up nose. "Hey, wanna see a picture of a girl who's got it all?" Jason said. He walked over to Eric's bunk. "Look at this." He held out a rumpled photo signed, "Love, Cindy."

Eric grinned, "I can't imagine what a pretty girl like this could see in the likes of you."

"The lady obviously has taste," Jason replied. He stared at the picture for a moment, his mind obviously miles away. "Lights out in ten minutes," the familiar voice called.

"Seems like the only words I ever hear are `Lights on' in the morning and `Lights out' at night," Jason complained. "All the rest is hard work and frustration."

"We'll all attend church services this morning. Fall out in formation, you got fifteen minutes," Baulkner said. Groans were heard from different parts of the barracks. "What's your feeling toward church, Eric?" Jason asked.

"I go regularly. Although I think of myself as a free soul."

"Me too. If I gotta be anything, it's a free soul," Jason said.

"I don't believe in anything I can't see," Ted added.

"I don't see God, but I believe in him," Jason added. "You've got to believe in something, especially in this place." The men went to church in fatigues, the dress of recruits. Services were peaceful and relaxing, although strange in a military atmosphere. Sunday the squad wrote letters and did their laundry.

Eric wrote his folks, Karen and Frank. The letter to Alice, he saved for last.

> *Dear Alice,*
>
> *I received your letter. I don't want you to worry. It isn't that bad here. The hardest part is missing you. I'll write when I can, but they keep us very busy. In a way, that is best. We don't have much time to think. I miss you so much. In fact, just the other night I fell asleep wondering how many freckles you have on your nose. I'll write again soon.*
>
> *Love you, Eric*

The following morning, the squad took its first turn at KP. After a hard fourteen-hour day, several guys refused to lie on their bunks for fear they might not make it back up before showering. Jason groaned. "I need to be somewhere else, anywhere but here." He flopped on his bunk.

The squad began to shape up the last week. "Just think, in a couple days we'll get a twelve-hour pass," Jason sighed. "I've gotta see if there's still life out there."

"It'll be great," Eric admitted, "Maybe a good meal and a couple of beers. I'll leave the girls to you guys."

"You might as well be married," Ted added.

"At Christmas I probably will be."

"You gonna invite me?" Jason asked.

Eric smiled. "You'll probably be my best man."

A big grin spread across his face. "If I'm the best man, why is she marrying you?"

"Because she's in love with me," Eric said.

"Sounds like reason enough to me."

Before going on a pass, Baulkner assembled the entire barracks. "The last couple of days I've heard some rumblings. Now hear this! Discrimination will not be tolerated. The Air Force is not concerned about your nationality, social position, or anything else. You are here for one reason and that is to complete basic training. Any questions?"

The recruits were loaded on buses and taken to Dennard, Texas. Eric, Jason and Ted got off the bus, with the warning of Baulkner's voice ringing in their ears.

At the street corner, Jason said, "How about a couple of beers? Let's see now—in the name of tradition, let's head left." Ted and Eric laughed at the ritual that decided their movement, even away from the base. "There appears to be a lounge just ahead. Let's bless 'em with our presence," Jason said, with a big grin.

"Great," Eric said. He opened the door, letting Jason and Ted lead the way. It took a couple minutes to adjust to the dimly lit bar after coming out of the bright sunlight. A long bar, lined with stools was on the right, and booths and small, individual tables to the left. The end of the bar led to an adjoining room, with booths surrounding the walls and tables in the center. Scenic western paintings surrounded the dining room with indirect lighting, which gave the room its own attractive atmosphere.

"Place looks a little deserted," Jason said. "I'll guess one-thirty in the afternoon isn't their busiest time."

"I'm sorry, but I must see your identification," the waitress said. She stared at Ted. She quickly checked them and smiled, glancing at their hair. "What'll it be, gents?"

"Beers, and don't let these haircuts fool you," Jason said.

She smiled and added, "They're not."

"That identification thing always happens to me," Ted sighed.

Jason laughed. "Hey, someday you'll appreciate it. Let's face it. We're marked men."

Eric rubbed the top of his head. "I think it's obvious. I gotta hunch they're used to guys like us around here."

When the waitress returned, Jason said, "We hail from the great state of Illinois. That do anything for you?"

"Not at the present," the waitress replied. "Welcome to God's country."

A little later Jason whispered, "If she can dish it out, she outta be able to take it." He motioned for her. She started putting the empties on a tray, but Jason held onto his.

"One guy told me, they chose the most barren, desert-like country in the U.S. for training bases, what else would it be good for," Jason said. "However, where they came up with the name of Texas, I don't know."

The girl quickly glanced around. "I guess I asked for that, but be careful. Some of these guys don't have much of a sense of humor. You could start a small war. Listen, I'm sorry, my name is Libby. I did not mean to offend you guys. Let's start over."

Jason winked at her. "I'm sorry, too. I had to see if you could take it."

"Three more rounds sound about right," Ted told her.

"I just had to bring out her finer points," Jason said.

"I'd watch what I said about Texas," Eric warned. "We don't need any more training that's not on our schedule."

"Hey Libby," Jason said, "How about recommending a good restaurant?"

"Monsento Rose, four blocks to your right, and one straight ahead. You can't miss it."

Jason gave her a dollar tip. "Here honey, buy yourself a yellow rose. You could, after a reasonable time, end with a dozen."

Libby laughed. "For somebody who talks so much, do you really ever say anything?" Jason grinned sheepishly. "I can't be sure. See you later." She shook her head.

"Thanks for the tip," she said. "Don't get lost."

"That girl has possibilities, but she needs my guidance," Jason said as they left the bar.

"Libby's right," Jason said, a little later at the restaurant. "These red and white checkered tablecloths really give this place a pleasant, comfortable, homey touch."

"The candle helps too," Eric said. He glanced at the western pictures surrounding the paneled walls. 'Talk about atmosphere!'"

A young, dark-haired waitress with big brown eyes and a sly smile brought menus. She placed glasses of ice water and a basket of rolls on the table. "I'll be back a little later to take your orders." She smiled, and then left.

After they had eaten, Jason leaned back, took a sip of coffee and smiled. "What an improvement over the mess hall. That's the best chicken dinner I've had in a long time, a very long time."

The waitress returned. "Is there anything else?" She looked at Ted and smiled.

Ted, who seldom drank coffee, ordered refills all around. "She's a pretty one. How about coming back here before we go back to the base?"

"Sure," Jason said. "But you're gonna have to work a lot faster."

They left the restaurant and went to the movie. The boy still got the girl, but this time it was on horseback. "Would you believe it, it's only about eight o'clock," Jason said. "How about a couple more beers?"

The Bull Head Lounge was crowded. They walked to the back of the noisy, smoke-filled lounge. "I wonder where my girl is," Jason said. Another waitress stopped at their table, but suddenly Libby seemed to come out of nowhere. "I'll take care of these three. I know how to handle 'em," she said, "How was the movie?"

"How did you know?" Ted asked. "Oh, I get it."

"You guys in basic all follow the same pattern. Let's see now," she began, her green eyes shining. "A few beers, good meal, movie, and a few more beers before heading back on the bus. It is just so obvious. I don't mean to put you down."

"Three beers," Jason said, and then added, "Did you miss me?"

51

She broke into laughter. "Yes. Nevertheless, I managed to overcome it."

"Hey, it's almost ten," Ted slurred. Several beers later, Ted was trying to sing and keep time with the organist. Jason tried flirting with Libby, but she was on the move. "Another round," Ted called, losing time with the music.

"One more and you guys better take off," Libby said, "No getting into trouble."

"Maybe you should hold their hands," yelled a voice from the booth behind them, followed by laughter and giggling. Ted turned to see the couples. "What have we here? One of the air base's finest?" said one guy. "Does your mother know where you are?" the other guy nudged the girl beside him.

"Screw you, and the horse you rode in on," Ted yelled.

Eric and Jason broke into laughter. The guy with small eyes and a stiff black haircut stepped over to their booth, forcing Libby back.

"All right you guys—no trouble!" she said.

The people at the surrounding tables stopped talking, sensing a disturbance.

"He didn't really mean anything," Jason said, "Why don't you go back to your booth. Besides, you started it." Turning to face Libby, he said, "We'll have that last round."

"Tell your friend to apologize."

"Sure, and Ted, while you're at it," Jason said, glancing at the girl beside him, "ask him why in the hell didn't he leave his horse outside." The guy swung, but Jason quickly shoved his elbow in the guy's stomach. He doubled over and fell on the floor.

The girls screamed and the surrounding people backed away from their tables with the skill of previous experience. The other guy jumped up and Eric leaped up to meet him.

"*What in the hell's going on here?*" Baulkner's voice roared as he walked up to them.

Ted stretched to his full five-foot-seven and tried to explain. He looked at Baulkner with the slow deliberation of a guy who has had too many, trying to pretend he was sober. "You guys are everywhere!" Ted said.

"How many beers have you men had?" Baulkner asked.

"Five or six," Ted admitted, "and we're gettin' ready for another round."

Baulkner stared at Ted and tried to keep a straight face. Behind him, Corporal Avery laughed. "All this after five or six beers?" Baulkner shook his head then said to the guy who was picking himself up off the floor, "These men are my responsibility. I'll take care of them. From what I could see you asked for it."

"You're spyin' on us," Ted said, still trying to control his tongue.

"I check the bars to keep guys like you clowns from gettin' in trouble. You sure you need another beer?" Baulkner asked, no longer trying to hide his smile.

"I've gotta keep up with these guys," Ted mumbled.

"Last round, then coffee and the bus," Eric said.

"I'm holding you to it. Don't make me come back here!" Baulkner said, and then smiled.

"Let's see how you handle your booze tomorrow."

"Ted, let's go to the restaurant. What'll that girl think if you're loaded?" Jason asked. He put five dollars on Libby's tray. "Keep the change. I don't want you to forget me."

She smiled and said, "I don't think I could. Thank you and take care of yourselves."

"Easy Ted," Eric said. He opened the door to the restaurant.

"Hello, may I help you?" the waitress asked, and then took their order.

As the waitress walked away, Ted said, "I don't think I'm getting anywhere."

She placed their orders on the table; Ted looked at her and took a deep breath. "Would you mind if I ask your name?"

The girl glanced at him, smiled and then she whispered, "Marie."

"I'm at the air base," Ted said. "I—I'd like to see you again!"

"I'll be here," she answered softly, then hurried away.

"Marie," Ted murmured. "If I'm lucky, I'll dream about her tonight. I'm gonna talk to Sergeant Baulkner about this. Didn't he say if we had any problems we should talk to him 'man to man'?"

Marie came back to refill their cups. Ted could not take his eyes off her. He took a deep breath and asked, a little too loud, "Will you go to the movies with me sometime?"

She whispered softly, "I'll have to think about it."

Later, Ted's voice sang out over the noise of the bus. "Did you see how she looked at me when I said, 'I'll see you later, Marie?'" Ted said. The look in her eyes told him she really hoped he would.

Her parting smile sealed the promise.

CHAPTER FIVE

"ALL RIGHT—UP AND AT 'EM! You've had your pass. Time to hit it! Formation in ten minutes." The familiar voice brought the men back to reality.

Ted threw back the covers, leaped up and grabbed his head. "I can't believe I drank that much." Jason and Eric looked at each other and laughed. "I gotta feeling they're really going to put the pressure on today," Ted groaned.

"Fall in! Forward march," Baulkner shouted, and they began to move. "Column left harch, your left," he said "your left, your left, right, left." Baulkner and Avery led close - order drills and a full day at the rifle range. They marched back in formation. Avery shouted, "Sound off—*I got a girl who lives in the West,"* and the squad echoed, *"I got a girl who lives in the West."* Then the sergeant again, *"She's got mountains on her chest."* And the echo: *"She's got mountains on her chest."* After arriving back at the barracks, Avery shouted. "Squad *halt!* Dismissed."

Eric sensed the squad coming together. For the first time, after a very long, hard day, a sense of cooperation and pride showed in the squad's faces.

"I've gotta talk to Sergeant Baulkner," Ted said after his shower. "I mean, if the guy was trying to kill me, he would have succeeded today." He knocked on Baulkner's door. About half an hour later, he came out and slowly went to his bunk.

"What happened?" Jason asked.

"He couldn't give me a pass, but he did listen and said he'd help me. He offered to personally drop in at the restaurant and take a letter to Marie. The sergeant knows her and her father, who owns the restaurant. How about that!"

"That's great," Jason said. "We only have a little more than five weeks to go."

Ted forced a smile. "That's what he said. If it was that important to me, we could write, talk on the phone, and really get to know each other by the end of basic."

Eric read a letter from his folks, then opened a letter from Alice.

> *Dear Eric,*
>
> *I hope you're still holding up. I've been spending time with Karen and Frank. They know how much I miss you. They have the cutest apartment. I've eaten dinner at your house, and your family's very pleasant, but we all miss you.*
>
> *Five and half more weeks. I can barely wait to see you.*
>
> *I'm closing now. Here's the only picture I have. Write when you can.*
>
> *Love you, Your Alice*

Jason wandered over and Eric handed him the picture. "She's very pretty. Especially those blue eyes. I can't wait to meet her. I can't see how a guy like you got her."

"It surprises me too, believe me. You will meet her at Christmas," Eric said.

"Lights out in ten minutes," the call rang out.

Eric picked up the stationery.

> *Dear Alice,*
>
> *To say I miss you won't ease what's in my heart. I'm always thinking of you. I'll make this letter short, but I want to give you something to think about.*
>
> *I'll have about twelve days at Christmas; I know that isn't much time. If you're not doing anything special, I thought maybe you'd like to get married.*
>
> *Love you, Eric*
> *P.S. Love your picture!*

The next four and half weeks moved quickly. Things began to shape up when word got around that Baulkner stood up for them in the Bull Head Lounge. Ted became one of the sergeant's biggest fans. Baulkner meant it when he said he would back up his men. The whole squad voiced their determination to win the honor squad.

Finally, the last week of basic training arrived. The squad was really clicking, with the hardest training behind them; all that remained was a little precision and fine-tuning.

Eric opened Alice's letter with a feeling of change.

> *Dear Eric,*
>
> *In a little while, you'll be coming home. I don't want to worry you, but you should know. I'm pregnant. I've known since Thanksgiving. You have no idea what I've been going through, but I had to tell you before you came home. I think mother knows, because I've been sick in the mornings, but she's never mentioned it. I'm glad you asked me to marry you before you knew.*
>
> *I didn't want to tell you this way. Nobody else knows.*
>
> *Love you always, Alice*

Eric folded the letter and hurried to the PX. He grabbed the phone and placed the call.

"Alice, this is Eric. Don't worry—Everything's going to be all right. I'll be home in a week, and we'll handle it together. We'll get married as soon as possible. Keep your chin up. I'm almost on my way. I love you."

"Jason," Eric said, the minute he got back to the barracks, "let's get Baulkner that award and get home."

"You know I think we really gotta shot at it. The way our squad is shaping up is unbelievable." A few days later, the squad marched in their review with pride showing in every man. Baulkner got his award and assembled the men for the last time. He walked from one end of the formation to the other.

"Each man won this award and that's what's important," Baulkner said. "I know I've been called everything you could think of. However, it fired you up to do more than you thought you could. That's my job. When I turn out a top squad, it makes it all worthwhile. Those of you who are assigned to this base will have your equipment moved to your job assignments. Now—get the hell outta here. Dismissed!"

A few minutes later, the barracks was in turmoil. The squad yelled and shook hands, congratulating each other, while at the same time packing. "Do you realize we've got a twenty-hour head start?" Jason said. "I'm packed. How about you guys?"

Eric grabbed his B4 bag. "Give me ten minutes."

"I'm hurrying fast as I can," Ted said.

The minute they arrived in town, Eric said, "Let's drop off our bags at the train station. We have about an hour before we can leave. I guess we'd better go see Libby and Marie."

The evening crowd hadn't started at Monsento Rose yet. Marie smiled the moment they walked in the door. "The three of us are stationed here, until some technical schools open up," Ted said. He took Marie's hands in his. "I'll be back in about twelve days. I feel I know you so well after our phone conversations."

Marie blushed. "I feel the same, Ted."

Her father congratulated them.

"I have to leave in a few minutes," Ted said, looking at her father. "I'd like to kiss Marie goodbye—with your permission, of course!"

"Right here in front of everyone?" she whispered.

"Go in the back," her father said, and then laughed. "I guess you boys'll be happy to get home for Christmas."

"More than you know," Jason said. When they returned, Ted's face was as red as Marie's was. "I'll write you, Marie."

———————

"Three fast beers, Libby!" Jason said. "You're lucky. I'm gonna be stationed here for a while."

"This must be my day," she said, unable to suppress a smile.

"I'll be gone twelve days," Jason began, "I want a kiss from you." She didn't respond. "Libby—time's running out. We have to catch a train. Hey, lady! Where's your Christmas spirit?"

Jason gently kissed her, and dropped a five-dollar bill on her tray. "See you after the holidays. Merry Christmas."

Jason leaned back in the club car and nursed a beer. "Man, it feels so much better riding this train home."

"I'll go along with that," Eric said. "I've got a lot to think about."

"Count me in," Ted said, and broke into a rare smile.

When the train finally pulled into Cutler City, Ted picked up his bag and said, "I'll pick Jason up for your wedding. I'll call you."

"Merry Christmas, Ted."

"The same to you guys." He saluted, and flashed his boyish smile.

Eric and Jason settled back on the bus. Dark clouds let loose a mixture of rain and snow. "I never thought I would appreciate this kind of weather," Jason said.

"Yeah, it kinda takes on a new meaning."

"Wyler," The bus driver yelled over the noise of a very cheerful and festive crowd.

"Here's my number," Jason said, "Merry Christmas, buddy."

"Same to you. I'll call you," Eric said. After the bus pulled out, he gazed out the window at the rain changing to light snow.

He relaxed, feeling the release of the last three months. It was like a dream.

The noisy, crowded bus was filled with the excitement of the approaching holidays. A group of college kids sang Christmas songs, interrupted by self-conscious laughter and the excited applause from students and passengers alike.

The bus crossed the bridge, and began the long slope before entering the edge of town. The driver worked his brakes as the bus rounded the corner. "Benford," he shouted.

The dismal, late-afternoon sky blew light snow against the familiar lighted blocks of storefronts as the bus rounded the corner of the bus station. The courthouse square brought an awareness of home he never realized. Benford, with its rough-edged traditions and small town people, took on a new appreciation.

Eric stepped off the bus with a new meaning to the spirit of Christmas. The driver removed his bags and they exchanged holiday greetings. He picked up his B4 bag and walked through the small park, decorated with snow and Christmas lights. A block later, he entered his father's shop.

"Eric, you're home!" his father exclaimed.

"I got a head start," Eric said. He grabbed the phone.

"I'll close shop while you make your call."

"Hello, Mrs. Dawsher. Would you have Alice call me at home?"

"Eric, I'm surprised you're home this early," she said.

"Yes, I just got in. It's great to be home."

His father opened the front door. "Hey Martha, look who's here!"

"Eric! You're home." His mother rushed around the table and hugged him.

"Alice is a pretty young thing," his father said. "She was with Karen and Frank one evening. If I were thirty years younger . . ."

"The way you talk," his mother said, trying to hide her smile.

Eric picked up the phone the minute it rang.

"Oh, Eric, I'm so glad you're home!" Alice said. "I'll meet you at Grover's as soon as I can after I get off work."

"Great. Oh, by the way—I love you."

"I love you. Until then."

His mother looked him over carefully and then said, "You've lost weight."

"Believe me, I'm in good condition. This roast is terrific," Eric said. "It's great to taste good food again." His mother beamed.

"I'll see you later, I gotta meet Alice."

Eric looked at the snow-covered branches of the large oak trees along the familiar street. He was early, so he took his time, enjoying the familiar sights. The snow was tapering off, but it seemed colder. He entered Grover's, glanced around, and sat at the counter.

"Welcome home Eric—coffee?"

"Yes. How 'ya doing, Jeff?"

"Great—especially this time of year." The place seemed deserted except for a few people in the back. Suddenly Eric felt a tap on his shoulder. He turned around to face someone vaguely familiar. "Eric Silkwin? You probably don't know me. Name's Claude Stratman. I'm a reporter for the Benford *Daily News*."

"Stratman. I remember you led Benford into the basketball semi-state finals four or five years ago. You guys sure played a terrific game," Eric said. "I tried to contact you before I left."

"Yes, I know. Let's get a booth in back," Stratman said. "I have not followed up on the rumor of a girl being healed in your church. I've been told you would agree to an interview."

"That's correct."

"I realize it's been about four months. It's still a good story, although, after all this time I'm not sure where to go with it."

Eric hesitated and stared at the tall, blond, blue-eyed basketball hero with the receding hairline and said, "What exactly would you like to know?"

"I thought about doing a story. Nevertheless—As I said before, it's a little late. Have you done any, err, healing since then?"

Eric lit a cigarette and Stratman frowned. Evidently, he was still in condition, Eric thought. "No. I've been busy the last three months."

"I can imagine. If I drop the story, will you promise me an exclusive if you are involved in a similar situation?"

Eric didn't offer an immediate reply, and then said, "You have a deal."

"From what I've heard you keep your word. I do also. Off the record, would you want to comment at all on the incident?" Stratman asked.

Eric explained the incident in as much detail as he could remember.

"Somehow," Stratman said, "I thought it would be more . . ."

"Fascinating?" Eric said.

"Good choice of words. I don't mean that . . ."

Eric grinned. "It's all right. Maybe it was blown out of proportion."

"Maybe. I did talk to a Bryan Silkwin, who insisted there was nothing miraculous about the incident. He referred to nature correcting itself."

"Sounds like Bryan. Maybe he's right," Eric said.

Stratman looked at his watch, and then said, "I'm on a deadline. Not that I have anything special, but it's my job. Maybe something big in the future."

"Maybe," Eric said. He followed the young reporter up front and suddenly realized Stratman never cracked a smile. Eric got a coffee refill, lit another cigarette, and relaxed as the sound of Christmas music filled the drugstore.

"Beautiful song, I love this time of year," Jeff spoke again.

"Sure is. It's great to be home."

"Buy a girl a drink, soldier?" Alice asked. She put her hand on his shoulder. She wore a dark blue coat with a matching hat, which held flakes of snow beginning to melt. He looked into her big blue eyes, which seemed to widen when she was happy or excited. This moment he would remember for the rest of his life. "Eric . . . ."

"In your case, I might." He quickly kissed her cheek. "Sorry. I couldn't control myself." He grinned. "Jeff, how about bringing us a couple of hot chocolates in the back?"

"My pleasure."

Alice looked at his hair and smiled. "It hasn't quite grown out," Eric said. He shrugged and rubbed his head self-consciously.

"Looks good to me," she whispered.

"Do you have any idea how long I've waited for this moment?" Eric said.

"Me, too. I'm on vacation until after New Year's. I—we—" She looked down. "Eric, you must understand. I didn't want it this way."

"Look at me," he said softly. He cupped her chin in his hand. "We love each other. Nothing else matters. I'll call Reverend

Langtree tonight. It's only six-thirty. Tomorrow we'll get our marriage license and blood test."

"What will your folks think?"

"I talked to them about you earlier. My father said if he were thirty years younger, I'd have competition. The only thing I know for sure is three months is a long time."

"It has been for me, too."

Eric went in the phone booth with Alice anxiously waiting at his side while he called Reverend Langtree. He explained the situation. "Yes, I understand. We appreciate it. We'll talk to you later. Yes, I know. We thank you very much."

"It's settled," Eric said. "He'll marry us whenever we're ready." He grinned. "He mentioned marrying another couple under the same circumstances. I imagine he was referring to Karen and Frank. You see—It's not all that bad."

"I'm glad that's settled," Alice said. "You don't know what's been going through my mind the last few days."

"Don't worry about it, Alice. Good night, Jeff," Eric said.

He smiled, "You two look good together."

"We belong together," Eric said. When they stepped outside it was snowing again. He looked up at the sky. "It's beautiful, isn't it?"

Alice laughed, "Why yes. You didn't happen to hit your head in training, did you?"

He grabbed her around the waist. "Come here, you."

"Eric, there are people everywhere. I think . . ." He took her in his arms and kissed her.

Finally, she slowly pulled away. "Why, Eric Silkwin—I do think you are trying to seduce me on Main Street," Alice sighed.

"The way we're carrying on, we'd better get married right away."

"Eric, do you mind if I go home alone? I should tell my parents myself."

"If you're sure. Call me if you need me." Suddenly, without another word, she rushed down the street. He watched her turn, smile at him, and wave. It was a moment he would never forget. As Eric was walking home, he saw Bryan.

"Hey Eric, When did you get back?"

"A few hours ago, I just talked to Alice and now I'm heading home."

"When do you have to go back?"

"In about twelve days or so."

"Have you heard that waitress from Mabel's cafe is pretty sick?" Bryan said. "I heard she's in the hospital with acute pneumonia."

"I'm sorry to hear that. If I get a chance, I'll stop and see her," Eric said.

Bryan's expression changed to that crooked grin of his. "You think you can heal her?"

"I don't know, but I would like to help. I have to get going, Bryan. I'll see you later."

Eric's parents were waiting in the living room when he opened the front door. He said slowly, "I've got something to tell you. I—"

Ellen walked in the door before he could continue. After the initial surprise, she put her arms around him and kissed him, which surprised him. "I'm so glad to have you home. You look great," she said, with a big smile. She rubbed her hand through his hair.

"Eric has something to tell us," their mother said, with an edge of impatience in her voice.

"I asked Alice to marry me while I'm home."

His mother stared at Eric in disbelief. "What are you talking about? Why so soon?"

"Is she pregnant?" Ellen asked.

"Yes. I thought I'd better tell you right away. I talked to Reverend Langtree earlier."

"How long have you known?" his father asked, trying to keep a straight face after glancing at the expression on his wife's face.

"About a week. I asked her to marry me before she told me she was pregnant."

"First Karen and Frank, now you and Alice," his mother sighed, and took a sip of wine. "I've known she liked you for a long time, but I never thought . . ."

"I think I'll give Karen and Frank a call."

"Eric!" Karen shrieked into the phone. "You're home! Get over here. I'll put some coffee on. Our address is 328 West Elm Street."

The snow had stopped and the night was calm. Eric started to knock when the door flew open. Karen threw her arms around him and kissed him. She smiled and looked him over. "Hmm, not too bad, I guess," she said.

Frank shook hands with Eric. "Welcome home. Come in the kitchen and we'll talk over coffee."

Eric looked around the apartment. "Cozy and comfortable—something I've missed."

"What do you think of the Air Force?" Frank asked.

"I'm not sure. I'm due back at Landish Air Base in twelve days. How's it going with you and the lock factory?"

"Things are looking up. I received a raise and a better job."

"Frank, don't be so modest," Karen said. "He's in the model shop. That education and training really paid off."

"What it amounts to is, they are designing new models and expanding their line. The job opened up and I lucked out."

"That's great. I'm glad to hear it," Eric said. He sensed a new confidence in Frank, even in his conversation.

"Have you seen Alice yet?" Karen asked Eric.

"Earlier this evening, I asked her to marry me."

Karen and Frank looked at each other. "Kind of sudden, isn't it?" she finally asked.

"Just the opposite. It's a little late I'm afraid."

"You mean?" Karen's mouth opened wide. "You!"

Eric grinned. "I never thought I'd see you at a loss for words. I told the family earlier. You want to come to a small wedding after Christmas?"

Frank grinned. "I think we can make it."

"Mind if I call Alice?" Eric glanced at the clock.

Karen laughed. "The phone is our only extravagance. Mother made sure we had one."

"Hello, Alice, how did it go?"

"I told them, Eric." She sounded relieved. "It wasn't as bad as I expected, although mother is a little shocked. My father's off work until after New Year's, so we can talk together tomorrow. Did you tell your family?"

"Yes. Everything's going to be all right. What time do you want me to come over tomorrow morning?" He paused. "Alice?"

"About nine. Eric, I'm still embarrassed."

"Don't worry about it. I'll see you tomorrow."

"Until then."

"Would you and Alice like to come to dinner tomorrow evening?" Karen asked. "Say about six."

"If you're sure it's not too much trouble. I'll bring Alice and a bottle of wine."

"Sounds great. Our furniture is what you call early junk," Karen said with a laugh, "but its home."

"You heard anything from the church?" Eric asked.

Their expressions changed. "The last I heard," Frank said, "they agreed to drop it, because of the service. Claude Stratman was nosing around for a while, but evidently he couldn't get anywhere. I've heard rumors, but I think it's tapered off. It's best forgotten."

"I talked to Stratman earlier," Eric said. "I don't think he'll be any trouble."

"Oh, by the way," Karen said, "there was a strange lady and a very weird-looking young man asking about you, I've never seen in church before."

"I can't imagine who they were," Eric replied.

When Eric stepped outside it was snowing again—a light snow, with big flakes and no wind. After arriving home, Eric looked around his room. After three months of barracks life he hadn't realized how much he missed his home.

Next morning Eric joined his family at breakfast. "Good morning, everyone," he said. "I'm going to meet Alice and her parents this morning."

"You should be kind to Alice's parents," his mother stressed. "They're nice people, and she's the youngest daughter. Has Alice said anything about her sister? I've heard rumors and..."

"She mentioned her briefly. I'd better get going," Eric said. "Wish me luck."

Eric stepped out in the morning air and took a deep breath. The streets were almost clear and the sun was fighting its way through clouds. Most of the local people were off work until after New Year's. It was a good feeling.

Christmas decorations surrounded the long redwood ranch home, which was decorated with lights strung around the picture window and the front porch railing. Two medium-sized elm trees, with traces of snow-covered branches, looked bare compared to the cedar trees with brightly colored lights. "I hope the Christmas spirit and a little understanding dwell inside," Eric whispered to himself. He slowly climbed the front steps and knocked.

Alice opened the door, obviously forcing a smile. "Hello Eric. Come in," she whispered.

He was wondering whether to kiss her when her parents joined them. After a tense moment, Eric and Alice's father shook hands.

"Let me take your things," Alice's mother said. He could see redness around her eyes. "I thought we might talk over a cup of coffee. Last night Alice told us about you two's predicament. Is there anything you want to say?"

"I'm sorry it's under these circumstances," Eric said, "but we love each other."

"That's the important thing," said Alice's father, looking at his wife. "You look sharp in that uniform; don't you think so, Edith?"

"Err, yes. I guess so. What do you think, Alice?"

"I think he's handsome any way." Alice blushed. "I mean . . ."

"We know what you mean, dear." Alice's father turned away quickly—but not before the flash of a smile appeared. Eric quickly changed the subject.

"We've talked to Reverend Langtree and he agreed to marry us when possible."

"Under the circumstances, the sooner the better," Mrs. Dawsher said firmly. "There's so much to do in such a short time with the holidays and all." She bit her lower lip.

"I know this is hard for you, Mrs. Dawsher," Eric said.

"It isn't as if we had a choice. You must realize our daughter's happiness means everything to us. I can only imagine what Paula will say about this, err, situation."

"We'd better get going if we're gonna get our license and blood tests," Eric said. He hesitated at the door and added, "I'm going to make Alice happy. Trust me."

Alice's father put his arm around his wife, who was on the verge of tears. "Please bear with us. This is a difficult time for us."

Eric could only nod.

After they took the test, Eric explained their urgency.

Later, at Grover's, Alice smiled as the waitress brought a cheeseburger and a double order of French fries.

"We're invited to Karen and Frank's for dinner tonight," Eric said while drinking his coffee.

"That'll be pleasant. I have Christmas shopping to finish."

"I hope you can be ready by five-thirty, or I'll have to help dress you," Eric said.

"Sounds interesting," Alice said. "It has been three months, hasn't it?"

"I did have a twelve-hour pass about halfway through basic."

Her eyes widened. "What did you do on your pass?"

"Five-thirty," he said, and quickly walked away. After fighting the crowds, Eric finished his shopping and headed home.

Eric placed his gifts under the Christmas tree, headed for the bedroom, and fell asleep. Suddenly, a brilliant ball of white light appeared. *"Don't lose hope,"* the crippled little girl said. *"We're drawing nearer to you. Keep praying and have faith. We're closer than you know."*

"Eric, wake up. You were mumbling about something terrible in your sleep," his mother yelled. "You told me to wake you in an hour."

He looked around his bedroom, trying to recall the details of the dream. "It was the little Indian girl; she told me to keep praying."

"I've been wondering about this girl," his mother asked. "Who is she, and where does she come from? Sounds very strange to me."

Eric decided to get it all out in the open. "It was an Indian that offered me the gift of healing—I would imagine from our Cheyenne ancestors."

It was as if his mother was suddenly struck dumb. Finally, she managed to speak. "You mean your *father's ancestors*! You'd better wrap yourself in the protection of the Christ light."

"I know their compassion and sincerity is beyond questioning," Eric replied.

"There has to be more to this," his mother said. "I'll have to read my Bible."

After his mother left, Eric heard his father say, "Is this a private conversation or can anyone join in?" He continued, "Eric, I had a feeling you had something on your mind." He poured himself a cup of coffee and joined his son at the table. "I thought I'd better fill you in on a couple things. I have heard rumors—the way I understand it, some members of a couple local churches seemed upset. I know your healing shouldn't affect them—but it does. I felt you should know."

"I'm glad you told me, "Eric said.

"I would guess they are afraid their members might stray and look for a quick fix for their problems. In a way I understand. Everybody's looking for some kind of miracle."

He took a sip of coffee and continued. "I think it's affecting Karen and Frank. They haven't said anything—It's just the impression I get. I can understand Nathan Winslow and Alice's folks—especially her mother."

His father put his hand on Eric's back and said, "I'm about done with my lecture. Of course it affects Bryan—but that's to be expected. Just be ready for anything that might come your way. I'll help as best I can, but the decision has to be yours." He hesitated a moment, then he added, "You're going to have enough trouble as it is."

CHAPTER SIX

THE DOORBELL RANG. Alice immediately opened the door. Her smile was a welcome sight. "Come in Eric, I want you to meet my Uncle Paul. Uncle Paul, Eric Silkwin."

The ruddy-faced, heavy-set man smiled and rose from the table and extended his hand. "I've heard so much about you, I had to meet you," he said, with a big, booming voice.

"My pleasure, sir."

"I understand you got together through an attempt at healing, after Sunday school class. I am an outspoken man. Although it is almost unheard of, I would normally recommend you consider an abortion, rather than ruining two lives, but I will reserve judgment. I never married myself, but then I never met anyone special. If you will excuse me, I have to be going. Eric, it has been a pleasure. I guess I'll see you here for dinner tomorrow evening."

"It's been a pleasure, sir. As for being outspoken, I wouldn't want it any other way."

"I suspected that."

"He's one of my favorite men," Alice said after he left. "Although he has the reputation of being a maverick."

"He has a forceful, domineering way about him," Alice's father added.

"I like the way he lays it on the line," Eric said. "We'd better go. It's getting late."

On the walk to Karen and Frank's, she would look at him, smile, and turn away as if embarrassed. Her shyness was one of the things that he loved most about her.

"It's starting to snow again," Alice said as she stuck her tongue out to catch a snowflake. Eric looked at her, and she joined him in laughter.

"Welcome," Karen said. She took their coats and added, "Alice, you look so pretty. And Eric, well.... If you can find something that will support you, you'd better grab it. It's a matter of necessity on a budget. Follow me, and I'll show you our baby clothes."

Frank expressed a newfound enthusiasm about his new job. It was the first time Eric remembered him being excited about anything in years, but he felt there was something else on their minds.

He was right.

"You still wrapped up in this healing thing?" Frank asked, with his usual awkwardness. "Alice's knee was one thing—but that could've been a fluke, or act of nature like Bryan says." Eric noticed Karen watched his reaction carefully.

"I'm not sure. I haven't thought about it for some time."

Frank looked at Karen, then Eric. "I thought it was just a passing thing. I mean . . ."

"Frank takes his new job seriously," Karen interrupted. "It's hard to explain to people you're in contact with every day. You know, they could interpret this as—who knows!"

"I thought it was just your way to get next to Alice," Frank added quickly, with an awkward attempt at humor. "I'll admit we have mixed feelings about this healing thing of yours. Sometimes it's hard to explain!"

Karen and Frank could never hide their emotions.

"The dinner was great, but we have to get going," Eric said. He looked at Alice, and broke out in a big grin, and then quickly added, "What're your parents gonna think if I bring you home tipsy?"

"They'll see I'm happy and in love," Alice said.

"I'd hate to have to top that one," Karen said, with a forced smile.

The minute they were outside, Alice said. "I felt the tension. Evidently Karen and Frank have had some reaction from the church incident at work and the church."

72

Eric stopped suddenly and faced her. "Have you?"

"Maybe a little ridicule at the office, but nothing I can't handle," Alice said. "I experienced the healing, remember? I don't know if I should tell you, but that reporter Claude Stratman did question me one afternoon." Alice continued, "He was very pleasant and didn't pressure me after I told him I had no comment."

"I've talked to Stratman. He's just doing his job."

"Look at the Christmas decorations on these houses," Alice said. "Imagine how much happiness must be inside. If people could keep that feeling all year—wouldn't it be wonderful?"

"I've never heard you talk so much," Eric said. "You're really wound up tonight, aren't you?"

"Do you mind? Am I talking too much?"

"I like it," he said. "I never knew you liked poetry."

"How'd you know?" Alice asked.

"I would guess the book of poems on the coffee table is yours."

"I love reading them. It is as if I am in another world. Well, I'm home," Alice said when they walked up the front steps. Almost at once, they saw her parents through the kitchen window. "I can't very well ask you in tonight, I . . ."

"It's all right. We'll have our time."

"Shhh! Let him sleep," Eric heard his mother's voice outside his door. He dressed and went to the kitchen. The sound of Christmas music flooded the house.

"It's good to see you in real clothes again," his mother said to Eric.

"I got to go along with that. I'm tired of uniforms."

"I met Alice's uncle, Paul Dawsher," Eric said.

"He's a rich and powerful man," Howard said. "I've heard he's in real estate, politics, and I don't know what else. He does have a reputation of being fair and very outspoken."

"He doesn't mix words," Eric agreed. "I can't believe Alice's uncle and father are brothers."

"Don't let Alice's uncle overpower you," his father said.

————————————

It was a clear, chilly day. The snow left everything looking clean and fresh. Eric waved at a car that honked, although he did not know the driver. It was that kind of day.

When Alice greeted him at the door, her blue eyes sparkled. He stepped inside, kissed her, and said, "You look great."

She smiled when she took his topcoat. "Dinner won't be ready for about half an hour."

"Is there anything I can help with? I've picked up a little experience the last few weeks."

Alice laughed. "Mother, Eric volunteered to help in the kitchen."

Alice's mother appeared in the doorway and said, "I think we can manage. I would think you two have a lot to discuss."

"You think we'll get our blood test results the day after Christmas?" Alice asked.

"I think so. If not, I'll ask your Uncle Paul to apply some pressure."

Alice looked out the window. "He would, too. Speaking of Uncle Paul, he's here."

They watched her uncle remove brightly wrapped packages from his black Lincoln. Alice and Eric helped him. He leaned over to kiss her, glancing at Eric. "You don't mind, do you son?" His booming laugh filled the room.

"I can relate to that," Eric replied. When they shook hands, Paul laughed louder.

"Alice, are you going to have a highball?" her father asked.

"Of course. After all, Daddy, I am about to become a married woman. We're celebrating more than Christmas, you know."

"That's my girl," Uncle Paul shouted. "What day are we getting you two married?"

Alice's mother said, "Thursday, the twenty-eighth, at three in the afternoon. It's not as if we had any choice!"

"If you have any trouble getting those results," Alice's uncle interrupted, "call me."

When Eric finished the last of his apple pie, he said, "This is one of the most delicious meals I've ever eaten."

"The boy's right, Edith. Outstanding!" Uncle Paul added.

The rest of the afternoon, the conversation revolved around the wedding. Suddenly her uncle looked Eric in the eye and said, "I'm afraid my curiosity is getting the best of me. Eric would you mind going into more detail and explain this healing procedure?"

"I'll explain as best I can, but there's a lot I don't understand myself."

Alice, her uncle, and her parents listened carefully. Finally, Uncle Paul spoke. "I've read about these things, but the personal touch always brings things to life."

Eric explained, "I had a dream, about an Indian and a little girl. The little girl had twisted legs. The Indian offered me the gift of healing if I so desired it."

"I can imagine the pressure you must feel," Alice's father said.

"This little girl," Alice's mother said. "I can't possibly see how she could be a part of our . . . I mean, I don't understand the abnormal influence she seems to have on you. I guess we should be thankful the publicity I feared wasn't as bad as I thought. We can't understand what the connection is with this little girl, and why it's so important to you!"

"I'm not sure I can explain it," Eric said.

"It's touchy," Uncle Paul added. "I'll help in whatever way I can. You kids want to use my cabin in Wyler? Alice always loved it so much."

She looked at Eric. "The cabin is really pleasant—a wood burning fireplace and just about everything."

"Whatever makes you happy," Eric said.

"I'll get the Legion hall for the reception," Uncle Paul said. "I'll have the food catered. That way you and Eric's family can get acquainted."

"That could get expensive, Paul," Alice's father said.

"It's my wedding present. The food at the cabin has been taken care of. You see? It's all settled." Alice kissed him and he beamed.

"You've always spoiled me."

"My pleasure," Paul said. "Lawrence call me and let me know how many people to expect. I'll see you kids at the wedding."

After he left, Alice's father said, "That brother of mine never ceases to amaze me."

"I'll help with the dishes," Eric said. "My training shouldn't go to waste."

"We can do the dishes later," Alice's mother said.

"How am I supposed to feel like one of the family?"

Alice took his hand to lead him to the kitchen. "Tell me, P.F.C. Silkwin, are you experienced in washing or drying?"

"If I remember right—pots and pans were my specialty." He quickly kissed Alice on the nose as she tied an apron around his waist. Her parents watched from the doorway, which brought on a rare smile from her mother.

After finishing the dishes, Eric said, "It's been nice, but I'd better be going."

Alice walked him to the living room. "This was a pleasant day, wasn't it?"

"Yes. It's just the beginning." He quickly kissed her nose. "When you and I are together, how can it be otherwise?"

Alice broke into a big smile. "I'll take your word for it. You sure like to kiss my nose."

"I'm crazy about your nose, freckles, and all."

"How'd it go?" Eric's father asked.

"Great!" Eric explained, "Alice's uncle offered the use of the Legion hall and the cabin."

The thought of Rita in the hospital kept occupying Eric's mind. He whispered to himself, "*I need your guidance.*"

Later that evening Eric decided to go to the hospital. "I'll see you later. I have to take care of something." *How could he explain the overpowering feeling leading him to Rita*? He felt a power beyond his control urge him forward. He knew what he had to do. "I hope you're with me," Eric whispered to himself. He took a deep breath before entering the hospital.

The nurse behind the counter attempted her best professional smile.

"What time does the gift shop close?"

"Eight," she replied, looking up with a hint of annoyance. Eric lit a cigarette and walked over to the window, staring out at the cold, bleak day. Even the snow, which had looked so white and clean, was slowly becoming dingy and dirty.

He walked back to the counter

"What's the name of the patient?" The nurse asked.

"Rita Luckner," Eric said.

"She's in Room 112. She's had very few visitors." The nurse's voice revealed compassion. Maybe he was wrong about her smile.

"What kind of flowers do you suggest?" he asked.

"Some carnations might be nice."

"Thanks again." Eric walked into the gift shop.

Later, on his way upstairs, the nurse nodded her approval. He paused outside her room, took a deep breath, and walked in. The woman to his left smiled, as Eric walked around the screen separating the beds.

The patient in the bed turned to face him. Rita's eyes were sunken behind a lifeless complexion. He had to move closer before she could recognize him. "Eric, is that you?" she said.

"Yes it's me." He tried to smile.

"Crank up this damn bed so I can get a good look at you." Eric cranked until she nodded her approval. A sudden hacking cough overtook her. The nurse, who was attending the other patient, rushed to Rita and gave her a drink of water.

"Just give me a couple of minutes," Rita gasped. "The flowers are so pretty."

"Let me take care of those for you," the nurse offered.

"How long you going to goof off in here?" Eric asked.

"Not long, I hope, although I feel lousy." Rita still had her spirit. "I've got the flu or something. I never had anything like this before. I get so weak."

Eric leaned close to her and whispered, "You know about the healing I gave the girl at church?" He looked into her eyes, with what he hoped was strength.

"Yes, the whole town does. The girl, is she all right?"

"Great. In fact, we're getting married this coming Thursday at three."

"You're getting married in a week, and you're up here with me? If it were anyone else, I would not believe it. I guess you came to invite me to the wedding at the last minute?" For the first time, a slight smile crossed Rita's face.

"Not exactly. This is a little awkward: I came to give you a healing."

Eric gripped the healing stone in his pocket for a moment.

She tried to smile. "I have to warn you I don't have much faith. I wish I did." She fought the tears in her eyes. "If there's any way you could help me, I'd be grateful."

Eric put one hand on her forehead and the other behind her neck. He could feel the power flow through him stronger than ever before. The room was quiet except the usual activity in the hallway and the buzz of equipment.

"Your hands are so warm," Rita whispered. "I feel heat going through my body. It's a warm, tingling sensation." Within a few moments, perspiration broke out on her forehead.

"Just try to relax," Eric said, "and let the power flow through you."

"The heaviness in my chest is really leaving. It's—it's much better. I can't believe it!" She stared at him in disbelief. "Your eyes, Eric—they're different! They're much brighter somehow."

"Take your hands off her!" The nurse, suddenly standing behind him shouted. "I'm going to get a doctor."

"I gotta go," Eric said. "You're going to be all right."

"How can I ever thank you?" Rita asked.

"Wish me luck on my honeymoon."

"The best ever," Rita said.

————————————

The next morning, Eric opened his father's shop. A half hour later, Eric noticed a distinguished looking man standing near his father's shop entrance. "Are you Mr. Eric Silkwin?" the man asked.

"Yes" Eric said, trying to recognize the vaguely familiar face.

"I'm Dr. Edward Emmery." He was a tall broad-shouldered man with gray eyes. "Maybe I should explain. Reverend Langtree and I have spoken briefly about you."

Eric returned his smile and said, "Won't you come in?"

"Just for a couple minutes, I'll come right to the point. I would like to arrange a brief meeting this afternoon if possible. I was on duty yesterday. I saw you rushing out of Mrs. Luckner's room."

Eric did not answer, so Emmery continued. "It can be beneficial to all concerned. Dr. Raymond Hedwick asked to be present. Naturally, all conversation will be held confidential."

Eric had the distinct impression he could trust this man. "Wouldn't this type of association hurt you?"

"We feel it warrants discussion. I assure you we are not on a witch-hunt. Three this afternoon would be convenient."

"I'll be there."

Eric's father came in the shop after lunch. Eric told him about the doctor and that he was going to meet with them this afternoon. "What else was I supposed to do? He saw me at the hospital."

His father shook his head, and looked Eric straight in the eye. "It seems to me you do not have a choice. Watch what you say and keep your guard up."

Eric sat in Dr. Emmery's office glancing at a magazine, but could not concentrate.

"Sorry we're late," Dr. Emmery said. "Eric, meet Dr. Raymond Hedwick."

"How do you do?" Dr. Hedwick said. His cool blue eyes and tight-lipped smile implied immediate authority. He shook hands and quickly released Eric's hand. "Sherry, we are not to be disturbed, unless of course it's an emergency."

Eric sat in front of the large oak desk and looked around the room. His eyes moved from one to another of several framed diplomas hanging from dark, expensive paneling. "We are aware of your, err, religious experiences, especially concerning, uh, healing," Dr. Emmery said. "Would you mind telling us, in your own words, your involvement?"

Eric explained reading the Bible. He tried to put into words how it came alive for him. The doctors listened carefully. "I know how foolish this must sound to you," he said, self-consciously. "It's the only way I can explain it, and try to make any sense at all."

"Do you believe you have the power to heal?" Hedwick asked.

"No. I feel it's a power working through me."

"Do you consider this power to be of divine origin?" Emmery asked. "We do not ask these questions to imply ridicule."

Eric hesitated, trying to find the right words. "I'm not sure. Naturally I like to think so."

Dr. Hedwick pressed forward. "You must have something to base it on—some sort of a spiritual contact, perhaps?"

"I don't see how it can be anything else," Eric said, suddenly resentful of his own feeling of being self-conscious.

Hedwick's smirk was evident. "This is an age-old problem," he said. "Individuals have a right to their own religious beliefs. However, sometimes it takes the place of seeking proper medical treatment."

Eric felt the smile spread across his face. "You came to me. Other than mild curiosity, what do you want from me?"

Dr. Emmery's smile faded.

"I believe healings of this type are over-emotional reactions that replace some form of proper medical treatment," Dr. Hedwick said. "Have you ever thought of being under some form of hypnosis, consciously or unconsciously, that makes you vulnerable to an overactive imagination?"

Eric was becoming frustrated and a little irritated. "I feel there's much more to it than hypnosis or imagination." *How could he explain his guidance, and why should he have to?* "All over the world there has been documented evidence that confirms healings."

Dr. Hedwick expressed irritation. "In the interest of time, we'll explore that later. Were you involved with the waitress at the hospital?"

"Yes, you know that. Otherwise, I wouldn't be here."

"We tried to get information from her," Dr. Emmery said with a trace of a smile. "She essentially told us where to go."

"We believe your sincerity is misplaced," said Dr. Hedwick, whose expression never changed. "Sometimes that can be the most dangerous kind. There is always the danger of a patient ignoring medical treatment because of misplaced faith in unorthodox healing."

Dr. Emmery glanced at his watch. "Would you consider us monitoring your next healing?"

"I can't promise anything. I'm in the Air Force for three years, so that's unlikely."

CHAPTER SEVEN

LATER THAT AFTERNOON, IN A BOOTH at Grover's drugstore, Eric sat facing a serious-minded Claude Stratman. "I have your background," he said, and then he examined his notes. "My future interviews will hopefully bring all this together."

"I'm sure; don't expect too much." Eric sipped his coffee and, to Stratman's obvious discomfort, lit a cigarette. "What is your reaction to the doctors?"

Eric thought a minute, and then said, "Naturally I understand their concern. Let's face it—it was uncomfortable."

"Is there anything you wish to tell me that you couldn't discuss with them?"

"Nothing beyond what I've already told you."

"Let's move on," Stratman said. "Your church members, from what I've heard, seemed divided. Is there anything more you can tell me about your church history, including speaking in tongues and your devotion to the Bible? You must admit that is unusual for someone so young. It's my understanding some of your members support you—while others seemed to think it would be better if you ...." Stratman's voice trailed off.

"I understand what you're trying to say. I'm well aware of their feelings, but I must choose my own way."

"How does your family feel about your decision?"

"Mixed feelings. I'd rather leave them out of it—at least for now."

"Fair enough," Stratman said. "I assume your church takes a negative view of your unorthodox healing?" He hesitated and flashed his rare smile. "Although at one time you were considered special. Any comment?"

"No. You got it about right."

Stratman glanced at his watch. He picked up the check and said, "I have a feeling you're destined for more. I'll be around. Congratulations on your marriage."

"Thank you," Eric said. Stratman suddenly flashed his smile before maneuvering his way among the customers, as he skillfully made his way to the front of the drugstore.

Church services were just getting under way when Alice and her parents called Eric aside. "Paula called and expressed her regrets. They can't make the wedding," Alice's mother said. "Henry's sick. She said they would surprise us in the near future and…"

"I know what his sickness is," Alice's father interrupted. "He's probably hung over."

"In a way I'm glad," Alice said with the sound of relief. "It's my wedding, and I don't want to answer needless questions, let alone face her. I can't say I'm sorry."

"I must admit I'm somewhat relieved myself," Alice's mother said. "Paula can be so outspoken and demanding."

"That's an understatement if I ever heard one," her father added.

They started entering the church, when suddenly a woman appeared before him. "Young man, you are under an evil influence!" the woman yelled. Her face took on the appearance of someone deranged. "I'm here by the mercy of God to ask you to repent!"

Nathan Winslow, Mrs. Dunley, and several other members of the congregation surrounded him. The woman, along with a young man chanted: "Repent! Repent!"

Eric saw Alice trying to work her way through the crowd followed by her parents. "We know about your affair with the waitress in the hospital!" the woman screamed.

"*Affair!*" Eric yelled at the couple. "What are you talking about?"

Reverend Langtree fought through the crowd, and faced the strangers. "This is a house of worship. I must ask you to join our service in a peaceful manner or leave."

The woman, whose face was contorted, stared at him for a moment. "You are a minister. How can you be a part of this charade?"

Reverend Langtree looked the woman in the eye and said, "I do not stand in judgment, nor should you."

The young man waved his hand and raised his voice at the surrounding audience. "You must! You're responsible for your congregation."

"We're leaving," the woman replied. "However, before we go, I want this man to tell me by what right he has to heal in the name of the Lord!"

Eric looked the woman in the eye, and calmly said, "I am a child of the living God, and so are you. I have my belief and you have yours. What right have you to condemn me?"

"It's my duty to defy you! You are leading the righteous to a path of moral decay and spiritual destruction, defacing the Lord's name," the wild-eyed woman shouted. "You have not seen the last of us!" The woman and young man stormed out of the church.

"Please return to your seats and let's return to the service," the reverend said. The stunned congregation slowly filed back, some shaking their heads. Others mumbled to themselves or each other, not sure what to think or say.

Later that afternoon Eric talked with Alice and her parents. "I can't explain it, but I had to help that waitress."

"Who in the world were those people, especially that woman shouting with that strange-looking young man?" Alice's mother asked. She fought her tears and took control of herself. "The wedding must go on! What choice is there? Another scandal!"

"I never saw that woman before," Eric said. "Evidently they are some religious fanatics."

"What's done is done. Edith is right! The wedding *will* go on as planned," Alice's father said. "We'll get through this thing. It will just take a little time."

Alice's mother burst into tears and left the room.

Eric arrived home to find Bryan talking to his parents.

Just about that time, the phone rang, Eric answered.

"Eric, its Frank, Karen and I were just thinking about going for a ride. We were wondering if you and Alice would like to go with us."

"Hey, I am just happy to get out of the house. Let me call Alice, I'm sure she feels the same way. Alice was telling me there was somewhere special she wanted to go, maybe we could take a ride there."

Karen opened the car window, and a late afternoon breeze blew through her strawberry blond hair.

Frank followed Alice's directions beyond the city limits. It was a surprisingly warm and sunny day for December.

"This is the place," Alice said. "These people are friends of the family——I used to come here when Paula and I were small. My parents always bought their chickens and all our farm products from here."

"I've been past here several times," Frank said as he pulled into a long, winding driveway. They all stared at the older brick house, which stood out among the tall oak trees in the massive front and side yards.

"Yeah—the Bingman place," Karen said softly.

A moment later, a tall, thin man with intense blue eyes shook hands with Karen, Frank, and Eric. He flashed a big smile and put his arms around Alice. "It's so nice to see you again. I see you brought some friends with you, young lady."

After introductions, Mr. Bingman invited them in the house for coffee. "Alice Dawsher," Mary Bingman said, "this is such a pleasant surprise. I remember when you and your older sister were here with your folks a few years ago. You were a little thing. My, how you've grown—and so pretty, too." She brushed her gray hair over her shoulder; her soft brown eyes twinkled. They sat at a large oak dining table just off the country-sized kitchen. "I take it your sister and family are well."

"Yes. I don't know if you remember, but I promised you years ago when I was small, that when I got married, I would introduce you to the man I was going to marry," Alice said. She took Eric's hand in hers.

The elderly couple congratulated Alice and Eric, while Karen and Frank looked on with amusement.

Mr. Bingman laughed. "I remember now—I used to tease you about getting married!"

After delicious chocolate cake and fresh coffee, Mr. Bingman said, "I don't know if you heard or not, we're moving out East to be near our daughter, her husband, and our grandchildren."

Mr. Bingman took his wife's hand in his. "It's going to be hard to leave this place. It has been good to us." He paused a moment, then continued, "We raised two children here; our boy was killed in the war. Mary, let's show them the rest of the house."

They walked into the living room, among furniture that belonged to another era. The picture of a young man in uniform stood out from several pictures on the top ledge of the large brick fireplace. The man gazed at the picture for a moment, his eyes becoming misty. "That's our son," he said softly.

"Well, I think we better be going. Thanks again," Eric said.

"It was our pleasure, feel free to come back anytime. We enjoyed meeting you," Mr. Bingman said. "If you like—-walk around outside and get a feel of the place that has been so good to us for years."

They walked among the big oak trees, which took a large part of the side yard. Eric noticed an old swing under the tree, and the remains of a sand box. The weeds almost covered the rotting boards and faint traces of scattered sand. The big rope, tied to an old tractor tire, was frayed and strained by the gentle breeze. Eric couldn't help but wonder how many memories revolved around that particular area; maybe a small boy who enjoyed one of the best times in his life.

Early Christmas morning, Eric's family followed their tradition of snacking around the Christmas tree when the phone rang. Ellen motioned for Eric. "Hello, Linda? Yeah, I got home Wednesday evening." After Eric hung up the phone, he said to the family, "I told Linda I'd drop by later on today for a few minutes."

They exchanged presents. Later, in the afternoon, Eric's family, along with Karen, Frank—and even Bryan, who was with a pretty girl named Liza—welcomed Alice and her parents.

"Why don't we go in the kitchen?" Ellen said. "We girls can sit at one end of the table and the men at the other, that way; we can get a word in occasionally."

"As if we could keep you from it," Eric said.

"You look great, Karen," Ellen said.

Frank said, "It's hard to believe we're going to be parents."

"It's real, all right," Karen said, patting her stomach.

"It'll be here soon enough," Frank added. "The kid will probably keep us up most of the night."

"Yeah—you now, and the baby later," Karen said, which brought laughter.

"Why the sudden rush into marriage, cousin?" Bryan asked. "I guess Alice will go away with you after the marriage?"

Eric spoke slowly and clearly. "No, she's going to stay here and get ready for our baby."

Bryan's mouth was wide open.

"Liza, are you enjoying your Christmas?" Ellen quickly interrupted.

"Yes. My brother is home from the Army." She smiled, and added, "He's a secret admirer of yours. He used to work in the shop at Mullaird's."

"You should have asked him to come along for dinner," Ellen said. "What's his name?"

"Johnny," Liza said to Ellen. "Would you like to meet him?"

"Yes, but I'm afraid there's only leftovers," Ellen said.

"For some reason, I don't think he'd mind." Eric saw Ellen blushing, which was unusual. Liza and Bryan hurried out the door. Eric's mother came in the kitchen, followed by Alice's parents. "We've worked out the details. It'll be a small wedding Thursday at three o'clock, with the reception at the Legion Hall," Eric's mother said.

"We must be going, now that everything is settled," Alice's mother said.

"We're going to take off too," Eric's mother added, "Mary Maynard and Walter invited us over this evening. Don't forget, there's Christmas Service at church tonight."

A short time later, they heard the door open. Bryan entered, followed by Liza and a soldier. "Everybody, I'd like you to meet Liza's brother, Johnny. I'll start with Frank Karland and his wife Karen, my sister. Eric and his soon-to-be bride Alice, and of course, Eric's sister, Ellen."

Sergeant Johnny Bowers stood a little under six feet, with light brown hair and an easy smile. "I'm happy to meet you. I did not want to intrude, but I could not resist meeting Ellen," he said, and sat down beside her. She turned to face him, smiled, and asked, "When do you have to go back?"

"I have to be in San Diego January twelfth, before going overseas."

"What do you do in the Army?"

"I'm in communications," Johnny said, looking at Ellen with obvious admiration. "I graduated from radio school in September. I have been fascinated with radios even before I went to high school."

"Did you work for Mullaird's before enlisting?" Frank asked. "Liza was telling us about your admiration for Ellen from afar. You obviously have very good taste."

Eric laughed. "Frank had a crush on Ellen too."

"I got what I wanted," Frank said.

"You'd better have," Karen added, but could not resist a smile.

"We should eat if we're going to church," Ellen said, rising from the table. "I'll reheat some of this stuff."

"Let me help," Johnny said. He joined Ellen, picking up dishes from the table and followed her into the kitchen.

"I think they would make a nice couple," Liza said. "Anybody else?"

"I agree, but I think nature will take its course," Karen said.

Ellen and Johnny returned from the kitchen.

"Eric, have you been to the hospital yet to see Rita?" Bryan asked.

"I saw her a couple days ago, and she seemed to be getting better."

"Do you think it had anything to do with you giving her a healing?" Bryan smirked.

Karen frowned. "Bryan, you are not going to start that again?"

"I'll admit I'm curious. How can Eric know whom he is getting involved with? I'm afraid, those dreams, or whatever he calls them, could be a form of possession."

"Drop it, Bryan!" Karen said. "We're trying to put that behind us. Eric is going to do what he chooses. I would think healing would involve higher forces."

Bryan's usual pale complexion turned red. "High spiritual forces!" Bryan said, ignoring his sister. "Just because Eric gave Alice a healing in church, everyone seems to think he healed her knee. Come on! Nothing personal, Eric."

"No offense," Eric replied with a grin.

"You ever heard of anything like that, Johnny?" Bryan asked.

"Yes, in fact, I was involved," Johnny said. "More of an observer than anything." Bryan's grin faded.

"Let me explain. A corporal and I became good friends. One day, we began talking about religion. He said he was a healer and . . ."

"A healer?" Bryan whispered.

"Yes," Johnny continued. "He explained as if it were the most natural thing in the world. He thought he could help this guy in the hospital, so he asked me to join him."

89

"What was wrong with the man in the hospital?" Ellen asked.

"The guy had severe headaches and he was in constant pain."

"And?" Bryan asked.

"The corporal asked if he could place his hands on his head. After staring at him for a moment, the guy said he was so miserable he'd try anything. The corporal told me to take the patient's hand and silently pray for strength. After the prayer, a feeling of peace came over me. I looked up and beads of sweat appeared on the guy's forehead. His attitude completely changed."

"Yes, and then?" Bryan pushed.

"'I'll be damned. My headache is gone for the first time in over a week,' the guy said. 'I can't believe it.' The corporal went back to his outfit. I never saw him again."

Everybody at the table fell silent.

"I can't believe regular people can heal," Bryan said. "What would be the point in doctors? The exception would be a minister, priest, or an officer of the church."

"Why just the church, Bryan?" Eric asked. "Do you think that automatically makes it right? You were so careful to make it clear—officers of the church. Why?"

"Because," Bryan shot back, "they'd have the proper authority and dignity necessary for the power of a religious body."

"How can you believe authority has priority over sincerity for healing?" Eric snapped back. "I'd think it'd be a person with a sincere compassion for the sick. It's not just a religious ritual."

"*Religious ritual*!" Bryan's face became red. "Eric, I don't understand how you could say such things! What's happened to you?"

"Bryan, everyone has a right to their own beliefs," Eric said. "There are things you don't understand."

"But the way you were raised. Our church...What don't we understand?"

"I still respect our church," Eric said. "I personally believe it could be an important part of the service. Winslow knows about my healing in the basement. I gotta hunch he don't mind, because of the increase in attendance."

Ellen interrupted. "Speaking of church, it's almost time."

"Would you mind if I joined you?" Johnny asked.

"I'd be honored," Ellen said.

"It's Christmas, Bryan. Let it go," Karen said sharply. "I am surprised Eric—religious ritual!? You have changed."

"Let us celebrate our Lord's birth with joy, love, and compassion for all. It truthfully is a blessed day," Reverend Langtree said. He stressed Jesus' teachings. A message that carried a Christian approach to everyday life. "Let's all accept this day, and all its blessings with a joyful heart. May God bless you each and every one."

"Meeting you was a pleasure, Johnny," Eric's father said. "I hope we see you over the holidays. We're gonna hurry on home."

"Are you a Protestant, Johnny?" Eric's mother asked.

"No, I'm Catholic, but I attend different services. I think we all really worship the same God."

"I'm sure," Eric's mother answered, although not too convincingly. "It's so pleasant walking tonight—even with the snow—it seems just right for Christmas, and everyone seems so happy." Eric's parents waved and strolled off into the night.

Frank hugged Karen. "I'm gonna take mother-to-be home and put her to bed."

"I'll bet," she said with a short laugh. "Eric, you mentioned getting together with your friends from the service."

"I'll call you."

Ellen took Johnny's arm. "You may walk me home, soldier."

"My pleasure," Johnny said. "I feel this day is an unexpected blessing for me."

"It's such a beautiful night," Alice said to Eric. "Look at those stars. I think one of them is winking at me."

"I don't blame it," Eric said.

"I hope you'll come in for a while," Alice said. "My parents are really trying to deal with this situation."

Alice's father met them at the door. "Come in, you two. It's cold out there. We're having hot chocolate."

Alice's mother surprised everybody by kissing Eric's cheek, and said, "The evening service was delightful, wasn't it?"

"Yes, it was," Eric said. "It's a beautiful evening—even the stars winked at Alice."

Alice blushed, but managed to laugh. "Oh, Eric."

A little later Alice's mother said, "I hope you'll excuse us, it's been a long day."

Alice put the hot chocolate on the coffee table then joined Eric on the couch. He put his arm around her. They watched the flickering lights on the Christmas tree in silence.

Eric rose to leave. "It's late. I'll pick you up in the morning. Merry Christmas, honey."

"That's the first time you called me that," Alice said. She pulled a small package out from under the Christmas tree. He opened the present. It was a gold cross and chain.

"Alice, its great—but you shouldn't have."

"I didn't know if you could wear it with those—what'd you call them?"

"Dog tags." Eric grinned. He unbuttoned his shirt. "Will you put it on for me?"

"It's my way of protecting you. I couldn't think of a better way."

"If you'll get my coat, I have something for you," Eric said.

Alice's eyes lit up with excitement. She tore into the brightly colored package. "I love it. You remembered," she said, and kissed him lightly as she ran her hand over the leather-covered book of poems. "It's beautiful." She moved into his arms.

He smiled, and kissed her. "It's because you're special. I'll see you in the morning."

Eric stepped into the night air. The sound of Christmas carols and the houses with brightly colored Christmas lights gave him a feeling of contentment.

A few feet from Linda's house, he saw a car drive into the driveway. Eric slowed, staying in the shadows. He heard car doors slam, and laughter as Linda ran toward her house with the man throwing snow at her.

Eric stepped up his pace. "*Good will to all,*" he said to himself.

"What is this?" Eric asked. His mother, dad, and sister were sitting in the living room, holding a glass of wine. Eric assumed Christmas spirit was only a part of it. "What do you think of Johnny?" Eric asked. From the change in her expression, he guessed right. Ellen had a glow about her he had never seen before.

"I like him. I think I knew it when I first met him."

"How are you and Alice getting along?" his mother asked.

"Not bad, considering we're getting married in a couple days," Eric said. "If you want to see my Christmas present you'll have to come over here. I promised I wouldn't remove it."

"It's beautiful." His mother ran her hand over the cross. "I'll be so proud to have Alice as my daughter-in-law." And then, with deep emotion, she added, "Johnny is Catholic, Ellen." She paused for comment.

"I think we can overlook that," Eric said, winking at Ellen.

"First Karen and Frank. Now you and Alice," their mother said. "Reverend Langtree must think us Silkwins are something,"

"We are," Eric said.

"Well, I guess we're something, all right." His mother laughed until tears clouded her eyes. "I don't know what's wrong with me. This isn't like me at all."

"We know, we know," Eric's father said.

"Oh, we're acting so foolish, but I'm enjoying it," she said. She rubbed her hands over her new sweater. "It's gettin' late, and I'm very tired."

"Me too," Ellen said. "It's been a long day and I—"

The phone rang, startling them. "I'll get it," Ellen said. "Hello. Yes, Eric's here. Just a moment."

"I'm going over to Linda's for a few minutes. I'll be right back." He grabbed his jacket and quickly walked out.

———

"Merry Christmas Eric," Linda said, greeting him. "Won't you come in?" He had almost forgotten how attractive she was. "You look fabulous as always," he said.

93

"Thank you." They sat together on the couch. She bit the end off a cookie. "I have to be careful," Linda said, continuing with her favorite topic of conversation. "The way I've eaten the last few days, my figure will go right out the window."

He looked her over carefully, and then added, "I'd say you've nothing to worry about."

"Thank you. How do you like the Air Force?"

"I'm not sure. At least basic is over."

"So much has happened," Linda said. "I heard about you and Alice, but I had no idea your relationship was this serious." When he refused to comment, she continued. "I'm happy for you both," she said. "Are you still involved in this—What do you call it? Healing?"

"There are times I'm not sure one way or the other."

"I can imagine," she said with a short laugh.

"What about you and Bill Hausler?"

Linda was no longer smiling. "Bill? I think I love him one minute and then . . ." Eric heard a car pull up in the driveway. Linda looked out the window. "He's back. We had a misunderstanding. Please, don't leave."

When Linda opened the door, she ducked away from Hausler's attempted kiss. "Bill, you remember Eric Silkwin from high school? You were three years ahead of us."

"Oh, yeah." He walked over to Eric, who rose to shake hands. It was obvious he had been drinking heavily. His movements were controlled, but his speech gave him away. "Let's see now," Hausler said, "the last time I saw you, you were boxing at school. You still box?"

"Not lately. Are you still in college?"

"Yes. I'm studying en-GUN-eer-ing," deliberately mispronouncing the word. "Doesn't Linda look great?"

"She's as lovely as ever."

"I hear you're tying the knot Thursday. Isn't it a little odd to be here with Linda, instead of the girl you're going to marry?"

"I asked him to come over," Linda said.

"You two wouldn't be getting a little something going before the wedding, would you?"

Eric quickly jumped to his feet. "You know better than that!"

Hausler's face was flushed, his voice spit out the words. "We'll eventually tangle, Silkwin, but not in front of Linda on Christmas day. Meanwhile, stay away from her." Eric and Hausler stood close together, face to face until Linda stepped between them.

"I'll talk to you later Eric," Linda said. When she faced Hausler, her face was red and her voice much louder than usual. "As for you, Bill, you leave and don't come back until you sober up and apologize!"

Bill glared at her, mumbled something, then quickly grabbed the doorknob, rushed out and slammed the door behind him.

"I'm sorry. I'm afraid his Christmas party got the best of him," she said. "Usually he's not like this at all."

"Forget it. Merry Christmas, Linda."

CHAPTER EIGHT

ALICE AND ERIC WAITED OVER AN HOUR for their marriage license. "It's late. I have to call Jason and Ted," Eric said. "Would you like to eat lunch?"

"Not really," Alice replied. "I want to shop on my own."

"All right, I'll see you later this afternoon."

"Until then," Alice said.

"You're home early," Eric's mother said.

"We got our license, so everything's set. Alice is shopping for baby clothes."

Eric grabbed the phone. "Hello, Jason, It's Eric. Yes, I had a great Christmas. Okay, I'll see you about five-thirty tonight." He hung up and called Karen. "Is this the lady of the house?"

"Close enough," she said with laughter in her voice.

"Jason and his girl are coming over this evening," Eric said.

"How about we get together at our apartment," Karen replied. "Wait, what's-his-name is saying something. . . Frank wants to go out and eat."

"Sounds good to me."

Eric tried to call Ted, but could not reach him.

There was a knock on the door. "Walter is here," Eric's mother said.

Walter Blanchard, his father's best friend, was sensitive, intelligent, and forty-two-years old. Two years ago, he met a teacher named Brenda. They fell in love almost at once. He was an accountant at Mullaird's Corporation, and considered to be on his way up. She became ill and died of pneumonia overnight. He went to pieces and was never the same.

Eric walked into the dining room and they shook hands. "Walter, it's great to see you."

His hunched shoulders and the gray in his thick black hair seemed more obvious in the last few months. He was still an accountant at Mullaird's, but his career stalled, and he had not seemed to care until lately. Eric assumed the reason being was his interest in Linda's mother.

"How do you like the Air Force, Eric?" Walter asked.

"All right, but leaving Alice will be rough."

"I imagine you're getting ready for the big day."

"Yes, everything is so hectic. You caught me at a bad time," Eric said.

Eric glanced at his watch, "I'm sorry Walter, but I have to go. I'm pressed for time. I enjoyed seeing you again. You're invited to our wedding, its Thursday at three o'clock."

"I wouldn't miss it. Don't keep that young lady waiting."

Alice answered the door. "My parents went visiting," Alice said. Her hair was not completely dry when he leaned over to kiss her. She smelled of cologne, and Eric guessed she was fresh from a shower.

"You smell good."

"Would you like something to drink?" Alice asked.

"Actually, I had something else in mind."

They made love with a passion that took complete control. Later Eric returned from the bathroom and saw Alice with her hands on her hips, looking carefully around the bedroom. "There, everything's the way it was." Alice sighed, and with a look of total concentration said, "Let's go in the kitchen—you know, natural-like." Eric laughed.

"What's so funny?" She tossed a potholder at him, and they both laughed. "I'm sorry," she continued, "but we have to get serious." Alice hurried around the table, and her robe came loose. She quickly tied it back together. "Don't even *think* about it!"

He laughed. "I'm trying very hard not to. Are you sure we haven't got enough time?" Eric said.

"You damn fool," she said, unable to control her laughter. "I think we're both a little crazy."

"It's healthy to be a little crazy," he said.

"Come on Eric—Would you like whipped cream on your pie?"

"Yes, dear, I'll have that whipped cream on my pumpkin pie."

"I'll show you." She pointed the can of whipped cream at him. Suddenly, the cream shot from the can directly into his face.

"*Oh—Oh damn!*" Alice screamed. She dropped the can and grabbed a towel. Eric looked at her, torn between shock and laughter. At the same moment, they heard the front door open. "Oh, you're eating. We did not . . . "'Alice's mother stopped. Her mouth flew open as she watched Alice trying to wipe the whipped cream off Eric's face and shirt.

"Let me dear, you're supposed to wet the towel first," Alice's mother said. She grabbed the towel and hurried over to Eric.

Her father shook his head and laughed. "I'm sorry, kids. You should see yourselves."

Alice watched with a look of total frustration. "I just—It wasn't on purpose. I was just playing around and . . . ."

"Eric, hold still. Take your shirt off. I'll clean it for you."

"I'm so sorry," Alice cried. "I really didn't mean to . . . my finger slipped."

"It's all right, Alice," Eric said. Her expression amused him. He never felt as close to her as he did that moment. He removed his shirt and sat at the table eating pie in his undershirt, watching Alice, who finally got herself under control.

"I guess it was amusing," Alice admitted, nibbling at her pie.

"If it was so funny, I'll let you explain it to my mother," Eric said.

Eric watched how her expression changed with her moods. Alice sighed. "How can I explain something like this?"

"I've called everyone I want to invite to the wedding," Alice's mother said. "Did you think of anyone special you wanted to invite?"

"No," Alice said. "Eric didn't get here until a little while ago, and we haven't had time."

Alice's father gave Eric a shirt. "I think I better go home and change," Eric said. "Thanks for the shirt, pie, and especially the whipped cream."

Alice stuck her tongue out at him.

"*Alice!* Shame on you," Her mother screamed.

Eric laughed. "I forgive her."

"Of all the pictures I've taken, what I'd give to have one of you with that whipped cream on your face, and Alice's expression. It would be priceless," Alice's father said.

"Why daddy, I've never seen you so—so . . ."

"Silly?" her mother said with a rare smile.

"See you later," Eric said as he kissed Alice lightly. "Don't forget we're getting together with Jason and his girl and Karen and Frank. We're going to meet at my house around 5:30."

"Until then."

"What happened to you," Ellen said. "Where in the world did you get that shirt?" Eric laughed and explained the whole thing.

"You mean Alice squirted you with whipped cream?" Eric's mother asked, "That poor girl."

He explained that Alice's parents walked in just after it happened. Eric's father laughed so hard tears came to his eyes.

The phone rang and Ellen answered it. "It's Alice," she said.

"Hello Eric. If you're not busy, can you meet me where I was shopping this morning, I have a decision to make. It won't take long, but it's important to me."

"Ok, give me about twenty minutes." Eric returned to the dining room. "Alice wants me to meet her downtown right away."

Eric fought his way through the crowd. When she saw him, she broke out in laughter, and held up two baby outfits. "What do you think?"

"I think they're both nice. What's the big decision?"

"One's pink and one's blue," She said, staring at him. "Don't you know one's for a boy and the other's for a girl?"

"I'm with you so far," Eric said. "Why don't you buy both? We can use one for this baby and save the other for the next."

"The next?" she whispered. "Okay, I'll buy them both."

"I'll buy 'em," Eric said. Alice held his hand as he reached for his wallet.

"I insist." Alice said. "This is important to me."

"Even if we have twins—a girl and a boy—we're covered."

"Oh, Eric, you're just being silly." She stopped talking for a moment. Her expression changed. "You don't really think so do you? Twins?"

"You never know," he shrugged.

"It's snowing again while the sun's coming out," Alice said. "Isn't that something?" Eric's answer was to take her hand in his. When they reached her house, she started inside, and he swatted her behind. "Careful mister," she said. "That's already taken."

When Eric arrived home, Ellen was reading in the living room. She looked up. "How did the shopping go?" she asked.

"I think Karen's enthusiasm has rubbed off on Alice," Eric answered.

"Speaking of Karen, I felt a little tension at church between you, Karen, and Frank."

Eric did not answer, so Ellen continued, "You have to understand Karen and Frank's concern about your being involved in some unusual situations. Frank has a new outlook with his job, and then there is the baby to consider. His association with you because of your reputation does not exactly help his position with the Lock Company. You seem to embrace things which create controversy. As for Bryan, he's always trying to stir up something. It's been that way since we were kids. Ignore him, and this healing thing involving all of us may disappear."

A knock at the door startled them. Ellen looked out the window. "Your friends are here. I will get it." Ellen opened the door, with Eric behind her.

"Welcome—I'm Ellen, Eric's sister."

"Pleasure meeting you; you're prettier than he is," Jason said. "Meet my girl, Cindy."

"My pleasure," Eric said. "I've heard so much about you."

"Alice is on her way here."

"Why don't we let these guys make their plans?" Ellen said. Cindy followed Ellen into the kitchen.

"My cousin Karen and her husband Frank are coming over in a little while," Ellen said.

A few moments later, they returned to the living room to join Eric and Jason. Ellen glanced at her watch. "I have to leave and I'm running a little late. I am meeting Johnny, I'll see you later." She grabbed her coat, and broke into a big smile.

Karen walked in, with Frank's giant shadow looming behind her.

Jason shook hands with Frank. "He's a big one," Jason said, and turned to face Karen. "You're a pretty one."

"Why, thank you. It's a pleasure to meet you."

A few moments later, Eric laughed and said, "That's Alice's knock." He let her in and took her coat and quickly kissed her. Alice openly beamed. "I hope I'm not late."

"No, Karen and Frank just arrived." He led her into the dining room. "Alice, I'd like you to meet Cindy Korran and Jason Corkland."

"You're even prettier than the picture Eric showed me in basic," Jason said.

Eric pulled out a chair for her. "Frank, you watch and take notes," Karen said.

"Whatever you say, dear."

"This wedding is Thursday at three, right?" Jason asked.

101

"Yes," Alice said. "The reception's at the American Legion hall, and the honeymoon's going to be at my Uncle Paul's cabin. It's on Lake Tanner, near Wyler."

"That sounds wonderful. How lucky you two are," Cindy said.

The couples had dinner at Mabel's Cafe, and then went to a movie.

"I just love Gregory Peck," Cindy said. "He's so . . ."

"Dreamy," Karen added.

"Yeah. I guess he's all right," Jason said, which brought on more laughter.

"This is our humble home," Karen said, leading their guests into their apartment. "Just make yourselves comfortable." She turned on the radio. Karen lifted her glass of wine in a toast, and by the time the music filled the room the couples were dancing.

Later, Jason said, "It's been great, but we have to be going. We'll see you Thursday about noon. I'll try to get hold of Ted. Come on, gorgeous, I've gotta get you home."

A few minutes later, after Alice and Eric left, Alice said to Eric, "I like your friends."

"Karen and Frank didn't seem as upset as they were the other day," he said. "Either the pressure has worn off, or they decided to ignore the whole thing."

"Whatever the reason—It's good. I admit I feel the wine a little." She giggled. He kissed her, and when she reached the top of the steps—she blew Eric a kiss—and almost lost her balance. When she recovered, she rushed into the house.

"Wake up. It's your wedding day," his mother shouted.

"I'm getting up. Just make sure the coffee's strong," Eric said.

Bryan came rushing into the house. "I've got fathers' car. As if it wasn't bad enough being in the paper, it's all over town about you and that waitress at the hospital!"

"No comment. I've got this wedding on my mind."

Ellen glared at both of them. "I'm going to take my turn in the bathroom. It takes me longer to put myself together."

"We're ready, Bryan," Eric's mother said. His father mumbled something about being overdressed as they went out the door.

———————

Later, after they arrived at the church, Alice and Eric exchanged their vows. He placed the ring on Alice's finger, and kissed her. She was stunning in an orchid dress. After the wedding ceremony, they walked down the aisle. A few moments later, they quickly took photos and greetings from relatives and friends.

Later at the reception hall, Alice led her favorite uncle on the dance floor. He smiled with pride. After the dance, they joined Eric, who said, "I want to thank you for everything."

"My pleasure, son" Uncle Paul replied.

"Sorry I couldn't make the ceremony." Eric turned to see Ted with a young girl by his side. He yelled over the noise of the crowd. "I'd like you to meet Nancy Blanke," Ted said.

"Welcome to our wedding—I'm glad you could make it," Eric said.

"Oh, I'm just having the best time." She hung on Ted's arm as if he would suddenly vanish. "I just love weddings, they're so—you know."

———————

"I can't believe it——they actually showed up," Alice's father said to himself.

"Eric, I would like you to meet Paula and her husband Henry. Edith is around here somewhere."

"We saw mother earlier," Paula said. "She is with Alice and a group of other people by the side entrance."

Paula offered her hand. She had the same facial features as Alice, although her makeup was heavier. She was a little taller, with dark flowing hair around her shoulders. "I'm not sure how I should feel about you," she said, looking into his eyes. Her breath reeked with the smell of beer.

Her husband Henry stepped forward and put out his hand. "Congratulations, Eric," he said. He was at least six feet tall, with thinning light blond-hair showing signs of receding. Rimmed glasses covered his dark brown eyes. "Call me Hank. How about a beer?" he asked with an expression that bordered on unwelcome anxiety.

"No, thank you," Eric said. "I have several things to take care of."

"I would imagine," he said. "How about you, honey?"

"Maybe it'll help—I hear you're the young man who put it to my sister!"

"*Paula!*" Alice's father shouted.

"Sorry, Dad. Sorry Eric. That remark was uncalled for. This is just so unexpected and I'm not sure how to handle this," Paula said. Eric could see the softness in her eyes that revealed anything but the hardness she was portraying.

"I think I'd better join my husband in the kitchen," Paula added.

Paula and her husband returned, each with a bottle of beer. "I seem to be saying all the wrong things——not that it would be the first time," Paula said.

"Congratulations, Eric," Linda said.

Eric led her away from everyone. "You look lovely."

"Thank you. Bill promised me we would leave right away. He's had too much to drink, as usual," she said with disgust. "I want to wish you and Alice the best."

"Hey, Eric," Jason said. "I'm driving; let me know when you're ready to go."

"I'm ready," Eric said, "if I can find Alice."

"Hey, Eric!" Bill Hausler said, "You've got yourself quite a girl here."

Linda, close to tears said, "Bill, are you ready to go? You promised."

"No," Bill shouted, "I'm not ready yet; you dance with Eric. You're old *friends,* aren't you?"

The musicians were on break and his voice echoed through the hall.

Alice walked up to them. "Hi, is everybody having a good time?" Then Frank walked over, asking "Is there a problem?"

Hausler pulled his arm away from Linda, and faced Eric. "You stay away from Linda."

He swung at Eric, who easily sidestepped Hausler's attempted punch, causing Hausler to lose his balance.

"Don't let this spoil your honeymoon," Linda cried.

"It won't," Alice said firmly.

Eric put his arm around Alice. "You're quite a girl."

"I know," he heard her say as they walked away. Alice and Eric acknowledged all guests before they left. "I'll never forget this," Alice told her uncle.

"Seeing you two together is all I need," her uncle said. "You had better get going. There is plenty of food and drinks waiting at the cabin. All you have to do is build the fire."

———————————

A light snow began to fall as Jason drove away. "Looks like the snow is changing into a mild blizzard," Jason grinned. "We're gonna have to hurry, or we might be forced to spend the night."

"Don't you wish," Cindy said.

———————————

Jason maneuvered the car next to the cabin's front door. Alice opened the door and turned on the lights. While everyone looked around, she opened the refrigerator and held up a bottle of champagne.

Jason said, "Hey, this cabin has even got a shower in the bathroom. Your uncle sure knows how to live."

Alice laughed. "That's my uncle." The fire roared as they sipped champagne. Cindy raised her glass. "Alice and Eric, I toast your happiness for years to come."

"I'll second that," Jason said, and looked out the window. "It's snowing hard. We'll see you tomorrow night and have our own special New Year's Eve party."

"This is what you've been waiting for, huh?" Alice whispered. "I think I'll slip into something more comfortable, as they say in the movies."

Eric poured a drink, lit a cigarette, and stared into the fire. All kinds of thoughts crowded his mind for attention. He smelled her perfume just before she touched his shoulder. He tossed the cigarette into the fire, turned around and looked at her. The light from the flames danced through her hair, changing the reflection of light across her face. Her rose-colored pajamas came alive in the flames. "Pajamas," Eric said, with a grin.

"Yeah. If you want me, you're going to have to peel me like an orange."

Eric reached for her. "There's nothing I would rather do." She was in his arms. With each touch, their passion ruled the moments until their togetherness exploded in ecstasy.

"I'm happy-tired," said Alice. "I want to wake up with you holding me."

He kissed her and asked, "What're you thinking?"

"The agony of the indecision I went through while packing," she said. "You don't know how important this was to me. I did not know what I should wear tonight. You think—"

"I couldn't imagine it being any better."

"You'll see the nightie tomorrow night."

"I can't hardly wait."

"You'll have to. I'm worth it."

"I have no doubt," she heard him whisper, and a smile crossed her face just before she fell asleep.

Eric awoke with the sun in his eyes. "What're you doing?" Alice asked, pulling up her covers. Bright morning sunlight streamed through her curly hair.

"I was counting the freckles on your nose," Eric said. "I've already got the coffee on."

"I feel strange. You have been watching me sleep. Let's get up for coffee—Would you please turn your head?"

"Turn my head?"

"Please Eric. I feel different this morning."

He laughed and said, "All right." He left the bedroom and sat at the table, sipping his coffee. Moments later, she walked slowly out of the bedroom wearing her pajama top and a big grin. "What do you think?"

"It sure looks good to me," Eric said, and reached for her.

She kissed him lightly, and then said, "If you can keep your hands off me I'll fix our breakfast." Alice lit one of Eric's cigarettes and coughed as tears came in her eyes. "How do you smoke these nasty things?"

"You get used to it," Eric said. "This is the first time I've had breakfast by candlelight."

"Isn't this romantic? Lets get dressed and go outside. It's beautiful out." She paused. "Do you think we could build a fire outdoors and roast marshmallows? It'll be fun—a winter picnic." Her eyes grew larger with her smile.

"Sounds great," Eric said.

They walked along the lake hand in hand, stopping occasionally to hold each other and melt the winter cold. Alice looked around her. "See how the sun glistens off the snow on those cedar branches." She ran around the grill and kissed him. In a few moments, flames broke the chill. "See, I knew we could do it. I'll get the marshmallows. We'll have a great time."

He pushed his hat back. The day was surprisingly warm. It had quit snowing, and the sun peeked through a couple clouds. It was a beautiful day.

"Eric. I—I said a prayer of thanks for us this morning."

"So did I," Eric said. "I have every day."

"You say nice things." She beamed, eating her third hot dog.

After lunch, at her insistence, he helped her build a snowman.

Later in the evening Alice said, "It is getting late. I've got to take my shower."

"Without me?" Eric said.

"You mean—together?" She turned red. "I never took a shower with anyone before."

"I'll give you five minutes." Eric waited until he heard the shower running, then walked into the steam-filled bathroom. She stood there with a big towel draped around her. "I'm ready to try," she said as the towel hit the floor. Eric quickly joined her. "I don't think there's room," he said. "Oh, I guess there is!"

A little later, Alice dried off, and quickly put on her robe. "We made it, didn't we? We had better start our dinner. You'd better peel these potatoes while I get the rest of the food ready. It won't be long until everyone's here."

They worked together as day faded into late afternoon. Alice wore a yellow dress that accented her eyes. "Am I easy on the eyes?" she asked Eric, and spun around for him to see. "I bought it especially for tonight." Her large eyes softened. "You'd better hurry. I just heard a car."

Eric looked out the window. Frank parked his dad's station wagon. Karen, Frank, Liza, and Bryan got out. "Eric, aren't you dressed? You men are something else," Alice said. She hurried to the door. "Welcome to our humble cabin."

When another car arrived, Eric welcomed Ted, Cindy, Jason, and Nancy. Jason walked to Alice and handed her a small package. He then handed Eric a package. "From what I've heard," Jason said, "this might come in handy."

"You first, honey," Eric said. Alice carefully unwrapped the package. She blushed, then took the can of whipped cream and turned toward Eric. He jumped back and everybody laughed. "I'd better set it on the table," she said. "These spray cans and I don't get along too well."

Eric opened his package to find a towel, soap and wash cloth. He laughed and placed them near the can, "Just in case," he said.

After dinner, they all went for a walk beside the lake until dusk closed in. The evening sun shone through the trees with a reddish glow as the sunset swept the sky. "What a place," Frank said. Karen slipped up behind him and stuffed some snow down his neck. He jumped to chase her. The women ended up in a snowball fight with the men. Everybody laughed and tumbled around in the snow as darkness closed in.

Eric threw two more logs on the fire. The couples huddled together around the fire as music from the radio drifted through the cabin. They danced and later regrouped in front of the fire and stared dreamily into the flames. A silence fell over the group as the time to leave drew near. Eric put his arm around Alice's shoulder and she whispered, "We have to start back. I better start to pack."

"I can help," Eric offered.

"Let me, please." She went into the bedroom.

Eric tried to smile. "Last round, everybody."

"The table is cleared and everything's in reasonable shape," Karen said. Even she could not change the mood that took control. Eric went to the bedroom and put his hand on Alice's shoulder. He tried not to call attention to her tears.

"Let's join our guests. We had a great honeymoon, didn't we?" Alice asked softly.

"The best," Eric said. They threw out the remaining logs in the fireplace and locked the cabin door. Jason, Ted, Cindy, and Nancy waved as they left.

Alice put her hand on their snowman. "Poor guy. We didn't even name him."

The drive back to Benford was strangely silent. "It's almost one-thirty," Karen said when they stopped in front of Alice's house. "Leave the bags. We'll take care of them tomorrow."

"The key should be under the mat," Alice said. She switched on the light, and then noticed a note by the telephone. "Mother and dad are at Uncle Paul's. They figured we'd want to be alone." Alice looked relieved, then grinned. "How'd you like to shower in my territory?"

With a big smile, Eric replied, "You mean this gets even better?"

———————

"Wake up, Eric." Alice kissed him. "I'm afraid it's time to get up."

They finished breakfast and were sipping coffee when Alice's parents entered the house.

"Good morning," Alice said. "We have coffee ready, although we've finished breakfast."

"Good morning. We've already eaten, but the coffee smells good," Edith said. She seemed to be in an unbelievably happy mood. They sat around the table and talked about the honeymoon.

A half an hour later the conversation seems to have run its course. Eric shook hands with Lawrence, while Edith hugged him. The early afternoon stillness soon faded away with the sounds of kids and a dog, deeply involved in a snowball fight in a nearby field. "I'm trying to be brave about your leaving," Alice said. "I-I'm not very good at it, but I refuse to spoil dinner."

The minute they walked in the house, Martha said, "We've been waiting for you. Let me hug my new daughter-in-law."

"How about a glass of wine for a toast?" Howard said.

"You toast everything!" Martha said. "But I'll join this one. Did you have a pleasant honeymoon?"

"Yes," Alice said. "We built a snowman and had a picnic. I don't know why I said something like that. I'm a little nervous."

The door flew open. Johnny rushed in with Ellen, followed by Karen and Frank. "You're just in time to toast the newlyweds and have dinner with us," Eric's dad said.

"We timed it that way," Karen said.

Tension grew as the afternoon faded into evening. Karen and Frank wished Eric well and left. Eric turned to his folks. "I'm going to say goodbye."

"Write and pray," his mother said. "You know we're here if you need anything."

Ellen put her hand on Eric's shoulder and said, "You be sure and take care of yourself."

When they arrived at the bus station, Eric said to Alice, "Don't worry about anything. We'll never really be apart."

"Remember, I'm the girl who loves you," Alice said with tears in her eyes. "I'm not gonna cry." The bus pulled in just as they reached the station.

"Love you," Eric whispered. He put his arms around her and kissed her.

"I told you I wouldn't cry," she said, and quickly turned away when he boarded the bus. Eric looked out the window and waved to the blue-eyed, curly-headed girl who waved back. He stared out the window as the familiar landscape passed out of sight.

CHAPTER NINE

"WYLER, FIFTEEN MINUTES," THE DRIVER CALLED.

Cindy waved to Eric while the driver tossed Jason's bag on the bus. "Here we go again," Jason said. "I'm not going to let myself get down, because there's nothing I can do about it."

"You don't let many things get to you, do you?" Eric said.

"What good does it do?" Jason said. "Life's a succession of changes. I think circumstances control many of our decisions. Let's face it—Cindy's quite a girl, but I'm afraid of getting too close. It's a long, complicated story. I'll tell you about it some time." A short time later, the bus pulled into Cutler City. They grabbed their bags and headed for the train station.

"Ted didn't seem too happy at your wedding," Jason said. They bought their train tickets. "Something's bugging him. I gotta hunch it's Marie."

"There he is," Eric said. "We've only got about ten minutes so we might as well board. Hi, Ted, how was your Christmas?" Eric said.

"Okay, but I'm looking forward to seeing Marie. I wrote her over Christmas. Nancy's talking marriage and our parents are pushing us together. When I told my parents I was in love with Marie, they encouraged Nancy more than ever."

Two young girls entered the car and sat across the aisle. The girls glanced at the guys, whispered to each other, and laughed.

A big smile crossed Jason's face. "Maybe this won't be such a bad trip after all. You think those young ladies would join us?"

Jason turned to Ted. "I know better than to ask Eric. Hey, Ted! I need you. You're not letting me down, are you?"

"I'll think about it," Ted said. Jason smiled and approached the girls. A few minutes later, he returned with a big smile. "Ted, I asked them to join us for dinner. They go to school in Dennard. You with me, buddy?"

"I guess so. Contacts could be important."

"When the dining car opens, we'll pick 'em up. You can join us, Eric."

"No thanks, I've got a lot of serious thinking to do. I'll wait until the crowd thins out." Eric looked outside at the darkness closing in. A mixture of rain and snow beat against the window as a lonely, familiar feeling crept over him.

"Last call for dinner," the porter announced. Eric waved off Jason and Ted's invitation in the dining car. "What will you have, sir?" the waiter asked.

"I'll have a hamburger and a beer," Eric said.

"Do you mind if I join you?" a tall, thin, young girl with light brown hair asked. "I'm afraid I waited until the last minute. I—I thought there'd be plenty of empty tables," She stammered and stared at him through wire-rimmed glasses.

"No need to apologize. I had the same idea." Eric glanced at her book as the waiter took her order. He could sense her discomfort. He tried a smile.

"It's journalism," she said. "Do you know anything about it?"

"Absolutely nothing," Eric replied.

"I go to the University in Dennard. This is my last year. I'm sorry. I do not mean to ramble. Sometimes I am so rattled, I get carried away. I get nervous when I meet someone for the first time."

"No problem. My buddies and I are going back to the base after Christmas leave." Eric told her about Alice. She listened intently. "I've only known you for about an hour, yet I find myself telling you things which I usually don't talk about," he said. "You're easy to talk to, although you're shy."

"I know. It is something I have to overcome. Being a journalist is important to me. I enjoyed talking to you. I am afraid it has been a very long day for me. If you will excuse me, I am tired. Meeting you was delightful."

"It was my pleasure. Good night." Eric returned to the coach. He relaxed and lit a cigarette, watching the passing countryside. He reached inside his shirt, touched the cross, and found himself wondering about the little girl in his dreams just before falling asleep.

Eric jumped when Jason shook him. "Hey, you've gotta help me! Ted's sick in the toilet. I can't get him out! If he don't pull the damndest things I ever heard of."

Eric groaned and walked to the rear of the car, and knocked on the bathroom door. "Ted you all right?"

People began to stir and complain about the commotion. He heard Ted moan, and then yell through the door, "I don't know if I'm going to make it. I think I'm going to die and I'm not sure I care."

Jason looked at Eric and they laughed. "You can't die," Jason said, "You've got a big future ahead of you, and a date with Uncle Sam."

"Now's a hell of a time to be funny," Ted yelled, which brought on laughter from some passengers and groans from others.

"Serves him right," some woman said.

"Lady, why don't you go back to sleep, and pretend you have a heart," Jason said.

She poked the guy next to her, and yelled, "Harry did you hear what that soldier said?"

"Yeah," Harry said. "Why don't you go back to sleep?"

"How dare you talk to me that way!"

Eric saw a porter approaching. "Ted, if you don't come out of there, they're going to throw us off the train."

"What's going on here?" he asked. "You're upsetting everyone in this car."

"My buddy's sick. Can you get us something?" Eric asked.

"All right, but you get him out of there before I return." He left, shaking his head.

"Ted, if you don't come out now, we're coming in to get you," Eric said. They heard him move as the door slowly opened.

"Here's some Bromo and an ice bag," the returning porter said. "I'd better not have to come back here again."

Eric overheard a lady tell another, "These servicemen are always causing trouble. I just can't understand them." He glanced at her and knew she never would.

"Easy, Buddy, you'll make it." When they got back to their seats, Ted whispered, "I slept with Nancy. I will probably have to marry her. Do not mention this to Jason. He'd never understand."

Eric stared at Ted and wondered who seduced whom.

When Jason returned, he said, "Ted, here's some water. Drink this Bromo. I'm gonna bring you back to life. Hold this ice bag. It will give you something to do."

––––––––––––––

Eric awoke with the sunrise. He went to the dining car, ate breakfast, and tried to relax. On the way back to his seat, one girl asked, "How're your buddies?"

"They're both out of it. You must have had some party."

"They drank too much," one of the girls said. She looked back at the wiped-out warriors. "We'll buy dinner," the other girl added. They looked at Ted and laughed, "if you can find some way to put him back together again."

"I'll bring Teddy back to life," Jason said.

Ted stirred and moaned. "My head hurts," he said. "I feel terrible." He grabbed his head with both hands and moaned again.

"You've gotta shape up," Eric said, "We'll be in Dennard around one."

The train continued through the countryside. It seemed like only moments later Jason appeared. "Come on, Ted, the girls are buying," Ted moaned as he slowly got out of the seat. Eric leaned back, and dozed off. A few minutes later, he woke up and saw the girl he met in the dining car smile at him.

"We meet again," she said.

"It looks like it. Would you like to join me for dinner?" Eric asked.

"I'd like that. We should be in Dennard in about an hour. An enjoyable dinner would be pleasant before, who knows what? She blushed "Why did I say that?"

115

"You're right," Eric laughed. "I'd like a good dinner and some pleasant conversation before I face the unknown."

She whispered, "You miss your wife already, don't you?"

"Very much. Do you have anyone special?"

"No. I'm career-bound." She paused a minute. "I'm afraid I married too young, and it didn't work out. He had both feet on the ground, but I had a dream. We had nothing in common."

"Nothing's wrong in following a dream. Where would this country be without them?"

"We'll reach Dennard in a few minutes. We had better get back. My name is Gail Jacoby. Maybe we can be friends. Here is my phone number. I know how dreadful loneliness can be."

"Name's Eric Silkwin."

"It's been delightful meeting you, and good luck."

The train slowly moved into Dennard. Eric, Jason, and Ted picked up their bags and boarded the bus to the base. The men sat silently as the bus pulled up to the familiar front gate. Two sergeants were waiting for them when they got off the bus. One of the sergeants checked off Eric's and a couple other guys' names. "You men follow me," he said.

The last time Eric saw Jason and Ted, they went in a different direction.

The three of them entered an orderly room and stood at attention. "You men are assigned to the Air Force Police. Sergeant Hanley, take these men and get them squared away. You men will be on duty at zero eight-hundred hours tomorrow. You're free until then." He finally smiled. "My name's Lieutenant Shredder. Dismissed."

The sergeant led them to the barracks. Eric unpacked his B4 bag, checked his equipment, and straightened his footlocker. He remembered Baulkner's words about base assignments before they left after basic. Eric saw a guy approach the bunk next to him. "Hi. My name's Everett Snively."

"I'm Eric Silkwin."

He stared at Eric through steel-rimmed glasses, and extended his hand. "I know how you feel. I've only been here three weeks, myself."

"It's really not all that bad," Snively said. "Police work is mainly a matter of falling into routine. This assignment's supposed to be temporary."

Eric stared at the guy he found hard to imagine in the Air Force police. He was a little over five feet and about a hundred thirty-five pounds. "The barracks chief is Sergeant Hanley," Snively said. "Watch out for him." He leaned closer and whispered, "Hard-nose Hanley, they call him. Lieutenant Shredder is all right, but he mostly lets Hanley run things."

P.F.C. Snively got dressed in his class-A uniform and continued, "I'm off-duty until tomorrow. Here he comes now. I'm going into town, see a movie, and have dinner. See you later, I gotta catch a bus." He hurried out the barracks door.

Sergeant Hanley checked his clipboard. "Deakes, Parris, and Silkwin, follow me."

They headed toward the Air Police orderly Room.

"I am Staff Sergeant Higgins," he said with a cold, tight smile. *Here's a man who loves his work,* Eric thought. "Welcome men. I know you are not here by choice, but that's the way it is. Read these regulations carefully." He paused for effect. "You will be expected to know them at my request, and . . . ." Eric noticed the clerk-typist grinning at them. Sergeant Higgins turned to face him. "What's so damn funny?" Higgins demanded.

"Nothing, Sarge." The clerk stared down at his typewriter.

"Look at me when I'm talking to you!" Higgins said. "This is one of the wise guys in this squadron, and there are others." Eric thought immediately of Jason. "You men are excused until eight hundred hours. Get some chow, and familiarize yourself with the base."

The three left the orderly room. They stared at the barbed wire that topped the chain link fence. It enclosed two barracks in the back. Searchlights covered the surrounding area at each corner of the stockade. "I've gotta feeling we're getting the shaft," Deakes moaned.

"That's for sure," Parris muttered.

"Hey, you guys," someone yelled when the three walked in the barracks door. "Our relief is here." Several guys introduced

117

themselves. They explained the worst thing about police duties, other than a certain sergeant, was the routine.

"How long before we can get a tech school or get out of here?" Parris asked.

"I've been in this outfit more than eight months. They turned down all my requests for a transfer. It's a hard outfit to get out of. I don't want to discourage you, but . . ."

A strange silence fell over the barracks. "I'm gonna have a few beers," Deakes said. "If I'm gonna deal with a headache tomorrow, it's gonna be from something other than this lousy assignment." He stormed out of the barracks.

"I don't think he likes our outfit," one guy said. "He's not the first. If he's not careful, he'll be in the stockade looking out. It can always get worse. I have been in the air police more than a year. I am marking time for a month and a half. You can bet I won't re-enlist."

After Eric and Parris left the chow hall, they went to the PX. "Well, look who's here," Parris said, pointing to Deakes. "Our comrade in arms. Mind if we join you?"

Deakes had a silly grin on his face. A look of someone who has had too many, but thought he had everything under control. "Welcome," he said. "How was chow?"

"Better than basic," Parris said.

"That wouldn't take much. A couple more beers and I'll level off," Deakes said.

Eric finished his second beer. "That's enough for me," he said. "It just makes things worse."

"There's a grain of truth to that," Deakes said.

"I'm going to the movies," Parris said. "You guys coming?"

"No," Deakes slowly replied. "The guy'll probably get the girl, and I can't relate to that tonight."

"I'm going back to write letters," Eric said. "See you guys later. Take it easy, Deakes."

"I'm mellowing out," he admitted. "Maybe one more, then I'll go back to the barracks and try to forget this nightmare."

Eric walked back to the barracks and composed his letter.

Dear Alice,

We got in about 1:30 this afternoon, so I'm getting settled. I'm in the AP's (Air Police). They took Jason and Ted in a different direction, I have no idea where or what they are doing. I really don't have anything else to say, except I miss you. Take care of yourself and the little one. Write when you can.

Love you always, Eric

"How's it going?" Snively said.

Eric glanced up. "You're back early."

"I'm not one for drinking," Snively shrugged. "I'm a Christian." Eric didn't know what else to say, but felt a reply was expected. "Dinner and a movie sound good," he said.

"I had a ham dinner and saw a Judy Garland movie."

"Judy Garland, huh?"

"Yeah, I sure like—here comes Hanley," Snively whispered. The barracks suddenly became silent except for Deakes and Parris, who flipped towels at each other. Sergeant Hanley was medium height and stocky, with close-cropped dark hair. His every move suggested the control of a career man. Hanley watched Deakes and Parris, then snickered, "Let's hope you guys have this much enthusiasm on duty tomorrow."

Eric finished his letters. He undressed and hit the sack. He noticed Snively reading a small Bible. Eric opened his Bible, and settled back to relax.

Sergeant Hanley wandered over their way. "Reading the Bible again, huh, Snively? I guess it takes all kinds."

"It helps me," Snively murmured.

Hanley snorted and glanced at Eric. "Looks like you two have something in common. Knock it off, you two," the sergeant told Deakes and Parris. "Lights out in ten minutes."

The next day, Eric realized what the guys meant. The job was routine—taking prisoners to chow and work details. "Stockade duty is the worst," Snively said one evening after chow. "You walk from one end of the stockade to the other. It's best if you train your mind to think of something else to overcome the boredom."

119

"Hey, Eric," Jason called. "You in here?"

"I'm afraid so," Eric yelled. Jason and Ted headed for Eric's bunk. Jason slapped Eric's back. "We've been looking all over this damn base for you," he said. A big grin spread over his face. "So you're in the Air Police?"

"Yeah, what can I say? I'll take it one-step at a time. Anyway, it's great to see you guys. What're you two doing?"

"Ted and I are cooks in training. Ain't that a gut?" Jason said, and then broke out in laughter. "Why do you think we eat in the PX? I asked the sergeant for a three-day pass. If he hadn't been laughing so hard, he'd have kicked my ass from here to breakfast."

Eric introduced them to Deakes, Parris, and Snively. "We're going into town tomorrow night," Jason said. "Can you make it?"

"Yeah. I'm off duty at sixteen hundred hours."

Jason grinned. "I'd rather be a cook than an AP. I guess we'll have to put up with this crap until we can get tech schools."

Sergeant Hanley wandered over. "You guys're in the service—what—five months or so? You think you just go off to school," he said with clenched teeth. "Ask these guys how long they've been waiting."

"We'll make it. You've gotta have faith," Eric spoke up.

Sergeant Hanley grinned. "Oh, yeah, the faith. Maybe there'll be an opening for a chaplain's assistant."

"Do you really think so?" Eric said

"They've got some churches in town," Hanley said with a wicked grin. "I wanted to make sure you guys knew."

"Naturally, I plan on visiting them." Eric said and then winked at Jason.

"You're goin' to church on your pass?"

"Sure," Jason said with a straight face. "I'll have a couple of beers, but I've no intention of missing services. You just cannot underestimate the power of a religious service. It makes you feel like you can handle anything that comes your way."

"I can't believe you guys." Hanley shrugged. "If you hit the bars, you might get lucky, pick up a woman. In your case, I should say girls. You do like girls, don't you?"

"You'd better believe it," Jason said. "You get acquainted in church and you don't have to blow all that money on booze."

Hanley's smile faded. "I get the feeling you're a wise guy putting me on." The sergeant walked back to his bunk.

Jason laughed. "We had him going."

"Be careful," Eric warned Jason. "He's a rough one, I hear."

"Nobody asked him to butt in," Jason added. "What's with the guy, anyway—some kinda inferiority complex?"

Hanley charged back to Eric's bunk. "I heard that," he said. The guys suddenly turned down their radios as attention focused on their end of the barracks. Deakes and Parris snickered. Hanley stood directly in front of Jason. "The service is a big joke to you, isn't it? Fun and games? That's what you think, boy? You guys really get me!"

Jason's grin vanished. "It's a joke all right," he said, "thanks to a recruiter I'm gonna pay a visit to when I get home."

Eric quickly interrupted. "Hey, tomorrow's payday . . . maybe we can unwind a little."

"Here's our barracks number," Ted said. "Come on, Jason, we've got to get back. I don't want to get restricted."

"Drop by our barracks," Jason said. "We'll head in town." His big grin was back.

They received their pay the following morning, and as usual, dice and poker games broke out in the barracks. Eric checked the duty roster and discovered that he and Snively had another shift before being relieved. Jason and Ted were almost as disappointed as Eric was.

"Damn!" Jason sighed. "Hanley's giving you and Snively the shaft. Ted and I had planned to stay in town. I heard the minute you get off duty, you better get outta sight or off the base. We'll see you later."

"I'll meet you tomorrow morning. I'll be on the first bus into town," Eric said. Jason sighed and then added, "I guess that's the way it has to be."

"Hey Silkwin, you got an emergency call in the orderly room," a voice said. Eric awoke to face a flashlight in his eyes. He grabbed his fatigues and ran to the orderly room, praying there was nothing wrong with Alice or the family.

He recognized Jason's voice right away. "Eric, I've some bad news—the AP's picked up Ted!"

"What're you talking about?" Eric yelled.

"It's a little hard to explain at this time. He got drunk, and took a swing at this AP. I called to see if you could cover Ted on that end. What else can I do? That guy is something else. I'm beginning to think he needs a keeper!"

"Why in the world would Ted swing at an AP?"

"Marie's father died and Ted flipped out," Jason said. "We got a hotel room, and Ted started carrying on about her father. I could see we weren't gonna get much sleep, so we went after a couple of six-packs. Anyway, we drank a beer on the way back to the hotel. Those guys seemed to come outta nowhere."

"What time did this happen?"

"A little after one. They were gonna let us off," Jason continued. "But when one of the guys reached for Ted's six-pack, he took a swing at him. It was ridiculous. The guy sidestepped Ted's swing and grabbed him. Ted cussed the Air Police out. I mean what else can I say? I knew Ted could pull some good ones, but this—anyway. I couldn't talk him out of it."

"I'll check the stockade and do what I can," Eric said. "See you in the morning."

"We shouldn't have rented that damn room," Jason said.

Eric entered the stockade orderly room. A sergeant he barely recognized asked, "Can I help you?" He looked up from the novel he was reading, obviously disappointed with the interruption.

"How soon do they bring a guy in when they pick him up?"

"Depends on the kind of trouble. Got a buddy of yours in trouble, right? What'd he do?"

"He took a swing at one of the APs." The sergeant shook his head. "They tried taking his six-pack of beer. It was after hours. He's really not a troublemaker. You'll see what I mean."

The sergeant stretched, got up and refilled his coffee cup. Eric helped himself to coffee, took a seat next to the sergeant and lit a Camel. "How long has he been in the service?"

"We just finished basic together." Eric heard the Jeep drive up. When the APs brought Ted in, he looked pathetic. "What's the complaint?" the sergeant asked.

"P.F.C. Faulkland was drinking beer after hours," the guy said. "We tried to take his beer, and he took a swing at me." Ted glanced at Eric, and then stood helplessly with his head down.

"What've you got to say for yourself, Faulkland?" the sergeant asked.

"I lost my head for a minute," Ted mumbled.

"The other guy with him didn't give us any trouble. We were going to let 'em off with a warning until this guy swung at me."

"I have to file a report," the sergeant said, and motioned to Eric. "This guy is a friend of his. He's in our outfit."

"Can I be excused?" Ted moaned. "I'm gonna be sick."

"In there!" The sergeant yelled. Ted ran for the latrine. "I hate to put him in the stockade. What do you guys think?" One of them shrugged. "The swing didn't amount to anything. We talked to him on the way out here, and we believe its outta character."

"All right, I'll put it down as a warning." The sergeant turned to Eric. "Silkwin, get him back to his barracks. Scare the hell out of him. Make sure he knows he lucked out."

"I'll get the point across, loud and clear," Eric said. "Thanks, guys."

"You're lucky Hanley wasn't duty sergeant tonight. He'd throw the book at him."

"I know. Thanks again."

Ted came out of the latrine. "Can I sit for a minute? I don't feel so good."

The sergeant and the two men exchanged grins. "Your buddy's going to take you back to your barracks. I'd better not hear about you pulling this kinda crap again. You read me, Faulkland?" The sergeant yelled so loudly that Ted jumped.

"Yes, *sir*," Ted moaned. He tried to snap to attention, but failed miserably.

Eric took him to his barracks. "You got any idea how lucky you are? Ted, you hear me?"

"Yes," Ted replied. "I'd appreciate it more if I felt better." Eric tried hard to keep from laughing.

"Tomorrow morning I'm gonna meet Jason. How about you?"

"If I can survive this night, I'll be glad to," Ted mumbled.

The next morning Eric entered Ted's barracks and shook him. "Up and at 'em." Ted sat up, grabbed his head and moaned. "I don't know why I did such a stupid thing. Those guys could have killed me. Even the idea of the stockade scares me. I—I—" Suddenly Ted jumped out of his bunk and rushed to the latrine. A few moments later, he returned. "There's no way I can make it. I'll have to call Marie later."

When Eric arrived at the hotel room, Jason was patiently waiting. "I didn't think Ted would make it. I've met some characters in my life, but he's a new breed. You never know what he's gonna do next."

"What can I say? Ted is Ted," Eric said.

"He's lucky you're in the APs."

A few minutes later, they tried to relax over coffee at a little cafe a couple blocks from the hotel. Eric felt a touch on his shoulder. "Remember me?"

"Yes," Eric said. He introduced Gail to Jason, and asked her to join them.

"I would love to, but I'm on my way to work," she said.

"I'll walk you. Jason has to go back to the base."

"I'll see you, Eric. My pleasure, Gail," Jason said, and then added, "Can you believe it? What a night!" Eric explained the incident to her while they walked along the street.

Just before Gail entered the drugstore, she said, "I would love to spend the afternoon with you, but I can't get out of work."

"I should be getting back to the base anyway . . . I just had to get away for a while."

She put her hand on his arm. "Maybe we could have dinner, go to a movie, or have a couple beers. Call me sometime, but don't wait too long."

"I—I'll be looking forward to it," Eric said.

CHAPTER TEN

THE FOLLOWING MONTH WENT BY QUICKLY. Eric and Snively polished their combat boots with determination. They worked mechanically, buffing the tips to a high luster. Ferguson, a lanky, moose-faced corporal with a big mouth, joined them. He put his hand on Snively's shoulder. "I hear you're gonna baby-sit the window bandit at the hospital."

"Yes," Snively said. "I'm not looking forward to it."

Deakes and Parris wandered over from the other side of the barracks and leaned against the raw wood post next to Snively's bunk. "Who's the window bandit?" Deakes asked.

"A guy from supply squadron. They've been after him for months. The local police caught him the other night," Ferguson said. "His head looked like he'd been in a car wreck. You oughta see him! Two long, jagged gashes over the top of his shaven head. Police say he rammed his head against the bars."

Ferguson flashed a twisted grin. "No way. Gory, huh, Snively? Look at it this way—you need the experience."

"It didn't seem to upset you too much," Eric said.

"Not really. It took the edge off the regular, boring duties," Ferguson said. "Now, picture this: You're sitting there trying to read when suddenly this guy—who's supposed to be in a coma—is staring straight at you." Ferguson was enjoying the attention. "You don't know if he sees you, what he's thinking, or what he's going to do next."

Snively's face suddenly became pale.

"What would you do if he got up and started walking outta the room?" Parris asked.

Ferguson's mouth twisted into a bitter grin. "I'd put a couple more gashes on his head." He rubbed the back of his huge, hairy hand and looked at Eric with small, close-set eyes. "Almost like going on the warpath—huh, Silkwin?"

Eric stared at him for a moment, then uttered: "Shove it, Ferguson!"

"I'll see you later," Ferguson said. "I need a few beers. Duty like that can drive a guy to drink." He broke into laughter, and then directed his attention at Eric and Snively. He laughed and sang "*Go Onward Christian Soldiers.*"

After Ferguson left, Parris said, "Why would a guy who'd just pulled that kind of duty be in such a good mood?"

"He probably saw someone kick a dog on his way back from chow," Deakes said. "Guys like him really get to me. He's got his nose so far up Hanley's ass, if Hanley suddenly turned a corner, he'd break it off."

After frustrated laughter, Deakes returned to his bunk and Parris left the barracks. "I don't know how I'm going to handle this!" Snively said. He sat on his bunk, with his head between his hands, obviously counting the minutes until he had to report to the base hospital.

"Don't mind Ferguson—You know the kind of guy he is," Eric said. "He's just trying to shake you up."

"I think he got the job done," Snively said. A few minutes later, Parris stormed into the barracks and broke into a big smile. "Hey Snively, you're off the hook. I just came from the orderly room. We have to take the prisoners on the grass cutting detail."

Snively breathed a sigh of relief. "What about the—"

"They transferred the guy to the hospital in town," Parris said. "Some kind of complications."

"You really lucked out, buddy!" Eric said. He heard Snively whisper, "Thank God."

Eric opened the first of two letters. The last name on the return address surprised him. He grinned as he read, "Ellen Bowers."

Dear Eric,

I'm a very happy married woman. I fell in love with a guy named Johnny. I should've written you before, but you know me. Johnny and I were married January 8. We only had a three-day honeymoon, but I have never been happier.

Alice and I see each other often. She misses you, but keeps busy. The feared publicity hasn't taken place— thank God. That woman who caused such a scene has not returned. As for Claude Stratman, he has not pursued anyone, including Alice and her parents. Keep your chin up.

Your big sister, Ellen
P.S. Johnny was worth waiting for.

He opened Alice's letter. He grinned to himself when he noticed Alice's style changing.

Dearest Eric,

I can feel our baby. It's a special feeling. The way he kicks, it would have to be a boy. You'd be proud of me. I miss you—it's the nights that are worse. I know we'll make it past these times. Mother and I are closer than ever. We are making baby clothes. I will close now, because I cannot think of anything else to say.

All my love and prayers are with you.
With love Alice and our little one.

For the next two months, Eric and Jason made occasional trips to town and gym workouts, which helped pass the time. Eric and Jason's boxing sessions drew a crowd. Jason's appearance was deceiving. He was strong and aggressive. What he lacked in experience, he made up for in determination.

One evening, Eric was working out on the heavy bag. Jason watched for a while, and then asked, "I'd hate to be that bag. What's got you so uptight? Is it Alice?"

Eric stopped, grabbed a towel and wiped sweat from his face "That's only a part of it." He felt depression absorb him like a living thing. "It's a combination of things."

"I got a hunch you're referring to Hanley and the APs."

"You got that right."

Jason said, "Let's grab a shower and go to the PX."

They got their beers and found a booth. "I'm gonna tell you about my father," Jason said. "He worked like a dog all his life on his farm, and to this day, he's in debt. There was always something he couldn't control. If it wasn't the weather, it was something else."

Eric watched the intensity in Jason's face build.

"I know you've wondered about my attitude toward Cindy," Jason continued. "My definition of a dangerous girl used to be one you wanted to hang around after you got outta bed." His smile quickly faded. "I'll get us another beer," he said. "While I'm unloading on you, I might as well tell you the whole story. Sit tight."

Eric could see the pain in Jason's eyes. When he returned, his face took on a look of anxiety. Jason took a sip of beer and looked into Eric's eyes. "When my mother died four years ago, my father, strong as he is, fell apart," he said. "In a way, he died with her."

Jason paused, staring at the bottle of beer. "We never got along," he continued. "He could never understand why I couldn't put my heart and soul into that hopeless farm. After my mother died, we just went through the motions. Nobody could take her place, so my father shut everyone else out."

Eric interrupted. "Four years? Didn't he meet anyone?"

"Not until last year. We couldn't talk. All I could see was trouble and heartbreak. All he could see was building his dream." Jason's smile turned cold as the story progressed. "I remember two or three years ago, I'd lay awake at night and hear him crying in the next room. I didn't see him, but I knew he held her picture."

Eric looked down at his beer to avoid Jason's eyes. "Enough hearts and flowers. I'll see you later," Jason said.

For the first time, Eric felt he really understood Jason.

128

The next four weeks, Jason and Eric continued workouts. Ted insisted on joining them, and worked as a handler. "Hey, Nancy's not pregnant," he said. "You don't know how I've worried these last few months."

"Oh yes we do!" Jason and Eric said together.

Ted and Marie became inseparable.

The next evening Eric, Jason, and Ted entered the barracks. With payday still a few days off, blaring radios and letter writing occupied most of the men. Jason plopped on Eric's bunk. "You still uptight?" he asked.

"Yeah. I can't seem to shake it off. One thing for sure—I've had it with the APs!"

"I figured that," Jason added.

"You're not gettin' outta this outfit," a voice called from the front of the barracks. "You get in the Air Police. You're stuck."

"I won't accept that!" Eric's voice carried over the sound of the radios that drew immediate attention. Sergeant Hanley wandered over and shouted, "The only way you'll get out of the air police is with a court martial."

Eric did not reply.

Hanley grinned at Eric. "I saw you with that tall blond with the wide-rimmed glasses. She's not the greatest, but she looks like she's built for action. Can't she satisfy you?" he shouted, then laughed and walked back to his bunk.

"There goes living proof that stripes don't necessarily mean brains," Jason said.

Hanley quickly turned to face him. "You talking to me?"

"No more than I have to." Suddenly the guys turned down the volume on the radios. All attention focused toward their bunk area. Hanley walked up to Jason. He spit out his words. "I knew you were a wise guy the first time you walked in this barracks," he said.

"Wait a minute," Jason answered. "You're the one who butted in."

"I knew you were a wise ass. You got anything besides a big mouth?" Hanley shouted.

"There's only one way to find out—if you wanna take off those stripes," Jason yelled.

Hanley's voice sounded like a wounded animal. "You got it, punk. Would you like to step behind the latrine?"

"What're we waiting for?"

"Drop it Jason," Eric said slowly. "This is between me and Hanley and we both know it. I'm sick and tired of you and your golden boy, Ferguson, giving me and Snively every lousy detail, and any extra duty you can think of! I've had it! If you're determined, let's get on with it."

"Wait a minute Eric," Jason said.

"Tell you what punk," Hanley shouted. "When I finish with Silkwin, I'll take you on."

For the first time Jason grinned. "I think you'll have your hands full with Eric. You should've settled for me."

Eric said to Hanley. "How about the gym. With witnesses?"

Hanley's face was twisted by rage. "What's the matter? Afraid of a real fight?"

"*Outside*. You got it!" Eric shouted in Hanley's face.

Jason whispered, "You don't have an edge in this one, buddy. He outweighs you by at least twenty pounds."

"Whatever," Eric yelled. "This has been coming on since I got here. It had to happen, and I'm in the mood for it."

The men made a circle behind the latrine. A sergeant who volunteered to referee brought the opponents together in the center of the jeering crowd.

"No rounds," Hanley sneered. "The man down for the count of ten loses."

"Agreed," Eric said. They went to opposite sides and removed their shirts. The referee waved them in. Hanley roared in like a bull, swinging a right, which Eric ducked. Eric fired a jab, feinted a right and knocked Hanley's head back with another jab. The sergeant's nose bled, which only enraged him. He circled Eric, slipped his jab and drove a right to his stomach. Eric doubled over, Hanley fired another right, but Eric backed away and countered with a left hook. Hanley bobbed and weaved then threw a left hook. Eric blocked it and dug his left into Hanley's stomach. He grunted, and pushed away. Hanley feinted a left, threw a right, and Eric hit the ground. He took an eight count on one knee, and then got to his feet. Eric shook his head trying to clear the cobwebs. The sergeant asked him if he wanted to continue. He nodded, and moved quickly left to right. Hanley rushed in, throwing a wild left hook. Eric grabbed and held on. Hanley started another left hook, but Eric stepped back and landed a right to the midsection. Hanley groaned and held. He pushed Eric away and fired a right, which caught Eric flush, and knocked him to the ground. Eric tried to clear his head and get to his feet, but he felt his legs weaken and fell back to the ground.

Suddenly the roar of the crowd faded.

"What's going on here?" Lieutenant Shredder pushed through the crowd. "Every man back to the barracks on the double! I want you men in front of my desk in ten minutes. You read me?"

"Yes, sir," Eric and Hanley replied in unison.

"Ten minutes!" Shredder walked off sternly. They entered the latrine and dunked their heads under the faucets.

Jason rushed in with Ted behind him. "I got ice from the mess hall," Ted yelled. "I took off before it was over. I couldn't watch."

A few minutes later, they stood at attention in front of Lieutenant Shredder. "I want an explanation. Who's first?"

"We were boxing, sir," Eric said. He felt the pain set in.

"That's right sir," Sergeant Hanley added.

"Why didn't you go to the gym, sergeant?" Shredder looked from one to the other, carefully watching their reactions.

"It was late, sir. The men were settled in."

"If that's the case, I can assume the demonstration's over?"

"Yes, sir," they spoke in unison.

"Sergeant Higgins, drive these men to the base hospital. Have them patched up. Take my Jeep. Dismissed." Eric and Sergeant Hanley climbed into the Jeep.

The doctor applied minor treatment to both men. "What happened to you two?"

"We were boxing, sir."

The major grinned. "From appearances, I suggest both of you should concentrate more on defense rather than offense."

"Yes, sir," they said. After they returned, both went to the latrine, and ended up staring into the mirror. "I want to ask you a question, Sergeant Hanley."

"Yeah, what's that?"

"What did we prove?"

Hanley rubbed the side of his jaw, looked in the mirror, then turned back to Eric. "Not a damned thing."

They entered the barracks and heard the guys whispering. Eric felt the dull, throbbing ache in his head. He thought about the stupidity of it all. He fell asleep right away. Later when he woke up he felt the pain shoot through his ribs. Eric reached for an ice bag then heard Snively's voice. "You all right? Sergeant Hanley left early."

Eric groaned and he sat up. He took a pill and held the ice bag to his head. "He's lucky. I gotta get this shift in, and then I've got forty-eight hours off."

"Hey Eric!" Jason's voice called. "We wanted to make sure you were still alive. You feel up to shooting the bull?"

"Your eye's turning blue. At least it isn't closed," Ted said.

"I'll take a crack at 'em," Jason said. "I won't make the same mistake you did."

"What mistake was that? I was too busy to notice." Eric tried to grin, but he winced instead.

"When you cut his eye, you backed off," Jason said. "You don't have the killer instinct."

"I know." Eric stuck his hand in a bucket of ice. "Forget it. He's not someone you want to fool with. He's not as awkward as he appears," Eric said. "He's strong and he hits hard."

"Let's change the subject," Ted said. He broke out in a big smile. "Marie has accepted my marriage proposal and I'm going to let my family know. She has agreed to go home with me in May or June. We're getting married with or without my family's blessing. I'm about to become my own man, and it's about time my family understands that."

"Congratulations Ted," Jason said, slapping Ted on the back. "I gotta admit, when you and Marie get together, it's like there's no one else around. Tomorrow's payday. Tomorrow night, we celebrate. We'll see you later."

Eric picked up his mail, surprised to see a letter from Linda.

> *Dear Eric,*
> *I hope this letter finds you well. Bill and I split up. He went east to take a job with an engineering firm. Eric we could always talk. Am I really so self-centered and unrealistic? Bill said I was like a mannequin who suddenly came to life. If I am out of line, let me know. You said we would always be friends. I am taking you at your word."*
> *Your friend, Linda*

Hausler was close to being right, Eric thought, but in some strange way, Linda and I always needed each other. He didn't want her hurt. He put the letter aside and fell asleep.

"It's almost three o'clock," Snively said. "You were really out. You needed the rest. The whole squad was talking about the fight."

After Eric went through the routine, he wondered why the shift seemed so much longer than usual. When his relief came on duty, he called Gail to ask her to meet him at the Bull Head Lounge tomorrow. Exhausted, he then climbed in his bunk and fell asleep. The next morning, after being paid, he noticed that the usual poker and crap games were going full blast. "Let's move out," Jason said. "You look a little better, but you've still got a ways to go."

When Eric, Jason, and Ted arrived at the Bull Head Lounge, Gail was waiting for them. "I'm surprised at you, Eric," she said, with a faint smile.

"It had to happen, there was no other way."

When Marie walked in the lounge, Ted's face brightened. He pulled back a chair for her. "I have to get back to the base in a couple of hours, but I couldn't resist seeing you for a little while," he said.

Marie looked at Eric, and Ted told her about the fight. "I'm sorry. I hope you feel better."

"I'm fine, Marie," Eric said. "Let's get outta here" They walked toward the park by the river. The weather was beautiful, it was almost a perfect day. They sat at a picnic table, making sandwiches and drinking beer. "I gotta catch the bus," Ted said. "I'll see you later." He quickly kissed Marie and, with a sandwich in one hand and a beer in the other, took off. After lunch, the girls went for a walk along the lake. "What's really on your mind?" Jason asked.

Eric told him of the dreams: the healing of Alice and the waitress, and being questioned by the doctors. He explained the trouble and the pressure he had caused the family. Jason listened carefully and looked out over the lake at the girls. "A couple times Cindy and I went to a medium," Jason said. "We were told some pretty amazing things. Cindy doesn't mention it too often, but she takes it very seriously, believe me. As for me, I haven't had that much experience."

"I think it all started with my grandmother, and the sign she saw on me when I was born," Eric said. "My mother insists it's a spiritual gift not to be denied. The rest of the family is ...."

"I was a little shocked when you first mentioned it," Jason said. "But knowin' you, now that I think of it, I'm not all that surprised. A spiritual gift has to be an awesome responsibility. Believe me, I have enough respect for the Bible and it's teachings to take'em seriously."

"That's what makes it so hard!" Eric said.

"I would think there has to be a good reason for it," Jason said. "As for dealin' with those who oppose you—you can't avoid that."

"You're right, of course," Eric said.

"I've always believed everyone has to play the cards that life has dealt you," Jason continued. "That's not a cop out; it's what's called our destiny, if that's the right word for it. If I know you, you'll do what you think is right. I'd like to go into this a little more, but right now I think we'd better knock it off. The girls are about to join us."

"What are you guys looking so serious about?" Gail asked.

Jason laughed. "Life in general, you know—Goin' home in about a month. Eric is gonna be a father and Marie and Ted— who really knows!"

"I've never heard you mention your home, Jason" Gail said.

"Let's see, how can I describe Wyler? It has two taverns, a few stores, a pool hall, and two churches. What else can I say? The most exciting thing to do Saturday nights is to watch the A&P truck unload, and trying to make out in the movie theater balcony."

Everyone joined Jason in laughter as he continued. "Maybe I exaggerate. All the people know each other. They're not a bad bunch. They are usually there for each other."

"Hey guys—Marie and I have to get back to work," Gail said. Late evening approached as the flickering shadows took over the picnic benches. The air turned cool as they started back toward town. "You think it's all right for friends to hold hands?" Gail asked.

"I guess so," Eric said. He felt relieved when they were back in town. "I think we should take off. We'll see you girls later."

"It's none of my business, but Gail," Jason said to Eric "Maybe it's my imagination, but . . ."

"She's a good friend. Nothing more."

The next day Eric, Jason, and Ted returned to Bull Head lounge. Jason's face lit up when he saw Libby. They moved toward their usual table. "If it isn't Illinois' finest," Libby said. "The movie's over?"

"Libby," Jason said, "you're cuter than words can describe."

She laughed. "I never know what to expect from you. You're something else."

135

Jason watched Libby as she walked away. "That girl should get a patent on her figure," Jason said. "I think I'm in love with two women." Eric and Ted just laughed.

"Here you are, gents," Libby said upon returning. "I get a feeling you guys are out for a big one tonight."

Jason raised his glass of beer. "That woman can read my mind, for the good times. Hey guys—cheer up. Home is just around the corner."

"I'll drink to that," Ted added.

Libby returned. "How are you men doing?"

Jason looked at her and said, "I'm glad we've built our love on a solid foundation." She only smiled and left for the late evening crowd.

"Eric, you think faith and religion would work for me?" Ted asked. "I know it would be important to Marie, although we've never discussed it—I definitely need something." He shook his head. "I don't know how to tell you this Eric, but—look who just walked in the door."

"I only worked for a couple hours," Gail said. "The manager didn't need me. Looks like a party." She pulled back a chair and joined them.

"We have quite a group here," Libby said. "Beer all around?"

"Yes. This round's on me," Gail said.

When Libby returned to their table, Jason spoke up, "Libby, how about a date tomorrow?"

"Let me consider it," she said. "In the meantime, you guys better behave."

"Yeah, we know," Ted interrupted, almost knocking his beer over. "Hey Eric—I'm gonna build on this faith thing—I believe I'm beginnin' to feel somethin'!"

Jason looked at Eric and shook his head. They both laughed. "Ted, I think you've had enough. You gotta admit, you get carried away."

"What're ya talkin' bout?" Ted yelled over the sound of the music.

The afternoon faded into evening, and the crowd became jammed. The smoke-filled lounge became so crowded that people were standing at the bar. Occasionally Ted joined the organist in song. "I gotta experience this special religious feeling."

"Hey, aren't you guys overdoing it?" Libby asked Jason.

"You never gave me an answer," Jason said, lighting up one of Eric's Camels.

"Hey, Libby," Ted yelled. "How about giving my buddy a break?"

Libby looked at Ted, smiled, and then faced Jason. "All right," she said, "*if* you can stay out of trouble tonight. I mean it, Jason."

"This'll be our last round. Where shall I meet you?" Jason said.

"You can pick me up at my apartment. Here's my address," Libby said, writing on a slip of paper.

"Ted," Jason beamed, "I think I underestimated you."

Ted laughed, "I think it came from my decision to convert." Suddenly his mood changed. "When I saw that wreath on the door after Marie's father died, I promised myself if Marie was all right, I'd accept her belief. And I'm going to do it."

Jason smiled and said to Libby, "I'll see you tomorrow morning."

She yelled over the noise of the crowd, "You behave yourself."

"I'm a happy man," Jason said after they walked out the door. Gail took Eric's arm. They walked slowly down the street. Just ahead, the Salvation Army choir sang at the corner.

"I'll prove my Christian love," said Ted, who suddenly rushed to a woman in the group. He threw his arms around her, and she screamed.

He looked stunned.

Jason and Eric rushed to catch up with him when the woman screamed again. Suddenly, a police officer appeared from around the corner. "What's going on here?" the officer shouted. He grabbed Ted's arm. The woman stopped screaming when she saw the officer.

"Did you see that? This soldier grabbed me. He threw his arms around me!"

Ted struggled for control of his voice, but finally mumbled, "I was just expressing Christian love. This lady misunderstood my—"

"You've been drinking!" the woman screamed. "How dare you speak to me of Christian love?"

"But, you don't understand," Ted said, panic entering his voice. "It's my way of—"

"You attacked me on the street. In front of everybody!" the lady shouted.

A crowd soon gathered around them. Several people laughed while others watched with curiosity. Eric stepped in and talked to the police officer. He tried to explain to the lady Ted's intentions, and the emotion he felt, after seeing the wreath at Monsento Rose.

"I think I should call the APs," the officer said.

Suddenly Ted's face began to turn into a pale, sickly expression.

CHAPTER ELEVEN

JASON TOOK THE OFFICER TO ONE SIDE and said, "Ted's had a few beers. He's a very emotional guy. I'll admit, he gets carried away on occasions. We were talking about the importance of Christian love, and what it would mean to the girl he's about to marry."

The officer didn't seem impressed.

"Tell you what," Jason said. "You take a good look at the woman and tell me if you believe he was actually making a pass."

The officer smiled in spite of himself. "If she won't press charges, I'll drop it."

Jason thanked the officer and turned to the woman. "The officer agreed not to press charges, if you'll forgive Ted's behavior."

She hesitated. Jason quickly pressed his advantage. He told her about Marie's father. "I'm sure Ted would apologize."

"It's not necessary to beg," the woman said slowly.

Ted sighed with relief and pleaded to the woman. "I apologize. I don't know why I do these stupid things." When they moved along, he said to Eric and Jason, "you guys saved my life."

Jason grinned. "You didn't do so bad yourself, with that converting line of yours."

Gail whispered to Eric, "I can't believe you and Jason got him out of that."

Later that evening, Marie joined everyone. After they had dinner, Marie and Ted left to be alone before he returned to the base.

"Ted has to get some control over his emotions. It's been quite an evening," Eric said.

"We'd better get you back to your apartment."

After Eric and Jason returned to the base, Eric opened a letter that was on his bunk.

> *Dear Eric,*
>
> *I've some bad news. Uncle Paul died suddenly. He had a heart attack last week, and never regained consciousness. He was so special. I loved him like a father, but I realize... these things happen. I saw Karen and Frank last week, their baby's due soon. I miss you. One day just follows the other. If it wasn't for our little one, I don't know what I'd do. Hope you're well and happy under the present circumstances. I'm ending now. Until then.*
>
> *Love Alice and the little one.*

A few days later, Eric, Jason, Gail and Libby attended church. "I'm sorry, it just wasn't my kind of sermon," Jason said. "I'd hate to be in that guys' sights on one of his off days. No offense, girls."

The girls looked at each other, and just started laughing.

"What'll we do now?" Gail asked. "Libby, what do you think?"

"It doesn't matter," Libby said. "I suppose a walk would be nice, but it's only a suggestion." Jason couldn't get over how she seemed so different—almost shy. It was a warm, beautiful evening. The sun moved slowly behind the trees, casting reddish shadows across the area.

Eric and Jason sat on a park bench, watching the girls walk along the riverbank. "Isn't Libby something?" Jason asked. Eric smiled at him.

"I thought you weren't getting involved," Eric said.

"I'm not kidding myself. Libby's not really interested in me. She only agreed to go out to get me off her back for a while," Jason said. He gazed out over the river. "Besides, when we're out here like this, my thoughts always go back to Cindy and home."

"Time to get back, guys," Gail said. They walked the girls back to their apartments as the evening shadows brought on a feeling of loneliness.

"Hey, Eric, I'll see you at the bus station later," Jason said, as he took Libby's hand.

When they arrived at Gail's apartment, Gail asked, "You're not coming in?"

"No. It's late." *It would be so easy to take advantage of her,* Eric thought.

"OK, Goodnight my friend."

———————

At the bus station, Eric saw Jason running around the corner. "That was close," Jason said after stopping to catch his breath. "When I get around Libby, I can hardly leave."

Once they boarded the bus, Jason stared out the window at the darkness. "It was a great day, wasn't it?" he said. "Gail is quite a temptation. That has to be rough on you, Eric."

"Just a little less than a month to go," Eric said. "Tonight, that seemed so far away."

"You'll make it," Jason said. "Pour on the gym workouts." Then he added, "I told you about my dad meeting someone. I'm gonna ask if they'd agree to a double ceremony with Cindy and me. Wouldn't that be something? A father and son wedding?"

"That would be great. You'd like that, wouldn't you?" Eric said.

"More than you know, Eric. I'm glad he found someone. His last letter came across so different. Oh, by the way, I'm going camping Monday, so I'll see you Tuesday." A big grin spread over his face. "Maybe one last Camel, you know, to wrap up the evening."

141

After they returned to the barracks, Eric read his Bible until he drifted off to sleep. He saw the little girl in his dreams draw closer. She stood in a ball of brilliant white light, which suddenly changed to a dark, murky color. Eric saw tears running down her cheeks.

He woke up and glanced at his watch; it was around 2:20 a.m. He finally fell back to sleep wondering what that could mean.

The next day was routine like so many others, yet somehow different. Eric went to chow and tried to shake off the depression. His mind kept going back to the dream. He started to eat when he overheard the conversation across the table. "Did you hear about the guy who drowned in the river this afternoon?"

"No." The others stopped eating. "What's the guy's name?"

"Corkland, I believe. I didn't know him."

Eric dropped his fork. He looked up at the guys across the table, took a deep breath. "What did you say the guy's name was?"

"Corkland, I believe. Did 'ya know him?"

"Yes." Eric felt like he'd been kicked in the stomach. He felt stunned as nausea overcame him. He left the mess hall, walked back to the barracks and flopped on his bunk.

"I just heard," Snively said. "I can't believe it. I'm sorry."

Eric heard Ted screaming the moment he entered the barracks. "Eric! You hear about Jason? He drowned! God, I can't believe it."

"I heard a few minutes ago."

Ted sat on the bunk beside Eric, twisting his fatigue hat and fighting back tears. "I just can't believe it!" he sobbed. "I'm sorry, I got to get outta here!" He rushed out the barracks.

"I understand," Eric heard himself say. *So that's what the dream meant.* He stared off into space. It was an emptiness he had never felt before.

Deakes and Parris expressed their sympathies. After a few awkward moments, they went back to their bunks. Eric left the barracks and entered the chapel. He bowed his head and said a prayer for Jason, Jason's father, and Cindy. "Can I help you, son?" the chaplain asked quietly. He put his hand on Eric's shoulder.

"You've heard about the guy who drowned at the river?"

"Yes, a terrible thing," the chaplain said, and sat beside him. "I assume he was a friend of yours, and you're trying to accept or understand why it had to happen. Are you religious?"

"Yes. I was brought up in church. But there are things I have a hard time accepting."

"In the Bible or the church?" the chaplain replied.

"Both. All my life I've heard God's will used for tragedy. I've never been able to accept it. It doesn't fit the compassionate God I believe in."

"Have you ever been through something like this before?"

"The only one I can think of is my grandparent's death several years ago," Eric said. "I don't remember exactly how I felt. You'd think after all my years in the church and studying the Bible, I'd have the strength and guidance to deal with this."

"All your years," the chaplain briefly smiled. "It's an emotional shock. You'll be able to put it in a proper perspective in a few days. Time is the best healer of all."

"I don't mean to be disrespectful, sir but, that's not the answer I'm looking for. There has to be—something more."

The chaplain shook his head. "I don't know what it could possibly be. We don't know why these things happen. We must accept, with faith, God's will. I don't know what else I can say. I'm sorry I can't be of more help."

"I'm sorry too, sir." Eric walked out. He felt hollow and empty.

When Eric got back to the barracks, Ted was waiting. He looked Eric in the eye, "I need something! Some kind of explanation. I mean—oh I don't know what I mean!" Ted said.

Eric had none, but just said, "Let's go to the PX and have a couple beers."

"Beer?" Ted had a strange expression on his face. "Don't you mean church?"

"I've been there," Eric said, "It's not the answer."

"Eric, this is not like you."

After arriving at the PX, Ted took a sip of beer and said, "It's the way Jason would have wanted it."

Eric remembered Ted's desire for accepting religion for Marie. "Don't get the wrong idea," Eric told Ted. "Religion is still one of the most important things in my life. I'm frustrated. Sometimes what I've been led to believe and what I feel don't . . . I've missed something. I can't explain it."

"Maybe that's why," Ted said with tear-filled eyes. "I have such a hard time accepting—I dunno! Be careful, Eric. You can't change anything. You're not yourself. Even I see that."

"Ted, I'm going to town. I just need to get away for a while." Eric ended up at Gail's apartment. When she opened the door, she was immediately in his arms.

"Oh, Eric! I heard about Jason on the radio a couple of hours ago. Isn't it terrible?"

"More than you know," Eric said, "I came to invite you out."

She stared at him. "Promise me after a couple drinks you'll go back to the base."

The Bull Head Lounge wasn't crowded. A jukebox blared in the background. Gail looked at him, and whispered, "I wish I had the answers you're looking for."

"At least Libby's not working tonight," Eric said as he ordered them a beer. "I guess that's something to be thankful for."

"Bitterness won't help," Gail said. "Wouldn't it be better to go to church?"

He waved to the waitress for another round. "I talked to the chaplain. He didn't have the answers. Nobody has the answers."

"What'd you expect? You're in shock," Gail said. "I'm surprised at you with your religious background. Can't you accept the chaplain's explanation?"

"No. Not now," Eric said slowly.

Gail looked in his eyes. "You're a strange one. Sorry, that was uncalled for. You're looking for answers that don't exist.

Let's get out of here; this isn't helping. I'll walk you to the bus station. You've got Alice and the baby to think about." She took his hand, and said, "You're the most sensitive guy I ever met. Everybody needs someone sometime. This is your time."

Eric didn't answer. When they reached the bus station, he said, "You're quite a girl."

"I've been trying to get that across for some time," Gail said, and then added, "I'm just a friend who's here for you."

"Maybe, just maybe, that's why I had to come to town. I'll see you later."

Eric gazed out the bus window at the darkness. He wondered if Jason's father or Cindy knew. Eric walked to the barracks and slipped in his bunk. *Maybe Gail was right,* he thought. *Who am I to question the chaplain or anybody else?* The pain and exhaustion finally led to sleep.

Early the next morning, Eric woke to someone shaking him. "Silkwin, you're wanted in the orderly room."

"At ease, Silkwin," Lieutenant Shredder said when Eric arrived. "I understand you were a close friend of the man who drowned yesterday. Aren't you from the same part of Illinois?"

"Yes, sir, that's correct."

"I understand, also, your wife is expecting a baby very soon."

"A month and a half, sir," Eric said.

"Would you be interested in serving as an escort to ship the body home?" Lieutenant Shredder asked. He studied Eric closely. "You understand of course, there would be another man with experience—Sergeant Hanley."

Eric felt chills running down his back. Taking Jason home would be difficult, but the thought of seeing Alice again drew him closer to accepting that assignment. "Yes, sir. Jason and his girlfriend attended my wedding. They live only twelve miles from my home."

Lieutenant Shredder slowly raised his head. "You understand, the most time we could allow you, other than travel time, would be about thirty-six hours."

"I understand, sir."

"Check with Sergeant Hanley. Get your gear ready and be prepared to leave. You'll be on special assignment. Dismissed!"

"Yes, sir." Eric saluted, and left. He rushed to the barracks. Sergeant Hanley was packing. He looked up. "I'm sorry about your friend." His eyes showed sincerity.

"I know we're pressed for time, but I'd like to talk to Ted. I could eat at his mess hall."

"Make sure to take an extra class-A uniform for the burial service. I've been through this before. One bag'll do it. You'd better take off for chow. I'll meet you in the orderly room, and sign for our allowance." Hanley glanced at his watch. "You've got forty minutes."

Eric remembered Ted was on duty and he rushed to his mess hall. "I've gotta talk to Faulkland. It's an emergency," Eric told the guy checking passes.

"What're you doing here?" a pathetic-looking Ted asked.

"I've gotta catch a train in a few minutes—I'm taking Jason's body home."

"Oh, God!" Ted moaned.

Eric explained, and then glanced at his watch. "I gotta hurry. It's a chance to see Alice."

"I don't envy you. How much time will you have at home?"

"I'm not sure. Lieutenant Shredder said the most would be thirty-six hours. Sergeant Hanley's responsible, so he'll get the orders . I'll take what I can get."

"It still seems unbelievable." Ted picked at his food.

"I know. You explain to Marie and Gail, and try to get yourself out of the dumps."

Ted tried to smile. "Do what you can for Jason's father and Cindy. They must be going out of their mind."

Eric winced. "I'll try. Take care of yourself."

"You men will be due back at twenty-two hundred hours Friday," Lieutenant Shredder said, glancing at Eric. "That's the best I can do."

"Yes sir." Lieutenant Shredder turned to Hanley. "You know the routine. Get squared away. The corporal will drive you."

They pulled into the station. Hanley and Eric watched the men loading the casket. A warm drizzle and gloomy overcast fought the sun for control. They walked to the car with the casket. Eric felt chills when they entered. "You want the first shift?" Hanley asked.

"If you don't mind."

"I'll get our gear squared away and relieve you in two hours. Try not to let this get to you. We've a long way to go." Eric looked out the train window, but could not keep his eyes from returning to the casket. The train jerked and moved forward. He stared at the flag-draped casket, but could not resist running his hand along the smooth surface. "*Who ever thought we'd end up like this?*" He felt the pain and sting of tears. Eric could still hear Jason's voice. "*Things are finally turning around for us.*"

"Ready for chow?" rang a voice, and Eric jumped when the car door suddenly opened. Sergeant Hanley walked in. "I've got a fifth of whiskey. This is against regulations, but the man who wrote the regulations probably never pulled this kind of duty." In the dining car, Eric sipped coffee and gazed out the window.

Sergeant Hanley joined him. "I checked everything and locked the car door." He set a brown bag beside him on the floor. "First you eat. When you get ready, I'll give you a couple of shots." Eric ate, surprised at how hungry he was. He pushed his glass of water toward Sergeant Hanley. "Not too much. It doesn't take much for me."

"You'll need it. The roughest part is yet to come. I've pulled this duty before and you never get used to it." He took a drink out of the paper bag. If the porter noticed, he never said anything.

"I'll make it," Eric said. He took a drink and felt the burning sensation. "I thought if I could keep my mind on my wife, it'd be easier, but it's not working." He took another drink. "Can you believe it? Now that I'm going to see Alice, I can't get my mind off Jason?"

"You're in shock. You don't want your friend's death to interfere with seeing your wife."

Eric stared at him. "That's quite an explanation," he said.

"For a sergeant, you mean. Let's say I'm a student of human nature. It's not out of a textbook that deals with theory," Hanley said. "Real life comes from experience." He finished his whiskey and poured two shots in Eric's glass. "That's the last one for a while. I'll take the next watch; try to get some sleep. This should help."

"Every one of these seems like the first one," Hanley went on. "I'm telling you this to prepare you. You never know what'll happen." Eric tried to relax. He was aware of people around him, but the faces seemed distant, as if he were in a dream. He finally drifted off to sleep.

Sergeant Hanley shook him. "Silkwin, wake up. I see the whiskey did the job. "

Eric sat up and glanced at his watch. "I must have passed out. At least I rested. I'll take over." Eric sat by the casket. He watched the miles of monotonous landscape and sleepy little towns. He wondered how many lives struggled between the joy and uncertainty of life. He tried to control his thoughts as the train rumbled through the countryside.

Day slowly passed into night. They locked the door and went to the dining car, eating with little conversation before settling down for the night. When Eric awoke, Sergeant Hanley sat staring out the window. "I was getting ready to wake you. We should reach Cutler City in less than three hours. I'll take the first shift. I figured you'd want to be with him before we get in."

"I'd like that," Eric said. After they ate, Sergeant Hanley went back to the car. Eric lingered over a cup of coffee and a cigarette. Eric relieved Sergeant Hanley.

"We've got a little over an hour," the sergeant told him.

Eric put his hand on the casket. He remembered Jason's words: "Sometimes I think our lives are planned for us." *Was Jason aware of what was going on? How could consciousness die and fade into nothing?* He felt a weakness in his legs. The tension he feared the most closed in.

"We're coming in the station soon," Sergeant Hanley said. "You want a couple shots?"

"Yes. My knees feel like they're buckling." He gulped down a shot.

"The trick's to take just enough," said Hanley, taking a swig himself. "The funeral parlor and his father have been notified. They'll pick up Corkland's body and take it to Wyler. We'll ride with them."

"One more," Eric whispered. "I think I'm going to need it." He looked at the casket, as if he were seeing it for the first time. He suddenly felt numb. His feelings seemed paralyzed. After they pulled into the station, a hearse pulled alongside the train. A thin, older man with slightly stooped shoulders and a woman with gray streaked hair watched the men unload the casket.

Hanley and Eric walked over to meet them. "Excuse me, sir," Sergeant Hanley said. "Are you Jason Corkland's father?" The man turned slowly and nodded. "I'm Sergeant Stuart Hanley, and this is P.F.C. Eric Silkwin."

The man extended a trembling, weather-beaten hand. Suddenly, he said, "Eric, yes. Jason mentioned you several times. Now I remember—he and Cindy attended your wedding in late December, didn't they?"

Eric tensed. "Yes. I'm so sorry."

"Excuse me," Jason's father said. "I don't know where my manners are. This is Miss Emma Norton." She nodded, and held his hand. "Cindy's under sedation. She went to pieces. She and Jason were very close, you know."

Eric could only nod. He was amazed at how closely his father resembled Jason. Eric thought, the same facial features and red hair now darkened with age.

Several minutes later Eric and the sergeant joined Jason's father in the hearse. Eric started to say something, but his voice wouldn't respond. "The funeral's at eleven o'clock," Jason's father said. He could not seem to take his eyes off the casket. He turned to Eric. He said, "We should be there in a few minutes."

"Jason was a good airman, sir," Sergeant Hanley said, trying to take the man's attention away from the casket.

"I'm glad. We couldn't get along, but most of that was my fault. When my wife died, I ignored him. Pretty soon, we couldn't talk." He tugged at his tie, which he was obviously uncomfortable wearing. "Jason had his way about him too—he got his stubbornness from me. I hope you don't mind my carrying on like this," he said. "It's my way of coping."

"We understand," Sergeant Hanley said carefully.

"Thank you for bringing my son home. I wish I could've talked to him, to try to—" he sobbed, then suddenly straightened up and looked straight ahead. Eric looked at his face, which showed hard times, and his eyes, which revealed strong, stubborn pride.

"I talked to Jason the night before the accident," Eric said. "He told me he finally understood how the loss of his mother affected you. He was happy because you found someone to share your life. He mentioned a father-and-son wedding."

"What I wouldn't give to have that happen. When I think of all the opportunities we had to become close, it makes me . . . Why do we always learn too late?"

Eric spoke quickly. "It was very important to him you had someone."

He forced a smile. "This lady and I are getting married soon. Do you think he'd know?"

"Yes. He'll be there in spirit. I can't tell you how I know, but I do," Eric said.

The church sermon was brief. Cindy stared straight ahead. Sergeant Hanley and Eric stood at attention until the service ended. When the pallbearers moved forward, Cindy suddenly jumped up, and ran to the casket. She viciously ripped away at the casket. "I can't let him go!" she screamed. Hanley rushed from one side, Eric from the other. "Let me go!" Cindy cried, struggling. They restrained her until Jason's father and Miss Norton took her back to her seat.

Suddenly she appeared calm, with an unusual expression and a slight smile on her face. Eric felt nausea grip his stomach. The ride to the cemetery was like something in slow motion and unreal. Eric stared out the window, trying to control his emotions. He stared at people along the street, who, out of curiosity, stopped long enough to view the procession.

The graveside service was brief. Jason's father and Miss Norton supported Cindy. When it was over, Sergeant Hanley and Eric followed Cindy, Jason's father, and Miss Norton. Eric turned back to see the workers lower the casket. He performed his final tribute between him and his friend: He saluted.

A little later, Jason's father extended his hand. "Thanks for being a good friend to my son," he said. Eric nodded, unable to speak. Cindy stared through him without a hint of recognition. Suddenly she stood before him, "Jason's gone ... he's just gone," Cindy cried with tears streaming down her face. Eric took her in his arms, knowing how useless the gesture was. He knew nothing could help her now, but the passage of time.

When the hearse stopped at the funeral home, Sergeant Hanley and Eric got out and walked to the tavern next to the bus station. "When's the next bus for Benford?" Eric asked.

The bartender hesitated a moment then said, "In about twenty minutes."

Eric got to a phone. "Alice," Eric shouted, noticing his handshake. "I'm in Wyler. You heard about Jason?"

"Yes. It was in our paper. I am so sorry. How did—?"

"I'll explain later. I'm in Wyler at Jason's funeral. The bus is leaving in about ten minutes. Meet me at the bus station. I don't have much time. I'll see you soon."

Eric returned to the bar and finished his drink. "You're welcome to come along, Sarge," he said.

"No, thanks," Hanley said. "I have my way of winding down. I'll get a room and a bottle. Be back by twenty hundred hours. Listen, it's over. Shove off before you miss the bus." Eric got his ticket and boarded the bus. He closed his eyes and tried shutting out the voices of people around him. "I hope I made you proud Jason," he whispered to himself. "I tried my best."

Suddenly a sense of peace seemed to touch him, and then he thought he heard a soft, faint distance voice say, "Thanks, Eric."

Before arriving in Benford, Eric could not get the voice out of his mind. Could it really have been Jason's voice, or was it his imagination? Would he really ever know?

CHAPTER TWELVE

"BENFORD IN TEN MINUTES," the driver called, inter-rupting Eric's haunting thoughts of Jason's voice. He watched the familiar sights as the bus moved into town. When the bus rounded the corner of the bus station, he saw Alice waving.

She rushed to meet him. Eric kissed her and took her hand in his. "I'm so sorry about Jason," Alice said "How long do you have?"

"We've got about thirty-two hours."

Howard rushed to meet them the minute they entered his shop. "They took Karen to the hospital early this morning," He said.

"We better go to the hospital," Eric said. "Frank probably needs support."

———————————

They met Frank in the hall of the hospital. "Hi Eric, Alice, I'm so glad you came," said a tired and nervous-looking Frank. "I didn't get much sleep last night. What're you doing home?"

"I was assigned to escort Jason's body home."

"I figured as much. Rough, huh. I'm really sorry about Jason."

"Mr. Karland?" the nurse interrupted. "You're the father of a six-pound, nine-ounce baby boy. Mother and baby are doing fine. You may see them in a few minutes."

"It's a boy. I'm a father!" Frank hurried down the hall.

Eric smiled and took Alice in his arms.

"I wish I could take away the pain in your eyes," she said.

"It will be okay. This is Frank and Karen's time."

Frank returned to the waiting room. "Karen said for you two to get in there right now. She and the baby are doing great. I can't believe I have a son!"

They walked in the room to see a pale but happy Karen reaching out to them. "Just wait till you see him," Karen said. She looked exhausted, but glowed with her usual dose of energy. "They're going to bring our son out in a few moments."

When the nurse placed the baby in Karen's arms, she whispered, "meet Bruce, Isn't he just precious?"

"Oh, yes," Alice said, with tears in her eyes.

The nurse returned the baby to the nursery. Eric took Karen's hand. "I'm happy for both of you. He's terrific."

"Thanks Eric. Frank said you had only a little over thirty hours. I'm sorry things weren't better for you because of Jason."

Alice changed the subject, "I have a surprise for you Eric. We own a certain cabin on a lake near Wyler. Uncle Paul left it to us." She paused for a moment. "He came to visit a couple days after you left. I told him how happy we were."

"I'm stunned," Eric said.

"Frank's going to drive you there," Karen said. "I can't have him hanging around here all the time. You two better get going, and make the most of the time you have."

"See you later, Mama," Frank kissed Karen.

"Alice, let's stop by your parents' house for a little while and then tomorrow afternoon spend some time with my folks. Karen's right. Time's slipping away."

Edith packed a few groceries while Eric and Frank had a beer with Lawrence. "Paul wanted you two to have the cabin," Lawrence said. "I've a hunch he had that in mind for some time."

On the ride to the lake Eric did most of the talking. He explained his Air Police work and told them about the funeral. Finally, they saw the familiar driveway that led to the cabin.

"I'll pick you up around one o'clock," Frank said.

"Come here, lady. I'm gonna carry you over the threshold." He picked her up before she could resist. "I couldn't wait to hold you in my arms."

When they made it inside, Alice said, "Eric, why don't you start the fire so we can get cozy? You know, it is not going to be the same. I'm—"

He pulled her to him and whispered, "You're you. That's all I need."

Alice grinned. "You say the nicest things. How about bacon and eggs, and maybe later me?" She fixed dinner, with music drifting through the cabin. "You know, seeing that little bundle in Karen's arms made me realize what we have to look forward to."

He stared into the fire for a moment, tiptoed up behind her. "I want to be near you. If you're wondering, you're still special."

Alice's eyes softened. "Help me set the table. You have a nice way with words, mister. So what do those Texas girls think of you?"

Eric resisted the urge to smile. "The only ones I know are Gail, who I met on the train. Other than Libby, who works in the Bull Head Lounge, and Ted's girl, Marie, who I wrote you about."

"Hmm," Alice said. "Tell me about this Gail."

"She went with us to the movies and a picnic, but there was never anything . . ."

"I trust you Eric. Actually, I had a couple of movie dates. Bryan took me. It was a little embarrassing for him, but he knew I was lonely."

"Let's see what you've learned the last five months," Eric said.

While Eric was eating, Alice watched him carefully. "What do you think?"

"They're delicious. The best I've ever had," he said. "Let's have coffee by the fire."

"Give me a couple minutes and I'll be back before you have a chance to miss me," Alice whispered. "I want to shower and slip into something special for you." The flames danced, making shadows that forced Eric's mind to wander. He felt Alice's freshness before she touched him. He turned to face her. "What do you think of my new pajamas?" she said.

"I like 'em. I guess it's true what they say: A woman who's expecting has a special glow about her." Alice cast aside the new pajamas, and they made love in front of the flames.

"I needed that," Eric said slowly as he took her in his arms and stared into the fire.

"If you feel like talking about Jason, I'm here for you," Alice said. "I still see the pain in your eyes." Eric told her about Jason's father, the funeral, and Cindy.

"It was difficult for me too, when Uncle Paul died. He was like a second father." They held each other close, watching the flames until they began to die.

Eric woke up and reached for her. The aroma of coffee filled the room. He walked to the door and watched Alice. "How do you manage to look so pretty this early?"

"I've been up over half an hour working on myself. I refuse to let you see me looking like a wreck before you leave."

"What are you doing now?"

"Fixing my husband's coffee." Eric wrapped his arms around her. Suddenly, he felt a swift ripple under his hand. "Alice, the baby's poking me!" he said.

She laughed. "The baby is saying hello. That happens all the time."

"It's great waking up with a pretty girl fixing me breakfast."

"She'd better be me. I'm the jealous type, you know."

"I've told you about Gail. If my spending time with her bothers you, I'll . . ."

"It's all right, as long as it's friendship. If she were here in town, I would not stand for it. I know you get lonely, but if she ever tempts you . . ."

Eric told Alice when he learned about Jason. "She was someone I could talk to. She told me to keep thinking of you and the baby."

"She sounds like a real friend," Alice said.

"Come on honey; let's get outside for one of your nature walks."

155

The day was beautiful, and not a cloud in the sky. Trees were unfolding their leaves and wild flowers were everywhere. The sun glistened over the lake, which shimmered like silver, reflecting off the water. "From a winter wonderland to a spring garden," Alice said as she sighed and gazed over the lake. "Isn't it beautiful?" Her eyes glowed. "Remember our snow fight?"

"Yeah, I remember," Eric said. "It's one of the things that kept me going."

"We'd better clean the grill and get the charcoal started," she said. "Frank'll be here before long." She scrubbed the picnic table while he got the fire going.

They saw Frank's car before they heard it, which was unusual.

"How're you doing, buddy?" Frank asked. "By the way, mother and son are doing great. Did you notice anything different?"

"The car. I didn't hear it before I saw it."

"I bought a new muffler and tailpipe this morning. I was off from work anyhow. I was kinda embarrassed when it fell off in the hospital parking lot. I had to do something."

Eric laughed. "What did you do?"

"I threw the works in the trunk and drove to the parts store. It was a little overdue anyway." He watched the hamburgers sizzle on the grill. "Do those ever smell good!"

"Watch these. I'll get us a beer," Eric said.

"My pleasure." Frank smiled as he took the spatula. "They're almost ready. Hi, Alice. Hope you enjoyed your stay. Karen and the baby are doing fine."

"That's great," Alice said, and handed Frank a beer. "They're done. I'll do the honors." As they ate, Frank talked about the baby, and Alice listened to every detail. Eric glanced at his watch. "It's time to head back." They cleaned up and locked the cabin.

When they arrived at Eric's house, they saw Ellen.

"Congratulations Ellen," Eric said. "I hope you and Johnny'll be very happy."

"We were for a few days. It seems there's never enough time but, I guess you two know about that." Ellen glanced at Alice, and then continued. "Johnny's on his way overseas. The funeral must have been difficult."

Eric only nodded. After dinner, they sat around the table talking. "A toast," Eric's father said, and held up a glass of wine. "To Alice and Eric, Ellen and Johnny, and, of course, to the new parents, Frank, Karen, and their baby boy."

"Bryan and Liza are here," Eric's mother said.

"How long will you be home?" Bryan asked.

"I have to leave this evening and catch the seven o'clock bus."

"Rita's back working at Mabel's Cafe," Bryan said, watching Eric carefully. "Not only that, I saw her at church."

"Rita? In our church?" Eric shook his head. "I'm surprised."

"She comes often," Bryan added. "Her husband's back. It's too bad your so-called healing or whatever you call it brought about the incidents at your father's shop."

"What incidents?" Eric asked.

Bryan saw the expression on Eric's father, and quickly faced Eric. "Somebody wrote controversial messages, among other things, on the shop window."

"It didn't amount to anything," Eric's father quickly added.

"Why don't people just mind their own business?" Eric snapped.

"We didn't want you upset," his mother said, glaring at Bryan. "Isn't it bad enough you had to escort one of your best friends to his final resting place?"

"The day before Jason's death, I was depressed," Eric said. "That night, the little girl appeared to me. She had tears in her eyes. The next day I heard about Jason drowning."

"You see how important your calling is," Eric's mother shouted. "Do you think we're gonna let some narrow-minded people keep us from fulfilling your destiny?"

157

"Mother's right," Eric said. "We'll face these things one at a time. If I didn't think it was important I wouldn't go through with it."

"Your dedication seems to be taking quite a toll," Bryan said. "Is it really worth it?"

"Maybe that's the other side of the sword," Eric said slowly.

He saw the expression on Bryan's face. "Can't you understand this abnormal obsession you have with healing affects all those around you!" Bryan said.

Frank never said a word. The room was unusually quiet. After a few tense moments, Ellen asked, "How's Cindy, considering the circumstances?"

"In shock," Eric said slowly. "She looked right through me."

A few tense moments later, Liza, Bryan, and Frank left with few parting words. Eric knew the time was getting short. After saying goodbye to his mom and dad and Ellen, he felt the loneliness inside him. He wondered if Alice felt the same way. He could tell she was trying so hard to accept his leaving.

They left the house strolling hand in hand. "Listen, honey," he said. "Why don't you quit work soon? Promise me you'll get lots of rest and take a trip or two to the cabin."

"I will," she said. "Don't let Bryan upset you. You take care of yourself and be careful around Gail. If anything happens, it'll never be the same for us."

"Believe me, I know now how lucky we are," Eric said. He thought of Jason and Cindy. When he saw the bus, he put his arm around Alice and kissed her. "Take care of yourself, honey. Write when you can." Eric boarded the bus and watched Alice as she waved with her usual enthusiasm, fighting back the tears in those big blue eyes.

"Wyler in five minutes," the driver called. Eric watched out the window as Sergeant Hanley handed his bag to the driver.

"I see you made it," the sergeant said. "You're a lucky man."

"Believe me," Eric said "I appreciate it now more than ever."

A spring rain swept the windows when they pulled on the main highway. Eric glanced at Sergeant Hanley. "You never met a special person?"

"A few years ago. The only woman I ever loved was killed in a car wreck. I still think about her every once in a while," Hanley said. "When it happened, somebody once told me that time heals. I'm still wondering how much time." He turned away to watch the rain streaking down the window.

"Cutler City, ten minutes," the driver called.

The men got their bags and boarded the train. "Thanks for the chance to spend a few hours at home," Eric said. "There were times I didn't know if I would make it."

"You done well," Sergeant Hanley said. "It's over. Let it go."

"You men did a fine job," Lieutenant Shredder said. "You'll resume your duties at zero eight-hundred hours tomorrow. I hope you enjoyed seeing your wife, Silkwin." The lieutenant studied Eric carefully. "I hope it has a positive effect."

"Yes sir, I'm sure it will," Eric replied.

"Dismissed." Lieutenant Shredder returned Eric and Hanley's salute.

They took their bags to the barracks and unpacked. A few minutes later Eric walked into Ted's barracks. Ted jumped off his bunk and smiled. "Am I ever glad to see you. Let's go to town. Everyone'll want to see you. How's Alice?"

"Wait a minute," Eric said. "I'll tell you everything."

After a few moments, Ted stared at him, and said. "The funeral was rough, huh?"

"Yes," Eric said slowly. "There's something I gotta take care of. We have a half hour before the bus leaves."

When he entered the little chapel, the priest recognized him. "I've been thinking about you," he told Eric. "I heard you were assigned to accompany your friend home."

"I want to apologize for my attitude," Eric said.

"No apology necessary. There were times when I wished for any other duty—but we both know better than that, don't we?"

"Yes, sir. Talking to you helped me more than I realized."

"I appreciate your telling me," the priest said.

When he returned to the barracks, Eric filled Ted in on what happened at the funeral and how Cindy reacted.

"Why do you think she would do such a thing?" Ted wondered.

"Probably the reality of never seeing Jason again."

Ted shook his head. "I went to the chapel and prayed for Jason," he said. "I felt I should do something. I mean—coming from a guy who doesn't believe in anything he can't see." Ted nodded and then added, with a catch in his voice, "It was the only thing I could think of to do. You think it made a difference?"

"Yes I do. Let's go to town," Eric said, "Have a couple of beers and shake off this mood."

The Bull Head Lounge was not as crowded as usual. They hesitated at the bar, then walked back to the booth. Eric looked up to see Libby. She tried to smile. "I'm so sorry about Jason," she said. "I'll miss him. He had that special knack for cheering me up."

"How about changing the subject?" Ted said. "I'm sorry, I didn't mean—"

"It's all right, I understand," Libby said. She faced Eric. "How's the father-to-be?"

"All right. If it gets crowded in here, we'll move to the bar. Right now, we'd like to sit in our regular booth."

"No problem. It's slow tonight; would you mind if I join you guys for a few minutes?"

In a few minutes, she returned with their beer and joined them. "I remember the first time we came here. It seems so long

160

ago," Eric said. He put a quarter in the music selection box. The music cut through the lounge's unusual stillness.

"I was assigned to escort Jason home," Eric said. "And I did get to see Alice for a short time."

Libby smiled. "I like the way your eyes light up when you mention her name."

"The baby's due in about five weeks. I'm taking off early. How about that guy of yours?"

"We split up. At least for now," she said slowly. "Thanks for the beer, guys. I guess I'd better get back to work."

"Jason really liked you Libby. That last Sunday meant a lot to him."

Libby had tears in her eyes. "I'm so glad."

"Jason was right. That guy who left you has to be a damn fool."

After Libby left, Ted snapped out of his daze. "I'm a little worried about my family accepting Marie. Nancy claims she can't live without me. My well-meaning parents are afraid she'll do something stupid, like commit suicide. Can you imagine that?"

"You think she would go through with it?" Eric asked.

"Knowing her, she just might. She's kinda kooky. My family, as you probably guessed, is well off. My father is an executive with a large insurance firm—you know, the country club set and the whole bit."

"Don't you have a college education?"

"Three years. I am reasonably educated, but as my father put it, spoiled silly. He would not believe me when I said I was joining the Air Force. After enlisting, he said, maybe it would make a man out of me. I found out later he'd opened the door for me at his firm."

"What in the world are you doing in the Air Force?" Eric asked.

Ted smiled. "You know me, one of those wild, sudden impulses. I guess I had to prove to myself I could survive. I felt smothered and cramped—from Nancy as well as my parents."

Eric shook his head, then commented, "In some ways, my situation is much the same, except for different reasons. It's the first time I've heard you talk about your family, other than a reference to Nancy."

"How about another beer, guys?" Libby asked.

"We'd better," Ted said. "Look who just walked in the door."

"I took off work," Gail said. "I passed my finals, I'm celebrating."

"That's great," Eric said. "You should be very happy."

"Of course! It's what I want, isn't it? Oh, don't get that look. I know my place. I'm just happy to see you back."

"Congratulations," Ted said, "If you'll excuse me, I'm going to see how Marie's doing at the restaurant. I can't be without her."

CHAPTER THIRTEEN

WHEN ERIC RETURNED TO THE BARRACKS, Snively was all smiles. He was packing. "Can you really believe it? I'm going to typing school in Mississippi," he said, with a big grin. "I leave tomorrow. I guess miracles do happen."

"That's great Everett," Eric said. He picked up the letter lying on his bunk.

> *Dear Eric,*
> *I hope this letter finds you understanding. I have not heard from you for some time. I need someone I can talk to that I can trust. Things have not exactly been going my way. I thought we could always talk to each other about anything.*
> *Evidently, you do not feel the same way.*
> *P.S. I am dating again.*
> *Your friend, Linda*

Eric took out some paper and began to write.

> *Dear Linda,*
> *I apologize for not writing sooner. At times, you seem so self-centered. Other times you're one of the most thoughtful people I've ever met. It's difficult to explain.*
> *I hope you find the right guy. When you do, it will be something special.*
> *I tried to answer your question honestly. You have so much to give.*
> *Sincerely, Eric*

He reread the letter and decided it was the best he could do.

"I'll miss you guys," Snively said. He turned in his equipment and shook hands.

"Good luck, Everett," Eric said. "You've got some breaks coming."

"Thanks." He looked down in that shy way of his. "I've got ten days before reporting. My girl and I are getting married."

"Congratulations on both counts," Eric said.

"Faith works, Eric! Whatever you do, don't lose heart."

"I won't," Eric said. "It's the one thing I have to hold on to."

"Congratulations, Silkwin," Sergeant Hanley said. "You never checked the bulletin board?"

"No. I came straight back to the barracks."

"*Corporal* Silkwin, I'm surprised at you." Hanley grinned. "You've earned it."

The next couple of weeks passed slowly. Jason's absence haunted them. Ted, who acted as handler with the sparring sessions, seemed distant. He admitted earlier that he was having a hard time shaking off his depression with Jason and Everett's absence. He kept looking over his shoulder, waiting for Jason's good-natured ribbing about his and Everett's so-called strategy.

Eric wondered why he had not dreamed of the little girl or the Indian in spirit. He tried to pull Ted out of his slump, but concluded that he had to deal with it in his own way.

"Eric, are you about ready to go to town?" Ted unrolled Snively's mattress and relaxed while Eric finished dressing.

"Just a moment Ted, I want to read Alice's letter."

> *Dear Eric,*
>
> *In about a week, you will come home. It has been a long couple weeks since I saw you last. I have been lying around the house with nothing to do. I think the baby is coming earlier than we thought. I am big as a barn. Everybody's so helpful. I am lucky to have so many people who care. With all these people around me, I still miss this guy in Texas. I am going to close now and eat. You know how I am. Love you. Until then,*
> *Your Alice*

P.S. The little one and I are sending you a few kisses. Try to catch a couple.

Eric folded the letter, leaned back, and smiled.

Sergeant Hanley came into the barracks and approached Eric. "I've been promoted and transferred."

"Congratulations, *Master* Sergeant Hanley," Eric said. "When do you leave?"

"Soon as possible. As always, I've mixed feelings, but I'm a professional. What the hell, in another week you'll be going home. You're going to be a father. If you handle it right, you'll have it made."

"Hey Eric, are you ready to go to town yet?" Ted shouted.

"Okay, let's get outta here. We've got ten minutes to catch the bus."

It was a beautiful day. The temperature was about seventy, with a clear and sunny sky. "I feel great today for some reason," Ted said. "I wish Jason were here too—Sorry."

Eric said slowly, "I was thinking the same thing. He is here with us in spirit! Don't ask me how I know, but I do."

Ted looked at Eric in a strange way and shook his head. "Marie's acting different," he said. "She is not going home with me. Something sure as hell happened."

"What'd she say?"

"She doesn't think our marriage will work out." He wrung his hands. "I don't understand what happened. She said something about a letter, somebody must have written her." When they got off the bus, Eric said, "Let me talk to Marie. I'll meet you at Gail's later. Try to get yourself together."

"All right," Ted replied.

Eric entered Monsento Rose and approached the counter. It was obvious Marie had been crying. "If you're here to talk about Ted," she said, "I'm afraid it will only make matters worse."

Eric tried a smile. "I'll buy you a cup of coffee and we can go in the back and talk."

She sighed as she came around the counter. Eric stared at her. "You see, I've got this guy who's crazy about this girl," he explained. "He's coming apart at the seams."

Surprise showed in her expression. "Ted's parents mentioned this Nancy," Marie said. "Their letter made a lot of sense."

"I've seen him with Nancy and I've seen him with you," Eric said. "He loves *you*, Marie."

"Sometimes that's not enough. I am not strong like you. Neither is Ted. I know him."

"Ted's strong in different ways. You gonna throw it all away? His furlough is only three weeks away. Why don't you go home with him? If it doesn't work out, you can still come home. Isn't it worth taking the chance?"

She looked away for a moment and then faced him. "You confuse me. I need time to think. You do make a good point, Eric. I will think about it and decide this weekend. Tell Ted not to pressure me. I am in no mood, believe me! I mean it." It was the first time he saw her dark eyes turn to glass.

"I'll make it clear," Eric said, and he stood up.

Marie's usually pleasant smile failed to appear.

He opened the apartment door. Ted jumped up and said, "Well?"

Eric explained, and tried to make it clear what she meant.

"Listen to Eric's advice Ted," Gail said, "Don't pressure Marie. Just enjoy being with her this weekend. It'll work out."

"I wonder what my folks said in that letter," Ted murmured.

"Forget the damn letter! Just let it happen," Eric said, disgusted with himself for losing his patience. Ted said little on the bus ride back to the base.

"This is it." Sergeant Hanley said. "I'm catching a plane in a few minutes." He smiled, shook hands and left.

Someone barged in and yelled, "Hey, Silkwin! You're wanted in the orderly room—on the double. Emergency!"

When Eric arrived, the clerk handed him the phone. Frank was on the line. "I don't know all the details, but they rushed Alice to the hospital," he said. "Can you catch a plane for Cutler City or any place nearby? I'll meet you."

"Wait a minute." Eric turned to Lieutenant Shredder. "Sir, my wife was rushed to the emergency room. Is there a plane I can get to Cutler City or anywhere near?"

"Sergeant! Check flight control," Shredder ordered. In a few moments, the sergeant said, "There's a plane that leaves for Cutler City in about two hours. It arrives at six-twenty p.m."

Lieutenant Shredder looked at Eric. "You got it," he said.

"Frank? I'll be in Cutler City at six-twenty."

"Good. I'll meet you. Don't worry."

"I've gotta hurry." Eric hung up.

"If you can be here packed and ready in an hour, we'll run you over to the flight line," the lieutenant said.

"Yes, sir," Eric said. He packed and rushed to Ted's barracks.

"Ted," Eric called. "Alice is in the hospital. I've got a flight in an hour and a half. Come with me to chow, we'll talk there."

"The baby's coming early huh? Relax, Eric. Just think, you'll be home in a few hours."

"I'd planned to be there with her," Eric mumbled.

"Good luck Eric," Ted said. "Call me."

Eric walked into the orderly room. "Good luck, Silkwin," Lieutenant Shredder said. He hopped in the Jeep. The driver headed toward the flight line. Eric boarded the plane, leaned back, and tried to relax. The plane taxied in Cutler City fifteen minutes early. Eric moved quickly to the terminal. Frank was waiting. He tried to read Frank's face.

"The last I heard," Frank began as he moved through the crowd, "you've a seven-pound, two-ounce daughter. They took the baby by Cesarean section."

Frank maneuvered his car into traffic and floored it. Soon they heard a siren and a flashing light as a police car pulled behind them. He pulled over. "I just picked this man up at the airport," Frank said to the officer. "I've gotta rush him to Benford Memorial Hospital. His wife's had an emergency."

"Follow me. I'll clear the way," the officer said. Eric watched the speedometer hit eighty and climb. He lit a cigarette and rubbed his forehead, fighting a headache. Frank's car pulled in the emergency entrance. Eric rushed to the information desk. "I'm Eric Silkwin. My wife—they said there was an emergency."

"Down the hall to the left."

Outside the emergency room, Alice's parents and his folks stood in the corridor. Their faces revealed shock and fear. When he saw the expression on Ellen's face, a chill ran down his back. "The doctor's with her now," she whispered.

Eric turned toward the emergency room. As he started in, the doctor was leaving. "You're the husband?" He asked. Eric nodded, and looked into the doctor's eyes. "I'm afraid it's her heart."

"I gotta see her." Eric rushed into the room. He felt his heart pounding as he stared down at her. He took her hand, and whispered, trying to steady his voice, "Alice, it's me, honey. I'm home." He felt her try to squeeze his hand. Eric put his hand over hers and repeated prayer for his strength to reach her. He pleaded for healing to touch her as he pictured it reaching her.

"Let her rest," the doctor whispered. Eric tried to remove his hand, but Alice held on. He looked hopelessly to the doctor, "She's not responding," he whispered.

Alice's lips moved, but no sound came. Eric leaned closer. He felt her hand go limp as the sudden, steady buzzing of the monitor startled him with fear.

The nurses quickly rushed him out the door. Ellen and his family rushed to him. A moment later, the doctor came out of the emergency room; his eyes were full of sympathy.

"I'm very sorry," the doctor said. "She's gone." Eric felt his legs weaken as his father grabbed for him.

"No! No!" Eric cried out.

His father started after him, but the doctor grabbed his arm. "Let him go to her. That's the least we can do."

"Oh, my God," Alice's mother cried. "Help us!" Her parents walked slowly toward the emergency room. Her father opened the door, and saw Eric draped over her. "Alice! Alice, don't leave me!" Eric screamed through tears. Alice's father quickly shut the door and turned to his wife. "Let him be alone with her for a while."

Frank rushed through the door. "She's gone. Alice is gone," Ellen cried.

Frank stood beside the emergency room, trying to shut out the deep cries from the other side of the door.

Eric moved through the next couple of days like a sleep-walker, his grief and pain an unrelenting torment that showed in every part of his being. Alice's father asked Eric to meet them before the funeral. "Edith asks that you would forgive her," he said. "She's lying down, she's not feeling well."

"I understand," Eric said. "I'm sorry."

"Paula and her husband just pulled up," Alice's father said.

As Paula approached Eric, he could see her eyes bordered on fresh tears.

"I've already made an ass out of myself the last time I met you. I'm sorry, I wish I could—I seem to be saying all the wrong things." Eric could see her pain. Her voice sounded close to hysterical.

Her husband Henry stepped forward and put out his hand. "I'm just sorry we had to meet again under these circumstances."

"I'm just not sure how to handle this, but I have to ask: What about the baby?" Paula said.

Eric hesitated a moment, then said, "I don't know. After the funeral, I'll pick up Colleen from the hospital. After that, we'll have to sort things out."

"Of course, I can't seem to manage my thoughts," Paula said.

A little after closing time, Howard Silkwin slowly lifted a bottle of wine. He held onto it as if it would suddenly vanish before his eyes. He took a swig, and then passed the bottle back to his old friend Walt. "I can't seem to help Eric," Howard said.

"I know what Eric's feeling," Walt said slowly. "Remember what I went through with Brenda? I thought my life was over.

Eric will pull through, but it'll take time—lots of time." Walt's eyes clouded over. He tipped the bottle, finished it, and then tossed it into the trash barrel.

"He's got that baby." Walt paused. "I don't know whether that's going to help him."

Eric's father turned to Walt. "He hasn't even seen the baby? He's never mentioned her that I know about." They both sat staring out the shop window, watching a slow, warm rain begin to fall. "I got to get home," Howard said. "The funeral is tomorrow."

Howard Silkwin walked into the kitchen. His wife Martha turned away from the stove and attempted a smile. "You and Walt already finished your wine. I can tell."

Howard did not answer for a moment, but then he asked, "Is Eric still with Alice's folks?"

"Yes," Martha said. "Sometimes he acts as if nothing happened. Then I look in his eyes and I can hardly bear to face him."

"I heard him rambling around the house the last couple of nights."

"Howie," she said softly. For the first time in three days, Howard Silkwin smiled. He wondered how long it had been since she called him that. "Has Eric mentioned the baby? It's so difficult to know what to say. Tomorrow will be the hardest. I don't know how he'll handle the funeral, and face the fact Alice is gone," she said.

The sound of the front door interrupted her. She looked for some sign of emotion in Eric's eyes. They went through the routine of the meal. Finally, Eric's mother said, "How's Alice's mother holding up?"

Eric spoke in a flat tone. "About what you'd expect," he said. "Lawrence has his hands full."

Martha finally asked, "Eric, what about your baby?"

"I was thinking about her today. I have to get her out of the hospital. I know."

"Your father and I want her here," his mother said. "She's our precious family. Nobody would welcome her or love her more than we do."

"I know. Just let me get through the funeral tomorrow."

"We'll make it," Howard said slowly. "There's no choice."

———————————

The funeral was set for ten-thirty, but people began to arrive about nine. Alice's parents and older sister Paula were waiting when Eric got there. Eric's parents just came in. Frank and Karen followed shortly. Karen hugged Eric.

The Dawsher living room was crowded with folding chairs placed in neat rows. Most of the furniture was taken out of the room or pushed against a wall. The corner where the casket rested contained flowers, mostly red roses and carnations.

A couple of wreaths also decorated the room, one from the insurance company where Alice had worked. Eric did not know where the other wreath came from and he did not bother to check.

Before the services, Eric recognized two of the women from church. "She doesn't look natural, does she?" one whispered. "Her smile doesn't look quite right," the other said. Both turned, embarrassed when they realized someone might have overheard them.

They were both right.

Reverend Langtree arrived a few minutes before the services. He opened with a hymn sung by the leader of the church choir. Langtree stood beside Alice's mother's piano. He spoke quietly and with assurance. The minister's affection and concern were evident in his words. The only sounds were Alice's mother weeping, nervous coughing, and the clearing of throats.

Eric stepped forward with Alice's parents. Paula and her husband walked to the casket. Paula reached in the casket and touched Alice's face, then cried out in anguish and pain. "Oh my God I'm so sorry for the things I said Alice! Please, I beg of you—forgive me!"

171

Her father and Paula's husband took hold of her, and led her away from the casket.

Her mother embraced her older daughter, sharing the pain and the tears.

Pallbearers lifted the casket. When they carried the casket from the room, Alice's mother reached out in a helpless gesture, then sat down and wept.

Alice's grave was near a small lake. It included several plots, including that of her Uncle Paul. Reverend Langtree offered his last solemn prayer. A ray of sunshine found its way through the trees and reflected off the corner of the casket, and then quickly vanished.

Eric stepped forward with Frank and Bryan. He placed his roses on the casket and whispered, "Until then."

They turned away and walked toward the car. When they were leaving the cemetery, Eric could not look at the men lowering the casket.

When they returned to the Dawshers' house, the women from the church prepared the table for dinner. The men sat in the living room talking about the events of the day. A little later, the guests ate in shifts at the dining room table. Gradually the guests began to leave. They were eager to be on their way. There was nothing else to do or say.

"I've a fifth of whiskey I haven't touched in years," Alice's father mumbled to himself. "I think it's time."

Eric's mother and father and Ellen were waiting at the house.

Ellen set two glasses on the table and poured a shot of whiskey in each. Eric downed his and poured another. "Don't worry. This'll get me through the night," Eric said. "Does this mean the Silkwins have feet of clay after all?"

Ellen downed her drink and poured another. "This is the last one for me, but I want you to know those feet of clay mean sensitivity—and caring deeply."

"Tomorrow we'll be stronger," their father said. "One day at a time."

Their mother spoke softly and slowly. "God has his reasons; it's not for us to understand. Remember Eric, he does not give us anything we cannot bear and overcome. What does not destroy us makes us stronger!"

"I wouldn't bet on it," Eric barely whispered.

The next morning he slept late. They ate lunch in almost complete silence. "I've called the hospital," Ellen finally said. "We can pick up the baby at one-thirty."

When they arrived at the hospital, Karen and Frank were waiting. Eric took care of the paperwork. The nurses prepared the baby. "We hate to see her go," the nurse said. Eric looked at the small, curly-headed baby with blue eyes, wrapped in layers of blankets.

When Eric arrived home, his mother said, "bring her into Ellen's room." Karen placed Colleen on the bed and pulled back the blankets. Eric's parents quickly slipped in around her. "She's so beautiful!" Eric's mother exclaimed.

"She's something, that's for sure," Eric's father said. "Imagine—our first grandchild."

"How about a beer?" Eric asked Frank.

"I'll have one, too," Karen said as they headed toward the kitchen. She stared into Eric's eyes. "She's beautiful."

"That she is," Eric said flatly.

"God, I hope I don't detect resentment," Karen sighed. She finished her beer just as someone knocked. Eric and Frank followed her into the living room.

"Come in, Paula," Karen said.

"Henry is helping dad move furniture," Paula said. "I just had to see the baby." Eric took her hand and led her in Ellen's room, and Karen followed. Paula looked into the bassinet and touched the baby's hand. "Oh she's so beautiful," Paula said.

"She has Alice's eyes." She faced Eric with tears in her eyes. "I didn't want to intrude, but we're leaving early tomorrow morning for Chicago. Henry has a job assignment that he cannot pass up. They don't come that often."

"I'm glad you came," Eric said. "Alice would like that."

"I have to think so. I want to apologize for my earlier attitude and remarks. With Alice's death, I said some things I should not have. I am not as strong as I seem. "

"I suspected that," Eric said.

"I had better be going," Paula said. "Henry's not too crazy about kids—any age."

"I'm sorry," Eric said.

"So am I, but that's another story." Paula looked down at the baby and smiled. Eric walked her to the front door. "I wish you the best," she said. "Maybe someday we can meet again."

"I hope so. You're welcome anytime." Her only reply was a smile.

"I feel sorry for her," Karen said after Paula left. A couple minutes later, the doorbell rang. It was Linda.

"I don't want to intrude," Linda said, "but Mother and I were out of town and we just heard what happened. We wanted to express our sympathy."

"Would you like to come in and see the baby?" Eric said. "My folks and Karen are with her now." Eric led her to the bedroom to join them.

"She is so beautiful," Linda said.

"Yes, she is." Eric replied.

Eric went back in the kitchen with Frank. "If it had been Karen instead of Alice," Frank said. "I would be out of my mind."

"There are times when I feel close to it, believe me," Eric said.

After supper, early evening faded into darkness. The family was in and out of Ellen's bedroom throughout the evening. Karen, Frank, Linda, and Eric sat around the table drinking coffee. "If I'm out of line Eric, let me know," Karen said. "We could drive to the cabin Saturday afternoon. Maybe it'd be better if you got out for a while."

"Yeah," Eric said. "I can't very well run away and hide."

The phone rang. "Eric, you have a call from the Twilight Tavern," Ellen said.

"What?" Eric asked. "I wonder what—Hello, this is Eric Silkwin."

The bartender yelled over the music in the background. "There's a lady here who's asking for you and someone named Jason. She's loaded and I don't want any trouble. She says her name's Cindy."

"I'll be right over," Eric said.

"Don't be too long. She's been hitting it pretty hard," the bartender said, and hung up. Eric wondered how Cindy knew he was home. He rushed back to the kitchen, "Frank, Cindy's at Twilight Tavern. She's drunk. She's looking for me and Jason."

CHAPTER FOURTEEN

FRANK LOOKED AT KAREN AND SAID, "I think we probably should try to get Cindy back home."

"You and Eric be careful."

"We shouldn't be too long," Eric said.

A blast of music and air thick with cigarette smoke greeted them as Eric opened the tavern door. He could not believe the woman sitting at the bar was the same girl he had met a few months earlier. "Hiya," Cindy said. She ignored the man beside her. "I came to see Alice and the baby." She suddenly stopped speaking, and glared at the man trying to talk to her. "Will you please leave me alone? These are my friends."

"I was all right when I was buying your drinks," the man said and reached for her. Frank quickly stepped between them. "Forget it, buddy," Frank said. The guy muttered something, and turned away.

Eric took Cindy by the arm and walked to a table. "Who's your friend?" She pointed to Frank. A strange little smile crossed her face.

"We've gotta get you out of here," Eric said.

"I need one more drink," Cindy yelled. "Hey, bartender!" Eric grabbed her when she turned to face the bar, and she almost fell off the chair. The bartender walked over and shook his head. "You folks gonna be responsible for her?" He had a face that

176

looked like he had been in several brawls, and on the losing end of most of them.

"I get a little mixed up when I've had a few," Cindy said. "Tomorrow, I'll see the baby and Alice. I don't know where Jason is. He's always wandering off somewhere!"

"That girl's going to need help," Frank said. "Hey bartender, can you get us a couple of black coffees?"

After they finished their coffee, Eric said, "Start walking her out, I'll settle with the bartender."

"Coffee's on me," the bartender said.

"Thanks, now let's get outta here!" Eric said.

Frank took her by the arm and guided her toward the car. Eric joined him.

"Cindy, I think we should get you home."

"I'm so sorry," Cindy said. "You've a wife and baby. I don't have anybody."

"How'd you know I was home?" Eric asked.

"Ted called. He's getting married in a couple weeks. He couldn't reach you. I told him I'd look you up. Somehow I got sidetracked. Don't know what I was thinking of. I remember thinking I'd have a couple, and call you about the wedding."

"You know, I loved Jason so much," she went on. "I don't understand why he had to leave me. I keep thinking it's a night-mare, and somebody will wake me. I'm still having a nightmare. I remember you told me we'd see Alice and the baby." Her eyes filled with tears. "Don't tell me I imagined that!"

Eric decided he should tell her about Alice.

"Alice is dead Cindy," Eric said slowly. The words sounded hollow as the feeling inside him.

"I don't understand. What happened? I'm so sorry."

"There were complications with her heart," Eric said.

"What—what about the baby?" Cindy asked.

"The baby's with my folks. Would you like to stop and see her before we take you home?"

"Yes, I would like too, but I don't want to impose."

"It's all right Cindy, it's on the way."

"Oh Eric, what's happened to us? And I was feeling so sorry for myself. Take me back to Texas with you. Wait! Don't interrupt me. I have to meet new people. Everything at home reminds me of Jason. I can't stay here! We can help each other. You don't look so great, either."

"What about your mother?" Eric asked.

"She doesn't care. She's shacking up with this guy. I have to have my own life," she pouted. "When do you think we could leave?"

"I'm not sure. I was going back early, but with Ted's wedding."

After arriving at Eric's house, they met Eric's mother at the door. "Mom, do you remember Cindy?" Eric said. "I wanted her to see the baby."

"Come in, you and Eric have had a rough time."

Ellen brought Colleen into the living room. "Oh, what a beautiful baby!" Cindy said.

"Isn't she something?" Ellen beamed.

"Eric, you're supposed to call Ted Faulkland," his mother said.

Ellen and Cindy took Colleen into the bedroom while Eric called Ted. "It's good to hear your voice," Ted said. "How're Alice and the baby?"

Eric paused a moment and then said, "Ted, Alice is gone. After Colleen was born, Alice had complications with her heart."

The stunned silence went on too long. Finally, Ted said, "I'm so sorry. I had no idea. Cindy didn't tell me. Oh, God, I feel so bad for you."

"Cindy didn't know. She's here with me now."

"Is Colleen Ok?" Ted asked.

"She's fine, my family has been helping me take care of her."

"I called to tell you Marie and I are getting married two weeks from this Saturday, but under the circumstances ...."

"I'll be there. Tell Marie I'm happy for both of you."

"I will. You take care of yourself Eric. See you in a couple weeks. Be sure to tell Karen and Frank they're invited. Again, I'm so sorry."

"Goodbye, Ted. I'm glad things worked out for you."

"Colleen finally fell asleep," Ellen said as they joined Eric in the living room.

"I'm gonna catch the first bus to Wyler," Cindy said. "I want to put things in order before I leave for Texas."

"Cindy, Frank and I can take you home."

"That's okay, I'm feeling much better. Frank if you could drop me off at the bus station, I'm sure I can make it home fine."

"You're going to Texas with Eric?" Ellen asked.

"Yes. I can get a part-time job, and go to school. How can I stay around here?" Cindy said. She hesitated at the door. "Call me in a few days. At least you have Alice's baby. If I could do it over, I'd have Jason's. It would be like keeping a part of him alive. How come we never realize what's important to us until it's too late? Nobody seemed to have an answer."

"I'm going over to Alice's house for while," Eric said. He walked up the familiar steps. He knocked, and thought about the times Alice had greeted him with her special smile. "Come in," Alice's father said. Eric looked around the living room, which was back to normal. It was as if nothing had happened. He tried to keep his eyes off the familiar couch.

"Just cream, right?" Alice's mother asked. "You'd think I would remember."

"Yes." Eric felt his stomach knot up. Then he realized she'd be this way for a long time. "I have to know what went wrong," Eric said. He stopped when he realized he was losing control.

"It was her heart," Alice's mother said. "I'm afraid it's from my side of the family. Don't blame yourself, or the baby." Eric could see her holding back the tears.

"Please don't blame that little girl," Alice's father said. "I get the impression that's what you're doing. You must realize what she meant to Alice."

"What are you naming her?" Alice's mother asked.

"Colleen. That's what Alice wanted."

"I'm so glad," she said. "I can hardly wait to see her when I'm a little stronger. Excuse me."

"How about a refill?" Alice's father asked.

Alice's mother returned with a shoebox. "Paul wanted you two to have the cabin. Maybe one day it could be Colleen's. Here are Alice's letters, and the book of poems. I took them to the hospital. I thought maybe she might—"

Eric could see where Alice must have gone over the letters several times. He flipped through the book of poems and quickly closed it. Sometime later, he would go through the letters. Much later.

"Come for dinner Sunday; there is a little girl who wants to meet you," Eric said.

"We'll look forward to it," Alice's father said.

There was nothing else to say. It was time to leave.

Eric hurried out of the house. He felt his own tears. He clutched the shoebox and walked slowly down the street. It was one of the most painful walks he had ever taken.

"How'd it go?" His mother asked when he entered the kitchen.

"Rough," Eric said. "I invited Alice's parents over Sunday for dinner so they could see Colleen." He took the box to his room, then entered Ellen's bedroom and watched Colleen. Ellen joined him and smiled. "You don't know what she means to me with Johnny away. You know me; I'm not one for running around." Suddenly she smiled. "I know somebody who needs changing." She placed Colleen on the bed. "You wouldn't want to ...."

"Can you give me a couple days?"

"All right Eric, but you can feed her. You need to get to know her. She needs her daddy."

"I think I can handle that." Ellen watched as he went through the motions.

Eric held Colleen while Ellen left the room. The feeling of Alice's presence overwhelmed him. "Alice! I sense your presence!" he said aloud. Suddenly, he saw Ellen and his parents standing in the doorway watching him.

"Who were you talking to? Colleen?" Eric's father asked.

"No, Alice. She's here. Somehow I know it."

His father smiled and said, "I wouldn't be a bit surprised. I'll bet she's here in spirit."

Ellen and his mother seemed lost for words.

"I'm going to lie down," Eric said. "Call me when Karen and Frank get here." The little girl appeared in his dream. When he looked into her face, she wiped away her tears, smiled and opened her arms. *"Look to your healing gift and those in need. You've been through the darkness. It's time to embrace the light."* She quickly vanished.

Ellen entered Eric's bedroom and lightly tapped him on the shoulder. "Eric, Karen and Frank are here."

The minute they entered the house, Karen ran to the bedroom to see Colleen. When she returned, she said. "Colleen's so cute. I might have a little girl of my own someday."

"You're not sure?" Eric asked.

Karen laughed and patted Frank on the shoulder. "Almost sure. I am going to have to find this man a hobby."

"Sounds like he already has one," Eric said. It was the first time he smiled in days.

"It's good to hear you laugh again. Would you mind if I called Linda?" Eric didn't respond.

Half an hour later, much to Eric's surprise, Linda joined them. When they pulled into the driveway of the cabin, Bryan and Liza were waiting for them. Eric felt the tightness in his stomach, when memories flashed through his mind.

"Oh, what a lovely place, and there's even a fireplace," Linda said.

Liza and Bryan cleaned the picnic table while Karen and Frank scrubbed the grill. "Why don't you show Linda around the place? We'll take care of the cleanup detail."

A little while later, Linda said to Eric, "Don't get upset, Karen means well."

Eric smiled. He looked off in the distance. "Love's hard to come by and even harder to keep."

"I think I'm beginning to know exactly what you mean," Linda said.

They picnicked as music from the radio filled the air. Everyone seemed relaxed as the evening began to close in. "You men better gather firewood soon," Karen said.

Frank stretched and grinned. "Hey Eric, you ever had any sergeants who could give orders as well as Karen?"

"Couple. They weren't as cute, but they had the same kind of growl."

Everybody laughed, including Karen, who could take it as well as dish it out. The evening took on a glow as the sun slowly moved behind the trees. The men cut some branches and built a campfire. A little later, the group roasted marshmallows and hot dogs.

"This is the way life should be," Frank said with a look of contentment. He put his arm around Karen and drew her close.

"Those stars look almost close enough to reach out and touch," Bryan said. He stared at the fire, and then looked at Eric. "I don't quite know how to ask you this, but I have to know. Do you feel that the healing power of yours has let you down? With Alice, I mean!"

"*Bryan*, how can you ask such a thing!" Liza shouted. "Hasn't he been through enough?"

"I'm just asking what we all want to know!" Bryan yelled back at Liza. "Whether you people will admit it or not!"

A sudden silence fell over the group, then Eric broke it. "Yes," he finally replied. "I felt let down because of Alice—even bitter. I'm not sure of anything anymore." An edge of desperation accompanied his voice. "What you don't understand is, it's much more than the little girl, who, naturally is only symbolic. I see people in my dreams crying out for help."

"Those dreams," Bryan said, "surely you have something more to base your guidance on. There has to be more of an explanation than what you just described."

182

"Nothing," Eric said. "It's a commitment. I can't explain it in words. I don't know if I can handle it anymore! What's *really* bothering you, Bryan? Let's get it out in the open for once!"

"What about me?" Bryan shouted, his voice bordering on panic. "I've given my life to religion and the church. More dedication than you ever have! Why should *you* be among a select group to receive spiritual gifts?"

Eric stared at Bryan. For the first time he realized what was eating away at him. The flickering light from the campfire revealed the frustration and anxiety on Bryan's face.

"I can't answer that! Do you think I enjoy this?" Eric said slowly, "I've asked myself the same questions many times. You don't realize what you're saying. You have no idea how frustrating it is. I didn't choose it!"

"Let's drop it," Karen said. "I know Eric—after what he's been through lately, he'll make up his own mind when the time is right."

"I'm sorry," Bryan said, his voice betraying him. "I obviously lost control of my feelings. It's embarrassing for me. I usually always have my emotions under control." Then he added, "I feel, somehow, I have failed. I have such an overwhelming curiosity and desire. I can't help it." He quickly looked away to avoid Eric's eyes.

"No apology necessary," Eric said.

"When're you going back to the base?" Frank asked.

"Probably after Ted's wedding in a couple weeks. I've been thinking about a hardship discharge. With Colleen, and my father's crippling arthritis, I've got more responsibility than I realized." Eric's attention returned to the flames of the campfire.

"Don't you want to be with your daughter?" Karen asked. "There's more to being a father than paying the bills! You can't blame your little girl for Alice. After all, you are a part of her creation. It wasn't her decision."

Eric didn't respond. He watched the flames cast a strange glow over Karen's face—but it failed to hide the tears in her eyes. "It's getting late," Karen said. "We have to get up early in the morning. We girls will take the cabin and you guys can camp out under the stars."

"We should start back about eleven," Eric said. "Alice's parents are coming over for dinner. I hate to bother you Frank, but would you drive me to the cemetery later. I'll walk back."

"Sure. It's almost a two-mile walk, you know."

"Maybe it's just what I need."

The girls fixed breakfast the next morning. After eating, they walked near the lake. The girls picked wildflowers while the guys relaxed, enjoying the morning until it was time to load the station wagon.

Liza thanked Eric. Bryan mumbled thanks but carefully avoided Eric's eyes. It was the first time he had ever seen Bryan lose his composure in front of anyone. Eric was the one person he wanted to avoid more than anything else.

After they arrived at Linda's house, Eric walked her to the door. She turned to face him. "I hope things work out for you. I had a nice time."

"I'm glad you enjoyed it," he said. "You're a special girl. I remember reading somewhere that nice things happen to nice people."

"If you need someone to talk to, or maybe a movie or something, call me," Linda said.

"We'll be back later," Frank said.

Eric walked in the house and picked up the telephone. "Hello Cindy. How are you doing?"

"I'm doing okay, I guess, considering everything."

"I'm glad you got to see Colleen. Well, if you're not sure about the wedding, why don't you give me a call later and let me know? Ted would be happy if you could come. Take care in the meantime."

Eric saw Ellen come out of her bedroom. "How's Colleen doin'?" he said.

"See for yourself. I think she needs her daddy."

He leaned over the bed and stared at the little bundle who was his daughter. "You have your mother's eyes, but then, you should have," he whispered.

"I got a letter from Johnny. He's in Japan." Then she added, "He said he misses me so much he can't tell me in words."

"I know what he means."

Eric heard a knock and rushed to the door. "Please come in," he said to Alice parents. "There's a young lady who's waiting to meet you."

Ellen placed Colleen in Alice's mother's arms. She beamed and said, "I know every grandmother in the world says the same thing, but you are the most beautiful baby in the world."

The feeling of depression during dinner was very evident.

"I don't like to bring these things up," Alice's father said. "But Alice's funeral expenses are already settled. She also had her insurance and savings account."

"Put everything in an account for Colleen," Eric said.

"I'm sure that would make Alice very happy. Thank you for inviting us over." Alice's father glanced over at his wife, "I must get Edith home, I can tell when she's about had it. We would like to see Colleen again."

"You are welcome anytime."

––––––––––

A little while later Karen and Frank arrived to take Eric to the cemetery. They drove around to the area near Alice's grave and stopped.

"Don't wait," Eric said, "I don't know how long I'll be here. I couldn't relax knowing somebody was waiting for me. I haven't talked to Alice since the funeral."

"I'm glad we're the only ones having this conversation," Karen said. "Someone else might not understand."

"Do you?" Eric asked.

"I'm not sure," Karen replied.

Eric walked up the slope toward Alice's grave. He watched Frank's car move slowly and circle the bend until it disappeared. The slow, labored walk to the gravesite was like a nightmare.

The sounds of the surrounding countryside vanished as if they failed to exist.

After a moment of silence, he ran his hand along the smooth surface of the newly carved headstone. Eric looked down and whispered, "Whoever thought it'd end like this? We had so much. Now, it's just our little one and me." He arranged the flowers, trying to keep his emotions under control. "It's strange. I can't get my thoughts together."

Eric stared at the late afternoon sun, glistening off the top of the trees. The day was calm and peaceful. The blue sky was broken up by masses of white fluffy clouds.

A sudden stillness seemed to engulf him.

He walked to a small stone bench nearby and lit a cigarette. Eric couldn't take his eyes off the grave.

"I know you are with us, I feel your presence. I hope you'll forgive the way I acted after you were gone. You know how much I loved you. Surely you'd—"

"Who are you talking to, soldier?"

Eric jumped. He turned to see a young girl with dark pigtails. She had big green eyes and a nose full of freckles. She stared at him, twisting her bare feet in the grass.

CHAPTER FIFTEEN

"I DIDN'T HEAR YOU," ERIC SAID. He snapped out of his depressing thoughts to face reality. He looked beyond the little girl and saw a group of people across the road gathered around a gravesite. "I was talking to my wife."

"Is your wife in there?" she asked, pointing to the freshly dug grave.

"Yes. I'm afraid she is."

"You think she can hear you?" She suddenly stepped beside him and put her hand on his shoulder.

"Yes, I do. At least, that's what I tell myself."

"I hope she can. You been crying?"

"Patsy—Patsy! Come back here this minute. You hear me!" Eric glanced up to see a much older girl running toward them from across the road. The girl paused to catch her breath, and then faced Eric. "I'm so sorry," she said.

"It's all right," Eric said.

"No, it isn't. Patsy, where are your shoes?"

"By Aunt Lennore's grave." The older girl grabbed the little girl's hand "I was just talking to this soldier," Patsy said. "His wife's in that grave there." The little girl pointed again.

The older girl blushed. "I—I don't know what to say."

"There's no need to apologize. She meant well." A big grin spread over the little girl's face, revealing a missing tooth.

"He was talking to his wife. He was crying, and I felt sorry for him."

"Come along. Mother and Dad will take care of you." She jerked Patsy along behind her.

Eric looked down at the faded flowers. "Guess I'll never understand why you had to leave me. Sometimes, I wake up at night, thinking it is just a nightmare. I'll bring you some roses before I leave." He glanced at his watch, surprised at how long he had been here.

Eric walked toward the cemetery's entrance. He picked up his pace, not looking back as he moved toward town. A green Ford sedan pulled up alongside him. "Young man, would you like a ride to town? We're headed that way," the driver said.

Eric saw Patsy motion to him. "If you're sure you don't mind," Eric said.

The woman let him in the back seat. "Our name's Quinlin. I'm Vivian, and this is my husband, George. You've already met our daughters Maxine and Patsy. I apologize for their interruption."

"No apologies necessary. Meeting Patsy was a bright moment in my day. My name's Eric Silkwin."

"We read about your wife in the paper. We're very sorry. You have a little daughter, don't you?" Mrs. Quinlin asked.

"Yes. Her name's Colleen."

"How old is she?" Patsy asked.

"Just a little over a week."

"Can I see her?" Patsy asked. "Please?"

"Patsy!" Maxine yelled. "You'll have to excuse her, Mr. Silkwin."

"Call me Eric. She's saying what she feels. I like that."

"You see, Tyler?" Patsy smiled at her sister. "We put flowers on Aunt Lennore's grave, only we don't talk to her like you did to your wife."

"I don't understand. Patsy calls you Tyler," Eric said.

"It's my middle name. It was to be my first name if I were a boy and middle name if I were a girl. It was my grandfather's." She blushed with pride, and then smiled, which brought to life the most incredible dimples he had ever seen.

"Did you go to Benford High?" Eric asked.

"Yes," Tyler answered. I was a sophomore when you graduated. I watched you box in school a couple times."

"Do you think your wife can see you too?" Patsy asked.

"I think so," Eric said.

"What're we going to do with this child?" Mrs. Quinlin said.

"Love her," Eric said. The car pulled into the outskirts of town. "You can drop me off anywhere; I live about four blocks down the street, but, I'd like a young lady"—Eric winked at Patsy—"to meet my daughter."

"Can we, Daddy? Please?"

Mr. Quinlin hesitated. "We don't want to intrude."

"My folks will be glad to meet you." They stopped in front of Eric's house. He saw his mother looking out the window. The moment they entered the house, Eric said, "I'd like you to meet the Quinlins. They were kind enough to offer me a ride."

Eric took Patsy's hand. "I promised this young lady she could meet Colleen."

Ellen came out of the bedroom. Eric introduced her. "You're pretty," the little girl said to Ellen, who took Patsy's hand and walked her toward her bedroom. "Why, thank you honey," Ellen said. "Follow me. I'll show you the real beauty around here."

"We shouldn't intrude," Mr. Quinlin repeated. He shifted his two hundred pounds from one foot to the other. He tugged at his tie, and then ran his fingers through his straight brown hair, which was graying at the temples. Eric's father stepped forward and shook his hand. "It's good to see some cheerful faces around here."

They filed into Ellen's bedroom and gathered around Colleen's crib. She was wide-awake and staring right back at them. "She's truly beautiful." Mrs. Quinlin smiled. "Look at those beautiful blue eyes."

"She surely is something," Mr. Quinlin said, then smiled at Patsy. "Seems like a short time ago our little one was about that size."

"What do you think of her, Patsy?" Eric asked.

Patsy's eyes widened. "She's pretty, but kinda small."

"You wanna hold her?"

"Sit on the bed honey, and be very careful. She's not a doll," Mrs. Quinlin cautioned, and then she brushed back her long dark hair. She smiled as her light blue eyes stared at Colleen. Her complexion had the same tanned, ruddy color as her husband, which suggested hours of work in the sun.

Ellen placed Colleen in Patsy's arms. "Oh, I'd like one of my very own," Patsy squealed.

"Not for a few years, I hope." Mrs. Quinlin chuckled.

The men gathered in the living room. "I've got hay to get in next week," Mr. Quinlin said. "I'm a little short of help."

"Eric could help us," Patsy said.

"I couldn't pay much," her father said to Eric. "Maybe we could work something out."

"I don't have any experience, but it would give me something to do over the next few days."

"It's hard work," Tyler said. "I drive the tractor." Her smile failed to hide the challenge in her dark brown eyes.

"Tell 'ya what—I'll help in exchange for transportation and meals."

"You've got a deal," Mr. Quinlin said. "You know, we start early—around six in the morning. I'll call you."

"Whenever you're ready," Eric replied.

"We have to be going. We've chores to do," Mr. Quinlin said, and smiled at Eric's mother and father.

Ellen said to Eric. "I've never seen dimples like that. I don't suppose she's the reason you volunteered? Don't give me that look. I know how you felt about Alice. If she were here, she'd tell you the same thing."

He did not comment, so Ellen added, "I don't want to hurt you, but the fact is you're barely twenty-one years old. You've an infant daughter and your whole life ahead of you."

After Eric still refused to comment, Ellen's voice softened. "I realize Alice has a place in your heart and always will. Eventually, you'll meet someone. She won't be taking Alice's place, but you'll need each other."

"You're quite a philosopher," Eric said.

"Aren't you going to check your daughter? Damn it, Eric, she's your daughter." She shook her head.

"I guess I'd better look in on Colleen. It's just—" He took off for Ellen's bedroom and Ellen followed.

"She needs changing, she's only wet," Ellen said. "How about it, Daddy?" Eric changed the baby with Ellen's guidance. "Not bad, huh?"

"I guess not." Ellen still seemed upset.

"It's more than just losing Alice," Eric said slowly. "I'm afraid to get close to Colleen. Wait, don't interrupt me! After Alice died, I was afraid something might happen to Colleen and I just couldn't take it." He turned to see his parents in the doorway.

Ellen said, "What a terrible feeling, I never thought of it that way. I don't mean to hurt you, but you do have to face reality." He walked out of the room.

Ellen and her parents looked at each other.

———————

That night Eric sat holding Alice's book of poems until the early morning light streaked through the window. The following morning he left early. Eric walked up the familiar steps and knocked. Alice's father answered the door with a surprised look on his face.

"I just wanted to stop by and say how glad I was that you came to see Colleen," Eric said.

"It meant so much to both of us," Alice's father replied.

"You don't look well, Eric. Can't you sleep?"

"I've had a little trouble. I'll be all right."

Alice's mother joined them and said, "Eric, there's something I want you to know. You made Alice as happy as we've ever seen her. For that, we're grateful. You've got Colleen, and you're still young. Probably, someday you'll eventually meet someone and remarry; we want you to know we understand that."

"My sister said basically the same thing last night," Eric said.

"She's right. Your family is worried. All the caring in the world isn't going to bring Alice back. If it would, she'd be with us now. Do you realize what I'm saying?"

"Yes, but it'll take a little more time," Eric said. He knew there was nothing more to say.

———————

Eric went for a walk. Mabel's Cafe was just finishing the lunch hour. There were only a few people at the counter. "What'll you have, handsome?" Rita asked.

"Coffee sounds about right," Eric said.

She sighed. "Let's sit in that back booth and talk. I need a break, my feet hurt. I was sorry to hear about Alice. I've so much to thank you for. I wish I could help you."

"You don't owe me anything," Eric said.

"Yes I do. You helped me. Did the doctors ever corner you?"

"Yes, we had a brief discussion. I explained as best I could, but I got frustrated. I don't think they took it seriously, and I don't blame them."

"But you made it happen," she countered. "I'll have you know I'm a churchgoing woman now. I'm grateful every day."

"*Your faith hath made you whole.* That's a quote, by the way," Eric said.

"The bitter young man who turned my life around. If I had the power, I would take that hurt out of your eyes. My husband and I attend church. I'll pray for you. I have this feeling it'll help, not because of me, but, I feel it's the only way I can repay you." Eric slowly raised his head to look into her eyes. "How's that new daughter of yours?"

"All right."

"What the hell kind of answer is that?" she yelled. A few of the remaining customers glanced their way. "You'll have to forgive me. Every now and then I backslide a bit."

Eric laughed. "No problem."

"Well, at least I got you smiling. You know, she's a part of you and Alice."

"I know. I guess I better be going. I've gotta help a farmer with his hay."

"You?" Rita laughed out loud. She quickly put her hand over her mouth. "A farmer, huh? Any daughters?" She raised her eyebrows and broke into a big smile.

"Two, actually."

"You know what they say about farmers' daughters."

Eric couldn't help but smile. "No, what?"

She laughed. "I think I'll let you find out for yourself."

"See you later," Eric said. He waved as he walked out the door.

When he got home, his mother told him Mr. Quinlin had called. Eric picked up the phone. "Hello, Mr. Quinlin. Tomorrow morning about six, I'll be ready," Eric said.

Eric and his mother walked in the bedroom. He looked at Colleen and spoke to her. "I gotta change you before you eat," he said. "This is a little different, so you're going to have to bear with me."

"I'll help, but you need the experience," his mother added.

After he finished changing her, he gave Colleen her bottle; suddenly Eric felt Alice's presence, and the sensation of a very light touch. "Alice, you're here!" he said, just as Ellen entered the room. "Eric, it's about time to eat," she said.

Eric sighed, placing Colleen back in her crib.

The meal was eaten in silence until their father spoke. "I hear you're working tomorrow. Fresh air, hard work and good food will make you sleep better, which you badly need, judging from the looks of you."

The phone rang. "Eric, it's for you," his mother said. Linda was on the line. "Would you like to join me at Grover's," she asked. "Maybe we could talk."

Grover's was noisier than usual, and the jukebox blared away. Linda was standing by the counter. "I just got here," she said.

"Let's get a booth," Eric said, leading her toward the back. "You've got something definite on your mind. I know you."

"Bill called me. He wants us to get back together. I promised I'd meet him next week. Naturally I have mixed feelings."

"Do you love him enough to put up with him?" Eric asked.

"I think so," she said. "I'm not sure."

"With you women, one can never tell," Eric said. She didn't comment. It was as if she had not heard him. Eric noticed, as always, several guys at the bar looking at her. He stared at her perfection. He wondered what she'd ever seen in him.

"Eric, did you really ever have any feelings for me?" Linda asked quickly. She twirled the straw in the soda. "Were you ever—"

"In love with you? I'm not really sure."

She stared into his eyes. "Were you? I sometimes had wondered about us." Linda looked down.

"You found someone else!" Eric said flatly, trying to ignore the giggling from the booth behind them. "Let's get outta here and go to a bar."

"Wouldn't that be a little strange—I mean under the circumstances. Alice has only been gone a short time," Linda said.

"Oh, my!" A guy's voice came from the booth behind them.

Eric took his eyes off Linda for a moment, and focused on the two guys in the booth. "Something bothering you?" he said, with an edge in his voice. The area suddenly became quiet. People stared in their direction.

The guy with the homely face rearranged it with a crooked grin, and asked, "Were you referring to—Wait a minute! I do believe we have an offbeat celebrity among us, if I'm not mistaken. Yes it's Silkwin the healer." Suddenly the guy realized he was the center of attention. "You looking for trouble?" he asked, his voice much louder. The girls peeked over the top of the booth, and then disappeared.

"No, but evidently you are," Eric said.

194

"Let's go," Linda said, with a hint of fear in her voice. She wanted no part of trouble—any kind of trouble.

"Oh, let's go," mocked the other guy. The girls laughed.

Linda stood and started to leave when one of the guys deliberately stuck his leg in the aisle. Eric calmly moved Linda aside, and then suddenly kicked the guy's shin. His scream filled the room. People at the surrounding tables quickly backed away. The other guy jumped up and hit Eric in the eye. Eric backhanded him, knocking him back in the booth. Linda backed away, her mouth open, but no sound. The homely guy started to reach for him. Eric slammed his head against the back of the booth. The girls drew back in shock.

"What's going on here?" the manager shouted. He looked at the two men, the girls, then he faced Eric. "Want me to call the police?"

"Those servicemen are always causing trouble," a woman yelled. "Imagine picking on those two boys."

"I won't put up with this!" the manager shouted. He again looked at Eric. "Want me to call the police?"

"Why don't you ask these people who started it?" Eric said. The manager's face reddened. A police officer suddenly appeared. The crowd closed in around them.

The officer looked at the two guys, then Eric. "Everybody settle down," the officer said. "Who started this?"

"This clown stuck out his foot and tried to trip my friend as we were leaving," Eric said.

The guy with the homely face shouted. "That guy back handed my buddy. He kicked me in the shin and—"

One of the girls pointed her finger at the guy with the homely face and said, he's telling the truth."

The officer reached for Eric's arm when a police sergeant broke through the crowd. "What's going on here?" he asked. He looked at the surrounding crowd. Nobody spoke. "All right! Let's break it up." People slowly went back to their tables.

"They're going to let that soldier leave?" One woman remarked, getting the full attention of the two women with her.

"That's the Silkwin boy. You're telling me that's the conduct of an 'if you can believe this'—a spiritual healer? Really!"

The man next to her said, "Those two got what they deserved." Eric could not help but notice the sergeant's grin.

"Sorry Linda," Eric said, "Let's get outta here and get a drink."

"I don't know. You're not the same guy," she said, as they walked down the street. A few moments later they reached Daily's, one of Benford's better taverns.

"A lot has happened in the last year," Eric said. "We're not kids anymore."

"Wait a minute." Linda took out a tissue, wet it and wiped his eye. "It doesn't look too bad."

"It's nothing. One of the guys had a ring." Eric shrugged, and then looked into her eyes. "If we're going to have this conversation, I need a drink." He put his hand on the door. "*Well?*"

"I guess a little wine would be nice," Linda said. They were greeted with the sound of music and conversation. "You really hit those guys, didn't you?"

"Just as hard as I could." He led her to a booth. The results were the same. She drew immediate attention from every man at the bar. For some reason, it bothered him more this evening than ever. The waitress flashed a professional smile, and took their order. Eric put his hand on Linda's. "I feel better. It's like I took some of the hurt and passed it onto those guys. Do you realize the envy of those guys at the bar?"

"You're terrible," she said, flashing her perfect smile. The waitress brought their drinks, glanced at Eric's eye and left.

"Now, what were we talking about?" Eric quickly downed the shot and beer. The warm feeling began to engulf him.

"You still say nice things." She took a couple sips of wine, and said, "How's your pretty little daughter?"

"Great." He motioned to the waitress. The waitress set another round on the table. He quickly downed them, and then said, "What're you really looking for, Linda?"

She took another sip of wine and said slowly, "I'm looking for happiness with a guy who wants to build a life together."

"I think you're asking the wrong guy if you mean living happily ever after." He felt the warmth of the whiskey.

"What are you smiling about?" Linda asked.

"Private thought," Eric said.

"I want to know," she insisted.

"I was thinking how perfect you always look. You never have a hair out of place. Linda, what you need is to be messed up a little."

She almost choked while sipping her wine, and then she burst out laughing. "You never could drink."

"That's true." Eric flashed a grin, and then motioned to the waitress. "Excuse me a minute, I gotta go," he said, slurring his words, suddenly aware he couldn't control his tongue. "I'll be right back." He went to the men's room. On the way out, he went to the jukebox. He punched selections until the machine clicked no longer.

"Don't you think we've had enough?" she asked. She slowly sipped her glass of wine. "Will you take me home after we finish this round?"

"Your desire is my command, besides, I've gotta pick up hay tomorrow—early." He grinned.

"You? Working in the hay fields? I don't believe it." She laughed. Her eyes were much brighter. "How'd you get involved in that?"

"I met a farmer and agreed to help him with his hay," Eric said. He stared at her and grinned. "Linda, can I mess you up a little?"

Her mouth flew open. "*What!*"

"You're perfect. It bugs me." He felt his control slipping. "What were we discussing earlier? Oh, yeah I remember now, you wanted to know if I liked you, loved you or wanted to sleep with you. I don't remember; we never seem to clarify that."

"You're getting drunk," she said.

"Wrong. Already am."

"Are you going to take me home?"

"Most certainly."

She laughed without amusement. Linda finished her wine, aware of the men at the bar, who had her undivided attention. "See any particular one you like?" Eric asked.

"You're getting nasty."

"Whaddyasay we take the long way home—by way of the park?"

"You never spoke like this to me before. What's happened to you? That's all you want from me, isn't it? A roll in the grass."

"Hay! Linda—hay!"

"What? Oh you know what I mean!"

"I wanna know if there's any feeling behind all that perfection."

"Of course I have feelings," Linda snapped.

"What kind, Linda? Could you really give of yourself?" She stared at him without comment. "You mean what's-his-name never got next to you, either?"

"That's none of your business." Her eyes blazed.

"Does this mean," Eric went on, "that you don't want to take the long way home?"

"No, and end up like Alice?" Suddenly, the perfection faded because of the expression on her face—a look he had never seen before. Her voice choked with tears and a combination of shock and sincerity. "Oh God, I'm so sorry I said that."

"So am I," Eric said slowly. He felt he'd been kicked in the gut, and for a moment was afraid he was going to be sick. He felt the tears in his eyes, which made him angry.

"Forgive me, I—" she barely whispered. He looked up, but she was gone before he could answer. Eric left the bar and walked down the street. He ignored the blare of traffic and the crowds of people. His torment was slowly turning into a rage of helplessness.

CHAPTER SIXTEEN

ERIC HESITATED A MOMENT then walked in the house. His parents, along with Ellen, Bryan, Karen, and Frank, sat at the dining room table. They stared at him. "Let's see now," Eric said, with a lopsided grin. "You're having a party and no one invited me."

"You're drunk," his mother gasped.

"I heard about the trouble at Grover's," Bryan said.

"Somehow that doesn't surprise me," Eric said. "I'm surprised everybody in town hasn't heard—they'll know by morning."

"You think it's funny?" Bryan asked.

"No," Eric replied slowly. "I can't seem to think of anything else right now."

"We wanted to drop over for a while," Karen said, trying not to laugh. "We didn't realize you were celebrating. What's the occasion?"

"I'm not sure, but I think I insulted Linda. I wanted to mess her up. Anyway, she left without me."

"What do you mean—mess her up?" Ellen asked.

"You know that look of perfection and never a hair out of place. Well, I wanted to mess her up a little." Eric grinned. "I also suggested we take the long way home through the park."

"You didn't?" his mother gasped. Karen laughed.

"I'm pretty sure I did."

"I'm surprised at you," Eric's mother said. "Linda's such a nice girl."

"That's why I wanted to mess her up."

Frank could not keep from laughing. Bryan wasn't laughing. "Didn't you get kicked out of Grover's?" he said.

"I was invited to leave. Linda and I were minding our own business. Suddenly, these clowns in the next booth started making remarks." Eric hesitated a moment. "She said, `are you ready to leave?' I said, 'Yeah.'" Eric paused to light a cigarette and take a sip of coffee.

"And?" Bryan asked.

"Let's see, where was I? Oh, yeah, we got up to leave and this guy stuck his foot into the aisle, and I'm here to tell you—Linda almost tripped. That upset me, so I kicked him in the shin, and he screamed. The other guy jumped up and hit me. This was from his ring." Eric pointed to his eye. "I backhanded him."

"You didn't!" his mother gasped. "Oh, Eric."

"Anyway, the manager asked us to leave. We were going to anyway, but the police came."

"The police?" Eric's father's smile suddenly faded.

"No one pressed charges. We just left and went to Daily's."

"It's good you're going to the farm tomorrow," Howard said. "I hope they work your—"

"We're gonna go," Frank said quickly. "You'd better get some rest, Eric. Believe me—I know about working the hay fields."

"I know," he said. "Maybe with this work, I can sleep."

"Oh, you will," Frank said.

"Are you going to Marie and Ted's wedding by yourself? I don't think Linda would want to go since she doesn't want to get messed up?" Ellen said jokingly.

"At this time, I can't really say for sure."

"Eric, you should take a good look at yourself in the mirror," his father said with disgust. "Come on Martha, we're going to bed."

Eric got a bottle from the cupboard, left the room for a moment, and then returned with his Bible.

"I am surprised at you! Whiskey and the Bible." Eric held the glass in his hand and stared at the bottle of whiskey.

"I'm not sure I need this," he said. "It won't solve anything."

"I'm glad you're sobering up," Ellen said slowly. "The first thing is to quit feeling sorry for yourself! I'm sure the help you are looking for is in that book you just opened." He followed her to the bedroom. Ellen paused, and then said, "Eric, you're coming apart. Don't you see that? You mentioned Alice's presence. How do you think she would feel about what happened tonight? It would break her heart."

He touched the blankets around Colleen. "I know. It's as if I can't seem to put things back together. Maybe if I get some rest, I can turn things around."

Later that night the Indian appeared. The smile and compassion became a look of rage. He spoke with the same strong penetrating voice. *"Does not your good book say, 'You cannot serve two masters, for you will love one and despise the other? I come to you with a heavy heart. Take time for your sorrow and go forward to your destiny. If your choice is to serve, get your life in order! I am the spirit of your great-grandfather."*

Eric was stunned.

"It's five o'clock," Eric's father said, shaking him. "Mr. Quinlin'll be here soon."

It was still dark. "I'm awake." Eric grabbed his head. He felt as if he had just gone to sleep. He dressed in fatigues, with the words of his great-grandfather haunting him. He didn't know if the haunting face of his great-grandfather was a dream, or his spirit had stood before him. His mother was fixing breakfast when he walked in the kitchen. He poured coffee and sat at the table. His mother said. "How do you feel, or should I ask?"

"I've had worse mornings, but I can't remember when." Eric was just finishing his second cup of coffee when he heard the truck. "I'll see you tonight—if I'm able."

Mr. Quinlin glanced at Eric's eye and asked, "Rough night?"

"Rougher than I expected," Eric said.

"I'm sending Patsy to school. She can help tomorrow," Mr. Quinlin said.

They drove in the yard where Tyler was waiting for them. She wore a long-sleeved shirt and blue jeans. A scarf hid her long, dark hair. "Morning," she said and grinned. "You look a little under the weather."

"Good morning," he replied. "Can't say that about you." It had to be one of the hottest mornings Eric could remember. He tried to ignore his headache and the dryness in his throat. He tied a handkerchief around his forehead to keep the sweat out of his eyes. Eric glanced up at the blazing sun, grabbed another bale of hay, and loaded it on the wagon. In a couple of hours, they stopped for a break. Tyler grinned at him and said, "Rough, huh?"

Mr. Quinlin looked him over carefully. "You gonna make it? If you can't, I'll understand."

"I'll make it," Eric said, although he felt terrible. "Just keep pulling the wagon." He stared up at the blazing sun. By noon, he was exhausted. He welcomed the relief when they hopped on the back of the wagon and Tyler pulled them toward the house. Eric watched Tyler grin at him and he suddenly felt a little better.

"I guess I've gotta feed you," Mr. Quinlin said. "Hungry?"

"I'm not sure—but I think so. If you would've asked me earlier, I couldn't handle it—but now I think I'll give it a shot."

Mr. Quinlin laughed. "At least you're sweating that booze out of you," he said. "I didn't figure you for much of a drinking man."

"I'm not, believe me. Last night got away from me. I seem to do all the wrong things lately." Eric was surprised at his appetite. "I don't remember ever eating this much before."

Quinlin paused a moment and said. "It's going to take time. You've been through a lot. You'll find your way. I'll bet the other guy doesn't look much better," he chuckled.

"I hope you're right about me finding my way."

"Tyler's boyfriend is going to help us this afternoon," Quinlin said. "That should take a little of the pressure off."

"He's not my boyfriend," Tyler protested. "He's a friend."

"Here he comes now," Quinlin said as a young man stepped in the door. "Darryl, I'd like you to meet Eric Silkwin. He's agreed to help us out."

Eric stood and shook hands. "Nice to meet you, Darryl."

"There was trouble at Grover's last night. Some soldier—" Darryl saw Eric's fatigues and his face turned red. "Sorry, I—"

"Forget it," Eric said.

Quinlin just laughed. They worked hard the rest of the day. The dusty afternoon put a golden color on the land. Eric felt stronger as the afternoon faded into evening. "You've done well," Mr. Quinlin said. "You wanna work tomorrow?"

"Yes," Eric said. "I think I'll really be able to sleep for the first time in a few days."

"We've got a spare room. You're welcome," Mr. Quinlin said.

"I'll stay." Eric winked at Patsy. "There's no reason you should drive me in town and pick me up again tomorrow."

"I'll help you tomorrow afternoon," Patsy said.

"I'd like that," Eric said, and Patsy giggled. "I think I'll turn in early."

Quinlin grinned. "A little tired, huh?"

"Yes, but I feel pretty good."

"How about Tyler and I going to a movie?" Darryl asked the Quinlins. "Eric, you're welcome to come with us."

"No, thank you. I need a relaxing evening. Besides I gotta call my folks."

After Tyler and Darryl left, Eric called his house.

"Hello, Ellen? I'm gonna stay here tonight. Yes, I survived." He laughed, and then added, "I'll admit I'm hurting a little. I miss Colleen; how is she? That's good." After hanging up the phone, he joined the Quinlins listening to the radio.

"Eric, you have a baby girl. How come you don't have a wedding and get another wife?" Patsy asked.

"Patsy, what's the matter with you?" Mrs. Quinlin asked. "You should stop and think before you ask. Sometimes people don't like to talk about certain things."

"How am I gonna know if I don't ask questions?" Patsy said. "If you got another wife, your baby would have a mom, too. I'd marry you if I was old enough."

"I appreciate the offer," Eric said, and patted Patsy's head.

"Come on, off to bed with you! Give your little mouth a rest," her mother said.

A moment later, they heard a truck. Tyler came in the door. "I thought you were going to the movies?" her mother asked.

"Too long a line. We went to Grover's for some ice cream," Tyler said. "Darryl said he'd be here early tomorrow."

"Grover's still in one piece?" her father asked.

"Why, yes—Oh, I see." She looked at Eric, and then laughed.

"George, you should be ashamed," Mrs. Quinlin said with booming laughter.

"There was a guy at the counter who said a soldier hit a couple fellows last night. He banged one's head against a booth."

"Believe me, they had it coming. They started it." Eric said.

Nobody spoke for a moment.

"I'd better dish out the ice cream," Vivian said.

"You must have loved your wife very much," Tyler said.

"Yes, very much."

"Then why were you with another girl at Grover's? I don't understand."

"The girl and I were friends even before I got married," Eric said. He hesitated a moment, then continued. "I was lonely. I wanted to talk to someone who I thought would listen and understand – someone who I thought would care. It's getting late, I think I better turn in."

When Eric joined them for breakfast, he was surprised at the array of food. "I've never seen a breakfast like this," he marveled.

"Dig in. You'll need strength," Mr. Quinlin said. "You're looking better this morning." Tyler joined them. "Good morning honey," her father said. "Eat up. Tractor drivers need their strength too, right Eric?"

"Right, especially one so pretty in the morning," Eric said. Tyler blushed and smiled.

"Come in, Darryl. You wanna join us for breakfast?" Mrs. Quinlin said.

"No thanks," Darryl said. "Maybe a cup of coffee."

"Time to get going," Mr. Quinlin said as he got up from the table.

Eric and Darryl worked hard all morning. The temperature had to be still in the eighties. Eric was amazed how much better he felt. They headed toward the house for dinner.

Eric saw Patsy getting off the school bus. He noticed her walking slowly toward the house with her head down as if she seemed upset. When he entered the house, he heard Mrs. Quinlin ask Patsy, "Are you all right, honey? Here you're out of school for a few days, but you look sad. What's wrong?"

"I don't wanna talk about it," Patsy said. "I'm going outside for a while."

"Don't. Stay. We're about to eat." She watched her daughter and then said, "I don't know what's wrong with that child."

Eric said, "I'm gonna try to talk to her." He slowly worked his way next to her under a shade tree. "Do you mind if I sit beside you?"

"I guess it's all right," she whispered.

"You know, friends help each other and talk things over. When you're sad, it affects everyone around you."

She glanced at him. "If I told you, you'd laugh at me."

"I may laugh with you, but not at you," Eric said.

She stared at him. She said softly, "I'm not pretty like Melissa Ann. She's taking my boyfriend away."

"I think you're pretty."

"You're just saying that to make me feel better. You're prej— preju—What's that word?"

"Prejudiced," Eric said seriously.

"That's it," she said. "I've a missing front tooth and I've got freckles—quite a few." She looked up at him slowly.

"That's what makes you special."

"Whaddya mean?"

"They're what makes you that special someone. Your personality is what lets people know who you are. If I were in your class, you couldn't keep me away from you."

Her face hinted at a smile.

205

"Alice, my wife, had several freckles right there." Eric put his finger on her nose. Patsy giggled. A gleam came back into her eyes.

"She did?"

"She surely did. I wouldn't have wanted it any other way. If you took those freckles away, she wouldn't have been my Alice. You see, that was a part of her I loved very much."

Her smile spread across her face. "Really?"

"Someday, you're going to meet a boy who'll love them and everything about you. Why don't you get rid of that long face and bring back that smile I like so much?"

"You didn't laugh," Patsy said. She looked Eric in the eye. "I was afraid you'd think it was silly."

"I knew it was important to you, the way you knew how I felt when I talked to my wife."

"I didn't at first," she confessed. "But I knew she meant a lot to you."

Mrs. Quinlin smiled as they walked inside. "There isn't anything serious between the two of you, is there?"

"Oh, Mother. Eric's too old, but I kinda like him."

The phone rang just as they started to eat. Mrs. Quinlin motioned to Eric. "I'm sober, don't get nervous," Cindy said. "I called your mother, and she gave me this number. Are you still planning on going to Ted's wedding?"

"Yes. Do you still want to go?"

"I would like to," Cindy said.

"That's great, you know Ted invited Karen and Frank."

"That's fine. Let me give you my address," Cindy said. "See you a week from this Saturday about three."

Eric hung up, and returned to the table. "That was Cindy, the girlfriend of a buddy of mine named Jason Corkland. He was in the service with me. He drowned a couple of months ago. She lives in Wyler."

"I think we read about that young man," Mrs. Quinlin said. "I'm so sorry."

"Ted, my other buddy from the service is getting married a week from Saturday and Cindy is going with me to the wedding. Seems like it's been one thing after another," Eric said.

"What do I owe you?" Mr. Quinlin said.

"How about a cold beer to go with that shade tree?" Eric replied.

"It's a deal. You do look better than you did a couple of days ago. I'll run you into town whenever you want."

"Terrific dinner," Eric said. "Right, Tyler?"

"Yes, Mother, very good," she said flatly. "I'm going outside."

Eric went outside and wandered over near Tyler. She saw him, and started back toward the house.

"Nice day," he said, when she walked by him.

She kept walking. He relaxed and took off his shirt. A moment later, Patsy joined him.

"Hey Eric, want a soda?" she said.

"No, thank you. I've a beer coming."

"Doesn't beer make you act funny?"

"Sometimes. Especially in my case."

"You've got two chains around your neck. How come you wear them?"

"This one's from Uncle Sam. The other's very special to me."

"From your wife, I'll bet," Patsy said. She searched his face. "I think Tyler likes you."

"She has a funny way of showing it."

"Oh, she's just being a girl."

Eric laughed. "You're something else."

"I was told to bring you this," Tyler said. A red ribbon held back her long, dark hair. Her dark eyes gleamed.

"Why don't you sit with me awhile? For being so damn pretty, I think you're a little bullheaded." Tyler tried not to smile, but her dimples gave her away.

"I'm not bullheaded," she said. "Besides, you shouldn't swear." She sat in the chair next to him.

Patsy joined them, handed Eric a glass, then giggled. "I think Mom and Dad are watching us out the window," she giggled again.

"Patsy, come here a minute," Mrs. Quinlin called.

"Tyler would you like some beer?" Eric asked.

"I don't know, I've never had any." Eric poured a little beer into the glass and handed it back to Tyler. She took a sip and frowned.

"This does taste different. A little tingly." She took another drink. He touched his bottle to her glass.

"Here's to you, kid," Eric said, and grinned.

"You're teasing me again."

"We'd better get back to the house," Tyler said.

"I'm afraid I'm leading your daughter astray," Eric told Mr. Quinlin when they walked in the house. "I gave her a little beer."

"It better only be a little," Mr. Quinlin said.

"Eric, you've a phone call," Mrs. Quinlin said.

"My cousin Bryan and friend Frank are coming to get me," Eric said. "They want to check out my work."

Eric and Mr. Quinlin walked in the yard. "You wanna come to our cookout a week from Sunday?"

"Yes I would like that very much."

After Frank drove up, Eric made the introductions. They chatted. Finally, Frank asked Mr. Quinlin, "How'd he do?"

"He worked hard. I admit I had to whip him into shape, but he made it."

"He looks a lot better than he did a few days ago," Frank said, "He needed it!"

"Eric, you don't have to worry about giving Mrs. Dunley a healing anymore," Bryan interjected. "She's moving out East to be with her sister. I forgot, these people probably don't know about your dreams or healings."

"Bryan!" Frank shouted.

"Not until now," Eric said, with a trace of irritation. "I was going to explain later."

George Quinlin stared at Eric.

CHAPTER SEVENTEEN

FRANK AND BRYAN DROPPED ERIC OFF at his house. The minute Eric walked in the house, Ellen said. "Well, look who's all sunburned and healthy. I think I even detect a smile."

"I feel great. Where's the love of my life?"

"Who?" Ellen asked. Frank and Bryan grinned.

"My daughter." Eric hurried to Ellen's bedroom, only to discover that Colleen was asleep.

"What happened?" Ellen asked.

"After spending time with Patsy, I realized what being a parent really means and how precious Colleen is. I was wrong, you were right—about feeling sorry for myself, I mean," Eric said. "I realized I needed to think of Colleen. I finally got it in my head that rejecting Colleen wasn't going to bring Alice back."

Ellen smiled. "You should've gone out to that farm before."

"That's what Frank said." Colleen woke up and Eric picked her up. "I hope you'll forgive me, little one. I didn't realize how much I've missed you."

"Here's her bottle," Ellen said. "Isn't she beautiful?"

"Yes she is," Eric said softly. "I've been such a fool. She has to understand I was confused and afraid of losing her."

"She does and knows you love her," Ellen whispered. The next two days Eric helped his dad at the shop and spent time with Colleen.

"Eric, did you decide if you're taking anyone to Ted's wedding?" Ellen asked.

"Cindy and I are going together."

Their mother walked into the room "We'll eat in about a half hour."

"I've got to take a shower and shave," Eric said. "Karen and Frank are coming in a little while. Karen wanted to meet Tyler so we're going to get together and go to a movie."

They started dinner when the phone rang. "It's for you, Eric," his mother said.

"*It's off*!" Ted shouted over the phone. "Can you believe it? Marie and I broke up. It didn't work out. I should've known." There was a stunned silence.

"I'm sorry, Ted. Maybe you can work it out."

"No way," he yelled. Eric suspected he was drinking. "You're still coming to the wedding, aren't you?"

"Are you drunk? I thought you said the wedding was off."

"Same wedding, different bride. I asked Nancy to marry me. I told her I thought I had made a big mistake," Ted paused. Eric sensed the disappointment in his voice. "Hello, Eric? Maybe that is the way it should be. I guess you're kinda shocked huh?"

"Yes. You gotta admit it's a little unusual—even for you."

Ted laughed. "See you a week from Saturday. Same time, same place."

"Cindy and I will be there," Eric said.

"Hey, that's great."

"Goodbye, Ted." During dinner, Eric tried to understand, but realized it was impossible. Ted was Ted. He leaned back and lit a cigarette. A few minutes later, he heard Karen and Frank.

"Eric, we're going to have to hurry and pick up Tyler so we don't miss the start of the movie," Karen said.

Patsy answered the door with her usual enthusiasm. "Hi Eric! Tyler's in her room trying to make herself prettier," she giggled. "Is she gonna be your girl now?"

"You're always putting Eric on the spot," Mrs. Quinlin said.

"I'm ready," Tyler said with a smile.

"Have a good time, honey," Mrs. Quinlin said.

Eric and Tyler walked to the car. Eric made the introductions. "Tyler, you've met Frank. This pretty girl is his wife, Karen, who also happens to be my cousin."

"My pleasure, Tyler," Karen said. "I like the way you introduce me Eric."

"By the way, how's Bruce?" Eric asked.

"Great. Mother is watching him so I can have a little time for myself." She turned to Tyler. "Why don't we talk later, and really get acquainted?" Karen said with her usual ability to put anyone at ease.

"I'd like that," Tyler replied.

When the movie finally ended, Karen remarked, "I like a good love story, but it makes me hungry. How about you, Tyler?"

Tyler laughed. "Yes," she said. "It does."

They drove to Cookie's Drive-In, a place near the city limits where malts and hamburgers were special—and tonight was no exception. "You wanna go inside?" Frank asked.

"Sure, Daddy. I want to play the jukebox. I feel like some music," Karen replied.

The place was crowded, as usual. After they found a table, Eric saw Linda and Bill Hausler across the room, huddled together. He avoided looking in their direction.

A little later, he was surprised when he heard Linda's voice over his shoulder. "I guess I owe you an apology," she said.

"We both said things we shouldn't have," Eric said slowly. "I'm sorry, too. How about if we call it even and remain friends?"

"Does that go for me, too?" Bill asked Eric.

"Sounds good to me," Eric replied. He introduced Tyler, and asked Linda and Bill to join them.

"Actually, we've just finished," Bill said.

"So, you're the farmer's daughter," Linda said. "She wouldn't have anything to do with your loading hay, would she?"

Eric grinned. "Let's say she made the job a lot easier." He explained how Patsy, Tyler's little sister, made him realize his feelings for his daughter.

Linda turned to Bill and said, "Eric's daughter is so cute."

After they left, Tyler remarked, "She's very pretty. She looks like a professional model."

"Yes, but she still needs messing up a little," Eric said. Karen laughed out loud, almost spilling her coffee. Tyler looked at Eric strangely. "I don't understand," she said.

"Sorry. It was my attempt at a little humor," Eric said. "Very little."

They drove Tyler home. "I had a nice time tonight," she added.

"Great. I think we both did," Eric said.

When Eric got home, he went to the crib. "Is she up?"

"Sleeping." Ellen put down her novel. "How did it go?"

"Great! I talked with Linda and Bill Hausler. We apologized to each other." Eric glanced at her book. "So you're reading Mike Hammer?"

"Frank encouraged me to read it," Ellen said. "He's talked about it so much. I must say, he's quite a character. As for you and Linda, its good you've made up." She changed the subject. "You know when Johnny walked in the kitchen Christmas Day, I knew he was the one. I don't know why I would mention that now. I guess it's because I had my mind on him a few minutes ago."

"I can understand that," Eric replied.

The following morning, Eric rose early and went to Colleen. Ellen was with her. "I figured maybe I should help," he said.

"You're right, and just in time. You can change her, but this time may be a little different," Ellen said with a knowing smile.

Eric placed his daughter on the bed and removed her diaper. "I see what you mean," he said. "What a mess." He turned his head. Ellen laughed as she took the dirty diaper.

"Wash her, and then sprinkle her little bottom with powder. That's all a part of being a father."

"I know. I think I'm getting the hang of it."

"Eric, there's something different about you," his mother said. "I can feel it. I think it has something to do with your dreams and healings." This was the moment Eric had been dreading. "You know about the crippled little girl, but you don't know about my great-grandfather coming to me in a dream." Eric said. "After talking to dad, I'm convinced the Indian Medicine Man is my great-grandfather."

His mother seemed to be, for a moment, at a loss for words. Finally, she said slowly, "How?" Suddenly she turned to her husband. She stopped when she looked into her husband's eyes.

"I believe my great-grandfather is one of God's instruments," Eric said. "As for the crippled little girl, I can only judge by their messages and my faith."

"I don't know what you expect from Eric," Howard said.

Martha hesitated a moment, then calmly said, "I perceive Eric as a modern-day apostle, a minister and healer representing the highest teachings of the Holy Bible."

Eric shook his head. "Modern day apostle!? Me?"

"My basis is my undying faith," Martha said. "It began the day you were born, and the vision of my mother. As for being spiritually pure, you have only to look at the example of Apostle Paul!"

"I think you're tearing Eric apart with something that's beyond our power to understand!" Howard said.

"Maybe," Martha said. "But I do find communication with your great-grandfather to be something less than a spiritual calling."

"This is something I must make my own decision on," Eric said with a hint of irritation. "I may look into a church that practices spiritual healing."

"I assume you're talking about either the Quinlins' church, or the church in Mayville," his mother said with an edge in her voice. "You're putting your spiritual destiny in the guidance of another human being that has left this world. Now it's another church."

"You're the one who told me I must follow my gift," Eric said. "Remember?" Again, his mother seemed momentarily speechless.

Finally, she whispered, "I'll have to pray about it!" She left the room without another word.

"I'm thinking about putting in for a hardship discharge. I gotta think of my obligation to Colleen. I don't know how long it will take."

"My arthritis is getting worse," his father said, "especially in my hands. How would you like to take over? I'll help for a while until you can make it on your own." He looked into his son's eyes. "It's a good business if you work at it."

"Sounds good Dad, let me think about it. What can you tell me about my great-grandfather? I had a vision of him. I got the impression he was a compassionate man with a great force working through him."

"I don't remember him very well," Howard said. "I was small when he died." He drifted off for a moment, and then he continued: "He was a giant of a man, moody, with a deep voice and big, hearty laugh. I have heard many stories of his healing, and his weakness for whiskey. I feel his gift, if that's what it was, carried many responsibilities and frustrations. Some said the gift was a curse; others, a blessing. I think it's more like a two-edge sword."

"I don't know what to say," Eric said slowly. His father's expression changed only for a moment, and then he said calmly, "I don't envy your pressure, but the choice must be yours. As for the calls and gossip, we'll survive, and I'm sure Karen and Frank will too."

Eric walked through the living room and saw his mother reading the only book that would ever control her life.

———————————

Later, Eric walked to Grover's drugstore, hesitated briefly, and then walked in. "Can I help you?" a young girl asked.

"Coffee," Eric said, "and I'd like to talk to the manager."

"Here's your coffee, sir. I'll get the manager." She hurried away.

When the manager approached, Eric said, "I came to apologize for the other night."

"It should be the other way around. I've been told you tried to walk away," the manager said. He smiled, turned to the girl behind the counter, and said, "Coffee's on me. Don't be such a stranger."

"Thanks." Eric said.

Eric arrived home just as Colleen awoke. He carried her into the kitchen, and she quickly grabbed her bottle. "Look at this," Eric laughed. "She's a regular chowhound."

Eric just finished feeding Colleen and putting her in the bedroom when Frank pulled up. "Mom, I gotta get going, I'm running late," Eric said. "Karen and Frank invited Tyler and me over for dinner."

Eric walked toward the house when Patsy answered the door. "Hi, Eric—I saw you through the window. You taking Tyler out again? You gonna marry her?"

"Come in, Eric," Mr. Quinlin said. "Don't mind her. She's a little wound up tonight."

Patsy sat beside Eric on the couch.

"Patsy, what will we do with you?" Mrs. Quinlin sighed.

"Love me like Eric said," Patsy answered.

After they got in the car, Frank said, "Hello, Tyler, Karen's still fixing dinner."

"I should be helping," Tyler spoke up.

"At the rate she's going, I'm sure you'll get a chance," Frank said.

A few minutes later, they arrived at the apartment. Karen wiped her hands on an apron. "Welcome to our humble apartment," Karen said. "I want to introduce you to our little guy." She led Tyler into the bedroom.

Frank said, "I don't understand about the wedding next Saturday. Ted's marrying this Nancy now?"

"Last I heard." Eric shrugged. "Evidently, Marie was hurt, probably by Ted's parents. He was drinking when I talked to him. If you know Ted, nothing he does will surprise you."

"It's strange, to say the least."

Frank and Eric followed Karen and Tyler in to the bedroom.

"Bruce sure is growing," Eric said. "He's quite a boy."

After dinner, Eric and Frank drank a beer while Karen and Tyler sipped wine. Later, Frank and Eric drove Tyler to her house. Eric walked her to the front door. "It was nice, the dinner, the company—everything. You're spoiling me," Tyler said.

"It's my pleasure," replied Eric.

"Good night, Eric," Tyler said.

Frank and Eric seemed wrapped up in their own thoughts on the way back to town.

———————

When Eric got home, he undressed and slipped under the covers. Alice entered his mind. He wondered whether it was guilt or depression. *"Don't go, Alice! Please, don't go!"*

He jumped when his father shook him. "Wake up!"

"Alice was here, Dad. I know she was. The strange part was she was running, and I still couldn't catch her."

"You were dreaming son," his father said calmly. "Try to go back to sleep. You're still being haunted by dreams. I guess it's only natural, but you shouldn't let them upset you."

Eric lay back and stared at the ceiling until he fell into a deep sleep.

CHAPTER EIGHTEEN

THERE WAS LITTLE CONVERSATION as Eric, Karen, and Frank drove to Cindy's house.

When they arrived at her address, Eric walked up to the little tan bungalow. He knocked and waited. She answered the door, and flashed a rare smile. "How do I look?"

"Stunning, I'd say," Eric said. She wore a lavender dress with a wide-brimmed hat. Everything about Cindy seemed improved, even her attitude. She showed no signs of the emotional upheaval she had survived.

"Why, thank you, Eric. I must say you look different in a suit."

"It's great to see you smiling again," he added.

———

As they pulled in front of the church, Frank asked, "You sure we've got the right place?"

"This is it. Let me check." Eric asked the two men by the church entrance. "Is this the Ted Faulkland wedding?"

"Yes, it's been called off," one of the men said. "We are supposed to send the guests to the American Legion on Sixth Street. It's been strange."

"When was it called off?" Eric asked.

"The wedding was canceled about ten-thirty this morning. Ted seemed relieved. He actually laughed about it. Can you believe it?"

"Knowing Ted," Eric said, "it doesn't surprise me. Thank you." He ran back to the car. "It was called off at the last minute. We're supposed to meet Ted at the Legion hall on Sixth Street. I have no idea what's going on, or what to expect."

"That's terrible," Cindy said. "Poor Ted."

Eric opened the hall door, clearing the way for everyone. The reception appeared to be well under way. Blaring music and air thick with cigarette smoke greeted them as they made their way through the crowded hall. "Hey, Eric!" Ted's familiar voice called as he tried to maneuver between overcrowded tables. "The wedding was canceled, due to lack of interest." He laughed. "Come on in. Eat, drink, and be merry. I paid for this damn thing, and we're gonna enjoy it."

"What happened?" Eric asked.

"What's to say?" Ted slurred. The drink he held was clearly not his first of the evening. "Nancy backed out at the last minute. She said she could tell I was still in love with Marie. You know something? She's right."

"What happened to Marie?"

"My folks—who aren't at this reception, by the way," he shrugged. "Hey! Who is this stunning blond? Cindy, is that you?"

"Yes it's me," Cindy said. "I'm sorry, Ted."

"Don't worry about it. Hey, I will survive. You're really looking sharp tonight, Cindy."

Eric didn't recognize most of the people he met. Soon the faces began to blend.

"Eric, old buddy, live it up. Hell, man, I am glad we're going back Monday . . . I am so sorry about Alice. Cindy and I both cried like a baby when we talked. What's happened to us?"

"I don't know, Ted. Sometimes I wonder myself."

"Hey, the reception's going great," Ted said. "The wedding? That's another story." Ted took another drink. Eric stared at the guy who, a few months earlier, couldn't stand the sight of whiskey. "I'm gonna steal Cindy away for a dance. Hey!" Ted grabbed Eric's arm. "You people get something to eat. We'll join you later."

They worked their way through the crowd to the adjoining room; the banquet tables were covered with a variety of food. "I feel sorry for the guy," Frank said.

"It's unbelievable," Karen said. Cindy and Ted showed up a little later. He was obviously drunk, and Cindy appeared to be on her way.

An hour later, Ted yelled, "Eric, old buddy, do you mind if Cindy and I keep each other company? I don't know if you'll understand this, but we kinda need each other."

Eric looked at Cindy, then Ted. "I do understand Ted. It's up to her. We have to leave soon."

"At least have a drink with us."

Ted poured shots. Frank waved it off. He and Karen had a beer. After they downed their shots, Eric studied Ted for a moment. He didn't know whether it was frustration, pity, or both. He could not believe this was the same guy he pulled out of the train toilet. "One more, Ted and we have to leave."

Cindy's eyes began to glaze over, "Teddy and I both love you," she said. "You know that, don't you Eric?"

"I know—friends forever."

"Eric, I wanna kiss you.

"Hey, you kiss him. I'll shake his hand."

On the way home, everyone seemed quiet. "Do you think Cindy and Ted will make it?" Frank asked.

"I wouldn't bet on it either way. They're a little shaky," Eric said. "I only hope they can comfort each other. We'll all make it one way or the other. We've got to! What choice do we have?"

"Your bitterness is showing, Eric," Karen said. "We'll see you for dinner tomorrow. Good night."

"Good night, Thanks for everything."

Eric opened the front door and walked in the kitchen. Ellen was sitting at the table drinking coffee. Their folks were evidently in bed. He walked into the bedroom and touched Colleen gently and left to join Ellen. She grinned at him. "You appear to have had a couple," Ellen said. Eric poured his coffee and explained what happened at the wedding. Ellen shook her head and said "I've never heard of anything like it. Tyler called earlier. She asked if you could call her back. Eric, are you trying to put Tyler in Alice's place? She's a young girl who could be easily infatuated," Ellen added. "How does she feel about you?"

"To tell you the truth, I have no idea. I haven't really thought about it."

Eric dialed Tyler's number. "Hi Tyler, it's Eric, Ellen said you called earlier."

"Hi Eric, how was the wedding?"

"Very interesting to say the least," Eric explained what happened.

"I was wondering if you would like to go to church with us tomorrow before the cookout. I think you need it."

"I think I'd like that," Eric said.

"We'll pick you up tomorrow morning," Tyler said. "See you then."

At breakfast the next morning, Eric told his mother he was going with the Quinlins to church. "I worry Eric," his mother said. "I've prayed and thought about what you said about being led. The Bible says, 'If you do not use the gift, you lose it.' I wouldn't want that to happen. The only thing I ask is keep praying for guidance. I know you've been through a lot, but it's so important."

"I'll admit I've had second thoughts about the gift since Alice died," Eric said. "I guess I should continue until I can figure things out." His mother seemed to be struggling between a smile of relief and a strange look of concern. Eric heard the Quinlins' car. He hurried out the door without another word.

He climbed in the back seat between Tyler and Patsy. "How lucky can a guy get, sitting between two pretty girls," Eric said, which brought on Patsy's giggling.

A group of people stood outside the church entrance. "Hey, Tyler!" a voice called. A young man with a big smile and curly brown hair joined them. "I've been waiting for you. I got home late last night."

Tyler introduced Eric to Jerry Yount. Jerry took Tyler's hand and said, "You sit with me. I've missed you so much." Jerry turned to Tyler's folks. "My parents and I would like to come over after church. I hope you do not mind. I couldn't wait to see Ty again."

"You're welcome, we're having a cookout," Mr. Quinlin said.

Patsy tugged at Eric's arm. "I'll sit with you."

"I think I'd like that," Eric said. Tyler and Jerry sat near the front of the church. Eric saw her looking at him, and he winked at her. She smiled and turned toward the front. When the sermon ended, Eric noticed a couple people going to stools on opposite sides of the room. There were two other individuals at each stool laying their hands on them. He turned to Mr. Quinlin and asked, "Is that a healing session?"

"Yes," Mr. Quinlin said, then looked closely at Eric. "I wondered about that the other day when your friend mentioned something about healing."

Eric watched the healing sessions closely and with fascination. After the service, Mr. Quinlin introduced him to Reverend Harold Webber. "Maybe we could talk later at the cookout," Webber said.

"My pleasure," Eric said. "I think I'd enjoy it."

The ride back to the Quinlins was uncomfortably quiet. Even Patsy appeared to be lost in her own thoughts. Finally, Tyler broke the silence by saying, "I didn't know Jerry was home."

"Tell him I'm just someone helping with the hay," Eric said. "I won't embarrass you." Eric suddenly wondered what he was doing here, he felt an uneasiness. Why would he feel threatened by Tyler's boyfriend? Eric started to think about what Ellen said, was he trying to put Tyler in Alice's place?

After they arrived at the house, Tyler hesitated and then said, "He's the boy I told you about. We had a fight before he left."

"How do you feel about him?" Eric asked.

"We were going steady before he left for college." Tyler looked down. "I'm not really sure." She watched a car drive in the yard. "They're here." The minute the young man got out of the car, he ran to Tyler. He took her hand in his.

"You still hanging around here?" he asked Darryl.

"Eric and I helped with the hay."

"Excuse us," Eric said. He grabbed Darryl by the arm, and they walked away. "If I could, I'd gracefully leave," Eric told Darryl. "This situation's all mixed up. It's a good thing I'm leaving. It's better this way."

"I don't know what to say," Darryl replied.

Patsy ran up to Eric and Darryl. "Time to eat. You two can sit with me." Most of the other guests were already seated.

Reverend Webber approached their table. "Mind if I join you? I finally figured out where I heard the name before. I'll admit it's a rumor, but there was something about a soldier who gave a healing to a woman in the hospital. Am I correct?"

"Yes," Eric said. Everyone at the nearby table stared at him.

"That's very commendable," the reverend said, then bowed his head. "Now the name's very familiar. I'm sorry about your wife."

"I can't picture you as a healer, Eric," Jerry said, watching Tyler's reaction.

"I can," Mrs. Quinlin interrupted. "I can't explain it, but somehow it doesn't surprise me."

"Silkwin," Mr. Yount said. "Weren't you the soldier who started the trouble at Grover's recently?"

"Yes," Eric said softly.

"They called the police," Mrs. Yount said. "It just doesn't seem to fit the image I'd imagine a spiritual healer to have."

Eric held back the sudden resentment he felt. "That's true," he replied. He noticed the surrounding people listening. "The death of my wife and best friend sent me into a troubled period. I drank out of depression and frustration. Now I'm trying to get my life together, especially for my daughter's sake. It isn't easy."

"Sometimes a sudden shock drives a person to desperation. Have you talked with a minister?" Mrs. Yount asked.

"Yes," Eric said. "They didn't seem to have the answers. Actually, it was this young lady who helped me realize my love for my daughter." He patted Patsy's head.

"Out of the mouths of babes," the reverend quoted.

"Who's taking care of your daughter?" Mrs. Yount asked.

"My sister and my mother." Eric hesitated a moment, then added, "I called the base last week and got an extension on my furlough. I'm putting in for a hardship discharge."

Mrs. Yount continued, "You couldn't have been in the service long. It seems strange you would enlist when you knew you were going to be a father."

Mr. Quinlin interrupted quickly. "I think we should let him off the hook for a while. His food's getting cold."

Eric nodded his appreciation. A little later, he saw Frank's car coming up the driveway. He noticed Karen was looking out the car window.

"I'll say goodbye now. My friends are here to pick me up. My folks planned a dinner this evening, and I want to go by the cemetery before I leave." Eric shook hands with Mr. Quinlin.

"Thanks for helping. You know you're always welcome," he said.

"Thanks for giving me a feeling of belonging," Eric said to Mrs. Quinlin. "Your family helped me at a trying time in my life."

Patsy came up to Eric, with a tear in her eye. "Is this goodbye?"

"Just for a little while, but I'll see you again. Remember what I told you." Eric bent over to kiss Patsy's forehead.

"I promise," she whispered.

"Darryl, thanks for being a friend."

Darryl nodded and said, "Goes double for me."

Eric looked Tyler in the eye. "I would like to kiss you too, but I won't embarrass you. I'll just shake hands."

"Well! I never heard of such a thing," Mrs. Yount said abruptly. "The nerve!"

Tyler's mouth opened, but no sound came. Suddenly, Eric turned and started across the yard toward the car. He heard her voice behind him,

"Eric," Tyler ran to meet him. "Wait! It's important you realize I'm not Alice!" she exclaimed. "I can't be her for you!"

"I know." Eric put his arms around her, and kissed her softly on the cheek. "It took me awhile. You knew all the time, didn't you?"

"Yes," she said, and slowly looked up at him.

"I hope you and Patsy will write to me," Eric said.

"We will," she said. "There are things about me you don't know. I'm very serious!"

Eric grinned. "I'll be looking forward to finding out." She turned and walked slowly back to the house.

"The boyfriend came back, I would guess, I saw a young man with his arm around Tyler," Karen said after Eric climbed in the car.

"It's for the best," Eric said. "I'm not ready to get involved."

"That makes sense, I was afraid you might—"

"Give me a few minutes at the cemetery; I have to talk to Alice before I leave."

Karen shook her head. The ride to the cemetery was silent. When Frank pulled in the entrance, a feeling in his gut stirred again. The car pulled around the circular drive and stopped. Nobody spoke for a moment. Then Eric said, "I won't be long."

"Take your time. We understand," Frank said.

Eric stood before the grave. The flowers were dead, like the hollow, empty feeling inside him. His mind flashed back to the funeral. *Has it been almost three weeks?*

"Alice, I miss you so much. I'm having a hard time figuring things out. Today is the day Colleen was suppose to be born. When you died, I felt the healing gift had failed me. I seem to be torn between the church, the family, and the healing gift." Clouds moved in and the sun faded away. "It looks like it's gonna rain. I'm a little nervous because I'm about to leave you."

Eric stared at the headstone, as if he was seeing it for the first time. "This is where I say goodbye." He bowed his head, and whispered, "Watch over our little one for me. Until then."

He walked slowly toward the car. "Is everything all right?" Karen said. "I guess that is a stupid thing to ask. I'm sorry."

"Saying goodbye to Colleen will be the roughest. I'm going to miss her so."

"It shouldn't be long before your discharge," Frank said.

"I hope you're right," Eric said. "That's what I have to keep in mind."

When they arrived at his house, Eric noticed Bryan's car. The minute Eric got out of the car, he said to Bryan, "No discussions tonight, I'm not in the mood."

Bryan said, "I just wanted to see you before you left."

Eric said, "I'm just a little uptight tonight."

Bryan tried a smile. "I do understand."

"We're all leaving right after dinner, so you can spend time with Colleen," Karen promised. "Don't worry. We'll watch over things."

The telephone interrupted the almost complete silence at the dinner table. His mother motioned for Eric. It was Linda.

"Hi Eric, I realize you are probably having dinner, but I wondered if I could drop over for a couple of minutes," she said. "I wanted to see the baby before you leave. That is, if it's not too much trouble."

"I'd like that Linda," Eric said.

"I'll see you in a few minutes," Linda replied.

Eric hung up and returned to the dinner table. "Linda's coming over to see Colleen—and hopefully me—before I leave."

"I'm glad you two are friends again," Eric's father said.

Bryan turned to Eric. "What about Alice's folks?" Karen stared at Bryan.

"I'd hoped they were doing better." Eric said. "I haven't seen them for a while. I wish I would have stopped over there and let them know they are welcome to visit Colleen anytime."

"Eric, don't worry," Ellen said. "I will talk to them."

"That's good," Eric said. "Right now I'm having mixed feelings anyway. Keep me posted on any crank calls, or anything else along that line."

"We will. It's not that bad. We'll work it out," Frank said.

"It's just that sometimes," Bryan added, "I think all this could have been avoided." When Eric refused to respond, Bryan continued, "I've had a few incidents at work. It's those guys you tangled with at Grover's—Dexter and Ilders, they work in the shop at Mullaird's. Buck Dexter is named after the late cowboy star Buck Jones. Can you believe it!"

"We have to be going," Karen said. She grabbed Bryan by the elbow. A few minutes later, Karen, Bryan, and Frank left.

"She's awake, Eric," Ellen said softly. "Take over."

"All right. In about an hour, that young lady and I are going to have a father-daughter talk. I want her complete attention."

Ellen smiled. "I think that'd be good for both of you." The knock at the door startled them. "It's probably Linda. I'll get it," Ellen said.

"Hey Linda! Look what I've got," Eric said. "Would you like to feed her?"

She looked from Ellen to Eric, then smiled. "Yes, I would," she said.

"Here, put this blanket on your lap, just in case," Ellen said.

Eric laughed. "Look at her, what a chowhound. You're looking sharp Linda."

"You mean not a hair out of place?"

Eric returned her smile. "Something like that. You look great holding a baby. You should have one."

"I'd better get married first. Oh, I mean—"

"Linda, it's all right. Don't be so sensitive. I just thought if you needed any help."

Ellen almost dropped her glass, but managed to say, "Shame on you Eric!" even though Ellen and Linda both smiled.

"All kidding aside, you'd make a beautiful mother."

"I consider that a compliment," Linda said.

"It was meant to be." Eric said sincerely.

She looked down at Colleen and said, "Bye, little sweetheart."

"You never talk to me that way."

"Oh, Eric, what shall I do with you?" The minute she said that, her face got red, and she got that familiar look on her face.

"You open for suggestions?" Eric asked.

Linda only smiled and kissed Eric's cheek. "Good luck, and you behave yourself."

"I'll do my best. You take care of yourself, Linda. Remember what I said about good things working out for nice people."

"I want to believe that," she said slowly.

She flashed her fabulous smile just before Ellen walked her to the door.

When Ellen returned, she noticed Eric seemed to be unusually quiet.

"You know that Silkwin edge," Ellen said, "You know what I mean, that supreme feeling of confidence you used to have. I haven't heard you mention that for awhile."

"I'm afraid that "Silkwin edge feeling" is going to take a little more time," Eric replied slowly.

CHAPTER NINETEEN

"YOU LOOK AHEAD, ERIC," HIS MOTHER SAID. "No matter what I've said, or the way I feel, the important thing is trust in your Bible. In all honesty, you made me aware of some things I should have known. I've apologized to your father. I should have never judged his grandfather. Who are we to judge God's plan? I guess we have to stumble and fall and pick ourselves back up and go with what we've learned."

"Look who's awake," Ellen said as she brought Colleen into the kitchen. "I'll bet she was waiting for her daddy."

When Eric looked at her, he felt a lump in his throat. He took her gently in his arms. "You and me, honey. We have to have a talk. Look at her smile. She can almost steal your heart away."

"She already has mine," Ellen said.

"If you'll excuse us," Eric said, feeling his eyes misting over, "I wanna lay down the law." He propped her up on the bed.

"Here, let me help you." Ellen bunched the pillows together and placed the baby in the middle. "I'll let you two talk."

"It's just you and I, kid," Eric said. "Losing your mother was the hardest thing I've ever had to face. I've had a difficult time coping with it, but I'll tell you all about that sometime when we can both handle it."

"I don't like to intrude," Ellen said, "but the young lady needs this if you're going to keep her attention."

Eric placed the bottle in her mouth. "Another thing," he said. "I love you very much. You are the most important person in my life. The hard part is going to be explaining what your mother was really like. I have the strongest feeling she's with us now." He hesitated a moment, then added, "I wonder if you can see her? I hope so, because it's so important to me." He watched a trace of a smile when he took the bottle out of her mouth.

Ellen came to the door. "Eric, it's late," she said. "Colleen knows you love her."

"I know. Your daddy will be home soon. I love you, little one." He kissed her forehead softly. "Until then." After saying goodbye to everyone, Eric walked toward the bus station.

Eric glanced at his watch, then walked into Mabel's Cafe and said, "A fast cup of coffee, please. I've got ten minutes, tops."

Rita glanced at him, and grinned. "How's that daughter of yours?"

"Your prayers have been answered, Rita. I finally realized what a fool I've been."

"I'm happy for both of you. The old man and I got our marriage together. Thanks for my life, Eric. I mean that."

"You're welcome, lady. I've gotta run. Uncle Sam is calling. With your prayers, I think we're even." With that, Eric went out the door.

The rain started just as the bus pulled in. Eric turned up his collar and hurried toward it.

The driver quickly took his bags and Eric boarded the crowded bus. He took the first window seat he came to. When the bus pulled around the corner, he looked back and waved to the curly-headed, blue-eyed girl who he knew would be waving back.

A picture of Alice flashed through his mind with a clarity that surprised him. He leaned back in his seat when the woman next to him spoke. "I'll bet you're waving goodbye to a special girl," she said softly. "I didn't notice anyone out there."

"She's there all right. She's my wife. We always say goodbye at the station," Eric said.

"It must be difficult saying goodbye."

"Yes it is." He leaned back and tried to relax, but Alice's words haunted him. *"I am not going to cry. I am a trouper who's saying goodbye to her husband."*

Eric cried for her, and then whispered. "Until then."

"Wyler in five minutes," the driver called. Eric looked out the window. The minute the bus pulled in the station, Cindy boarded the bus. "Just a minute, driver. This is important. Eric, where are you?"

Eric yelled over the noise of the passengers. "Over here."

She rushed up to him. "I'm not going. This letter will explain. Pray for me, and I will do the same for you. Write when you can."

She quickly kissed him, and then hurried off the bus. He tucked the letter in his pocket, and thought about Jason.

"Cutler City, ten minutes," the driver called. Eric snapped out of his daydream. He picked up his bag and looked around for Ted, then walked to the train station. "How soon does the train leave for Dennard, Texas?" Eric asked.

"In about twelve minutes," the ticket agent said gruffly. Then, he tried to smile. "I'm sorry. It's been a bad day."

"It's all right," Eric said. "I've had a few of those myself lately."

Finally, Ted rushed in. "That was close," he said, stopping to catch his breath. They put their bags away and settled back for the trip just as the train pulled out. "How's your daughter?" Ted asked.

"She's fine, but that's not what you really want to talk about, is it?"

"We'll talk later." Even Ted's boyish grin did not work. The little-boy look was gone.

Eric leaned back and lit a cigarette. Ted stared out the window. It was still raining, which added to the gloom.

"Let's grab these seats," a young man called to a couple of friends. He glanced at Eric and Ted, noticing their uniforms. "I wonder what Landish Air Force base is like," the first guy said to the others as they settled in.

"We're in. I guess we'll find out soon enough," The next one added. They stared at Ted and Eric, whispering among themselves.

"Just a year ago, those guys were me, you, and Jason," Ted said. "Strange, isn't it? The things that have happened since then."

Eric tried to smile, but his mood would not let it happen. "I hope they have better luck than we've had," was all he could say.

"I do, too. The club car should be open soon, if my memory serves me right," Ted glanced at his watch. A few minutes later, the porter took their orders. "I'm going to ask Marie to marry me; regardless of circumstances. I love her."

"Sounds reasonable," Eric said. "You and Nancy through?"

"Yes. I will not sweat out whether she is pregnant or not this time. If she is, it can't be mine." The porter brought their sandwiches and coffee. "I told my parents I was going to see Marie."

"Are you going to marry her in Texas?" Eric asked.

"If she'll have me. I should have done it in the first place. I knew Cindy was not going with us. I'll tell you about that later," Ted added.

"She gave me a letter," Eric said. "I hope she gets herself together."

"I prayed for you when Alice died," Ted said. The familiar misty-eyed look came over him, and then he added, "I knew how much you loved her."

"There are times when she's with me," Eric said. "I know it."

"If I could just believe things like that, I'd be happier."

They settled back and sipped beers. Ted started to speak his mind. "The night my wedding was canceled, Cindy and I stayed together in a hotel room. Both of us were drunk and, in our own way, trying to console each other."

He stopped for a second to clear his thoughts. "Nothing happened, Eric. I was trying to take a shower—just trying." He smiled, then quickly changed his expression. "I came out of the bathroom and she threw her arms around me, her eyes had a strange glazed look. Then she cried, 'Jason, Jason!' After crying out his name, she passed out. I ran back in the bathroom and got sick. I waited a few minutes, and went back in the room. She was asleep, so I climbed in bed and cried like a baby. I lay there until dawn, trying to think things through."

The three young men came in. Ted looked at them and said with a grin, "I wonder if they have any idea what they're facing."

"They'll find out soon," Eric said.

"Excuse me, corporal," one of the guys said. "You two from Landish Air Force Base?" Slowly, the other two joined him.

"Yes," Eric said. "I assume you guys are headed that way?"

"How is it?" One of the guys asked.

"It's not that bad," Ted said. "Basic's a little rough, but not as bad as you expect. Do not worry. You'll make it."

"Let's get a beer," one of the guys said. "We'd better live it up while we got a chance."

Eric smiled. "We know how you guys feel. Not long ago we were facing the same thing. I wish you the best of luck."

All three nodded. The recruits got a table, evidently living for the moment.

"One more, then I'm going back," Eric said.

"You mind if I hang around? Maybe I'll join those guys."

"No, go ahead. I'm going to try and get some rest," Eric said, and then he laughed, "Remember, I'm not going to try to get you out of the toilet."

"I think I can handle it a little better now," Ted said. "I will not be long; I just want to talk to those guys for a few minutes."

Eric relaxed. He took Cindy's letter out of his pocket.

> *Dear Eric,*
>
> *Going to Texas would not solve my problems. That is something I have to do myself. I know that now. We know what it is to lose our loved one.*
>
> *I met someone last week. He seems like a nice guy, but I've been through this before. I'm going to take time to heal, so we'll have to take one day at a time. I need your friendship and strength.*
>
> *Eric, you have to be the strong one. You and Ted were so close to Jason that I could not deal with it being around you two. I finally realized that.*

Ted will probably tell you about it.
P.S. Ted needs your help too.
As Always, Cindy

Eric stared out the window. He saw a few lights from an occasional farmhouse every now and then—a small town or two to break up the darkness.

"Those guys are a little nervous," Ted said when he returned.

"I'm gonna put in for a hardship discharge. My daughter and my dad need me," Eric said.

"You kinda caught me off guard with this discharge thing, but I can understand. What does it feel like—being a father, I mean?"

"It's hard to describe. There's nothing else like it. It's special."

"I'm gonna put the pressure on Marie to marry me right away. No waiting around for anything or anybody. If we're lucky, we can have a baby, too."

"I can only wish you and Marie the best," Eric said.

The next morning, when Eric awoke, Ted was not there. He shaved, cleaned up, and headed to the dining car.

"I thought I'd have a cup of coffee," Ted said, "then wake you for breakfast."

"Are you ready to order?" Eric asked.

"Yes." Ted looked at him and whispered, "You were moaning in your sleep. I heard you a couple times." Eric did not answer, so Ted continued, "You were calling out to Alice. You mumbled something about the little one. I felt like I was eavesdropping."

"I read Cindy's letter," Eric said, ignoring Ted's comment. "She said to be with us would remind her too much of Jason. She's probably right."

"I gotta go along with that." The hours passed quickly, it wasn't long before the train pulled in.

They watched the three recruits ready to face reality. Eric and Ted boarded the regular bus going into town.

"How about dropping in at Monsento Rose?" Eric asked.

"I like the way you think," Ted said, and added a big grin.

Eric opened the restaurant door. When Ted saw Marie, his eyes lit up. They sat at the counter where she couldn't avoid them. When Marie saw them, a smile crossed her face. "Hello, Eric. I was so sorry about your wife. My heart went out to you."

"Thank you," Eric replied.

Ted wandered over to the jukebox, and soon the soothing voice of Nat King Cole filled the restaurant.

"Hello, Marie," Ted said.

She turned slowly to look at him. "Hello, Ted. How are you?"

"So much in love with you I can't stand it." Although the restaurant was not crowded, a couple at the counter looked their way and smiled.

A slight redness filled Marie's face. "Please Ted, we're not exactly alone. Besides, I believe we had this discussion before. It wouldn't work out, there's too much against us."

"Marie—see me, not my family. *I'm* the one who loves you. Do you really think my family should have control over both our lives? I had to grow up and realize what my life would be without you. I haven't thought of anything else except you. Marry me—if you still love me."

The couple finished and Marie went to the cash register and took care of their check. When she returned, she looked into Ted's eyes.

"I love you Marie," Ted said. "If you don't accept my proposal, I don't know what I'll do. You know I can do some pretty crazy things sometimes." Ted smiled and attempted to get on his knees.

Her smile finally surfaced. "I'm well aware of that . . . Teddy! Don't you dare get on your knees!"

He straightened up for a moment and looked Marie in the eye. "I gotta have an answer now," he said. "I'm not kidding around."

Marie's smile broke through. "All right! When and where?"

"As soon as possible, wherever you want."

Eric calmly drank his coffee and watched the two of them go back and forth.

"I take marriage very seriously," she said.

"So do I, honey. Where do you want to hold the wedding?"

"It'd mean a lot to me to be married by a priest," Marie said.

Ted thought for a moment and said, "I'll make the arrangements."

"Nice to see you again Marie," Eric said. "I'm glad this is settled. You don't know what I've been putting up with."

"Oh, I got an idea," she said, matching Ted's smile. "How's that daughter of yours?"

"She's wonderful. The love of my life."

CHAPTER TWENTY

ERIC STOOD AT ATTENTION before Lieutenant Shredder. "Corporal Eric Silkwin reporting for duty, sir."

"At ease, Silkwin," Shredder said. He looked up slowly. "I was sorry to hear about your wife."

"Thank you, sir. I need to put in for a hardship discharge," Eric replied. "I have a three week-old daughter who needs me."

"I understand. Would this be considered an emergency?"

"Yes, sir. My sister works and takes care of her at night and my mother in the daytime. They have more than they can handle."

"I'll go through channels and notify you when we can start processing. In the meantime, report at zero eight-hundred hours for regular duty. Dismissed."

"Yes, sir," Eric said. He saluted.

He went to the barracks and unpacked. Parris and Deakes came over to express their sympathy. It was an awkward time. "We have to get ready for duty. Hang in there. We'll see you later," Deakes said.

Eric glanced at the bunk next to him. He wondered how Snively was doing. A few minutes later, Sergeant Higgins entered the barracks with one of the new guys he saw on the train. The sergeant introduced Private First Class Larry Damon.

The look on the newcomer's face told the frustrated story. After the sergeant had left, Eric said, "I know how you feel. A few months ago, I was in the same position."

The weak smile told him it did not help. "This isn't what I expected," Damon said. "I guess I'd better unpack. I'm going on duty in the morning. I surely never expected anything like this."

"If I can be of any help, let me know. I'll see you later." Eric walked out of the barracks toward the PX. He had some coffee, wondering why he was stalling. He dialed a familiar number. "Hello, Gail," he said.

"Eric! I was wondering about you. I'm so sorry about Alice. When can I see you?"

He hesitated a moment, then said, "I'm off until tomorrow morning. How about a beer and some small talk?"

"I'll meet you at the bus station," she said.

When the bus pulled in, Gail ran to him. "I'm so glad you're back. I missed you so much. Tell me about your baby."

"She's a cute, curly-headed beauty. She has her mother's eyes, and I think she's terrific."

Gail took hold of Eric's hand. "Libby got married last week. The only thing she told me was that she was crazy about the guy—and it just happened!"

"I'm glad to hear it. She deserved a break. By the way, can't you do anything about this weather? It's in the nineties."

Her only reaction was a big smile.

They went to the Bull Head Lounge and sat at their familiar booth. Eric ordered beers. "Tell me what's been going on with you. You just finished school, didn't you?"

"Yes. I am happy with my grades, and I am looking for a good job. My ex-husband finally made it. He still has his feet on the ground, but I think he is still interested in me. He is coming back in two or three weeks. His job is very demanding. I want you to meet him."

"It'll be my pleasure," Eric said. Gail did not volunteer what his job was, and Eric did not ask.

"What do you say I cook for you this evening," Gail said. "I know you're going to say we are already out, but it's something I want to do. I'm lonesome, Eric. If I asked you about Alice, would it hurt you?"

237

"No. I've been through hell. I'm on my way back. When Alice died, I flipped out. I feel I lost a part of me. My mother and sister are taking care of Colleen until I can get a hardship discharge."

"A discharge?"

Eric took in the expression on her face then looked down at his glass. "I'm going to take over my father's shoe repair shop. It's nothing as exciting as journalism."

"At least you have a job," Gail said.

Eric lit a Camel and looked into her eyes. "You're just out of school," he said. "You should give yourself a chance."

"I guess you're right," Gail said. "Let's get some beer and take it to my apartment."

"All right, but I'm paying. I insist. You cook, and we'll have it made."

She seemed unusually quiet until they arrived at her apartment. "Just set the groceries on the table," she whispered. "You know, sometimes I like to be held."

Eric lit a cigarette. This was something he did not want to deal with. She moved closer. He took her in his arms and she kissed him. Suddenly, he pulled away. "What's the matter?" she said.

"I'm sorry," he said slowly.

"I understand," Gail said. "I guess we'd better get busy fixing dinner." Eric watched her fight the tears in her eyes. She walked to the kitchen.

"It's me, not you," Eric said. "Can't you see that?"

"I'm trying to," Gail said. "I really am."

"Marie and Ted are getting married soon," Eric said, quickly changing the subject. "How'd you like to go to their wedding?"

"I think I would like that very much," she said slowly.

Dinner was tense, but after a few minutes, Gail's smile broke through. They kidded around and ended up washing dishes together. Finally, she turned to face him. "I don't expect you to fall in love with me, but sometimes I just get lonely."

Eric did not answer for a minute, and then he looked into her eyes, and took her in his arms. "We all do, Gail. Believe me, we all do."

"Maybe you'd better leave soon. It has been a nice day, and I do not want to spoil it. We are good company for each other, aren't we?"

"Yes. That's for sure." Just before starting out the door, he added, "Remember, we have this wedding."

"I'm looking forward to it." She tried to smile, but her tears were in the way.

The ride back to the base gave him a chance to think about his life. He could almost see his life unfolding before him. It was not going to be easy.

When Eric returned to the barracks, it wasn't long before Deakes walked over to his bunk. "There's a rumor you're putting in for a hardship discharge. You'll make it."

"The rumor's true," Eric told him.

Larry Damon joined Deakes and Eric. "I hope things work out for you. I just heard about your wife. I'm sorry about unloading on you. And I thought I had problems."

The following week Eric fell into a routine. He opened the letter from Tyler, and a good feeling came over him.

> *Dear Eric,*
>
> *This is my first letter to you. I feel a little strange about it. I hope you will bear with me. Patsy and I both miss you. She's already wondering when you're coming home. We are all working on the farm. Patsy's out of school and she says we have to look in on Colleen. I know how much you must miss her. I wanted you to know, I am seriously thinking about going back with Jerry to enroll in college. I feel this is something I must try and this would be my only chance.*
>
> *We are thinking of you, Tyler & Patsy.*

"Hey, Eric!" Ted's voice sounded throughout the barracks. "The wedding's set! It'll be a Catholic ceremony here on the base in about two weeks." The little-boy smile returned. "You are going to be my best man?"

"I'd be honored."

"It's been a while since I've felt this happy," Ted carried on. "We love each other too much for anything else to happen." Eric noticed Ted looking into his eyes for some kind of verification.

"You belong together," Eric said.

"Anything going on with you and Gail?"

"Just friends," Eric said. "There's this girl—Tyler."

Ted smiled. "I hope it works out for you. Hey Eric, I want to see us both happy. We have it coming. That's not too much to ask, is it?"

"No, it isn't," Eric said.

"I've gotta go on duty. You heard anything about your discharge?"

"Not yet. It may take a while. I'll just stick it out and get this buddy of mine married."

Ted beamed. "I'll see you later."

Eric read the postcard from Ellen.

Dear Eric,

I know you are wondering about Colleen, so I am dropping a few lines to let you know. She is doing great. She is laughing, and really starting to fill out. In fact, she is a little on the chubby side, but cute as ever. She says she loves her daddy, and misses him. I will close, with the thought you will be home soon.

Love from Ellen and Colleen

P.S. The Dawshers are doing better.

———————

The next week, attention revolved around Marie and Ted. Their wedding was closing in fast. Gail seemed to be in a better mood, with her ex-husband coming the following week. Eric decided to write to Tyler.

Dear Tyler,

I miss you and Patsy, too. Be sure to tell her she is with me in thought. My buddy is getting married a week from this Saturday. I think it is for real this time.

240

I hope so. They belong together. I understand how you feel about school and I'm glad you're not afraid to express yourself with me. It is important to me. I know you will make the right decision and whatever that may be, I will be happy for you.

I'm closing with you on my mind.

Eric

The following week, Eric stood beside a very nervous Ted Faulkland.

The ceremony was about to begin. "Do I look all right?" Ted said. "Check me out. I will be glad when this is over."

Eric laughed. "You look great," he said. "Relax. You'll make it."

Marie was striking as she walked slowly down the aisle. She never looked lovelier. Ted beamed as they stood together.

When the ceremony was over, the light in her eyes highlighted Marie's happiness.

"You're beautiful," Eric said softly. "I could hardly wait to kiss the bride. Ted's a lucky man."

The blush was one of happiness. "Thank you, Eric," she said softly.

Eric turned to Gail. "You look pretty sharp yourself, lady." Her only reaction was a smile mixed with sudden tears.

"I've a three-day pass," Ted said a little later. He held onto Marie's hand as if she would suddenly vanish. "We're going away. I'm not saying where."

Later the group went to the Avalon, Dennard's local nightclub.

"Would you like to dance, Gail?" Eric asked.

"I like it when you hold me," she whispered.

A little later, Ted asked, "Mind if I cut in?"

"Not if I can dance with the bride," Eric replied.

Eric and Marie moved out on the dance floor. "I married Ted because I love him. There's going to be trouble with his family,"

241

Marie whispered. "I'll deal with it. I only hope Ted is strong enough to stand his ground."

"Don't worry. He will be. He had to go through some things to make him realize what your love means to him. You love each other—that's the difference."

"I only hope that's true," Marie replied.

"Tell you what, I'm going to pass on some of my Silkwin confidence," Eric said. "I lost it for a while, but I'm trying very hard to get back."

Marie laughed. "I've heard about that. I will ask Ted to tell me more. We're going to need all the help we can get."

"I wish you both the best happiness possible." Eric embraced them, and then shook Ted's hand when they were ready to leave.

Gail and Eric strolled toward her apartment. "My ex called me. We're going to try to make our relationship work. I think I've always loved him."

"Hang in there. The best is yet to come," Eric said. "Anything worthwhile has to be fought for."

The next couple weeks, Eric followed routine. He was getting impatient. It had been over a month. After a long and exhausting day, he entered the barracks. He felt depressed until an excited Deakes called him. "Eric, you're supposed to report to the orderly room." A big smile surfaced. "This may be it."

"I'm on my way!" Eric said, and added a silent prayer.

"Corporal Silkwin," Lieutenant Shredder said. "Your discharge finally came through. You have to report to Captain Maingler at the base hospital. You should be able to get out of here very soon." Shredder stood to shake hands. "I hope things work out for you. Good luck, Silkwin. Dismissed."

"Thank you, sir."

"Take these papers and get over there right away."

―――――――――

"Corporal Silkwin reporting as ordered, sir."

"At ease, Silkwin," the captain said. "Relax. Your physical covered everything, unless you're aware of anything else—physically, I mean."

"None, sir." The officer signed his papers.

"Give these to your company commander. You're then free to leave."

"Thank you, sir," Eric said. He rushed the papers to the orderly room and turned in his equipment. Eric picked up the phone and called home. "Ellen, this is Eric, I only have a few minutes, I just wanted to let everyone know I am on my way home. I just got my discharge. I should be home the next day or so."

"That's great," Ellen said. "I'll see you then."

He packed what few things he was taking with him and went to see Ted. Eric realized he was about to face the hardest part of leaving. The glow of the honeymoon was still on Ted's face. He looked happier than Eric had ever seen him.

"Marie and I—we're very happy," Ted said. "You'd think we were still on our honeymoon. It's partly thanks to you."

"That's great. You know I'm happy for both of you. I'm *out,* Ted."

Eric watched the expression on Ted's face change. His smile slowly vanished, as if he had not understood. "You mean you're discharged?"

"Yes. I have been going through processing all day. I'm leaving later tonight."

"So soon? Listen to me. I'm sorry, Eric. It seems so sudden. Naturally I'm happy for you, it's just that—"

"I know. It happened all at once."

"At least we can have dinner together and a couple farewell drinks," Ted said slowly, "I'll get somebody to change shifts."

"I'd like that. I'll meet you at my barracks. I have a few loose ends. I'll see you a little later."

Eric finished the last details, turned in his bedding, and checked everything. Finally, Ted walked in. "I'm ready. You've only got this one bag?" Ted asked.

"Yeah. I think it's all I'm going to need. I turned in the rest to supply."

Their ride into town was a strange mixture of joy and sadness. After all this time, it was still hard to know what to say. "Ted, what're you doing here?" Marie asked.

"Eric got his discharge. He is leaving tonight. I thought we'd have dinner together."

Marie stared at Eric. "You're leaving tonight?"

"Yes. Listen—I gotta call the train station. You both look terrific." He returned moments later. "I've got about an hour and a half."

"You can call Gail, and we can have dinner here," Marie said. "Then a couple beers at the Bull Head Lounge."

A few minutes later, Eric returned. "She doesn't answer, she must be working."

Throughout dinner, the conversation was tense. It seems like there was so much to say and so little time. Eric was surprised when he looked at his watch. Suddenly the time was slipping away.

They entered the lounge and headed back to their familiar booth. "Evidently Gail's still not home. She isn't answering the phone at her apartment. You'll have to say goodbye for me. I hope she gets it together."

"I know what going home means to you. I just hate to see you leave," Ted said slowly. "All the times we've had. Through it all, even when times weren't the greatest, we had each other. They'll always be special."

"I know what you mean Ted. I'll never forget them either. You and Jason will always be a special part of my life," Eric said, then glanced at his watch. "I've gotta be leaving. Keep in touch. You know where I am. You are both very special to me. The minute you know you're coming home, call me."

"We will. Bye, Eric." Ted extended his hand. "It won't be the same."

"Just for a while," Eric said. He shook hands with Ted and put his arms around Marie. She kissed him. "We'll pray for you," she whispered.

Eric picked up his bag and glanced around at the familiar lounge. The sounds and memories closed in on him with amazing clarity. For a moment or two he could almost hear Jason's laughter. Before going out the door, the last thing he saw was a misty-eyed Marie and Ted with their arms around each other. He half-waved and quickly left.

Eric boarded the train with the feeling of joy and depression. The memories, good and bad, flowed through his mind like a succession of snapshots.

The train rumbled through the night. He leaned back and tried to relax, watching lights from the farmhouses and the sleepy little towns. "I hope I never have to say goodbye again to those whose lives are so important to me," he thought.

The minute Eric got off the bus, he took the familiar walk to his father's shop.

"Eric, we're happy you're home," his father said. "And this time, for good."

"It feels great. How's everybody?"

His father flashed a big grin. "Doin' good. Colleen's fine, she is healthy and growing like she's in a hurry. The Quinlins were here a few days ago. Frank stopped in this morning and asked about you. I guess his father's pretty sick. Anyway, he wanted you to call him when you got home. I'm ready to lock up."

When they arrived at the house, his mother hugged him and said, "I do believe there's a young lady in the next room waiting for you."

Eric felt butterflies in his stomach. He picked up Colleen and held her close. "Your daddy's home, honey. If you only knew how much I missed you." He carried her into the living room. The minute Ellen entered the house, she put her arms around him. "Welcome home, little brother. You look great."

"How's Johnny?" Eric asked.

"He doing all right. Marking time, he calls it," Ellen said, "He said he was due to come home in the next few weeks."

Their mother broke into a big smile and said, "Everybody coming home. That's good."

"That's great," Eric said. "Guess I'd better call Frank."

"Eric, I need to talk to you," Frank said on the other end of the line. "Karen and I will be over right away."

The minute they entered the house, Frank said, "I hate to bother you when you just got home, but my dad's sick. He's in the hospital. I wouldn't have known, except they called me." He hesitated a moment then he added, "You know my dad and I are not exactly on the best of terms."

"I tried to get Frank to go see him," Karen said. "But so far he won't listen to me."

"You should," Eric said.

Frank stared at Karen, then Eric. "You don't know what you're asking. We haven't talked since Karen and I got married—and very little before that."

"Don't wait too long," Eric said. "If something happens, you'll never forgive yourself."

"That's what bothers me," Frank said. "I'll think this over and talk to you tomorrow."

After Karen and Frank left, his mother said, "Frank should go see his father."

"It's gotta be his decision," Eric interrupted.

Eric called Tyler. "Where are you?" Tyler said. Her familiar voice sounded wonderful, even over the phone.

"I just got in a few minutes ago. Any chance I can see you this evening?"

"Wait a minute," Tyler said. A moment later, she was back on the phone. "Daddy's going to bring us in town. See you in a little while."

The minute the Quinlins entered the house, Eric kissed Tyler on the cheek. The expression on her face was priceless.

"I guess welcome home is in order," Mr. Quinlin said with a laugh.

"Are you going to kiss me, too?" Patsy asked.

"Come here, you."

The evening air was hot and dry. Tyler and Eric sat on the front porch, not saying anything for a moment, and then Eric said, "I didn't mean to embarrass you. The impulse—I got carried away."

"I can handle it," Tyler said. "Before we join the family, I have to tell you I did register for school. I probably will be leaving in the next week or so."

"Tyler, I will miss you," Eric said, "but your happiness is important to me." He could not be sure, because of the late evening shadows, but he thought he saw a smile on her face.

The next morning at breakfast, the phone interrupted the early morning silence. "Eric, it's Frank. My dad's worse. He's in intensive care in the hospital. He asked for you."

"You gonna meet me there, Frank?"

Frank's silence was getting to Eric. Finally, he said, "All right. I'll be there."

"It's not my idea being here or asking for you," Frank told Eric in the hospital waiting room. "My dad's kidneys are shot. He has cancer of the liver. He doesn't have anybody to blame but himself."

Frank's father looked like a stranger. Eric had not seen him for a long time. Although he still had a full head of hair, it was all gray. The lines in his face made him look much older than his sixties.

"Eric, haven't seen you in years," Frank's father said. "I heard about you giving healings." He stopped to catch his breath. "I knew when you were a boy there was something different about you." The nurse checked his chart and left. "I know I've had it," he said. "If you could just ease the pain a little. Sometimes it's unbearable."

The other man in the room glanced their way then returned to his magazine. Eric placed his hand on the man's head and lower back.

"What're you people doing?" the man with the magazine asked. He put on his glasses and stared. "I'll call the nurse."

"Mind your own business," Frank's father said. The man grunted and went back to his magazine. "I feel better," Ralph Karland said. "Thank you for easing my pain."

Ralph Karland turned to face his son, "Frank, we are going to have to talk very soon. Look at me!"

A look of pity and disgust was on Frank's face. He stared at his father.

"Don't wait too long," his father said. "I'm on borrowed time."

A little later Eric and Frank walked out in the fresh night air. "Maybe we should talk. How about joining me for a drink?" Frank asked.

"A little unusual for you," Eric said.

Smokey's bar was going full blast. The clock showed seven thirty-five. "I keep seeing my father's face, the way it was years ago," Frank said.

"We all make mistakes," Eric said. "He's sorry, Frank. He doesn't have that long and he's trying to make it right."

"He was responsible for my mother's death. How am I supposed to forgive that?"

"I know what it is to lose somebody. You keep asking yourself what you should have done or said. You have that chance," Eric said.

"You're saying I should forgive him because I'm a Christian?"

"No. He's your father, whether you're a Christian or not!"

Frank finished his beer and said. "I don't know."

"I wouldn't wait too long." Eric said.

"I'll have to think about it," Frank said. "What do you think the healing has done for him?"

"I have no way of knowing," Eric said. "I can only hope it helped."

During breakfast the next morning, his mother said, Eric you can help feed Colleen.

Ellen looked at him, and broke out in a big smile. His father looked at him, and then said, "It's all part of being a father."

"I know. Come here you little rascal, you. Hold still," Eric said. Colleen continued fussing. After a few moments, Eric looked around the table.

"Don't look at me," Ellen said. "I've got to get to work."

His mother flashed a rare smile, and added, "Me, too. Look at this kitchen."

"Somebody's gotta open the shop," his father added, with a big smile.

―――――――――――

The following week went quickly. Eric had a lot on his mind.

The next morning on the radio, the announcement was made, "Ralph Karland, age 63, passed away at three ten this morning, after several days of illness."

"I need to go for a walk," Eric said. As he was heading toward the door, the phone rang.

"Hi Eric, it's Tyler. I just wanted you to know I will be leaving tomorrow morning with Jerry for college. I'm so glad I got to see you before I left for school."

After a brief silence, Eric said, "Tyler, I'm glad you called me. I hope everything works out for you. Your happiness is important to me. Write me and let me know how everything is going. You take care of yourself."

"You, too, Eric."

CHAPTER TWENTY-ONE

"I'M GLAD WE HAD A CHANCE TO TALK," Reverend Langtree said. "It's been a while. Now that you are out of the service, do you have any immediate plans?"

"I imagine I'll take over the shoe shop part time—Dad's offered to sell it to me a little later. Other than that, I'm not sure."

"I heard on the radio this morning about Frank's father," Reverend Langtree said.

"We heard about it too. I don't know how Frank's going to handle it. I'm afraid he waited too long. Everything seems to be happening so fast. I felt like I had to get away for a few minutes," Eric said.

"You picked the best place," the reverend said. "I have an appointment with some people. You're welcome to stay here and relax. It may even bring about some of the answers you're looking for."

"Maybe for a few minutes," Eric said. He almost dozed off until he heard the front door open. A lady stood huddled just inside the door, grasping at her coat. A brief smile crossed her face. "I—I need your help," she said. "I'm not a regular church member."

"It doesn't matter," Eric said. "The minister's not here right now—If I can help you?" The woman moved slowly toward him.

"I've heard about your healings," she said. She relaxed a little "I've got this heart problem. I don't know if you heal those kinds of things. You pray?" Her eyes focused on him.

"Yes. Always. I wouldn't do it any other way," Eric said. "I assume you have a doctor?"

"Yes, but sometimes the pain—maybe you could help. Do you use departed spirits?"

"I think I do part of the time," Eric said. "Naturally, I can't be sure." He suddenly had the feeling something was all wrong. Her eyes shifted every few seconds around the room. She removed her coat to reveal a blue-gray dress with long sleeves. "Where do you do this healing?" she whispered.

"There's a healing sanctuary in the basement."

She grasped her chest. "Sometimes the medicine doesn't quite relieve the pain," she said.

"Is there something I can do to help you? Would you like for me to give you a healing?"

"What would I need to do?" the lady asked.

"Wait a minute," Eric said. He switched on the light and led her down the basement steps. He took her to a far corner of the basement, and sat her on a chair. Her clothes appeared more expensive than he first imagined. "Just relax and join me in prayer if you like." Eric lowered his head, and prayed. He moved one hand on the back of her neck and the other on her forehead. He suddenly felt tense and uneasy.

"It's my chest," she whispered. She stared at him with soft, dark eyes that almost disappeared in her taut, bony cheeks. She took his hand and placed it high on her breast. "That's better. The tightness is going away."

He waited a couple of minutes, and then removed his hand.

"I do feel better," she said. Before the woman left, she stared in his eyes, which appeared glazed. She opened her purse and took out a ten-dollar bill, and offered it to him. She had one of the strangest smiles Eric had ever seen.

"It's not necessary. I never take money for healing," Eric said. She ignored him and laid the bill on a chair.

"Use it for collection. Churches always need money," the lady said.

"You belong to a local church?" Eric asked when they returned upstairs. She never answered and quickly hurried out the door.

Eric put the bill in the collection box, relaxed for a moment, and left. When he arrived home, he still felt uneasy and unusually depressed. "I'm gonna take a nap," he told his mother.

"You look tired," his mother said. "Maybe you're coming down with something."

––––––––––

"Eric, wake up you have a phone call," his mother said.

He picked up the phone, trying to clear his head. "Hello," he said groggily.

"Eric, I've got a couple ladies and their companion here with a complaint against you," Sergeant Hullman said. "It seems like there is some confusion about a healing. I'm not sure I understand it, but I'd recommend you come to the police station rather than me coming to your house. The way I understand, it happened at your church."

"I get the picture. I'll be right there," Eric said. "I'll be back in a few minutes," he told his mother. He quickly left before she could question him.

––––––––––

When Eric arrived at the police station, he saw the woman he had seen at church. This woman was with a strange young man and another woman who he recognized as being the couple who had caused a major disturbance some time ago in his church. They were talking to the sergeant. "That's him!" the other woman said. She raved and ranted about the evils of his church. She held up her Bible in the air with a look of defiance.

The young man said, "He must be stopped from corrupting true Christians."

A distinguished-looking older man suddenly interrupted them. He was a tall, rugged man in his early sixties, with black framed glasses. He had graying hair and a mustache in a blunt

252

military style. He stared at both the women and their male companion. "My name is Harold Louis Hurley. This woman happens to be my wife—and her sister, and their companion." He shook his head with obvious disgust and said to Eric, "I am a lawyer who, I'm afraid, has been through this before."

"But Harry, this man put his hand on my breast, and—"

"Do you have any witnesses?"

"No." She raised her Bible and shouted, "God is my witness! Who else would I need?"

"My wife, her sister and their disturbed companion get carried away with their self-imposed crusades," Hurley said.

When Hurley looked at his sister-in-law, she said bitterly, "I tricked him. He is an agent of the devil. He put his hands on me and accepted money. He didn't heal me. I fooled him and he accepted my money. We are doing the Lord's work, and—"

"Anthony—did you witness anything?" Hurley asked her companion.

"No! Mary told me all about it! She would never lie. She's the most dedicated Christian in today's corrupt world."

Hurley's face reddened. "No charges will be filed against this man. It's clearly entrapment." He turned to face Eric, "Are you willing to put this incident behind you?"

"Yes, I think under the circumstances it would be best," Eric said.

"Then I sincerely apologize to you, Mr. Silkwin. Like I said, I've been through this before."

"I don't think they will give you any more trouble—from past experience, you may get a minor demonstration or a phone call. I would suggest you ignore them. The one exception might be that young man—Anthony, or whatever his name is. I really don't know very much about him."

"They were pitiful," Eric told his mother and father later that night. "I wasn't sure about giving her a healing, but I'd gone too far. That woman set me up." His voice became louder than usual. "I have to remember: no more healings without someone else present. I should have known better. Don't worry, I've learned my lesson."

His father expressed mild shock, but nodded his approval. It was the first time his mother seemed lost for words.

"I gotta call Frank," Eric said.

Karen answered the phone. "I'm sorry Eric, he won't talk to anyone. He's closed out everyone around him. From outward appearances, you'd never guess it would hit him so hard. You know the funeral will be Tuesday at eleven."

"We will be there," Eric said, and hung up the phone.

Eric thought to himself, it's not his father dying as much as it is Frank not forgiving himself.

———————————

At Karen and Frank's request, the Reverend John Langtree held the service.

The funeral for Ralph Karland took place on a hot, bright, sunny morning in an overcrowded, little white family church. Frank and Karen, along with their son Bruce, sat in stunned silence. Reverend Langtree spoke of love, compassion, and forgiveness.

"Frank Sr. was a citizen who had lived his life in our town, and had contributed to the Benford community in his own way," Reverend Langtree said.

Eric thought about Frank's father's life. He must have had his share of joys and sorrows as well as victories and defeats.

Eric and his family stood beside Karen and Frank as they watched the casket being lowered in the ground.

After the service, people gathered in groups. Eric greeted a few people—mostly the church's congregation.

"I'm sorry Frank," Uncle David put his hand on his shoulder. Aunt Grace, with tear-filled eyes took Frank's, hand in hers.

"It's finally over," Frank said after an awkward silence. "I knew it was coming and yet, when it happened, I couldn't believe it."

———————————

Later in the week, Karen called. "Eric, that reporter—what's his name—Stratman—asked us for information. You know—

you giving a healing to Frank's father. Anyway, Frank had all he could take and left the house. He said something about having a couple drinks. I don't know, he just hasn't been himself the last few days."

"I'll see what I can do." He returned to the table. "I told Karen I'd talk to Frank; evidently he's drinking."

"Doesn't sound like him," Eric's mother said.

Smokey's bar was not as crowded as usual. What crowd there was seemed to be getting well under way for the evening. Eric saw Frank at the far end of the bar and sat down next to him. Frank looked up with a slight grin and said to the guy next to him, "Well, I do believe we have a celebrity among us."

"How about we get a table in the back?" Eric said. "We need to talk."

Frank stared at Eric with pain and frustration written all over his face. "By all means—after you," he said.

"Karen called me. She's worried," Eric said.

"You know, I never ask much from life," Frank said slowly. "A fairly good job, a family, and a decent marriage—I have it all."

"Then why are you sitting here getting loaded?"

"My father. He left me the house," Frank said. He took a drink, and then added, "Come to think of it, who else would he have left it to?"

"You have to put it out of your mind and get on with your life." Eric said.

"You make it sound so easy," Frank replied with sarcasm in his voice.

"It isn't, and it never will be!" Eric said with an edge to his voice. "Stop and think what I've been through! You can only go on. There's no other way!"

"You're telling me I'm feeling sorry for myself?" Frank raised his voice.

"Yes. If I'm wrong, explain to me what good it's doing sitting here getting drunk."

Frank got an expression on his face that he wanted to make a point, but was not quite sure how to express it. "You think you have all the answers?" he finally said.

"If I had, I'd have avoided several things."

Frank took another drink of his highball. "By the way—What the hell am I supposed to tell that reporter running around?"

"That you know nothing about the healings I'm involved with."

"There's probably a lot of truth in that," Frank said, and then got that unfamiliar, rare grin on his face. "Shouldn't I say you're a little strange and always have been—especially where religion's concerned?"

Eric matched his grin. "That's up to you."

"You are, you know."

Eric lit a Camel and looked into Frank's eyes. "I know," he agreed.

Frank's face turned red. "Doesn't it bother you when people put their faith in you and they end up like my father?"

"Yes. It's a price you have to pay," Eric raised his voice. "That's what makes it so difficult."

"It shouldn't have to be this way," Frank said. He stared at Eric for a long moment, finished his drink, and left the bar without another word.

———————

On the way home, Eric stopped to see Rita. He could always appreciate her frankness and honesty. He felt he could rely on her understanding and bluntness as well as anyone he knew. "My involvement with healing is affecting the family—all in the wrong way," he said. "Even the local reporter is—I don't know—I'm not sure how far I should go with this."

He watched her carefully, but her expression never changed.

"Are you referring to that strange woman? Don't give me that look—probably everyone in town has heard about it."

"I can handle it," Eric said.

"I'm not ignoring your problem, Eric. Colleen's your base; the rest will fall into place. I have thought about the way you helped me," Rita said. "It really turned my life around. I will never forget it. A gift like that is rare, and only you can decide if the price you have to pay is worth it." She paused for a moment, and then continued. "Eric, I can't help you on this one. The answer has to come from within yourself—nobody can make the decision for you."

"I guess that's what I had to hear," Eric said. "I'll see you later."

In his sleep that night there were people of all kinds reaching out to him. Men, women, and children passed before him like a parade. Eric woke up in a deep sweat, staring out the window; it was morning already. Eric tried to gather his thoughts, wondering what his dream meant. He got dressed and went into the kitchen. His mother had already started breakfast.

As he reached for a cup of coffee, the doorbell rang. It was Karen and Frank.

"Eric, I want to apologize," Frank said. "I was outta line. I had a few and I shouldn't have said what I did. We've been friends too long to let something like this get in the way."

"Whatever comes our way, we'll handle it," Karen added.

"You don't know what it means to me to hear you say that."

Suddenly the phone rang. To Eric's surprise, it was Alice's sister Paula, inviting him and Colleen to have dinner with her and her folks. "She made it almost sound urgent," Eric told his parents.

"Paula must be back in town then," Eric's mother said. "I wonder why."

"I don't know," Eric said. "That's the first I've heard about it."

The Dawshers' house looked the same except for the "For Sale" sign in the front yard. Eric hadn't been by here in months, although he heard they were back in town.

Lawrence, Alice's father, answered the door with an unfamiliar smile. "Please come in; dinner will be ready soon. Paula and Edith are in the kitchen. We are just about ready to eat."

Paula came rushing out. "Eric, it's good to see you," she said, kissing him on the cheek. She reached for Colleen and said, "My how she's grown. What a beautiful baby."

Paula seemed to change not only in her appearance but in her personality. Edith, Alice's mother, looked much better than the last time he had seen her. She took Colleen in her arms at once.

Alice's mother explained their plans with a newfound enthusiasm. "We're moving out West. It's a new beginning for us," she said, and then added, "We discovered closeness with our relatives we didn't know existed. The worst part will be leaving this little angel here. Paula came to help us get things in order."

"My husband is away on business for a few days and I just wanted to help Mother and Dad and see you and Colleen," Paula said.

The small talk was as difficult as always. The conversations were still awkward and would be for some time. Eric felt self-conscious sitting on the familiar couch Alice and he had shared.

Edith Dawsher watched him closely. "Is there anyone special in your life, Eric?"

"I'm not sure. Colleen holds it together for me."

"It takes time," Lawrence Dawsher said.

"Eric, you look much better than the last time I saw you. I'm glad you and Colleen are doing okay," Paula added.

"We had to see this little angel before we leave next week," Alice's mother said. Paula hugged Eric and kissed Colleen.

"We will be back to see you and Colleen; just because we are moving doesn't mean we will be out of your life," Paula said with tears in her eyes.

Everything necessary had been said. It was time to leave.

CHAPTER TWENTY-TWO

IT WAS A DARK, RAINY DAY; fall was in the air. It had been unusually warm for November. Eric was wondering how the Dawshers were getting along. He thought about how much they must miss Colleen; she was almost six months old. He hadn't heard from Tyler in quite some time, and that was unusual. Things had been quiet concerning his controversial healings.

As Eric entered the house, his mother was sitting in her favorite chair, holding a letter. She was staring into space and seemed to be in shock. "Mom, is there something wrong?" he asked.

After a brief pause, she said, "Eric, I just got a letter from a Mr. Snipes. He was a neighbor of Grandma and Grandpa Walden. It seems your grandfather had passed away about four months ago. Apparently, Mr. Snipes had trouble locating us to let us know. I haven't seen your grandfather since your grandmother died. He just seemed to disappear. He wasn't even at your grandmother's funeral."

"I don't remember very much about Grandpa Walden," Eric said.

"According to Mr. Snipe's letter, he was working as a handyman and living with a lady named Elsa Crawford. I don't remember too much about her, except I remember your grandparents had traded goods back and forth during hard times. The way Mr. Snipes talked in the letter, goods were not the only thing being traded."

"Even though I haven't seen my father in a long time, I feel a void now that's he gone," she continued. "I do remember the good times before the Depression hit us so hard. He was a good man. I guess when things happen to us, it changes who we are."

Eric didn't know what to say; he was heading toward the bedroom to see Colleen when the phone rang. Tyler was on the line, announcing that she had gotten home the day before.

"Tyler, it's so good to hear from you," he said. "Are you home just for the holiday?"

"Not only for the holiday," she said. "I'm home for good, but I'll have to go into detail about that later." Eric seemed startled. "How about you Eric? What have you been doing the last few months?"

"Other than being surprised at this moment, mainly working, although there are some interesting things that I'd like to share with you later. Tyler, I'm really happy you're home, and I want to see you as soon as possible."

"How about tomorrow?"

"That sounds great. I'll pick you up?"

Eric arrived at the Quinlins a few minutes early. Tyler was looking out the window and noticed a car in the driveway. As Eric walked toward the house, Tyler opened the door.

"I like your car. Blue is my favorite color," Tyler said.

"It's a 1946 Ford," he boasted. "I've had it about a month. It sure makes it easier to get around. I'm really happy to see you. You look great. I've missed you. All of a sudden I'm getting hungry."

Tyler laughed. "I see things haven't changed with you. I've missed you, too, Eric."

Eric looked around. "Where is everyone?"

"Patsy's over a friend's house and my mom and dad had to go to town for something."

"Are you ready to take a test drive in my new car?"

"I can't hardly wait."

Grover's was a little crowded, which was expected at lunch-time. Eric and Tyler made their way to the back. The waitress came over and said, "What can I get for you two?"

Eric looked at Tyler, "What sounds good to you?" he said.

"How about a cherry Coke and a grilled cheese?"

"Make that two," Eric said.

"Eric, how is Colleen doing? How about your mom and dad?"

"Everyone's doing great. Colleen is really growing. My mom and dad are doing OK. I'm at the shop picking up more experience. My dad is getting kind of limited to what he can do. The Dawshers have moved out west to be with some family. Oh—by the way, I had an unusual experience."

"Sounds intriguing. What kind of experience was it?"

"This woman came to church and set me up for a phony healing session, and then accused me of making inappropriate gestures."

"You—what?" Tyler's expression revealed surprise and shock.

"I had to go to the police department."

"I won't see you on a wanted poster anywhere, will I?"

Eric laughed, "I hope not. The bottom line is that this lady was a little off, to say the least. It turned out that she had done this kind of thing before. There weren't any charges. Her husband, who is a lawyer, said this was entrapment and he apologized to me. I kinda feel sorry for the guy, really. Now, what about you: What drove you back home?"

"No similar experiences along that line," she said, "but I realized I made the wrong decision concerning school. I didn't want to devote my life to being a teacher. I'm not quite sure what I really want."

"Tyler, I don't know if any of us really know what we want. Sometimes we have to try things to see if they are right for us."

"As for Jerry, right now we're still good friends. But as far as getting serious, I'm just not ready for that at this time. How about you, Eric? Anyone special in your life?"

"There is one young lady I'm very attracted to; she keeps me grounded and I think it's pretty serious. We've known each other about six months."

"Do I know this person?" Tyler asked with a smile.

"Yes, you probably remember her; your sister comes over once and a while and checks on her."

Tyler laughed and then said, "Would her name happen to be Colleen?"

"Why, you do remember her?"

"I think it's great that things are going so well with you and Colleen," Tyler said.

The two parted after the meal, and Eric promised to call her again soon.

It was Sunday morning. Eric and his family arrived at church and greeted Reverend Langtree. The sermon seemed to be longer than usual this morning. After services, Reverend Langtree led Eric aside.

"How do you feel about giving a healing?" he asked Eric with a look of concern. "I know you're upset about that woman you told me about, but this is different. I will let Dr. Emmery explain."

"Hello Eric. It has been a while," Dr. Emmery said. "I heard you had been discharged."

"Yes, I'm home for good. I received a hardship discharge because of my daughter Colleen. Reverend Langtree said something about a healing."

"Would you consider letting us monitor a healing session?"

"Of course," Eric said. "Who is the healing for?"

"The healing is for Nathan Winslow, he has lung cancer," the doctor said. "You do understand this is confidential. Why don't we meet at the church tomorrow morning at ten o'clock, if it's alright with you."

"That would be fine," Eric replied.

The next morning Dr. Emmery opened the church door, followed by Nathan Lewis Winslow, the most influential pillar of the family church. Eric remembered when Winslow tried to discourage him from giving healings in church, although he supported Alice and him during their church healing incident. The short, overweight man's expression bordered on panic. Winslow extended his hand in a nervous, restless manner. "Eric, I hope you will forgive me," he said. "I'm a desperate man in search of a miracle."

"No apology necessary," Eric said.

"I have his complete medical record," Dr. Emmery said to Eric, "along with the more recent tests." The look in the doctor's eyes revealed the seriousness of Winslow's condition. "When you're ready, I'll monitor you."

Winslow sighed and placed his hands in his lap.

"Relax as much as possible," Eric said, and then he bowed his head in prayer. He mentally called forth the healing power. Nathan Winslow trembled. Eric concentrated on the ball of light entering the top of the man's balding head. He then placed one hand on his back and the other on his chest. Beads of perspiration appeared on Winslow's forehead. Winslow closed his eyes and the trembling ceased.

"Breathe deeper!" Eric said.

"It hurts, but I'll try," Winslow said. Emmery moved in closer, along with Langtree. The look on their faces showed intense concentration.

"Again!" Eric insisted.

Winslow took another breath—cautiously at first, then much deeper. A look of disbelief crossed his face. Eric stepped away, and Dr. Emmery examined him. "His breathing seems to be easier, but erratic," Emmery said. Winslow's complexion turned a crimson color. He wiped his forehead in a restless manner.

"The breathing is much easier," Winslow said. "I feel better, but very weak." He looked Dr. Emmery in the eye. "I really do."

"A good night's rest should come next." Eric said.

That night Eric spent almost the entire evening reading the Bible.

He lay in bed staring at the ceiling, between drowsiness and sleep, when a brilliant white light spread over his consciousness. He felt a sudden feeling of overwhelming joy. The little girl appeared. "*We are with you. Have courage for the road ahead. Mentally call upon me and I'll help as much as I can. My name is Tawnya*." The vision vanished as quickly as it came. He felt a power surge through his body just before falling into a deep, restful sleep.

The following evening, Eric again met with Dr. Emmery and Nathan Lewis Winslow at church. "Dr. Hedwick has decided to join us," Emmery said.

Eric could not resist smiling at the smirk on Hedwick's face. "This is no longer confidential," Eric said. "I'm not sure how it happened, but I'm afraid it's all over town."

"That seems to amuse you," Hedwick said, losing his control for an instant. "It could be a way of discrediting your so called healing power."

"Whatever! I am determined to find out."

Eric's hands suddenly felt independent of himself. The movement seemed beyond his control. Winslow's body began to vibrate as perspiration poured from his body. "The heat is almost unbearable," Winslow said.

"Just a little longer," Eric said. A moment later, he removed his hands and stepped back.

Winslow smiled weakly. "I'm limp as a rag, but my breathing is easier and the pain's almost completely gone."

Dr. Hedwick watched him and said suspiciously, "You could be on an emotional high."

"Nonsense!" Winslow bellowed. "I know what I'm talking about. I am the one who is going through hell. I must get off the painkillers until I talk to my son. I need a clear head."

Dr. Hedwick lowered his head. "Do you realize we could be opening the door for every kind of—"

"Make it public at my request!" Winslow shouted, "I'll sign any statement you have for the press and the public."

After the second healing session, Eric started back toward town when he heard a familiar voice.

"Eric, it's me Bryan. I heard you were giving Nathan Winslow a healing."

"That's true. Want to join me?"

They stopped under a street light. Eric could see the expression on Bryan's face. "Nathan Winslow—of all people." Suddenly realizing Eric's invitation, he said, "What do you mean, join you?"

"You have often mentioned how you'd like to be a part of this."

The expression on Bryan's face changed. "But what if something went wrong—like he died or something? How would I ever—"

"I think that's something you never understood. There are times you have to put yourself out on a limb," Eric said. "There are no guarantees. You do what you can. If you really want to help, I can call you."

"I don't know," Bryan said, looking away into the darkness. "Tell you what—I'll call you."

The following day Eric, had thought about the promise he made to Claude Stratman. He called him and left a message.

Two days later, Dr. Emmery called. "Mr. Winslow has checked into the hospital," he said with some urgency. "He is critical and insists on seeing you. The important thing is Winslow has been free from medication for the last two days. His son is here from out east. Please come to the hospital as soon as possible."

"I'm on my way," Eric said.

265

Drs. Emmery and Hedwick were waiting. "The prodigal healer returneth," Hedwick said.

Winslow was barely conscious, but motioned for Eric. His voice was low and labored. "You've helped me," he told Eric. "Don't think you've failed." He stopped to catch his breath, and then continued, "I had a chance to talk to my son without being drugged out of my mind." He went into a series of spasms. Eric left the room; his heart went out to the wife and son, who closed in around him.

Minutes later—which seems like hours—Dr. Emmery and Dr. Hedwick approached Eric. "He's gone," Emmery said.

Eric glanced back at Winslow's wife and son and left the building. Outside, he took a deep breath. A helpless, depressive feeling came over him.

Eric noticed a small crowd gathered around the front entrance. They waved placards with signs denouncing him. Others, however, supported him. He tried to get around them but they closed in on him, along with some reporters. A heavy-set woman grabbed the young woman beside her and pushed her aside. She shoved her way toward the front of the crowd and shouted, "Behold the devil's advocate."

The other woman came forward and challenged her. She shoved her placard toward her rival. The placard's words consisted of big bold black letters, with the message "The Lord's Instrument." The heavyset woman tried again to push the younger woman out of the way shouting, "Outta my way you, misled bitch!"

"How dare you talk to me that way, you—you slut!" The two women faced each other with looks that bordered on hatred to the delight of several people around them. The crowd broke out in laughter and shouts from different individuals supporting both women's viewpoints.

Suddenly a young man stepped forward to make room for an elegantly dressed woman who stepped out from the crowd. "Cast out your evil ways!" she shouted at Eric. "I'm here to lead you to righteousness!"

Eric noticed that she was the woman who protested at the family church. He stared at the arrogantly dressed woman of middle age, with auburn hair graying at the temples. He could sense her commanding presence. At her side was the same tall, thin young man who had accompanied her to his church. He had long blond hair and dark green eyes that almost disappeared in taut, bony cheeks. Even though the young man was a few feet from Eric, Eric could still see the burning intensity behind the young man's penetrating eyes.

"The righteous will overcome," the woman said.

Eric noticed Claude Stratman coming toward him. "Eric, I got your message about discussing your healing sessions," Stratman said. "What's going on here?" He turned from Eric and asked the woman, "Who are you?"

"My name is Mary Hurley. I am a very devoted Christian, speaking for the conversion of a young man confused or controlled by evil spirits. The Bible warns us of such things!"

"How do you know he's controlled by evil departed spirits?" Claude Stratman asked. "By what right do you have to condemn him—or anyone, for that matter?"

"I believe he has a negative influence over helpless, innocent people. I believe he's under a spell—'controlled,' I believe would be the correct word," Mary Hurley replied.

"But still, you have to admit," Claude Stratman interrupted, "He, like all of us, has a choice."

Eric saw Sergeant Allen Hullman push his way through the crowd.

"All right, let's break it up!" Sergeant Hullman shouted.

"We have a right to free speech and assembly," the young man with the penetrating eyes yelled in Hullman's face.

"And I have a duty to prevent an uprising or riot," Hullman said, "which I believe is about to happen."

The crowds began to slowly disperse. Part of the crowd mumbled to themselves as they slowly moved away.

The day after Mr. Winslow died, Eric entered the doctor's office. After an awkward greeting, Dr. Hedwick said, with obvious controlled patience, "We have checked the records carefully. We concluded that what change occurred was due to spontaneous remission. We have decided to cease monitoring your—err—healings."

"I agree," Eric said.

"Then you accept our conclusions? I assume you will cease this healing of yours?" Hedwick asked.

"No. I've thought it over carefully. I have nothing to prove to the medical profession. If the occasion arises, I'm going to heal under the banner of religion."

"Religion? Is it your sincere belief, or a form of protection, or both?" Hedwick asked. "Do you think you really made any difference in Mr. Winslow's case?"

Eric grinned. "Maybe both. Don't get me wrong, I do understand how something like this could affect your judgment and reputations. As for helping Mr. Winslow, I believe I helped him. He told me so, and that's good enough for me. I'm not the self-conscious guy who walked into this office several months ago, so don't try to intimidate me. As for how much difference I've made, I'm gonna let you think about it, and you will—believe me, you will!"

Dr. Hedwick smirked. "Intimidation is not our goal. Maybe you misunderstand your ability, or should I say—yourself."

"Maybe. I guess the future will tell," Eric said.

"Why religion, Eric?" Dr. Emmery asked.

"Because that is where my heart is."

Eric took his time walking home. The minute he opened the front door, he heard his mother, "Eric is that you? You have a call."

"Eric, this is Tyler. Is everything okay? I haven't heard from you, and you said you would call."

"I'm sorry, so many things have happened I don't know where to begin. If you are not doing anything, why don't I pick you up and maybe we could go for a drive."

"That sounds good Eric," Tyler said. "There are some things I would like to talk to you about."

Eric pulled up in the driveway. Tyler was waiting outside. "Let's take a ride," Eric said. "There's somewhere special I would like to take you."

"Sounds interesting," Tyler said. "Eric, tell me: What's been going on?"

"I don't know if you remember Mr. Winslow. He is our church board director, and he had been very sick."

"I don't really remember him," Tyler said.

"He asked if I could give him a healing, at least to help with the pain he was having, so he could talk to his son without being drugged."

"Were you able to help him?"

"This last week, I was at the hospital trying to help him. He was feeling better and was even able to get off his pain medication. Unfortunately, he took a turn for the worst and passed away yesterday."

"I'm so sorry," Tyler said. "At least you tried to do everything you could."

"As I was leaving the hospital, a large crowd of people formed and I was confronted by a woman that caused problems at church for me some time ago. She challenged my right to give healings. She and her friends were creating a scene outside the hospital, saying things like, 'Cast out your evil ways! I'm here to lead you to righteousness!'"

"What did you do?"

"I really wasn't sure what to do, and then the police came and broke up the crowd."

"The police! Did anyone get hurt?"

"Fortunately no. Hopefully this will be the end of this controversy. After this experience, I made the decision that I have to do what I think is right, and follow my conscience."

"I think I understand that," Tyler replied.

When Eric pulled up to the cabin, many memories came back to him. "Tyler, this is the cabin given to Alice and me by her uncle. This is where we spent our honeymoon."

Tyler didn't quite know how to react. "It seems like a very nice place," she said.

As they approached the cabin, Tyler took Eric's hand. "Could we just stay outside and talk?" she said. "There is something I need and want to tell you."

They sat down on a bench near the front entrance of the cabin.

"There's only one way to tell you this: I have a child!" she said. It was as if she could not hold back the words any longer. "I should have told you before." Eric looked into her tear-filled eyes and knew not to interrupt her. "He is four years old. I had to give him up for adoption."

Eric tried to take her in his arms, but she pushed him away. She buried her face in her hands, fighting to control the tears.

"I was raped in the barn when I was fifteen years old. The man was a transient, bum, or whatever you call them."

Eric could see the pain in her expression. He felt her helplessness as if it were his own. He felt anger and disgust. "What happened to the guy?" he asked.

"He just disappeared. Daddy and the sheriff searched for him. I remember Daddy saying if he got his hands on him, he'd kill him."

"I can believe that," Eric said softly. He wanted to hold her in his arms and comfort her, but she pulled away. Suddenly her voice took on a tone of control. "I missed a year of school and stayed with an aunt in Nebraska. I put the baby up for adoption, came back home, and returned to school the following year. Patsy was only about three or four. Naturally, she couldn't understand why I left."

"I can understand that," Eric said slowly. "If there's anything I can do to help you, let me know. It doesn't change the way I feel about you."

"I just couldn't wait to tell you any longer."

"Like I said, it doesn't change anything Tyler. I think we better get back. Would you mind if I stopped at the cemetery on the way home? Alice has been on my mind and I just feel led to stop there."

"I don't mind, but I'm not sure how Alice would feel about me being with you," Tyler said.

"I think she would understand," Eric said.

Several minutes later, when they entered the cemetery, they walked over to Alice's grave.

"I feel her presence—I really do," Eric whispered. "Alice, I hope you don't mind that I brought Tyler with me. There are a lot of things happening. It is a confusing time. I want you to know I will always love you and you'll always have a place in my heart. You'll always live in Colleen."

Tyler stood motionless, wanting to say something but not quite sure she should. She looked at Eric and somehow got the courage to speak. "Alice, I want you to know, I respect Eric and his love for you."

As Eric pulled into the Quinlins' driveway, he looked at Tyler. "Tyler, there is something I need to explain—I am sensitive to certain conditions. It is something that evidently has a purpose beyond my understanding. Naturally, it means living with controversy. After the demonstrations earlier, I'm sure you can understand."

"I am trying to understand, I'm just not sure how I will react to it."

"Fair enough," Eric said. "We have been honest with each other, and that is the most important thing."

"I think it's especially important when two people care about each other," Tyler said. She kissed Eric on the cheek and walked toward the house, glancing back to wave as he started to leave.

Eric felt a sense of relief he had not experienced in a long time. Someday he would tell Tyler about the vision he had of Alice standing near her, especially Alice's smile of approval.

A spiritual awareness filled him with the most comforting feelings he had ever experienced. However, for now, he was going to try to build a future with the girl whose smile brought to life the most incredible dimples he had ever seen.

Breinigsville, PA USA
11 October 2010
247106BV00001B/7/P